Serpent Mage

Bantam Spectra Books
by Margaret Weis and Tracy Hickman

THE DARKSWORD TRILOGY
Forging the Darksword
Doom of the Darksword
Triumph of the Darksword

DARKSWORD ADVENTURES

ROSE OF THE PROPHET
The Will of the Wanderer
The Paladin of the Night
The Prophet of Akhran

THE DEATH GATE CYCLE
Dragon Wing
Elven Star
Fire Sea
Serpent Mage

and by Margaret Weis

STAR OF THE GUARDIANS
The Lost King
King's Test
King's Sacrifice

THE DEATH GATE CYCLE

VOLUME ♦ 4

Serpent Mage

MARGARET WEIS

AND

TRACY HICKMAN

SPECTRA ™

BANTAM BOOKS
NEW YORK • TORONTO • LONDON • SYDNEY • AUCKLAND

Wei
C1

SERPENT MAGE

A Bantam Book / April 1992

Library of Congress Cataloging-in-Publication Data
Weis, Margaret.
  Serpent mage / Margaret Weis and Tracy Hickman.
    p.   cm. — (Death Gate cycle ; v. 4)
  ISBN 0-553-08310-4
  I. Hickman, Tracy.   II. Title.   III. Series: Weis, Margaret.
Death Gate cycle ; v. 4.
PS3573.E3978S47   1992
813'.54—dc20   *91-33881*
                                                          CIP

Published simultaneously in the United States and Canada

Bantam Books are published by Bantam Books, a division of Bantam Doubleday Dell Publishing Group,
Inc. Its trademark, consisting of the words "Bantam Books" and the portrayal of a rooster, is Registered
in U.S. Patent and Trademark Office and in other countries. Marca Registrada. Bantam Books, 666 Fifth
Avenue, New York, New York 10103.

PRINTED IN THE UNITED STATES OF AMERICA

RRH   0 9 8 7 6 5 4 3 2 1

Dedicated to my new granddaughter,
NATALIE BRIANA BALDWIN,
and to her mother and father,
DAVID AND JOYCE.

♦

—Margaret Weis

Dedicated to
DON and JERI ALLPHIN
with love

♦

—Tracy Raye Hickman

Do I dare

disturb the universe?

◆

T. S. Eliot,
"The Love Song
of J. Alfred Prufrock"

Chelestra

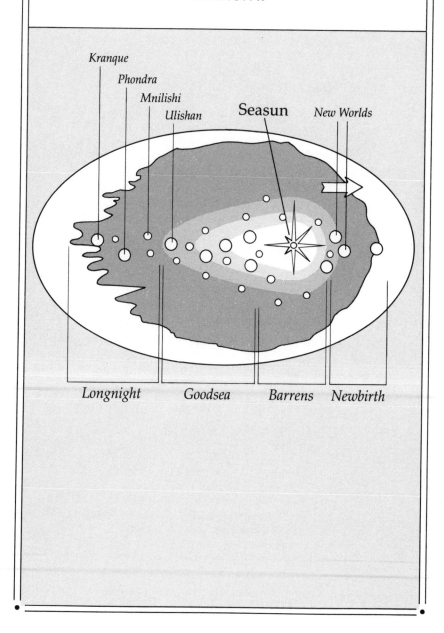

Cross Section of Durnai

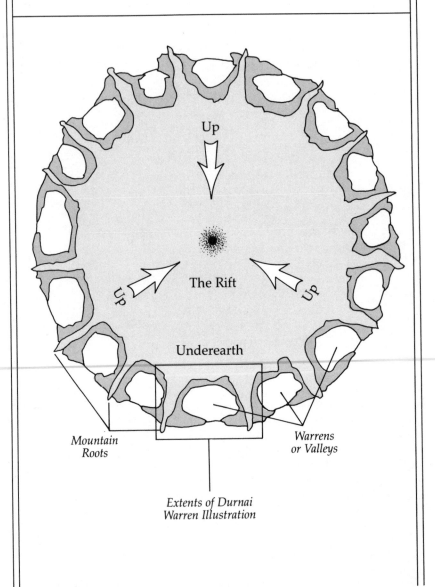

Up

The Rift

Up

Up

Underearth

Mountain
Roots

Warrens
or Valleys

Extents of Durnai
Warren Illustration

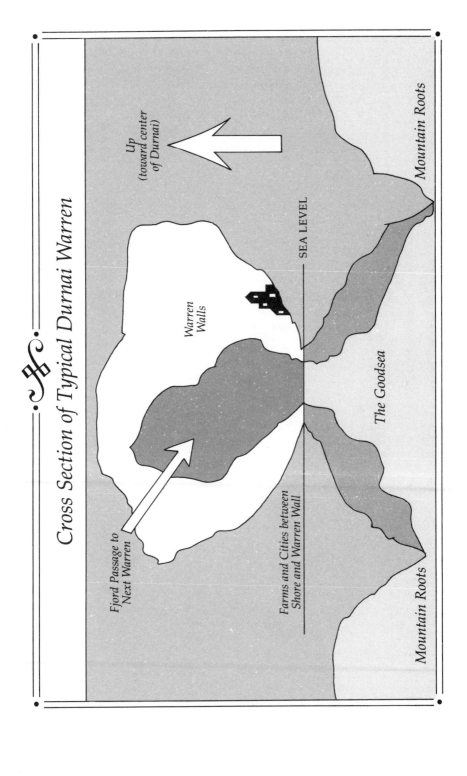

Cross Section of Typical Durnai Warren

Up
(toward center
of Durnai)

Fjord Passage to
Next Warren

Warren
Walls

Farms and Cities between
Shore and Warren Wall

SEA LEVEL

The Goodsea

Mountain Roots

Mountain Roots

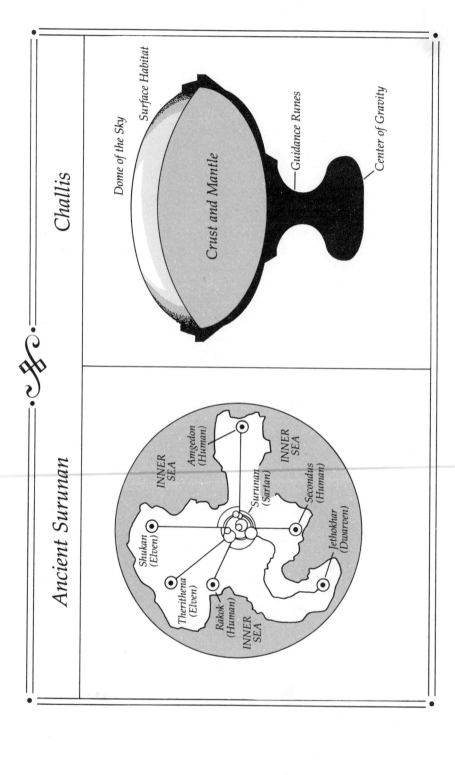

Ancient Suruman

Challis

PROLOGUE

I VISITED MY WRATH UPON HAPLO THIS DAY.[1] AN UNPLEASANT TASK. Few would believe me, but it grieved me to do what had to be done. It would have been easier, perhaps, if I did not feel in some part responsible.

When it became clear to me that we Patryns were nearing our time, when we were almost strong enough to be able to break out of this heinous prison into which the Sartan hurled us and move once again to take our rightful place as leaders in the universe, I chose one among us to go forth and learn about the new worlds.

I chose Haplo. I chose him for his quickness of mind, his independence of thought, his courage, his adaptability to new surroundings. And those, alas, are the very qualities that have led him to rebel against me. Therefore, I reiterate—in this way I am responsible for what has befallen.

Independence of thought. Necessary, I deemed, when facing the unknown territories of worlds created by our ancient enemy, the Sartan, and populated with mensch.[2] It was vital that he be able to react to any situation with intelligence and skill, vital that he not reveal to anyone on any of these worlds that we Patryns have broken free of our bonds. He behaved quite splendidly on

---

[1]Xar, *A Chronicle of Power*, vol. 24. The personal daily journal of the Lord of the Nexus. (Xar was not his real name. It is not a Patryn name at all, in fact, and is undoubtedly one he devised himself, possibly a corruption of the ancient word *tsar*, derived from *Caesar*.)

[2]The term used by both Sartan and Patryns to refer to the lesser races: humans, elves, dwarves. It is interesting to note that this word is borrowed from one of the many pre-Sundering human languages (probably German) and means "people."

two of the three worlds he visited, with a few minor lapses. It was on the third that he failed not only me but himself.[3]

I caught him just before he would have left to visit the fourth world, the world of water, Chelestra. He was on board his dragonship, the one he took from Arianus, preparing to set sail for Death's Gate. He said nothing when he saw me. He did not appear surprised. It was as if he had been expecting me, perhaps even waiting for me, though it seemed, from the disorder on board the ship, that he had been preparing for a hasty departure. Certainly there is much turmoil within him.

Those who know me would call me a hard man, hard and cruel, but I was bred in a place far harder, far crueler. I have in my long life seen too much pain, too much suffering, to be touched by it. But I am not a monster. I am not sadistic. What I did to Haplo, I did out of necessity. I took no pleasure in the doing.

Spare the rod and spoil the child—an old mensch proverb.

Haplo, believe me when I say I grieve for you this night. But it was for your own good, my son.

Your own good.

---

[3]References to Haplo's journeys to the worlds of Arianus, Pryan, and most lately to Abarrach, recorded in previous volumes of *The Death Gate Cycle*.

CHAPTER ♦ 1

THE NEXUS

♦

"DAMN IT! GET OUT OF THE WAY!" HAPLO KICKED AT THE DOG.

The animal cringed, slunk away, and endeavored to lose itself in the shadows of the hold, hide until its master's bad mood passed.

Haplo could see the sad eyes, however, watching him from the darkness. He felt guilty, remorseful, and that merely increased his irritation and anger. He glared at the animal, glared at the confusion in the hold. Chests and casks and boxes, coils of rope, and barrels had been tossed in hurriedly, to stand where they landed. It looked like a rat's nest, but Haplo dared not take time to rearrange them, stack them neatly, stow them away securely, as he had always done before.

He was in haste, desperate to leave the Nexus before his lord caught him. Haplo stared at the mess, ill at ease, his hands itching to sort it out. Turning on his heel, he stalked off, heading back to the bridge. The dog rose silently, padded soft-footed after him.

"Alfred!" He flung the word at the dog. "It's all Alfred's fault. That blasted Sartan! I should never have let him go. I should have brought him here, to my lord, let *him* deal with the miserable wretch. But who'd have guessed the coward would actually have nerve enough to jump ship! I don't suppose *you* have any idea how that happened?"

Haplo stopped, glowered suspiciously at the dog. The animal sat back, tilted its head, regarded him with bland innocence, though its tail wagged cheerfully at the sound of Alfred's name. Grunting, Haplo continued on his way, casting cursory glances to the left and right. He saw—with relief—that his vessel had sustained no lasting damage. The magic of the runes covering the hull had done its job, kept the *Dragon Wing* safe from the fiery environment of Abarrach and the lethal spells cast by the lazar[1] in their efforts to hijack it.

He had only recently come through Death's Gate and knew that he should not be going back this quickly. He had lost consciousness on the journey from Abarrach. No, *lost* wasn't quite the correct term. He'd deliberately cast it aside. The resultant undreaming sleep had restored him completely to health, healed the arrow wound he'd taken in the thigh, removed the last vestiges of the poison given him by the ruler of Kairn Necros. When he awoke, Haplo was well in body, if not in mind. He was almost sorry to have awakened at all.

His brain was like the hold. Thoughts and ideas and feelings were in a tangle. Some were thrust away in dark corners, where he could still see them watching him. Others were tossed in any which way. Precariously and carelessly stacked, they would come tumbling down at the slightest provocation. Haplo knew he could organize them, if he took the time, but he didn't have time, he didn't want time. He had to escape, get away.

He'd sent his report on Abarrach to the lord via a messenger, giving as his excuse for not coming in person the need to hurry after the escaped Sartan.

My Lord, You may remove Abarrach completely from your calculations. I found evidence to indicate that the Sartan and the mensch did once inhabit that hunk of worthless, molten rock. The climate undoubtedly proved too harsh for even their powerful magic to sustain them. They apparently tried to contact the other worlds, but their attempts ended in failure. Their cities have now become their tombs.

Abarrach is a dead world.

The report was true. Haplo had said nothing false about Abarrach. But its truth was polished veneer, covering rotten wood beneath. Haplo was almost certain his lord would know his ser-

---

[1]Lazar: the terrible necromancers of Abarrach, the Realm of Fire, whose living souls are trapped in dead bodies.

vant had lied; the Lord of the Nexus had a way of knowing everything that went on in a man's head . . . and his heart.

The Lord of the Nexus was the one person Haplo respected and admired. The one person Haplo feared. The lord's wrath was terrible, it could be deadly. His magic was incredibly powerful. When still a young man, he had been the first to survive and escape the Labyrinth. He was the only Patryn—including Haplo—who had the courage to return to that deadly prison, fight its awful magics, work to free his people.

Haplo grew cold with fear whenever he thought about a possible encounter between his lord and himself. And he thought about it almost constantly. He wasn't afraid of physical pain or even death. It was the fear of seeing the disappointment in his lord's eyes, the fear of knowing that he had failed the man who had saved his life, the man who loved him like a son.

"No," said Haplo to the dog, "better to go on to Chelestra, the next world. Better to go quickly, take my chances. Hopefully, with time, I can sort out this tangle inside me. Then, when I return, I can face my lord with a clear conscience."

He arrived on the bridge, stood staring down at the steering stone. He'd made his decision. He had only to put his hands on the sigla-covered round stone and his ship would break the magical ties binding it to the ground and sail into the rose-hued twilight of the Nexus. Why did he hesitate?

It was wrong, all wrong. He hadn't gone over the ship with his usual care. They'd made it safely out of Abarrach and through Death's Gate, but that didn't mean they could make another journey.

He'd prepared the ship in a slapdash manner, jury-rigging what he could not take time to carefully repair. He should have strengthened rune structures that almost surely had been weakened by the journey, should have searched for cracks, either in the wood or the sigla, should have replaced frayed cables.

He should have, as well, consulted with his lord about this new world. The Sartan had left written lore concerning the four worlds in the Nexus. It would be folly to rush blindly into the world of water, without even the most rudimentary knowledge of what he faced. Previously, he and his lord had met and studied . . .

But not now. No, not now.

Haplo's mouth was dry, had a foul taste in it. He swallowed, but it did no good. He reached out his hands to the steering stone and was startled to see his fingers tremble. Time was running out. The Lord of the Nexus would have received his report by now. He would know that Haplo had lied to him.

"I should leave . . . now," Haplo said softly, willing himself to place his hands on the stone.

But he was like a man who sees dreadful doom coming upon him, who knows he must run for his life, yet who finds himself paralyzed, his limbs refusing to obey his brain's command.

The dog growled. Its hackles rose, its eyes shifted to a point behind and beyond Haplo.

Haplo did not look around. He had no need. He knew who stood in the doorway.

He knew it by countless signs: he'd heard no one approaching, the warning sigla tattooed on his skin had not activated, the dog had not reacted until the man was within arm's reach.

The animal stood its ground, ears flattened, the low growl rumbling deep in its chest.

Haplo closed his eyes, sighed. He felt, to his surprise, a vast sense of relief.

"Dog, go," he said.

The animal looked up at him, whimpered, begged him to reconsider.

"Get," snarled Haplo. "Go on. Beat it."

The dog, whining, came to him, put its paw on his leg. Haplo scratched behind the furry ears, rubbed his hand beneath the jowl.

"Go. Wait outside."

Head lowered, the dog trotted slowly and reluctantly from the bridge. Haplo heard it flop down just outside the doorway, heard it sigh, knew it was pressed as close against the door as was possible to do and still obey its master's command.

Haplo did not look at the man who had materialized out of the twilight shadows inside his ship. Haplo kept his head lowered. Tense, nervous, he traced with his finger the runes carved upon the steering stone.

He sensed, more than heard or saw, the man come near him. A hand closed over Haplo's arm. The hand was old and gnarled, its runes a mass of hills and valleys on the wrinkled skin. Yet the sigla were still dark and easily read, their power strong.

"My son," said a gentle voice.

If the Lord of the Nexus had come raging aboard the ship, denouncing Haplo as a traitor, hurling threats and accusations, Haplo would have defied him, fought him, undoubtedly to the death.

Two simple words disarmed him completely.

"My son."

He heard forgiveness, understanding. A sob shook Haplo. He fell to his knees. Tears, as hot and bitter as the poison he'd swallowed on Abarrach, crept from beneath his eyelids.

"Help me, Lord!" he pleaded, the words coming as a gasp from a chest that burned with pain. "Help me!"

"I will, my son," answered Xar. His gnarled hand stroked Haplo's hair. "I will."

The hand's grip tightened painfully. Xar jerked Haplo's head back, forced him to look up.

"You have been deeply hurt, terribly wounded, my son. And your injury is not healing cleanly. It festers, doesn't it, Haplo? It grows gangrenous. Lance it. Purge yourself of its foul infection or its fever will consume you.

"Look at yourself. Look what this infection has done to you already. Where is the Haplo who walked defiantly out of the Labyrinth, though each step might have been his last? Where is the Haplo who braved Death's Gate so many times? Where is Haplo now? Sobbing at my feet like a child!

"Tell me the truth, my son. Tell me the truth about Abarrach."

Haplo bowed his head and confessed. The words gushed forth, spewing out of him, purging him, easing the pain of the wound. He spoke with fevered rapidity, his tale broken and disjointed, his speech often incoherent, but Xar had no difficulty following him. The language of both the Patryns and their rivals, the Sartan, has the ability to create images in the mind, images that can be seen and understood if the words cannot.

"And so," murmured the Lord of the Nexus, "the Sartan have been practicing the forbidden art of necromancy. This is what you feared to tell me. I can understand, Haplo. I share your revulsion, your disgust. Trust the Sartan to mishandle this marvelous power. Rotting corpses, shuffling about on menial errands. Armies of bones battering each other into dust."

The gnarled hands were once again stroking, soothing.

"My son, had you so little faith in me? Do you, after all this time, not know me yet? Do you not know my power? Can you truly believe that I would misuse this gift as the Sartan have misused it?"

"Forgive me, My Lord," whispered Haplo, weak, weary, yet feeling vastly comforted. "I have been a fool. I did not think."

"And you had a Sartan in your power. You could have brought him to me. And you let him go, Haplo. You let him escape. But I can understand. He twisted your mind, made you see things that were not, deceived you. I can understand. You were sick, dying. . . ."

Shame burned. "Don't make excuses for me, My Lord," Haplo protested harshly, his throat raw from his sobs. "I make none for myself. The poison affected my body, not my mind. I am weak, flawed. I no longer deserve your trust."

"No, no, my son. You are not weak. The wound to which I was referring was not the poison given to you by the dynast, but the poison fed to you by the Sartan, Alfred. A far more insidious poison, one that affects the mind, not the body. It inflicted the injury of which I spoke earlier. But that wound is drained now, is it not, my son?"

Xar's fingers twined through Haplo's hair.

The Patryn looked up at his master. The old man's face was lined and marked with his toils, his tireless battles against the powerful magic of the Labyrinth. The skin did not sag, however, the jaw was strong and firm, the nose jutted out from the face like the tearing beak of a fierce flesh-eating bird. The eyes were bright and wise and hungry.

"Yes," said Haplo, "the wound is drained."

"And now it must be cauterized, to prevent the infection from returning."

A scraping sound came from outside the door. The dog, hearing a tone of dire threat in the lord's voice, jumped to its feet, prepared to come to its master's defense.

"Dog, stay," Haplo ordered. He braced himself, bowed his head.

The Lord of the Nexus reached down, took hold of Haplo's

shirt, and, with one tear, rent the fabric in two, laying bare Haplo's back and shoulders. The runes tattooed on his flesh began to glow slightly, red and blue, his body's involuntary reaction to danger, to what he knew was coming.

He clenched his jaw, remained on his knees. The glow of the sigla on his body slowly faded. He lifted his head, fixed his gaze, calm and steadfast, upon his lord.

"I accept my punishment. May it do me good, My Lord."

"May it do so indeed, my son. I take no joy in the giving."

The Lord of the Nexus placed his hand on Haplo's breast, over his heart. He traced a rune with his finger; the nail was long, it drew blood from the flesh. But it did far worse to Haplo's magic. The heart-sigla were the first links in the circle of his being. At the lord's touch, they began to separate, the chain started to break.

The Lord of the Nexus drove the wedge of his magic inside the sigla, forced them apart. A second link slipped from the first, cracked. The third slid off the second, then the fourth and fifth. Faster and faster, the runes that were the source of Haplo's power, his defense against the power of other forces, broke and splintered and shattered.

The pain was excruciating. Slivers of metal pierced his skin, rivers of fire coursed through his blood. Haplo closed his mouth against the screams as long as he could. When they came, he didn't know them for his.

The Lord of the Nexus was skilled at his work. When it seemed Haplo must faint from the agony, Xar ceased the torment, talked gently of their past lives together, until Haplo had recovered his senses. Then the lord began again.

Night, or what the Nexus knows as night, drew its blanket of soft moonlight over the ship. The lord traced a sigil in the air; the torture ceased.

Haplo fell back on the deck and lay like one dead. Sweat covered his naked body, he shook with chills, his teeth chattered. A residue of pain, a flash of flame, a stabbing of a blade, surged through his veins, wrenched from him another agonized cry. His body twitched and jerked spasmodically, out of his control.

The Lord of the Nexus bent down and, once again, laid his hand on Haplo's heart. He could have killed him then. He could have broken the sigil, destroyed it past any hope of repair. Haplo felt the lord's touch, cool on his blazing skin. He shivered, choked back a moan, and lay rigid, perfectly still.

"Execute me! I betrayed you! I don't deserve . . . to live!"

"My son," whispered the Lord of the Nexus in pitying tones. A tear dropped on Haplo's breast. "My poor son."

The teardrop closed and sealed the rune.

Haplo sighed, rolled over, began to weep. Xar gathered the young man close, cradled the bleeding head in his arms, rocked him, soothed him, and worked the magic until all Haplo's runes had been rejoined, the circle of his being reestablished.

Haplo slept, a healing sleep.

The Lord of the Nexus took off his own cape, a cloak of fine, white linen, and drew it over Haplo. The lord paused a moment to look at the young man. The remnants of the agony were fading, leaving Haplo's face strong and grim, calm and resolute—a sword whose metal has been strengthened by being passed through the fire, a granite wall whose cracks have been filled with molten steel.

Xar laid his hands upon the ship's steering stone and, speaking the runes, started it upon its journey through Death's Gate. He was preparing to leave when a thought struck him. He made a quick tour of the vessel, keen eyes peering into every shadow.

The dog was gone.

"Excellent."

The Lord of the Nexus left, well satisfied.

CHAPTER ♦ 2

SOMEWHERE BEYOND

DEATH'S GATE

♦

ALFRED AWOKE, A FRIGHTFUL YELL RINGING IN HIS EARS. HE LAY perfectly still, terrified, listening with fast-beating heart and sweaty palms and squinched-shut eyelids for the yell to be repeated. After long moments of profound silence, Alfred came at last to the rather confused confusion that the yell must have been his own.

"Death's Gate. I fell through Death's Gate! Or rather," he amended, shivering at the thought, "I was *pushed* through Death's Gate."

If I were you, I wouldn't be around when I woke up, Haplo had warned him . . .

. . . Haplo had fallen asleep, fallen into one of the healing sleeps vitally necessary to those of his race. Alfred sat in the lurching ship, alone except for the dog, who lay protectively near its master. Alfred, looking around, realized how alone he was. He was terrified, and he tried to combat his fear by creeping nearer Haplo, seeking company, even if it was unconscious.

Alfred settled himself beside Haplo, occupied himself by studying the Patryn's stern face. He noticed that it did not relax in repose, but retained its grim, forbidding expression, as though nothing, not sleep, perhaps not even death, could bring perfect peace to the man.

Moved by compassion, by pity, Alfred stretched out a hand

to smooth back a lock of hair that fell forward over the implacable face.

The dog raised its head, growled menacingly.

Alfred snatched his hand back. "I'm sorry. I wasn't thinking."

The dog, knowing Alfred, appeared to accept this as a plausible excuse. It settled back down.

Alfred heaved a tremendous sigh, glanced nervously around the lurching ship. He caught a glimpse through the window of the fiery world of Abarrach falling away from them in a confused swirl of smoke and flame. Ahead, he saw the rapidly approaching black hole that was Death's Gate.

"Oh, dear," Alfred murmured, shrinking. If he was going to leave, he had better get going.

The dog had the same idea. It leapt to its feet, started to bark urgently.

"I know. It's time," Alfred said. "You gave me my life, Haplo. And it's not that I'm ungrateful. But . . . I'm too frightened. I don't think I have the courage."

Do you have the courage to stay? the dog seemed to ask in exasperation. *Do you have the courage to face the Lord of the Nexus?*

Haplo's lord—a powerful Patryn wizard. No fainting spell would save Alfred from this terrible man. The lord would prod and probe and drag forth every secret the Sartan had in his being. Torture, torment, lasting for as long as the Sartan remained alive . . . and the lord was certain to ensure his prey lived a long, long time.

The threat must have been sufficient to drive Alfred to action. At least that's what he supposed. He remembered finding himself standing on the upper deck, without the slightest notion how he had come to be there.

The winds of magic and time whistled around him, grabbed disrespectfully at the wisps of hair on his balding head, set his coattails to flapping. Alfred gripped the rail with both hands and stared out, horribly fascinated, into Death's Gate.

And he knew, then, that he could no more hurl himself bodily into that abyss than he could consciously end his own miserable and lonely existence.

"I'm a coward," he said to the dog. Bored, it had followed him up on deck. Alfred smiled wanly, looked down at his hands, clinging to the rail with a white-knuckled grip. "I don't think I could pry myself loose. I—"

The dog suddenly went mad, or so it seemed. Snarling, teeth slashing, it leapt straight at him. Alfred wrenched his hands from the rail, flung them up in front of his face, an instinctive, involuntary act of protection. The dog struck him hard on the chest, knocked him over the side. . . .

What had happened after that? Alfred couldn't remember, except that it was all very confused and all extremely horrible. He had a vivid impression of falling . . . of falling through a hole that seemed far too small for a gnat to enter and yet was large enough to swallow the winged dragonship whole. He remembered falling into brightly lit darkness, of being deafened by a roaring silence, of tumbling head over heels while not moving.

And then, reaching the top, he'd hit bottom.

And that's where he was now, or so he supposed.

He considered opening his eyes, decided against it. He had absolutely no desire to see his surroundings. Wherever he was, it was bound to be awful. He rather hoped that he would lose himself in sleep, and if he was lucky, he wouldn't find himself again.

Unfortunately, as is generally the case, the more he tried to go back to sleep, the wider awake he woke. Bright light shone through his closed eyelids. He became aware of a hard, flat, cool surface beneath him; of various aches and pains in his body that indicated he'd been lying here for some time; of being cold and thirsty and hungry.

No telling where he'd landed. Death's Gate led to each of the four worlds created magically by the Sartan following the Sundering. It led also to the Nexus, the beautiful twilight land meant to hold the "rehabilitated" Patryns after their release from the Labyrinth. Perhaps he was there. Perhaps he was back on Arianus. Perhaps he hadn't really gone anywhere! Perhaps he'd open his eyes and find the dog, grinning at him.

Alfred clamped his eyes tightly shut; his facial muscles ached from the strain. But either curiosity or the stabbing pain shooting through his lower back got the better of him. Groaning, he opened his eyes, sat up, and looked nervously around.

He could have wept for relief.

He was in a large room, circular, lit by lovely, soft white light that emanated from the marble walls. The floor beneath him was marble, inlaid with runes—sigla he knew and recognized. The ceiling arched comfortingly overhead, a dome supported by delicate columns. Embedded in the walls of the room were row after row of crystal chambers, chambers meant to hold people in stasis, chambers that had, tragically, become coffins.

Alfred knew where he was—the mausoleum on Arianus. He was home. And, he decided at once, he would never leave. He would stay in this underground world forever. Here he was safe. No one knew about this place, except for one mensch, a dwarf named Jarre, and she had no means of finding her way back. No one could ever find it now, protected as it was by powerful Sartan magic. The war between the elves and dwarves and humans could rage on Arianus and he would not be part of it. Iridal could search for her changeling son and he would not help. The dead could walk on Abarrach and he would turn his back on all except the familiar, the silent blessed dead that were his companions once more.

After all, one man, alone, what can I do? he asked himself wistfully.

Nothing.

What can I be expected to do?

Nothing.

Who could possibly expect me to do it?

No one.

Alfred repeated that to himself. "No one." He recalled the wonderful, awful experience on Abarrach when he had seemed to know with certainty that some sort of higher power for good was present in the universe, to know that he wasn't alone, as he had supposed all these years.

But the knowledge, his certainty, had faded, died with young Jonathan, who had been destroyed by the dead and the lazar of Abarrach.

"I must have imagined it," said Alfred sadly. "Or perhaps Haplo was right. Perhaps I created that vision we all experienced and didn't know I created it. Like my fainting, or like casting that spell that took the magical life from the dead. And, if that's true, then what Haplo said was true as well. I led poor Jonathan to his death. Deceived by false visions, false promises, he sacrificed himself for nothing."

Alfred bowed his head into his trembling hands, his thin shoulders slumped. "Everywhere I go, disaster follows. And therefore, I won't go anywhere. I won't do anything. I'll stay here. Safe, protected, surrounded by those I once loved."

He couldn't, however, spend the remainder of his life on the floor. There were other rooms, other places to go. The Sartan had once lived down here. Shaking, stiff, and sore, he endeavored to stand up. His feet and legs appeared to have other ideas, resented being forced back to work. They crumbled beneath him. He fell, persisted in trying to stand, and, after a moment, managed to do so. Once he was finally upright, his feet seemed inclined to wander off one way when he actually had it in mind to go the opposite.

Finally, all his body parts more or less in agreement as to the general direction he was headed, Alfred propelled himself toward the crystal coffins, to bid fond greeting to those he had left far too long. The bodies in the coffins would never return his greeting, never speak words of welcome to him. Their eyes would never open to gaze at him with friendly pleasure. But he was comforted by their presence, by their peace.

Comforted and envious.

Necromancy. The thought flitted across his mind, skittering like a bat. You could bring them back to life.

But the dread shadow lay over him only momentarily. He wasn't tempted. He had seen the dire consequences of necromancy on Abarrach. And he had the terrible feeling that these friends of his had died because of the necromancy, their lifeforce stolen from them, given to those who, he now suspected, didn't want it.

Alfred went straight to one coffin, one he knew well. In it lay the woman he loved. He needed, after the horrible sights of the restless dead on Abarrach, to see her calm and peaceful sleep. He placed his hands on the outside of the crystal window behind which she lay and, fondly, tears in his eyes, pressed his forehead against the glass.

Something was wrong.

Admittedly, his vision was blurred by his tears. He couldn't see well. Hastily, Alfred blinked, rubbed his hands over his eyes. He stared, fell back, startled, shocked.

No, it couldn't be. He was overwrought, he'd made a mistake. Slowly he crept back, peered inside the coffin.

Inside was the body of a Sartan female, but it wasn't Lya!

Alfred shivered from head to toe.

"Calm down!" he counseled. "You're standing in the wrong place. You've gotten turned around by that terrible trip through Death's Gate. You've made a mistake. You've looked into the wrong crystal chamber. Go back and start over."

He turned around and tottered once more to the center of the room, barely able to stand, his knees as weak as wet flax. From this distance, he carefully counted the rows of crystal chambers, counted them up, then counted them across. Telling himself that he'd been a row too far over, he crept back, ignoring the voice that was telling him he'd been in exactly the right place all along.

He kept his gaze averted, refusing to look until he was near, in case his eyes might play another trick on him. Once arrived, he shut his eyes and then opened them swiftly, as if hoping to catch something in the act.

The strange woman was still there.

Alfred gasped, shuddered, leaned heavily against the crystal chamber. What was happening? Was he going insane?

"It's quite likely," he said. "After all I've been through. Perhaps Lya was never there at all. Perhaps I only willed her to be there and now, after all this time away, I can't call her to mind."

He looked again, but if his mind was truly behaving irrationally, it was doing it in a most rational manner. The woman was older than Lya, close to Alfred's age, he guessed. Her hair was completely white; her face—a handsome face, he thought, gazing at it in sorrowful confusion—had lost the elasticity and smooth beauty of youth. But she had gained, in exchange, the becoming gravity and purpose of middle age.

Her expression was solemn and grave, yet softened by lines around that mouth that seemed to indicate a warm and generous smile had graced her lips. A line down the center of her forehead, barely visible beneath the soft folds of her hair, indicated that her life had not been easy, that she had pondered much, thought long and hard about many things. And there was a sadness about her. The smile that touched the lips had not touched them often. Alfred felt a deep hunger and an aching unhappiness. Here was someone he could have talked to, someone who would have understood.

But . . . what was she doing here?

"Lie down. I must lie down."

Blindly, his vision clouded by his confused thoughts, Alfred stumbled and groped his way along the wall that held many crystal chambers until he came to his own. He would return to it, lie down, sleep . . . or maybe wake up. He might be dreaming. He—

"Blessed Sartan!" Alfred fell back with a hoarse cry.

Someone was in it! His chamber! A man of early middle years, with a strong, cold, handsome face; strong hands stretched out at his side.

"I *am* mad!" Alfred clutched at his head. "This . . . this is impossible." He stumbled back to stare at the woman who was not Lya. "I'll shut my eyes and when I open them, all will be well again."

But he didn't shut his eyes. Not trusting himself to believe what he thought he'd seen, he looked fixedly at the woman. Her hands were folded across her breast—

The hands. The hands moved! They rose . . . fell! She had drawn a breath.

He watched closely for long moments; the magical stasis in which they lay slowed breathing. The hands rose and fell again. And now that Alfred was over his initial shock, he could see the faint flush of blood in the woman's cheeks, a flush that he would never see in Lya's.

"This woman's . . . alive!" Alfred whispered.

He staggered across to the crystal chamber that had been his own, but was now another's, and stared inside it. The man's clothing—a plain, simple, white robe—stirred. Eyeballs beneath closed lids moved; a finger twitched.

Feverishly, his mind overwhelmed, his heart almost bursting with joy, Alfred ran from one crystal chamber to another, staring inside each.

There could be no doubt. Every one of these Sartan was alive!

Exhausted, his mind reeling, Alfred returned to the center of the mausoleum and tried to unravel the tangled skein of his thoughts. It was impossible. He couldn't find the end of the thread, couldn't find the beginning.

His friends in the mausoleum had been dead for many, many years. Time and again he'd left them, time and again he'd returned, and nothing had ever changed. When he'd first realized that he and he alone, out of all the Sartan on Arianus, had survived, he'd refused to believe it. He'd played a game with himself, told himself that this time, when he came back, he'd find them alive. But he never had, and soon the game became so exceedingly painful that he'd quit playing it.

But now the game was back on and, what's more, he'd won!

Admittedly these Sartan were strangers, every one of them. He had no idea how they came to be here, or why, or what had happened to those he'd left behind. But these people were Sartan and they were alive!

Unless, of course, he was truly insane.

There was one way to find out. Alfred hesitated, not certain he wanted to know.

"Remember what you said about retreating from the world? About no longer getting involved in other people's lives? You could leave, walk out of this chamber without looking back."

"But where would I go?" he asked himself helplessly. "This is my home, if anyplace to me is home."

Curiosity, if nothing else, propelled him to act.

Alfred began to chant the runes, singing them in a high-pitched nasal voice. As he chanted, his body swayed and he moved his hands in time to his rhythm. Then, lifting his hands, he traced the sigla in the air and, at the same time, formed their intricate patterns with his feet.

The body that was so incredibly clumsy when left on its own filled with magic and Alfred became, for an instant, beautiful. Grace flowed through every limb, radiance touched his sad face, bliss lit his smile. He gave himself to the magic, danced with it, sang to it, embraced it. Round and round the mausoleum he solemnly whirled, coattails flying, frayed lace fluttering.

One by one, crystal doors opened. One by one, those in the chamber drew their first breaths of air of an outside world. One by one, heads turned, eyes opened, gazing in wonder or confusion, loath to leave the sweet dreams that had entertained them.

Alfred, lost in the magic, noticed nothing. He continued his dance, weaving gracefully back and forth across the marble floor, feet moving in prescribed patterns. When the magical spell was cast, the dance coming to its end, he moved slower and slower, continuing the same graceful gestures, but smaller in scope. At last, he ceased to dance and, lifting his head, gazed about him, far more bewildered than those who had just risen from their dreams.

Several hundred men and women, all clad in soft white robes, had gathered in silence around Alfred, politely waiting for him to complete his magic before disturbing him. He came to a halt and they waited another respectful moment, to give him time to let go of the bliss and return to reality, tantamount to falling into an ice-cold lake.

A man, the same Sartan who had been in Alfred's crystal chamber, stepped forward. He was obviously the acknowledged spokesman of the group, for the others gave way deferentially, regarded him with trust and respect.

He was, as Alfred had seen already, a man in early midlife, and it was easy to see, from his appearance, how the mensch had once mistaken the Sartan for gods. His face was cast in strong lines; intelligence molded the features and lit the brown eyes. His hair was trimmed short and curled over his forehead in a fashion that was familiar to Alfred, yet he couldn't quite recall where he'd seen it.

The strange Sartan moved with a casual grace the clumsy Alfred envied.

"I am Samah," said the man in a voice that was rich and mellow. He bowed in respectful greeting, an old-fashioned, courtly gesture that had gone out of style long before Alfred's childhood, but had been occasionally practiced among the elder Sartan.

Alfred made no response. He could do nothing except stare, transfixed. The man had given his Sartan name![1] This either meant that Samah trusted Alfred—a stranger, an unknown—as a brother or that he was so supremely secure in his own magical prowess he had no need to fear another gaining ascendancy over

---

[1]Since the Sartan language is magic in and of itself, Sartan have two names: a private name which is magical and could possibly give another Sartan power over them and a public name that tends to nullify magic.

him. Alfred concluded the reason must be the latter. The man's power radiated from him, warming the wretched Alfred like the sun on a winter's day.

In ages past, Alfred would have given this man his own Sartan name without a thought, knowing that any influence such a man as this must have over him could only be good. But that had been an Alfred of innocence, an Alfred who had not seen the bodies of his friends and family stretched out in their crystal coffins, an Alfred who had not seen Sartan practicing the forbidden black art of necromancy. He longed to trust them, he would have given his very life to trust them.

"My name is . . . Alfred," he said, with an awkward bob.

"That is not a Sartan name," said Samah, frowning.

"No," Alfred agreed meekly.

"It is a mensch name. But you are a Sartan, are you not? You are not a mensch?"

"Yes, I am. That is, no, I'm not," Alfred floundered, rattled.

The Sartan language, as the Patryn language, being magic, has the ability to conjure up images of the worlds and environment of the speaker. Alfred had just witnessed, in Samah's words, a realm of extraordinary beauty, a realm made entirely of water, its sun shining in its center. A world of smaller worlds—landmasses encased in bubbles of air, landmasses that were themselves magically alive though now they slept, drifting in their dreams around the sun. He saw a Sartan city, his people working, fighting . . .

Fighting. War. Battle. Savage monsters crawling from the deep, wreaking havoc, bringing death. The vastly conflicting images came together with a crash in Alfred's head, nearly depriving him of his senses.

"I am head of the Council of Seven," began Samah.

Alfred gaped; the breath left his body as completely as if he'd been knocked flat on the floor.

Samah. Council of Seven. It couldn't be possible. . . .

It occurred to Alfred, eventually, by the man's frown, that he was asking a question.

"I—I beg your pardon?" Alfred stammered.

The rest of the Sartan, who had been standing in respectful silence, murmured, exchanged glances. Samah looked around, quieted them without speaking a word.

"I was saying, Alfred"—Samah's tone was kind, patient. It made Alfred want to burst into tears—"that, as head of the Council, I have the right and the duty to ask questions of you, not from mere idle curiosity, but, considering these times of crises, out of necessity. Where are the rest of our brethren?"

He glanced about eagerly.

"I . . . I am alone," Alfred said, and the word *alone* conjured up images that made Samah and all the rest of the Sartan stare at him in sudden, aching silence.

"Has something gone wrong?" Samah asked at last.

Yes! Alfred wanted to cry. Something has gone dreadfully wrong! But he could only stare at the Sartan in dismayed confusion, the truth thundering around him like the fearsome storm that rages perpetually on Arianus.

"I . . . I'm not on Arianus, am I?" Alfred squeezed the words out of the tight feeling in his chest.

"No. What put such an idea into your head? You are on the world of Chelestra, of course," said Samah sternly, his patience starting to wear thin.

"Oh, dear," said Alfred faintly, and in a graceful, spiraling motion, he slid gently and unconsciously to the floor.

CHAPTER ♦ 3

ADRIFT SOMEWHERE

THE GOODSEA

♦

My name is grundle.[1]

When I was a child, that is the first sentence I ever learned how to write. I'm not certain why I wrote it down here, or why I begin with it, except that I have stared at this blank page for a long time now and I knew that I had to write something or I would never write anything.

I wonder who will find this and read it? Or if anyone will. I doubt that I will ever know. We have no hope of surviving our journey's end.

(Except, of course, the perverse hope that a miracle will happen, that something or someone will come to save us. Alake says that to hope for such a thing, especially to pray for it, is wicked, since if we were saved our people would suffer. I suppose she is right, she being the most intelligent among us. But I notice she continues to practice her exercises in summoning and conjuration and she would not do so if she was practicing what she counsels.)

It was Alake who recommended that I write the account of our voyage. She says our people may find it, after we are gone, and take some comfort in it. Then, of course, it is also necessary to explain about Devon. All of which is true, but I suspect she

---

[1] *Dear Stranger,* a journal kept by Grundle Heavybeard, princess of Gargan.

gave me this task so that I would leave her alone and quit pestering her when she wanted to practice her magic.

And I suppose she's right. It's better to do this than to sit and do nothing except wait for death. But I have my doubts that any of our people will ever see this. I think it will more likely be some stranger.

It's odd for me to think a stranger may be reading this after I am dead. Odder still to find myself sharing my fears and doubts with a stranger, when I can't share them with those I love. Perhaps that person will be from another seamoon. If there are other seamoons, which I doubt. Still, Alake says it's sinful to think that the One might have made us and no one else. But we dwarves are great doubters, suspicious of anything that hasn't been around at least as long as we have.

I doubt that our deaths will accomplish anything.

I doubt that the Masters of the Sea will keep their word. Our sacrifice will be for nothing. Our people are doomed.

There. I've put it down at last. I feel better for it, though I will have to make certain now that Alake never sees this journal.

My name is Grundle.

It came much easier that time. My father is Yngvar Heavybeard, Vater[2] of the Gargan. My mother is Hilda. In her youth, she was said to be the most beautiful woman in all the seamoon. Songs have been made of *my* beauty, but I've seen a portrait done on her wedding day; I'm plain, compared to her. Her side whiskers came almost to her waist and were the honey color, which is extremely rare and prized among dwarves.

My father tells the story that when my mother stepped out onto the field of contest, the other contenders took one look at her and walked off, leaving her the unchallenged winner. My mother, I am told, was extremely put out at this, for she had practiced long at the ax-throw and could hit the target five times out of six. If I had stayed on Gargan, they would have been holding the marriage contests for me, since I'm near the end of the Time of Seeking.

That blot is a tear. Now I'm certain I can't let Alake see this!

---

[2]Father or king. The queen is known as Muter—mother.

I wasn't crying for myself, mind you. I was crying for Hartmut. He loves me very much. And I love him. But I can't let myself think about him or the tears will wash out the ink on the page.

The person who finds this will probably be astonished to discover a dwarf writing this account. Our people have little use for such matters as reading and writing and ciphering. Writing makes the mind lazy, according to my people, who each keep the entire history of Gargan in their heads, plus the history of their individual families. Dwarves, in fact, have no written language of their own, which is why I am writing this in human.

We keep excellent accounts in our heads, as well—a marvel to human and elven purveyors. I have yet to see the dwarf who couldn't tell to the grain how much money he or she has made in a lifetime. Some old graybeards will go on for cycles!

I myself would never have learned to read and write, except that I am—or was—destined to be ruler of my people. And since I would be dealing so closely with our human and elven allies, my father and mother decided that I should be brought up among them and educated in their ways. And (I think they considered this more important!) they wanted me to educate the humans and elves in our ways.

At an early age, I was sent to Elmas—the elven seamoon[3]— along with Alake, the daughter of the chieftain of Phondra. Alake is near my age mentally, if not in terms of actual cycles. (Humans lead such pitifully short lives, they are forced to grow up rapidly.) With us was Sabia, the elven princess, who joined us in our studies.

Beautiful, gentle Sabia. I will never see her again. But the One be thanked that she escaped this cruel fate.

We three girls spent many years together, driving our teachers to distraction and learning to love each other like sisters. Indeed, we became closer than most sisters I've known, for there was never any rivalry or jealousy between us.

Our only disagreements stemmed from learning to put up with the others' shortcomings. But our parents were wise in rais-

---

[3]One of many small, habitable landmasses created by the Sartan. Their name derives from the fact that these small moons orbit the seasun of Chelestra, albeit on the inside, not the outside.

ing us together. For example, I had never much liked humans. They talk too loudly and too fast, are too aggressive, and keep bouncing from one subject to another, one place to another. They never seem to sit still or take time to think.

Being around humans over a long period of time taught me to understand that their impatience and ambition and their constant need for hurry, hurry, hurry is just their way of attempting to outrace their own mortality.

By contrast, I learned that the long-lived elves are not lazy dreamers, as most dwarves consider them, but people who simply take life at their leisure, without a worry or care for tomorrow, since they are certain to have almost innumerable tomorrows left to deal with it.

And Alake and Sabia were good enough to put up with my blunt honesty, a trait of my people. (I would like to think it is a good one, but it *can* be carried to extremes!) A dwarf will always tell the truth, no matter how little anyone else is prepared to hear it. We can also be very stubborn, and once we dig in our heels we stay put and rarely budge. An unusually stubborn human is said to have "feet like a dwarf."

In addition, I learned how to speak and write fluent human and elven (though our poor governess was always offended by the awkward way I held my pen). I studied the histories of their seamoons and their differing versions of the history of our world, Chelestra. But what I truly learned was affection for my dear sister-friends and, through them, their races.

We used to plan what we would do to bring our people even closer together when we at last came to rule, each of us on our own seamoon.

Never to be. We none of us will live that long.

I suppose I had better tell what happened.

It all began the day I was to bless the sun-chaser. *My* day. My wonderful day.

I could not sleep for excitement. Hurriedly I dressed myself in my best clothes—a long-sleeved blouse of plain and serviceable fabric (we have no use for frills), an overdress laced behind, and stout, thick boots. Standing before the looking glass in my bedroom in my father's house, I began the day's most important task: brushing and curling my hair and side whiskers.

The time seemed all too short before I heard my father calling for me. I made believe I hadn't heard him, stood looking at myself with a critical eye, wondering if I was fit to be seen in public. You mustn't think that such attention to my appearance was all for vanity's sake. As heir to the Gargan throne, I'm expected to both look and act the part.

I had to admit—I was pretty.

I cleared away the pots of oil, imported from the elves of Elmas, and replaced the curling tongs carefully in their stand by the grate. Sabia, who has servants falling all over her (and who has never once brushed her own long blonde hair), can't get over the fact that I not only dress myself, but clean up afterward. We Gargan are a proud and self-sufficient people and would never dream of waiting on each other in a menial capacity. Our Vater chops his own fire wood; our Muter does her own laundry and sweeps her own floor. I curl my own hair. The only mark of distinction the royal family receives above all other Gargan is that we are expected to work twice as hard as anyone else.

Today, however, our family was to have one of the rewards for services rendered to the people. The fleet of sun-chasers had been completed. My father would ask the blessing of the One upon them, and I would have the honor of nailing a lock of my hair to the bow of the flagship.

My father yelled again. Swiftly, I left my room, hurried out into the hall.

"Where is the lass?" I heard my father demand of my mother. "The seasun will have passed us by. We'll be frozen solid by the time she's ready."

"This is her big day," said my mother soothingly. "You want her to look well. All her suitors will be there."

"Bah!" Father grumbled. "She's far too young to be thinking of such things."

"Perhaps. But what catches the eye now catches the head later," said my mother, quoting a dwarven proverb.[4]

"Hunh!" My father snorted.

---

[4]Dwarves make several stages of progression through life, beginning with the Time of Weaning, proceeding through the Time of Seeking, and advancing into the Time of Sense. Dwarves are not permitted to marry until they reach the Time of Sense, when it is considered that the hot blood of the

But, when he caught sight of me, his stomach puffed out with pride, and he said nothing more about my being late.

Father, I miss you so! Oh, how hard it is! How hard.

We left our house that is more like a cave bored straight into the mountain. All our homes and businesses are built inside the mountain, unlike human and elven structures that are built on the mountain slopes. It took me a long time to get used to living in the Elmas coral castle that seemed, in my mind, to cling precariously to the rock. I had dreams about its tumbling down the mountainside, carrying me with it!

The morning was beautiful. The rays of the seasun shimmered up through the waves.[5] The sparse clouds that floated over the warren caught the sun's glow. My family joined the throngs of dwarves walking down the steeply sloping path to the shore of the Goodsea. Our neighbors called out to my father, more than a few coming up to slap him on his broad stomach— a typical dwarven form of greeting—and invite him to join them in the tavern after the ceremony.

My father slapped stomachs in return, and we continued down the mountainside. When on land, the Gargan travel everywhere on their own two feet. Carts are meant to haul potatoes, not people. And although we dwarves have grown accustomed to the sight of elves riding around in carriages and humans using beasts to bear their burdens, most Gargans consider such laziness to be a symbol of the weakness inherent in the other two races.

The only vehicle we dwarves use are our famous submersibles—ships designed to sail the Goodsea. Such ships—the dwarves' pride—were developed out of necessity since we have

---

Seeking time has cooled into the common sense of adulthood. This is equivalent in human terms to about fifty years of age. After the Time of Sense, at approximately the age of two hundred, dwarves pass into the Time of Wisdom.

[5]The seasun's position relative to the seamoons makes it appear, to those standing on these particular moons, as if the sun is in the water beneath them. Light shines from the water, therefore, not the sky. The sky itself often appears a turquoise color that comes from mosses growing on the surface of the air-caverns of the seamoon.

an unfortunate tendency to sink like stones in the water. The dwarf has not been born who can swim.

We Gargans are such clever shipbuilders that the Phondrans and the Elmas, who once built ships of their own, ceased to do so and came to rely solely on our craft. Now, with the help of financing from the humans and elves, we had constructed our masterpiece—a fleet of sun-chasers, enough submersibles to carry the populations of three seamoons.

"It's been generations since we have been called on to build the sun-chasers," stated my father. We had paused a moment to look proudly down from the steeply slanting roadway to the harbor at sea level, far below. "And never a fleet this big, designed to carry so many. This is a historic occasion, one that will be long remembered."

"And such an honor for Grundle," said my mother, smiling at me.

I returned my mother's smile, but said nothing. We dwarves are not noted for our sense of humor, but I am considered serious-minded and sober even for a dwarf and my thoughts today were concentrated on my duties. I have an extremely practical nature, not a shred of sentimentality or romance (as Sabia used to comment sadly).

"I wish your friends were here to see you today," my mother added. "We invited them, but, of course, they are extremely busy among their own people, preparing for the Sun Chase."

"Yes, Mother," I agreed. "It would have been nice if they could have come."

I would not alter dwarven life-style for the trapping of the seasun, but I could not help envying the respect accorded Alake by the Phondrans or the love and reverence shown Sabia by the Elmas. Among my people I am, most of the time, just another dwarf maiden. I comforted myself with the knowledge that I would be able to tell my friends all about it and (I must be honest) with the knowledge that neither would have a lock of her hair on the bow of a sun-chaser!

We reached the harbor, where the gigantic submersibles floated at anchor. Now that I was near them, I was overawed by the immensity of the ships, the amount of work that had gone into creating them.

The sun-chasers had been built to resemble black whales,

their prows smooth and made of the drywood of Phondra, so-called because it is covered with a type of natural resin that protects it from water damage. Windows studded the hull, shining like jewels in the seasun. And the size! I couldn't believe it! Each sun-chaser, and there were ten of them, was nearly eight stadion[6] in length. I marveled at the size, but then, I reminded myself, they have to carry the populations of three realms.

The sea breeze rose. I smoothed my whiskers, my mother patted my hair into place. The crowd of dwarves gathered at the wharf made way good-naturedly for us. The Gargans, though excited, were orderly and disciplined, none of the boisterous shoving and pushing that one would have seen in a similar gathering of humans.

We walked among them, nodding to left and right. The dwarven men put their hands to their forelocks, a sign of formal respect, suitable to the solemnity of the occasion. The women curtsied and prodded their offspring, who were staring open-mouthed at the great submersibles and who could not be made to turn their attention from these wonders to such an everyday sight as their king.

I walked beside my mother, the proper place for an unmarried young dwarf maid. I looked straight ahead, endeavoring to keep my eyes modestly lowered, my mind on what I was supposed to do. But I had difficulty preventing my glance from straying to the two long rows of leather-armored, clean-shaven young men standing at attention at the end of the wharf.

All dwarven males, at the Time of Seeking, are expected to serve in the military. The best had been chosen to act as honor guard for the Vater and his family this day. It was one of the these young men who, more than likely, would win the privilege of being my husband. It wasn't really proper for me to have favorites, but I knew Hartmut would be able to easily defeat all comers.

He caught me looking at him and gave me a smile that made

---

[6]Dwarven standard of measure: 1 stadion = 620 dwarf feet. The stadion is also a dwarven footrace that commemorates the combined Times of the reign of the first two kings. Whether the race was named after the standard or vice versa is not known.

me go all warm inside. He is so good-looking! His russet hair is long and thick, his side whiskers are auburn, and his beard, when he is allowed to grow it after his marriage, will most certainly match. He has already attained the rank of fourclan master, a high honor for an unmarried dwarf.[7]

The soldiers, at a word from their marshall, brought their arms—axes, the favored weapon—up in salute, whirled them around, and thudded the axheads on the ground.

I noted that Hartmut handled his ax with far greater dexterity than any other dwarf in his clan. This boded well for the future since ax-throwing, chopping, and ducking determine the winner of the marriage contest.

My mother caught hold of my sleeve, gave it a sharp tug.

"Stop staring at that young man!" she whispered. "What will he think of you?"

I obediently shifted my gaze to my father's broad back, but I was very much aware of passing close to Hartmut, who stood at the wharf's edge. And I heard him thump the head of the ax on the ground again, just for me.

A small ceremonial platform had been erected for us at the bow of the flagship, lifting us above the crowd. We climbed up onto the platform. My father stepped forward. The audience, though it had never been making much noise, quieted immediately.

"My family,"[8] began my father, clasping his hands over his broad stomach, "many and many Times have passed since our people have been forced to make the Sun Chase. Not even the eldest among us"—a respectful nod to an elderly dwarf, whose

---

[7]Dwarven military service is organized around family clans whose young men serve together as a unit. Units, known as regos, are organized under the clan master. Hartmut commands a rego consisting of four clans, thus his title. Above him are the rego master, the marshall, the clan master, and, finally, the Vater.

[8]The dwarves on Chelestra believe that they are all descendants of the only two dwarves to have survived the Sundering and that they are, therefore, all related to each other. While the legend is highly suspect, it does help explain the solid unity of the dwarfs, who have a strong regard for family. In this sense, the royal family are viewed more as parent figures than as monarches.

beard was yellow with age and who stood in the place of honor at the very forefront of the crowd—"can remember back to the time our people chased the seasun and landed on Gargan."

"My father could remember it," piped up the old dwarf. "He made the journey when he was a little boy."

My father paused a moment, his thoughts scattered by the unexpected interruption. I looked over the heads of the crowd, back to the warren and its neat rows of bright-colored doors, and it occurred to me for the first time that I must actually leave this land of my birth and travel to another land, a strange land, a land that would have no doors leading into the safe, dark sanctuary of the mountain.

My eyes filled with tears. I lowered my head, ashamed to have anyone (particularly Hartmut) see me cry.

"A new realm awaits us, a seamoon large enough for all three races—humans, elves, dwarves—to live on, each in our own separate realm, but each trading, working together, sharing to build a prosperous world.

"The trip will be long," my father continued, "and tiring. And when we arrive, we face backbreaking labor and toil to rebuild our homes and businesses. It will be difficult to leave Gargan. Much that we love and value must, of necessity, be left behind us. But that which we prize and cherish above all else, we take with us. And that is each other. We could leave behind everything, every coin, every stitch of clothing, every cooking pot and cradle and bed, and, because we have each other, the dwarven nation would arrive at its destination strong and prepared to go forth and establish our greatness on this new world!"

My father, during his speech, had put his arm around my mother. My mother clasped hold of my hand. Our people cheered loudly. My tears dried.

"As long as we have each other," I said to myself. "As long as we are together, this new land will be our home."

I peeped shyly at Hartmut. His eyes were shining. He smiled at me, only for me. Everything was said between us in that look, that smile. The marriage contests can't be rigged, but most dwarves know the outcome in advance.

My father spoke on, discussing how, for the first time in Chelestran history, humans and elves and dwarves would be making the Sun Chase together.

In times past, we'd done the Sun Chase, of course, hastening after the seasun that drifts endlessly through the water that is our world. But then it had been the dwarves alone, fleeing the approaching longnight of ice that would slowly encase our seamoon.

I shoved the unhappy thought of leaving my homeland from my mind, began to think about the fun times aboard ship with Alake and Sabia. I'd tell them about Hartmut, point him out. Not that any human female or elven maid could properly appreciate how handsome he is.

My father coughed. I saw him staring at me. My mother nudged me in the ribs. I came back to the proceedings instantly, feeling my face burning. I held in my hand the lock of my hair, already cut and tied with a bright blue ribbon. My father handed me the hammer, my mother the nail. I took them both, turned to the broad wooden beam of the sun-chaser that towered high above me. The crowd was quiet, waiting for the chance to cheer wildly when the ceremony was completed.

Feeling all eyes (two eyes in particular) on me, I twined the ribboned lock of hair firmly around the nail, put the nail to the wooden hull, and was just about to rap the nail smartly with the hammer, when I heard a low murmur sweep through the crowd. It reminded me of the rising of the sea during one of the rare Chelestran storms.

My first thought, I remember, was one of extreme irritation that something or someone was ruining my big moment. Aware that the crowd's attention had been drawn from me, I lowered the hammer and glanced around indignantly to see what all the fuss was about.

Every Gargan—man, woman, and child—was staring out to sea. Some were pointing. Those shorter than the rest were standing on tiptoe, craning their necks to get a look.

"It figures," I grumbled, endeavoring to peer around the submersible and not having much luck. "Alake and Sabia have come after all, right in the middle of everything. Well, their timing was bad, but at least they'll be here to watch. I can always start over."

But I could tell by the expressions on the faces of the dwarves standing below me, who had clear view out to sea, that whatever was coming wasn't one of the gaily decorated swan ships we

build for the elves, or one of the sturdy fishing ships we build
for the humans. These would have been welcomed with much
beard-wagging and the occasional hand-wave, about as demon-
strative as dwarves ever get. Now beards were being stroked—
a sign of dwarven unease—and mothers were quickly rounding
up children who had strayed.

The marshall of the dwarven army ran to the platform.

"Vater, you must see this!" he shouted.

"Stay here," my father ordered us, and descending the platform, he hurried after the marshall.

The ceremony was obviously ruined. I was angry about that,
angry about the fact that I couldn't see a thing, angry at Father
for dashing off. I stood clutching the hammer and the lock of hair
and cursed the fate that made me a princess, left me standing on
this stupid platform when every other person in Gargan had a
clear view of what was going on.

I didn't dare disobey my father—a dwarf maid who did that
would have her side whiskers clipped in punishment, a humiliating experience—but surely it wouldn't hurt if I moved to the end
of the platform. Perhaps I could see from there. I had taken a
step and could hear my mother draw in her breath to order me
back when Hartmut jumped up onto the platform and ran to us.

"The Vater has commanded me to keep you and your daughter safe in his absence, Muter," he said, with a respectful bow
to my mother.

His eyes were on me, however.

Perhaps fate knew what it was about, after all. I decided to
stay where I was.

"What's happening?" my mother was asking anxiously.

"A disturbance in the sea, nothing more," said Hartmut casually. "An oil slick of some sort is spreading and a few people
thought they saw heads sticking up out of it, but I think they're
looking through the bottom of an ale mug. Most likely it's a
school of fish. The boats are setting out to investigate."

My mother seemed reassured. I wasn't. I saw Hartmut's eyes
stray to his marshall, watching for orders. And though he was
making a gallant attempt to smile, his face was grim.

"I think, Muter," he continued, "that until we establish just
what's causing this oil slick, it might be wise if you were to step
down from this platform."

"You're right, young man. Grundle, give me that hammer. You look silly standing there, hanging onto it. I'm going to go join your father. No, Grundle, you stay with the young guard."

My mother bustled off the platform and sallied out into the crowd after my father. I sent my thanks and my blessing after her.

"I don't think you look silly," Hartmut said to me. "I think you look splendid."

I edged closer to the young dwarf, and now that my hand was free of the hammer, it could accidentally find its way into his hand. The boats were putting off from the beach, their rowers pulling on the oars, shooting out to sea. We left the platform and, along with the rest of the population of Gargan, hurried down to the water's edge.

"What do you think it is?" I asked in a low voice.

"I don't know," said Hartmut, allowing his trouble to show now that we were alone. "We've heard odd tales all week. The dolphins report strange creatures swimming the Goodsea. Serpents whose skin is covered with oil that fouls the water and poisons any fish unlucky enough to wander into it."

"Where did they come from?" I drew nearer.

"No one knows. According to the dolphins, when the seasun began altering its course, it thawed out several seamoons that have been frozen for the One knows how long. Perhaps these creatures came from one of those moons."

"Look!" I gasped. "Something's happening."

Most of the dwarves in their small boats had ceased to row. Some had shipped their oars and sat motionless in the water, staring out to sea. Others had nervously begun to pull back for shore. I could see nothing except the oil on the water—a greenish, brownish slime that smoothed out the waves and left a film on the sides of the boats it touched. I could smell it, too; a noxious odor that made me sick to my stomach.

Hartmut gripped my hand hard. The water was starting to recede! I'd never seen anything like it—as if some gigantic mouth were sucking the water out from under us!

Several boats were already beached, left stranded on the wet, oil-coated sand. Those boats standing farther out were being sucked along with the water! The sailors pulled on the oars, battling frantically to halt their forward motion. The submersibles sank lower and lower, then, rocking back and forth, they struck bottom with a tearing, grinding sound.

And then, an enormous head soared upward out of the waves. Its skin was gray-green and covered with scales that glistened in the weak sunlight with an ugly iridescence. Its head was small, the same size as the neck. It seemed to be *all* neck, unless one counted the back part as tail. The serpent moved in a horrible, sinuous curve. Its eyes were green when it first looked at us, but then the eyes changed, began to glow a dreadful fiery red. The serpent drew itself up and up and, as it rose, it sucked the water up with it.

It was huge, monstrous. It seemed half the height of the mountain, at least.

I watched the seawater rush away from me and I had the sudden, frightening feeling that I was about to be carried out into it. Hartmut put his arm around me. His body, thick and stocky, was solid and reassuring.

The serpent reached what seemed an impossible height, then down it dropped, smashed headfirst into the flagship, punching a huge hole in the ship's hull. The seawater surged back to shore in a great wave.

"Run!" my father shouted, his voice booming over the shocked cries of the crowd. "Run for the mountain!"

The Gargan turned and fled. Even in our fear, there was no confusion or disorder, no panic. Elder dwarves, who couldn't move fast enough, were whisked off their feet by their sons and daughters and carried bodily. Mothers grabbed infants, fathers lifted older children to their shoulders.

"Run on ahead, Grundle!" Hartmut told me. "I must return to my command."

He raced off, hefting his battle-ax, to rejoin the army that was grouping at the water's edge, prepared to cover the people's retreat.

I knew I should run, but my feet seemed to have gone numb; my legs were too weak to do anything more than keep me standing upright. I stared at the serpent, who had risen, unharmed, out of the wreckage of the submersible. Toothless mouth gaping in what might have been a noiseless laugh, it hurled itself down on another ship. Wood splintered and broke apart. Other creatures that looked exactly like the first rose out of the sea and started to break apart the remainder of the submersibles and any other boat they could find. The waves created by the creatures thundered down on the shoreline, completing the destruction.

Boats capsized, hurling their crews into the water. Some were simply swallowed up, the dwarves on board disappearing in the oil-covered foam. The army stood fast against the serpents. Hartmut was bravest of all of them, advancing into the water, his ax raised in challenge. The serpents ignored them, contented themselves with smashing all the boats in the harbor—except one, the royal ship, the one we used to sail back and forth to Phondra and Elmas.

The serpent paused, looked at us and at the havoc its creatures had wrecked. Its eyes had changed from red to green, their gaze was flat and unblinking. It turned its head from side to side in a slow, sweeping gesture, and whenever its dread gaze touched any of us, we shrank beneath it. When it spoke, the other serpents behind it ceased their destruction to listen.

The serpent spoke perfect dwarven.

"This message is for you and your allies, the humans and the elves. We are the new masters of the sea. You will sail it only with our permission and our permission can be obtained only by paying a price. What that price is to be, you will be told later. What you have seen today is a sample of our power, of what will happen to you if you do not pay. Heed well our warning!"

The serpent dove back down in the water and vanished. The others followed, swimming rapidly through the bits and pieces of wood floating on the slimy surface. We stood looking at the ruins of the sun-chasers. I remember the silence that fell over the people. No one even yet wept for the dead.

When all were certain that the serpents were finally gone, we began the grim task of retrieving the bodies of those who had died—all of them, it turned out, appeared to have been poisoned. Once pure and safe to drink, the seawater was now coated with a foul oil slick that killed anything unlucky enough to swallow it.

And that was how all this began. There is more, much more, to my story, but I hear Alake coming through the ship, looking for me, calling to me that it's time to eat. Humans! They think food is the cure-all for every problem. I like my dinner as well as the next dwarf, but, just now, I don't seem to have much appetite.

I must end for the moment.

CHAPTER ◆ 4

ADRIFT, SOMEWHERE

THE GOODSEA

◆

ALAKE KEEPS INSISTING THAT WE EAT—TO KEEP UP OUR STRENGTH, she says. What she thinks we're going to need our strength for is beyond me. Battle these dragon-snakes as I suppose we should call them now? Three of us? I said as much to her; curse the dwarves for our blunt tongues.

Alake was hurt, I could tell, though she was kind enough to say nothing to me in rebuke. Devon managed to cover our awkward moment, and he even made us laugh, though that put us close to tears. Then, of course, we all had to eat something, to please Alake. None of us ate very much, however, and all of us—even Alake—were glad, I think, when the meal ended. She left, going back to her magic. Devon went back to doing what he is always doing—dreaming of Sabia.

And I will go on with my story.

Once the bodies of the dead had been recovered and were spread out along the shoreline, their families, having identified them, were led away by friends to be comforted. At least twenty-five people had been killed. I saw the mortician dashing about aimlessly, a distracted look on his face. Never before had he had this many bodies to prepare for their final rest in the burial vaults in the mountain.

My father spoke to him, finally calmed him down. A detail of soldiers was sent to assist, Hartmut among them. It was a heavy, sorrowful task and my heart went out to him.

I was doing what I could to help, which wasn't much; I was

too dazed by the sudden upheaval in my orderly life. Eventually I just sat on the platform and stared out to sea. The sun-chasers that had been left anywhere near intact floated belly-up in the water. There weren't many. They looked sad and forlorn, like dead fish. I still held the blue ribbon and lock of hair in my hand. I tossed it in the water, watched it drift away on the oil-coated surface.

My father and mother found me there. My mother put her arm around me, hugged me close. We stood long moments without speaking.

My father heaved a sigh. "We must take news of this to our friends."

"But how can we sink between the worlds?[1] What if those terrible creatures attack us?" my mother asked, frightened.

"They won't," my father said heavily, his gaze on the one ship the serpents had left unharmed. "Do you remember what they said? 'Tell your allies.' "

The next day, we sank down toward Elmas.

The elven royal city of Elmasia is a place of beauty and enchantment. Its palace, known as the Grotto, is built of pink and white filigree coral and stands on the banks of the seamoon's many freshwater lakes. The coral is alive and still growing. The elves would as soon think of killing themselves as they would of killing the coral, and so the shape of the Grotto alters on a continuing basis.

Humans and dwarves would consider this a nuisance. The elves, however, find it highly diverting and entertaining. If one room in the Grotto is closed off by the rapidly growing coral, the elves simply pack up their things and move to another that is certain to have been created in the interim.

Finding one's way through the palace is an interesting experience. Corridors that lead one place one day will take a person somewhere completely different the next. Because every room in the Grotto is certain to be one of surpassing beauty—the white coral glistens with an opalescent radiance, pink coral shines

---

[1]Dwarves use the more appropriate term *sinking* rather than *sailing* to describe travel in a submersible. Humans and elves prefer the ancient terminology.

warmly—it doesn't really matter to most elves where they are. Some who come to the palace on business with the king may wander the Grotto for days before making the slightest attempt to find His Majesty.

No business is ever pressing in the elven community. The words *hurry, haste,* and *urgent* were not in the elven vocabulary before they began dealing with humans. We dwarves never dealt with either until only recently in our history.

Such diversities in human and elven natures once led to serious clashes among the two races. The Elmas, though generally easygoing, can be pushed only so far before they push back. But, after several destructive wars, both races came to see that they could gain more by working together than apart. The human Phondrans are a charming, if energetic, people. They soon learned how to manage the elves, and now they wheedle and flatter them into doing what they, the humans, want. This noted human charm worked even on the dour dwarves. Eventually, we, too, were won over by them.

The three races have lived and worked together, each on their own separate seamoon, in peaceful harmony for many generations. I have no doubt that we would have continued to do so for many generations more, had not the seasun—the source of warmth, light, and life for the seamoons—begun to leave us.

It was human wizards, who love to probe and prod and try to find out the why and the wherefore, who discovered that the seasun was altering its course and starting to drift away. This discovery led the humans into a perfect flurry of activity, quite marvelous to behold. They took measurements and made calculations, they sent out dolphins to scout for them, and questioned the dolphins for cycles on end, trying to find out what they knew of the history of the seasun.[2]

---

[2]Humans were the first to communicate with the dolphins and learn their language. Elves think dolphins amusing gossips, entertaining conversationalists, fun to have at parties. Dwarves, who learned how to talk to the dolphins from the humans, use dolphins mainly as a source of information on navigation. Dwarves—being naturally suspicious of anyone or anything that is not a dwarf—do not trust the dolphins, however.

According to Alake, this is the explanation the dolphins offered:

"Chelestra is a globe of water existing in the vastness of space. Its exterior, facing onto the frigid darkness of the Nothing, is made of ice, fathoms thick. Its interior, comprised of the Goodsea, is warmed by the seasun, a star whose flames are so extraordinarily hot that the water of the Goodsea cannot extinguish them. The seasun warms the water surrounding it, melts the ice, and brings life to the seamoons—small planets, designed by the Creators of Chelestra for habitation."

We dwarves were able to provide the humans with information concerning the seamoons themselves, information gleaned from long Times tunneling and delving into the sphere's interior. The spheres are a shell of rock with a hot interior comprised of various chemicals. The chemicals react with the rays of the seasun and produce breathable air that surrounds the seamoons in a bubble. The seasun is absolutely required to maintain life.

The Phondrans concluded that, in approximately four hundred cycles' time, the seasun would leave the seamoons far behind. The longnight would arrive, the Goodsea would freeze, and so would anyone left on Phondra, Gargan, and Elmas.

"When the seasun drifts away," reported the dolphins, who had witnessed this phenomenon firsthand, "the Goodsea turns to ice that slowly encases the seamoons. But such is the magical nature of these moons that most vegetable and some animal life on them remains alive, merely frozen. When the seasun returns, the moons thaw out and are once more habitable."

I remember hearing Dumaka of Phondra, chieftain of his people, relating the dolphins' information concerning the seamoons to the first emergency meeting of the royal families of Elmas, Phondra, and Gargan, the meeting that took place when we first heard about the seasun drifting off and leaving us.

That meeting was held on Phondra, in the big longhouse where the humans hold all their ceremonies. We three girls were hiding in the bushes outside, eavesdropping, as usual. (We were accustomed to spying on our parents shamelessly. We'd been doing it since we were little.)

"Bah! What does a fish[3] know?" my father demanded scornfully. He never took to the notion of talking to dolphins.

"I find the idea of being frozen extremely romantic," stated Eliason, the elven king. "Imagine—sleeping away the centuries, then wakening to a new era."

His wife had just recently died. I suppose he found the thought of dreamless, painless sleep comforting.

My mother told me later she had a mental image of hundreds of dwarves, thawing out in a new era, their beards dripping all over the rugs. It didn't sound romantic to her at all. It sounded messy.

Dumaka of Phondra pointed out to the elves that while the idea of being frozen and coming back to life several thousand cycles later might indeed sound romantic, the freezing process itself had definite and painful drawbacks. And how could any of us be certain we would actually return to life?

"After all, we have only the word of a fish on that," my father stated, and his pronouncement brought general agreement.

The dolphins had brought news that a new seamoon, a much larger moon than any of ours, had just recently thawed out. The dolphins were only now beginning to inspect it, but they thought it would be a perfect place for us to live. It was Dumaka's proposal that we would build a fleet of sun-chasers, set off in pursuit of the seasun, find this new seamoon as did the ancients.

Eliason was somewhat taken aback by the terms *build* and *pursue*, which implied a considerable amount of activity, but he wasn't opposed to the idea. Elves are rarely opposed to anything; opposition takes too much energy. In the same way, they are rarely in favor of anything, either. The Elmas are content to take life as it comes and adapt to it. Humans are the ones who are forever wanting to change and alter and tinker and fix and make better. As for us dwarves, as long as we get paid, nothing else matters.

The Phondrans and the Elmas agreed to finance the sun-

---

[3]Humans and elves claim that the dolphin is not a fish, but a species similar to themselves, because dolphins give birth to their young the same way they do. Dwarves have no use for such a nonsensical notion. Anything that swims like a fish *is* a fish, according to dwarves.

chasers. We Gargan were to build them. The humans would supply the lumber. The elves would supply the magic that would be needed to operate the sun-chasers; the Elmas being clever with mechanical magics. (Anything to save themselves physical labor!)

And, with typical dwarven efficiency, the sun-chasers had been built and built well.

"But now," I heard my father say with a sigh, "it has all been for naught. The sun-chasers are destroyed."

This was the second emergency meeting of the royal families, called by my father. This time, we were meeting, as I said, on Elmas.

We girls had been left in Sabia's room to "visit" with each other. Instead, immediately on our parents' departure, we hastened to find a vantage point from which we could, as usual, listen in on their discussions.

Our parents were seated on a terrace facing out over the Goodsea. We discovered a small room (a new one) that had opened up above the terrace. Alake used her magic to enlarge an opening through which we could both see and hear clearly. We crowded as near this new window as possible, being careful to keep in the shadows to avoid being seen.

My father went on to describe the serpents' attack on the submersibles.

"The sun-chasers were all destroyed?" whispered Sabia, as wide-eyed as an elf, with their almond-shaped eyes, can get.

Poor Sabia. Her father never told her anything. Elven daughters lead such sheltered lives. My father always discussed all his plans with both me and my mother.

"Hush!" Alake scolded, trying to hear.

"I'll tell you later," I promised, squeezing Sabia's hand to keep her quiet.

"There's no possible way to fix them, Yngvar?" Dumaka was asking.

"Not unless those wizards of yours can turn splinters into solid boards again," my father growled.

He spoke sarcastically; dwarves have little tolerance for magic of any sort, considering most of it trickery, though they are hard-pressed to explain how it works. But I could tell that he was secretly hopeful the humans would come up with the solution.

The Phondran chief said nothing in response, however. A bad sign. Usually the humans are quick to claim their magic can solve any problem. Peeping from over the top of the window ledge, I saw that Dumaka's face was troubled.

My father heaved another sigh, and shifted his bulk uncomfortably in his chair. I sympathized with him. Elven chairs are made for slender elven buttocks.

"I'm sorry, my friend." My father stroked his beard, a sure sign that he was upset. "I didn't mean to bark at you. Those blasted beasts have got us by the side whiskers, though, and what we do now is beyond this dwarf to figure out."

"I think you're worried about nothing," said Eliason, with a languid wave of his hand. "You sailed to Elmas in perfect safety. Perhaps these serpents got it into their snakey heads that the sun-chasers were some sort of threat to them, and, once they smashed them to bits, they felt better about the whole thing and departed, never to bother us again."

" 'Masters of the Sea,' they called themselves," my father reminded them, his black eyes glistening. "And they meant it. We sailed here by their permission. I'm as certain of that as if I'd heard them give it me. And they were watching. I felt their green-red eyes upon me the whole way."

"Yes, I think you're right."

Dumaka stood up abruptly, walked over to a low wall of coral, and stood gazing down into the shining depths of the calm and placid Goodsea. Was it my imagination, or did I see now upon its surface a trace of shimmering oil?

"I believe you should tell them our news, my dear," said his wife, Delu.

Dumaka did not immediately reply, but kept his back turned, staring gloomily out to sea. He is a tall man, considered handsome by the humans. His rapid-fire speech, swift walk, and abrupt gestures always make him appear, in the realm of the easygoing Elmas, as if he were doing and saying everything in double-quick time. Now, however, he was not pacing or roaming about in frantic activity, trying to outrun the swift mortality that must inevitably overtake him.

"What's the matter with your father, Alake?" whispered Sabia. "Is he ill?"

"Wait and listen," said Alake softly. Her face was sad. "Grundle's parents aren't the only ones who have a fearful tale to tell."

Eliason must have found this change in his friend as disturbing as I did. He rose to his feet, moving with the slow, fluid grace of the elves, and laid a comforting hand on Dumaka's shoulder.

"Bad news, like fish, doesn't smell sweeter for being kept longer," Eliason said gently.

"Yes, you are right." Dumaka kept his gaze out to sea. "I had intended to say nothing of this to either of you, because I wasn't certain of the facts. The magi are investigating." He cast a glance at his wife, a powerful wizardess. She inclined her head in response. "I wanted to wait for their report. But . . ." He drew a deep breath. "It seems all too clear to me now what happened.

"Two days ago, a small Phondran fishing village, located on the coast directly opposite Gargan, was attacked and completely destroyed. Boats were smashed, houses leveled. One hundred and twenty men, women, and children lived in the village." Dumaka shook his head, his shoulders bowed. "All are now dead."

"Ach," said my father, tugging at his forelock in respectful sympathy.

"The One have mercy," murmured Eliason. "Was it tribal war?"

Dumaka looked around at those gathered on the terrace. The humans of Phondra are a dark-skinned race. Unlike the Elmas, whose emotions run skin-deep, so the saying goes, the Phondrans do not blush in shame or pale in fear or anger. The ebony of their skin often masks their inner feelings. It is their eyes that are most expressive, and the chief's eyes smoldered in anger and bitter, helpless frustration.

"Not war. Murder."

"Murder?" It took Eliason a moment to comprehend the word that had been spoken in human. The elves have no term for such a heinous crime in their vocabulary. "One hundred and twenty people! But . . . who? What?"

"We weren't certain at first. We found tracks that we could

not explain. Could not, until now." Dumaka's hand moved in a quick S-shape. "Sinuous waves across the sand. And trails of slime."

"The serpents?" said Eliason in disbelief. "But why? What did they want?"

"To murder! To kill!" The chieftain's hand clenched. "It was butchery. Plain out-and-out butchery! The wolf carries off the lamb and we are not angry because we know that this is the nature of the wolf and that the lamb will fill the empty bellies of the wolf's young. But these serpents or whatever they are did not kill for food. They killed for the pleasure of killing!

"Their victims, every one, even the children, had obviously died slowly, in hideous torment, their bodies left for us to find. I am told that the first few of our people who came upon the village nearly lost their reason at the terrible sights they witnessed."

"I traveled there myself," said Delu, her rich voice so low that we girls were forced to creep nearer the window to hear her. "I have suffered since from terrible dreams that haunt me in the night. We could not even give the bodies seemly burial in the Goodsea, for none of us could bear to look upon their tortured faces and see evidence of the agony they had suffered. We magi determined that the entire village, or what was left of it, be burned."

"It was," added Dumaka heavily, "as if the killers had left us a message: 'See in this your own doom!' "

I thought back to the serpent's words: *This is a sample of our power. . . . Heed our warning!*

We girls stared at each other in a horrified silence that was echoed on the terrace below. Dumaka turned once again and was staring out to sea. Eliason sank down in his chair.

My father struck in with his usual dwarven bluntness. Pushing himself with difficulty out of the small chair, he stamped his feet on the ground, probably in an attempt to restore their circulation. "I mean no disrespect to the dead, but these were fisher folk, unskilled in warfare, lacking weapons . . ."

"It would have made no difference if they had been an army," stated Dumaka grimly. "These people were armed; they have fought other tribes, as well as the jungle beasts. We found scores of arrows that had been fired, but they obviously did no harm. Spears had been cracked in two, as if they'd been chewed up and spit out by giant mouths."

"And our people were skilled in magic, most of them," Delu added quietly, "if only on the lowest levels. We found evidence that they had attempted to use their magic in their defense. Magic, too, failed them."

"But surely the Council of Magi could do something?" suggested Eliason. "Or perhaps magical elven weapons, such as we used to manufacture in times gone by, might work where others failed—no disparagement to your wizards," he added, politely.

Delu looked at her husband, apparently seeking his agreement in imparting further bad news. He nodded his head.

The wizardess was a tall woman, equaling her husband in height. Her graying hair, worn in a coif at the back of the neck, provided an attractive contrast to her dark complexion. Seven bands of color in her feathered cape marked her status as a wizardess of the Seventh House, the highest rank a human can attain in the use of magic. She stared down at her clasped hands, clasped fast to keep from trembling.

"One member of the Council, the village shamus, was in the village at the time of the attack. We found her body. Her death had been most cruel." Delu shivered, drew a deep breath, steeling herself to go on. "Around her dismembered corpse lay the tools of her magic, spread about her as if in mockery."

"One against many . . ." Eliason began.

"Argana was a powerful wizardess," Delu cried, and her shout made me jump. "Her magic could have heated the sea water to boiling! She could have raised a typhoon with a wave of her hand. The ground would have opened at a word from her and swallowed her enemies whole! All this, we had evidence that she had done! And still she died. Still they all died!"

Dumaka laid a soothing hand upon his wife's shoulder. "Be calm, my dear. Eliason meant only that the entire Council, gathered together, might be able to work such powerful magic that these serpents could not withstand it."

"Forgive me. I'm sorry I lost my temper." Delu gave the elf a wan smile. "But, like Yngvar, I have seen with my own eyes the terrible destruction these creatures brought upon my people."

She sighed. "Our magic is powerless in the presence of these creatures, even when they are not in sight. Perhaps the cause is due to the foul ooze they leave on anything they touch. We don't know. All we know is that when we magi entered the village, we each of us felt our power began to drain away. We couldn't even use our magic to start the fires to burn the bodies of the dead."

Eliason looked around the grim, unhappy group. "And so what are we to do?"

As an elf his natural inclination must have been to do nothing, wait, and see what time brought. But, according to my father, Eliason was an intelligent ruler, one of the more realistic and practical of his race. He knew, though he would have liked to ignore the fact, that his people's days on their seamoon were numbered. A decision had to be made, therefore, but he was quite content to let others make it.

"We have one hundred cycles left until the full effects of the wandering of the seasun will begin to be felt," stated Dumaka. "Time to build more sun-chasers."

"*If* the serpents let us," said my father ominously. "Which I much doubt. And what did they mean by payment? What could they possibly want?"

All were silent, thinking.

"Let us look at this logically," Eliason said finally. "Why do people fight? Why did our races fight each other, generations ago? Through fear, misunderstanding. When we came together and discussed our differences, we found ways to deal with them and we have lived in peace ever since. Perhaps these serpents, powerful as they seem, are, in reality, afraid of us. They see us as a threat. If we tried to talk to them, reassure them that we mean them no harm, that we want only to leave and travel to this new seamoon, then perhaps—"

A clamor interrupted him.

The noise had come from the part of the terrace attached to the palace—a part hidden from my view—being short, it was difficult for me to see out the window.

"What's going on?" I demanded impatiently.

"I don't know . . ." Sabia was trying to see without being seen.

Alake actually poked her head out the opening. Fortunately, our parents were paying no attention to us.

"A messenger of some sort," she reported.

"Interrupting a royal conference?" Sabia was shocked.

I dragged over a footstool and climbed up on it. I could now see the white-faced footman who had, against all rules of protocol, actually run onto the terrace. The footman, seeming nearly about to faint, leaned to whisper something in Eliason's ear. The elven king listened, frowning.

"Bring him here," he said at last.

The footman hastened off.

Eliason looked gravely at his friends. "One of the message riders was attacked on the road and is, apparently, grievously wounded. He bears a message, he says, which is to be delivered to us, to all of us gathered here this day. I have ordered them to bring him here."

"Who attacked him?" asked Dumaka.

Eliason was silent a moment, then said, "Serpents."

"A message 'to all of us gathered here,' " repeated my father dourly. "I was right. They *are* watching us."

"Payment," said my mother, the first word she'd spoken since the conference began.

"I don't understand." Eliason sounded frustrated. "What can they possibly want?"

"I'll wager we are about to find out."

They said nothing further, but sat waiting, unwilling to look at each other, finding no comfort in seeing the reflection of their own dazed bewilderment on the faces of their friends.

"We shouldn't be here. We shouldn't be doing this," said Sabia suddenly. Her face was very pale; her lips trembled.

Alake and I looked at her, looked at each other, looked down at the floor in shame. Sabia was right. This spying on our parents had always been a game to us, something we could giggle over in the night after they'd sent us to our beds. Now it was a game no longer. I don't know how the other two felt, but I found it frightening to see my parents, who had always seemed so strong and wise, in such confusion, such distress.

"We should leave, now," Sabia urged, and I knew she was right, but I could no more have climbed down off that footstool than I could have flown out the window.

"Just a moment more," said Alake.

The sound of slippered feet, moving slowly, shuffling as if

bearing a burden, came to us. Our parents drew themselves upright, standing straight and tall, disquiet replaced by stern gravity. My father smoothed his beard. Dumaka folded his arms
across his chest. Delu drew a stone from a pouch she wore at
her side and rubbed it in her hand, her lips moving.

Six elven men entered, bearing a litter between them. They
moved slowly, carefully, in order to prevent jostling the
wounded elf. At a gesture from their king, they gently placed
the litter on the ground before him.

Accompanying them was an elven physician, skilled in the
healing arts of his people. On entering, I saw him glance askance
at Delu; perhaps fearing interference. Elven and human healing
techniques are considerably different, the former relying on extensive study of anatomy combined with alchemy, the latter
treating hurts by means of sympathetic magic, chants to drive
out evil humors, certain stones laid on vital body parts. We
dwarves rely on the One and our own common sense.

Seeing that Delu made no move toward his patient, the elven
physician relaxed. Or it may have been that he suddenly realized
it would make no difference if the human wizardess attempted
to work her magic. It was obvious to us and to everyone present
that nothing in this world would help the dying elf.

"Don't look, Sabia," Alake warned, drawing back and attempting to hide the gruesome sight from her friend.

But it was too late. I heard Sabia's breath catch in her throat
and I knew she'd seen.

The young elf's clothes were torn and soaked in blood.
Cracked and splintered ends of bones protruded through the
purple flesh of his legs. His eyes were missing, they'd been
gouged out. The blind head turned this way and that, the mouth
opened and closed, repeating some words that I couldn't hear
in a fevered sort of chant.

"He was found this morning outside the city gates, Your
Majesty," one of the elves said. "We heard his screams."

"Who brought him?" Eliason asked, voice stern to mask his
horror.

"We saw no one, Your Majesty. But a trail of foul ooze led
from the body back to the sea."

"Thank you. You may go now. Wait outside."

The elves who had brought the litter bowed and left.

Once they were gone, our parents could give way to their feelings. Eliason cast his mantle over his head and averted his face, an elven response to grief. Dumaka turned away, strong body trembling in rage and pity. His wife rose and came to stand by his side, her hand on his arm. My father gathered his beard in great handfuls and pulled on it, bringing tears to his eyes. My mother yanked on her side whiskers.

I did the same. Alake was comforting Sabia, who had nearly passed out.

"We should take her to her room," I said.

"No. I won't go." Sabia lifted her chin. "Someday I will be queen, and I must know how to handle situations like this."

I looked at her with surprise and new respect. Alake and I had always considered Sabia weak and delicate. I'd seen her turn pale at the sight of blood running from a piece of undercooked meat. But, faced with a crisis, she was coming through it like a dwarven soldier. I was proud of her. Breeding will tell, they say.

We peeped cautiously out the window.

The physician was speaking to the king.

"Your Majesty, this messenger has refused all easeful medicine in order that he may deliver his message. I beg you listen to him."

Eliason removed his mantle at once and knelt beside the dying elf.

"You are in the presence of your king," said Eliason, keeping his voice calm and level. He took hold of the man's hand that was clutching feebly at the air. "Deliver your message, then go with all honor to the One and find rest."

The elf's bloody eye sockets turned in the direction of the voice. His words came forth slowly, with many pauses to draw pain-filled breaths.

"The Masters of the Sea bid me say thus: 'We will allow you to build the boats to carry your people to safety provided you give us in payment the eldest girl-child from each royal household. If you agree to our demand, place your daughters in a boat and cast them forth upon the Goodsea. If you do not, what we have done to this elf and to the human fisherman and to the dwarven shipbuilders is only a foretaste of the destruction we will bring upon your people. We give you two cycles to make your decision.' "

"But why? Why our daughters?" Eliason cried, grasping the wounded man by the shoulders and almost shaking him.

"I . . . do not know," the elf gasped, and died.

Alake drew away from the window. Sabia shrank back against the wall. I climbed down off the footstool before I fell.

"We shouldn't have heard that," Alake said in a hollow voice.

"No," I agreed. I was cold and hot at the same time and I couldn't stop shaking.

"Us? They want us?" Sabia whispered, as if she couldn't believe it.

We stared at each other, helpless, wondering what to do.

"The window," I warned, and Alake closed it up with her magic.

"Our parents will never agree to such a thing," she said briskly. "We mustn't let them know we know. It would grieve them terribly. We'll go back to Sabia's room and act like nothing's happened."

I cast a dubious glance at Sabia, who was as white as curdled milk, and who seemed about to collapse on the spot.

"I can't lie!" she protested. "I've never lied to my father."

"You don't have to lie," Alake snapped, her fear making her sharp-edged and brittle. "You don't have to say anything. Just keep quiet."

She yanked poor Sabia out of her corner and, together, she and I helped the elven maid down the shimmering coral corridors. After a few false turns, we made it to Sabia's room. None of us spoke on the way.

All of us were thinking of the elf we'd seen, of the torture he'd endured. My insides clenched in fear; a horrid taste came into my mouth. I didn't know why I was so frightened. As Alake had said, my parents would never permit the serpents to take me.

It was, I know now, the voice of the One speaking to me, but I was refusing to listen.

We entered Sabia's room—thankfully, no servants were about—and shut the door behind us. Sabia sank down on the edge of her bed, twisting her hands together. Alake stood glaring angrily out a window, as if she'd like to go and hit someone.

In the silence, I could no longer avoid hearing the One. And

I knew, looking at their faces, that the One was talking to Alake and Sabia, as well. It was left to me, to the dwarf, to speak the bitter words aloud.

"Alake's right. Our parents won't send us. They won't even tell us about this. They'll keep it a secret from our people. And our people will die, never knowing that there was a chance they might have been spared."

Sabia whispered, "I wish we'd never heard! If only we hadn't gone up there!"

"We were meant to hear," I said gruffly.

"You're right, Grundle," said Alake, turning to face us. "The One wanted us to hear. We have been given the chance to save our people. The One has left it up to us to make the decision, not our parents. *We* are the ones who must be strong now."

As she talked, I could see she was getting caught up in it all: the romance of martyrdom, of sacrifice. Humans set great store in such things, something we dwarves can never understand. Almost all human heroes are those who die young, untimely, giving up their brief lives for some noble cause. Not so dwarves. Our heroes are the Elders, those who live a just life through ages of strife and work and hardship.

I couldn't help but think of the broken elf with his eyes plucked out of his head.

What nobility is there in dying like that? I wanted to ask her.

But, for once, I held my tongue. Let her find comfort where she could. I must find it in my duty. As for Sabia, she had truly meant what she said about being a queen.

"But I was to have been married," she said.

The elven maid wasn't arguing or whining. She knew what we had to do. It was her one protest against her terrible fate, and it was very gentle.

Alake has just come in for the second time to tell me that I must sleep. We must "conserve our strength."

Bah! But I'll humor her. It's best that I stop here anyhow. The rest that I must write—the story of Devon and Sabia—is both painful and sweet. The memory will comfort me as I lie awake, trying to keep fear as far away as possible, in the lonely darkness.

CHAPTER ♦ 5

DEATH'S GATE

CHELESTRA

♦

CONSCIOUSNESS FORCED ITSELF ON HAPLO.

He awoke to searing pain, yet, in the same instant, he knew himself to be whole once more, and pain-free. The circle of his being was joined again. The agony he'd felt was the tail end of that circle being seized by the mouth.

But the circle wasn't strong. It was wobbly, tenuous. Lifting his hand was an effort almost beyond his strength, but he managed it and placed the fingers on his naked breast. Starting with the rune over his heart, slowly and haltingly, he began to trace, began to reconnect and strengthen, every sigil written upon his skin.

He started with the name rune, the first sigil that is tattooed over the heart of the squirming, screaming babe almost the moment it is forced from the mother's womb. The babe's mother performs the rite, or another female tribe member if the mother dies. The name is chosen by the father, if he lives or is still among the tribe.[1] If not, by the tribal headman.

The name rune does not offer the babe much magical protection. Most of that comes from the tit, as the saying goes, from

---

[1]Children are extremely valued in the Labyrinth and are raised by the Squatters. Runners, such as Haplo, would often father children but, due to the nature of their lives, could not stay with a tribe to raise it. Female Runners, becoming pregnant, would move into a Squatter tribe until the babe was born, then give it to one of the Squatter families to raise. Occasionally

drawing on the magic of either mother or wet nurse. And yet the name rune is the most important sigil on the body, since every other sigil added later traces its origin back to it first—the beginning of the circle.

Haplo moved his fingers over the name rune, redrawing its intricate design from memory.

Memory took him back to the time of his childhood, to one of the rare, precious moments of peace and rest, to a boy reciting his name and learning how to shape the runes. . . .

. . . "Haplo: 'single, alone.' That is your name and your destiny," said his father, his finger rough and hard on Haplo's chest. "Your mother and I have defeated the odds thrown for us already. Every Gate we pass from now on is a wink at fate. But the time will come when the Labyrinth will claim us, as it claims all except the lucky and the strong. And the lucky and the strong are generally the lonely. Repeat your name."

Haplo did so, solemnly running his own grimy finger over his thin chest.

His father nodded. "And now the runes of protection and healing."

Haplo laboriously went over each of those, beginning with the ones touching the name rune, spreading out over the breast, the vital organs of his abdominal region, the sensitive groin area, and around the back to protect the spine. Haplo recited these, as he'd recited them countless times in his brief life. He'd done it so often, he could let his mind wander to the rabbit snares he'd laid out that day, wondered if he might be able to surprise his mother with dinner.

"No! Wrong! Begin again!"

A sharp blow, delivered impersonally by his father with what was known as the naming stick, across the unprotected, rune-free palm of the hand, focused Haplo's mind on his lesson. The blow brought tears to his eyes, but he was quick to blink them

---

Runners, such as Haplo's parents, would cease their Run and move in with a Squatter tribe until the child was old enough to keep up with them. Such instances were very rare. The fact that Haplo has any memory at all of his biological parents is quite remarkable among Patryns.

away, for his father was watching him closely. The ability to endure pain was as much a part of this rough schooling as the recitation and the drawing of the sigla.

"You are careless today, Haplo," said his father, tapping the naming stick—a thin, pliable branch of a plant known as a creeping rose, adorned with flesh-pricking thorns—on the hard ground. "It is said that back in the days of our freedom, before we were thrown into this accursed jail by our enemies . . . Name the enemy, my son."

"The Sartan," Haplo said, trying to ignore the stinging pain of the thorns left stuck in his skin.

"It is said that in the days of our freedom, children such as you went to schools and learned the runes as a kind of exercise for the mind. But no longer. Now it is life or death. When your mother and I are dead, Haplo, you will be responsible for the sigla that will, if done correctly, grant you the strength needed to escape our prison and avenge our deaths on our enemy. Name the runes of strength and power."

Haplo's hand left the trunk of his body and followed the progression of the tattooed sigla that twined down his arms and legs, onto the backs of his hands and the tops of his feet. He knew these better than he knew the runes of protection and healing. Those "baby" runes had been tattooed onto him when he was weaned from the breast. He had actually been allowed to tattoo some of these newer sigla—the mark of an adult—onto his skin himself. That had been a proud moment, his first rite of entry into what would undoubtedly be a cruel, harsh, and brief life.

Haplo completed his lesson without making another mistake and earned his father's curt nod of satisfaction.

"Now, heal those wounds," his father said, gesturing to the thorns protruding from the boy's palm.

Haplo pulled out the thorns with his teeth, spat them on the ground, and, joining his hands, formed the healing circle, as he'd been taught. The red, swollen marks left behind by the thorns gradually disappeared. He exhibited smooth, if dirty, palms for his father. The man grunted, rose, and walked away.

Two days later, he and Haplo's mother would both be dead. Haplo would be left alone.

The lucky and the strong were generally lonely. . . .

♦

Haplo's mind drifted on a cloud of agony and weakness. He traced the sigla for his father and then his father was a bloody, mangled body and then his father was the Lord of the Nexus, whipping Haplo with the cane of the rosebush.

Haplo grit his teeth and forced himself to blink back the tears and bite back the scream and concentrate on the runes. His hand traveled down his left arm, to the sigla he'd drawn there as a boy and those he'd redrawn as a man and those he'd added as a man, feeling his strength and power grow within him.

He was forced to sit up, in order to reach the sigla on his legs. His first attempt nearly made him black out, but he struggled out of the whirling mists and peered through the blinking lights of his mind, choked back the nausea, and sat almost upright. His hand, trembling with weakness, followed the runes on thighs, hips, knees, shins, feet.

He expected, every moment, to feel the sting of the thorny cane, the reprimand, "No! Wrong! Begin again!"

And then he was finished and he'd done it correctly. He lay back down on the deck, feeling the wonderful warmth flow through his body, spreading from the name rune at his heart through his trunk and into his limbs.

Haplo slept.

When he awoke, his body was still weak, but it was a weakness from prolonged fasting and thirst—soon cured. He dragged himself to his feet and peered outside the large window on the bridge, wondering where he was. He had a vague memory of having passed through the horrors of Death's Gate again, but that memory was literally ablaze with pain and he swiftly banished it.

He was not, at least, in imminent danger. The runes on his body glowed only very faintly, and that was in reaction to what he'd suffered and endured, not reacting to any threat. He could see nothing outside the ship except a vast expanse of aqua blue. He stared at it, wondered if it was sky, water, solid, gaseous, what. He couldn't tell, and he was too light-headed from hunger to try to reason it all out.

Turning, he stumbled through the ship, making his weary way down into the hold, where he had stored his supplies. He ate sparingly of bread dipped in wine, mindful of the adage "Never break a fast with a feast."

His strength restored somewhat, Haplo went back to the bridge, dressed himself in his leather breeches, white long-sleeved shirt, and leather vest and boots, covering every sign of the telltale runes that marked him as a Patryn to those who remembered their history lessons. He left only his hands free, for the moment, for he would need to steer the vessel, using the magical runes of the steering stone.

At least, he assumed he'd need to steer the vessel. Haplo stared into the aqua-blue whatever-it-was that surrounded him and tried to make sense of it, but he might have been sailing into a dome of air that spanned all the vistas of his vision or about to fly smack into a wall covered with blue paint.

"We'll walk onto the top deck and take a look around, eh, boy?" he said. Not hearing the usual excited bark that always greeted this statement, Haplo glanced about.

The dog was gone.

It occurred to Haplo, then, that he hadn't seen the animal since . . . since . . . well, it had been a long time.

"Here, boy!" Haplo whistled. No response.

Irritated, thinking the dog was indulging in a raid on the sausages, as happened from time to time, Haplo stomped back down to the hold, prepared to find the animal looking as inno-cent of wrongdoing as was possible with sausage grease smeared over its nose.

The dog was not there. No sausages were missing.

Haplo called, whistled. No response. He knew then, with a sudden pang of loneliness and unhappiness, that the dog was gone. But almost as soon as he experienced the aching pain, which was in some ways almost harder to bear than the burning pain of his torture, Haplo felt it ease, then disappear.

It was as if his being were opened like a door. A cold, sharp wind blew in and coated with ice every troubling doubt and feeling he'd been experiencing.

Haplo felt renewed, refreshed, empty. And the emptiness, he discovered, was far preferable to the raging turmoil and con-fusion that had previously churned inside him.

The dog. A crutch, as his lord had always said. The lucky and the strong were generally lonely. The dog had served Haplo's purpose.

"It's gone." He shrugged and forgot it.

Alfred. That miserable Sartan.

"I see it now. I was duped, tricked by his magic. Just as my people were duped and tricked before the Sundering. But not now. We will meet again, Sartan, and when we do, you won't escape me this time."

Haplo, looking back, was appalled to see how weak he'd grown, appalled to think he'd actually doubted and attempted to deceive his lord.

His lord. He owed this new freedom from doubt, this new feeling of ease, to his lord.

"As my father punished me when I was small, so my lord has punished me now. I accept it. I am grateful for it. I have learned from it. I will not fail you, My Lord."

He swore the oath, placing his hand upon the name rune over his heart. Then he walked out, alone, onto the upper deck of the elven ship called *Dragon Wing*.

Haplo paced the deck, looked up beyond the tall masts with the dragon-scaled wings, leaned over the rail to stare far below the ship's keel, walked forward to study what lay beyond the snarling dragon's head that was the prow. He caught sight of something in the distance. Not much, nothing more than a dark splotch against the blue, but from the tingling of the sigla on his skin and the creeping feelings of dread shriveling his bowels, he came to the conclusion that he was looking at Death's Gate.

Obviously, then, he'd passed through the Gate, since he certainly wasn't in the Nexus. His lord must have launched his ship on its way.

"And, since I was preparing to travel to the fourth world, to Chelestra, the world of water, this must be it," Haplo said, talking to himself, comforted by hearing a voice break the silence that surrounded him like the endless aqua blue.

His ship was moving; he knew that much, now that he could fix his sight on a point—Death's Gate—and see it dwindle and grow smaller behind him. And he could feel, standing out in the open on the deck, the wind created by their forward motion blow strong against his skin.

The air was cool and moist, but Haplo assumed that there

must be more to a world of water than high humidity, and he again paced the length of the deck, trying to figure out where he was and where he was headed.

A world of water. He sought to envision it, although he was forced to admit that he'd failed in his attempts to envision the previous three worlds he'd visited. He imagined islands, floating on an endless sea. And once he'd imagined that, he couldn't very well picture anything else. Nothing else made sense.

But, if so, where were the islands? Was he, perhaps, in the air above them? But, if that was true, where was the vast expanse of water, glistening in the sun?

Haplo returned below decks to try to sort out the problem, see if perhaps the runes of the steering stone offered some clue.

But, at that moment, he found out what Chelestra was like. His ship slammed into a wall of water.[2]

The force of the impact sent Haplo toppling over backward. The steering stone jolted from its mountings and went rolling about the deck. Haplo started to regain his feet, froze, listened in astounded horror to a crack and a booming sound, like thunder. The main mast had snapped, broken.

Haplo ran to the window, stared out to see what was attacking his ship.

Nothing. He couldn't see any enemy, only water.

Something fell over the window, blocking his view. He recognized it as part of the dragon's-wing sail that helped guide the vessel. Now it flapped and fluttered helplessly in the water like a drowning bird.

Other crashes, occurring amidships, and the sudden trickling of small streams of water onto the bridge brought an unwelcome revelation. He wasn't under attack.

"The damn ship's breaking apart!" Haplo swore, stared about in disbelief.

It was impossible. Every plank, every beam, every mast and

---

[2]Although Chelestra is a world made up entirely of water, there are places where large pockets of gases collect to form gigantic bubbles. One of these bubbles surrounds Death's Gate, probably placed there purposefully by the Sartan, in order to allow time for the traveler to make the transition from one world to another, and to prepare his vessel for entry into the sea.

sail, every splinter of this ship, was protected by rune-magic. Nothing could harm it.

The *Dragon Wing* had sailed without injury through the suns of Pryan. It had survived the Maelstrom of Arianus, floated unscathed on the molten lava sea of Abarrach. A powerful Sartan necromancer had tried unsuccessfully to break its spell. The dread lazar had sought to unravel its magic. *Dragon Wing* and its pilot had survived them all. But water, ordinary water, was causing it to shatter like flawed pottery.

The ship was wallowing sluggishly, timbers creaking and groaning, straining to survive, then giving way. *Dragon Wing* was breaking apart slowly; it hadn't been crushed, but it shouldn't be breaking apart at all.

Haplo still couldn't believe it, refused to believe it. He stood up with difficulty, fighting to balance himself on the listing deck. Water sloshed over his ankles.

He turned to look for the steering stone, wondering briefly as he searched why it should have been knocked loose. It, too, was covered with runes, protected by sigla that guided the ship. If he could retrieve the stone, replace it, he could steer his vessel out of the water and back to what he now concluded must have been some sort of air pocket.

Haplo located the steering stone; it had rolled up against the bulkheads. Its rounded top was barely visible above the rising water. He waded toward it, reached down to pick it up. His hand paused. He stared at the stone.

It was smooth, round, and completely blank. The sigla were gone.

Another crash. The water level was rising rapidly.

This must be a trick of his mind, a panicked reaction to what was happening. The sigla on the steering stone were inscribed deeply, magically, in the rock. They could not, by any possible means, be washed away. Haplo plunged his hands into the water in an effort to retrieve the stone. He drew it out, speaking the runes that should have caused its magic to activate.

Nothing happened. He might have been holding a rock dug from his lord's garden. And then, glaring at the stone in baffled, angry frustration, Haplo's gaze shifted to his hands.

Water dripped from his fingers, his wrists, his lower arms,

ran from skin that was smooth and unblemished, as blank and bare as the rock.

Haplo dropped the stone. Oblivious to the water that was at his knees now, to the shattering crashes that told him *Dragon Wing* was in its death throes, he stared hard at his hands, tried in vain to trace the comforting, reassuring lines of the runes.

The sigla were gone.

Fighting a surge of panic that rose in him even with the level of the water, Haplo lifted his right arm. A trickle of the liquid streamed from the back of his hand—now bare—down his rune-covered arm. In amazed horror, he watched the drop of water slide down his skin, meander among the sigla tattooed on his flesh. In its wake, it left a clean trail of slowly fading, diminishing runes.

This, then, was what was happening to his ship. The water was dissolving the runes, wiping out any trace of magical power.

Unable to think of any explanation why the water should destroy the magic, Haplo could find no way to remedy the situation. His mind was in turmoil and chaos. Accustomed to relying all his life on his magic, he was suddenly rendered helpless as a mensch.

The water level on the bridge was high enough now to float Haplo off his feet. He felt a strange reluctance to leave the protection of his vessel, though he knew logically that it would very soon be able to offer no protection whatsoever. Its magic was diminishing, dying, even as his own magic was dying. The thought came to him that it would be better to die himself than to live like a mensch—or worse than a mensch, for some of them possessed magical skills, though on a very crude level.

The temptation to shut his eyes and let the water cover his head and end his anguish was a fleeting one. Haplo was angry, furious at what was happening to him, furious at whatever or whoever was responsible. He determined to discover who it was and why it was and make them pay. And he couldn't do that if he was dead.

Haplo gazed upward, hoping to see some sign of the surface. He became convinced that he saw light above him. Drawing in a last breath, he shoved aside the floating remnants of *Dragon Wing* and pushed and kicked his way through the water.

Powerful strokes of his arms propelled Haplo upward,

fended off the pieces of drifting plank and boards. There was definitely light; he could look down and see the contrasting darkness of the water beneath him. But, no sign of the surface.

Haplo's lungs began to burn; bright spots danced in his eyes. He could not hold his breath much longer. Furiously, driven by a panicked fear of drowning, he swam upward.

I'm not going to make it. I'm going to die. And no one will ever know . . . my lord will never know . . .

The agony became too great. Haplo could bear it no longer. The surface, if surface existed, was too far above him. He lacked strength to keep fighting. His heart seemed likely to burst, his brain to explode, his chest flaming with excruciating pain.

Muscles acted in reflex the brain fought against. Haplo's mouth opened. He sucked in water through nose and mouth and, feeling a strange warming sensation run through his body, assumed he was dying.

He wasn't, and that astonished him.

Haplo didn't know a lot about drowning. He'd obviously never drowned himself, nor had he met anyone who had and come back to describe the event. He'd seen drowned bodies, however, knew that when the lungs were filled with water, they ceased functioning, along with all the other organs of the body. He was considerably surprised to discover that, in his case, this was not occurring.

If it had not seemed too improbable, Haplo could have sworn he was breathing in the water as easily as he had once breathed in the air.

Haplo hung motionless in the water and paused to consider this unusual and perplexing phenomenon. The rational, thinking, reasoning part of him refused to accept it, and if he dwelt consciously on the fact that the next breath he took would be filled with water, he caught himself holding his breath again, terror rising in him. But if he relaxed and didn't think about it, the breath came. Inexplicably, but it came. And, to some part of him, it made sense. A part of him long, long forgotten.

You have returned to what was. This was how and where you began life.

Haplo considered this, decided he would puzzle it out later. Now all that mattered was that he was alive, irrationally, but he was alive. And living presented an entirely new set of problems.

The water might be air to his lungs, but that was all it was. Haplo could tell by the empty, gnawing sensations in his belly that the water could not nourish him, nor quench his thirst. Nor could it bolster his rapidly flagging strength. Bereft of the magic that might have sustained him, he would survive drowning only to perish of thirst, hunger, fatigue.

His head cleared. Relieved of the panicked fight to avoid death, Haplo studied his surroundings. He could see now that the light he'd hoped was sunlight appeared to be shining, not above him, but somewhere to one side. He doubted now it was the sun, but it was light, and, hopefully, where there was light, there was life.

Catching hold of a scrap of lumber drifting from the wreakage of *Dragon Wing*, Haplo struggled out of his heavy boots and most of his clothes that added weight and drag. He gazed ruefully at his bare legs and arms. No trace of the runes remained.

Haplo rested himself as comfortably as he could upon the board and lay there, floating in the water that was neither cold nor hot but so near his own body temperature that he had no sensation of it at all against his skin.

He relaxed, consciously refusing to think, letting himself recover from shock and fright. The water supported him, buoyed him up. He could see, from the hair streaming past his face, that the water had a motion to it, a current, a tide that appeared to be running the direction he wanted to go. This strengthened his decision. It would be easier to travel with the tide than against it.

Haplo rested until, slowly, he felt his energy return. Then, using the plank for support, he began to swim toward the light.

CHAPTER ♦ 6

THE HALL OF SLEEP

CHELESTRA

♦

THE FIRST WORDS ALFRED HEARD, WHEN HE MANAGED TO ROUSE himself from his fainting spell, were not propitious to his recovery. Samah was speaking to the assembled Sartan, who were—Alfred imagined since he was keeping his eyes shut—gathered around a fallen brethren, staring at him in amazement.

"We lost many during the Sundering. Death took most of our brethren then, but I fear that here we have a casualty of a different nature. This poor man has obviously been driven out of his mind."

Alfred kept quiet, pretending he was still unconscious, wishing desperately that were the case!

He sensed people around him, he heard them breathing, heard robes rustling, though no one else spoke. Alfred was still lying on the cold floor of the mausoleum, though someone had been kind enough to place a pillow—probably from one of the crypts—beneath his bald head.

"Look, Samah. I believe he is reviving," came a woman's voice.

Samah—the great Samah! Alfred almost groaned, swallowed it in time.

"The rest of you, back away. Don't frighten him," the male voice that must belong to Samah ordered.

Alfred heard pity and compassion in the man's voice and nearly wept. He longed to rise up, fling his arms around this Sartan's knees, and acknowledge him Father, Ruler, Patriarch, Councillor.

What holds me back? Alfred wondered, shivering on the chill floor. Why am I deceiving them, my own brothers and sisters, by lying here, pretending to be unconscious, spying on them? It's a dreadful thing I'm doing. He thought with a jolt, This is something Haplo would do!

And at this terrible realization, Alfred groaned aloud.

He knew he had betrayed himself, but he didn't feel up to facing these people yet. He remembered Samah's words, *I have the right and the duty to ask questions of you, not from mere idle curiosity, but, considering these times of crises, out of necessity.*

And what, wondered Alfred miserably, will I answer?

His head rolled from side to side, seemingly of its own volition, for he tried to stop moving and couldn't. His hands twitched. His eyes opened.

The newly awakened Sartan stood around him, staring down at him, no one making any move to assist him. They were not being cruel or neglectful. They were simply bewildered. They had never seen or heard one of their own kind behave in such a bizarre manner and had no idea what to do to help him.

"Either he's reviving or having a fit," said Samah. "Some of you"—he gestured to several young Sartan men—"keep near him. He may need to be physically restrained."

"That will not be necessary!" protested the woman who knelt beside him.

Alfred fixed his gaze on her, recognized her as the woman he'd seen lying in what he'd thought was Lya's crypt.

She lifted his hand in hers and began to pat it soothingly. His hand responded, as usual, of its own accord. Certainly *he* wasn't the one who commanded his fingers to tighten over hers. But he was the one who was comforted by her. She clasped his hand strongly and warmly in return.

"I thought the time of defiance was over, Orla," said Samah.

The Councillor's tone was mild, but there was a hard edge to his voice that caused Alfred to blanch. He heard the Sartan around him stir restlessly, like children of an unhappy home, afraid their parents are going to fight again.

The woman's hand on Alfred's tightened; her voice, when she spoke, was sad.

"Yes, Samah. I suppose it is."

"The Council made the decision. You are part of the Council. You cast your vote, as did the others."

The woman said nothing aloud. But these words came suddenly into Alfred's head, shared with him by the shared touching of their hands.

"A vote in your favor, as you knew I would. Am I part of the Council? Or am I merely Samah's wife?"

Alfred realized, suddenly, that he wasn't meant to hear those words. Sartan could speak to each other silently sometimes, but generally only those who were very close, such as husband and wife.

Samah hadn't heard. He had turned away, his thoughts obviously on other, more important matters than a weak brother lying stretched out on the floor.

The woman continued to gaze at Alfred, but she wasn't seeing him. She was staring through him, at something that had happened long ago. Alfred didn't like to intrude upon such private, unhappy thoughts, but the floor was getting awfully hard. He moved just a tiny bit, to ease a cramp in his right leg. The woman came back to herself, and to him.

"How are you feeling?"

"Not . . . not very well," Alfred stammered.

He tried to make himself sound as ill as possible, hoping Samah, hoping all these Sartan, would go away and leave him alone.

Well, perhaps not *all* of them. His hand was, he discovered, still clinging tightly to the woman's. Orla was her name, apparently. Orla, a beautiful name, yet the images it brought to him were sad ones.

"Is there anything we can do for you?" Orla sounded helpless.

Alfred understood. She knew he wasn't ill. She knew he was shamming, and she was upset and confused. Sartan didn't deceive each other. They didn't lie to each other. They weren't afraid of each other. Perhaps Orla was beginning to share Samah's view—that they had an insane brother on their hands.

Sighing, Alfred closed his eyes. "Bear with me," he said softly. "I know I'm behaving strangely. I know you don't understand. I can't expect you to understand. You will, when you have heard my story."

He sat up then, weakly, with Orla's assistance. But he managed to regain his feet on his own, managed to stand up and face Samah with dignity.

"You are the head of the Council of Seven. Are the other Council members present?" Alfred asked.

"Yes." Samah's gaze flicked about the chamber, picking out five other Sartan. The stern eyes came to rest, finally, on the woman, Orla. "Yes, the Council members are all here."

"Then," said Alfred humbly, "I beg the favor of a hearing before the Council."

"Certainly, Brother," said Samah, with a gracious bow. "That is your right, whenever you are feeling up to it. Perhaps in a day or two—"

"No, no," said Alfred hastily. "There isn't time to wait. Well, actually there *is* time. Time's the problem. I mean . . . I think you should hear what I have to say immediately, before . . . before . . ." His voice trailed off lamely.

Orla caught her breath with a gasp. Her gaze sought Samah's, and whatever tension had existed between them immediately eased and slackened.

The Sartan language, comprising, as it does, Sartan magic, has the ability to summon up images and visions that enhance the speaker's words in the minds of his hearers. A powerful Sartan, such as Samah, would have the ability to control these images, making certain that his listeners saw, as well as heard, exactly what he wanted.

Alfred, unfortunately, could no more control his mental processes than he could his physical. Orla and Samah and every other Sartan in the mausoleum had just witnessed astounding, frightening, and confusing sights. Sights that emanated directly from Alfred.

"The Council will convene immediately," Samah said. "The rest of you . . ." He paused, looked with troubled eyes on the other Sartan standing in the mausoleum, patiently waiting his command. "I think perhaps you should remain here until we know for certain how matters stand on the surface. I note that some of our brethren have not awakened. Find out if anything is amiss with them."

The Sartan bowed in silent, unquestioning acquiescence, and left to go about their duties.

Samah turned on his heel and headed out of the mausoleum,

heading for a door separated from the chamber by a dark and narrow hallway. The five other Sartan Council members came after him. Orla walked near Alfred. She said nothing to him, courteously refrained from looking at him, giving him time to calm himself.

Alfred was grateful to her, but he didn't think it would help.

Samah strode the hall with swift, confident steps, as if he had walked these floors only yesterday. Preoccupied as he was, he apparently didn't notice that his long, sweeping robes were leaving small trails in a thick layer of dust.

Runes over the door lit with a blue radiance as Samah approached and began to chant. The door swung open, wafting a cloud of dust up from the floor.

Alfred sneezed. Orla was looking about her in perplexed astonishment.

They entered the Council room, which Alfred recognized by the round table adorned with sigla, standing in the center. Samah frowned at the sight of fine, soft dust that completely covered the table, obliterating the runes carved upon its surface. Coming to stand beside the table, he ran his finger through the dust, stared at it in pondering silence.

None of the other Council members approached the table, but remained near the door, whose runelight, once the door had opened, was beginning to fade. Samah, with a brief word, caused a white globe that hung suspended above the table to shine with a radiant white light. He gazed ruefully at the dust.

"If we attempt to clean this off, we'll none of us be able to breathe the air." He was silent a moment, then shifted his gaze to Alfred. "I foresee the path your words will likely travel, Brother, and I must admit that it fills me with a fear I had not thought myself capable of feeling. I think we should all sit down, but—this one time—there will be no need to take our accustomed places around the table."

Pulling out a chair, he brushed it off and held it for Orla, who walked to it with steady, measured tread. The other Council members moved chairs for themselves, stirring up such a quantity of dust in the process that for a moment it seemed a fog had rolled in on them. Everyone coughed and uttered swift chants to help clear the air. Yet the entire time they talked, the dust drifted down and around them, covered their skin and clothing.

Alfred remained standing, as was proper when appearing before the Council.

"Please, begin, Brother," Samah said.

"First, I must ask that you grant me leave to ask you questions," Alfred said, clasping his hands nervously before him. "I must have answers myself before I can proceed with any assurance that what I am about to tell you is right."

"Your request is granted, Brother," said Samah gravely.

"Thank you." Alfred gave an awkward bob, intended for a bow. "My first question is: Are you an ancestor of the Samah who was Head of the Council during the time of the Sundering?"

Orla's eyes flicked quickly to Samah. The woman's face was exceedingly pale. The other Council members shifted in their chairs, some looking at Samah, others looking at the dust all around them.

"No," said Samah. "I am not a descendant of that man." He paused, perhaps considering the implications of his answer. "I am that man," he said at last.

Alfred nodded, breathed a gentle sigh. "Yes, I thought so. And this is the Council of Seven who made the decision to sunder the World, establish four separate and distinct worlds in its place. This is the Council who directed the fight against the Patryns, the Council who brought about our enemy's defeat and effected their capture. This is the Council who built the Labyrinth and imprisoned our enemies within it. This is the Council by whose direction some of the mensch were rescued from the destruction and transported to each of the four worlds, there to begin what you planned to be a new order, there to live together in peace and prosperity."

"Yes," said Samah, "this is the Council of which you speak."

"Yes," repeated Orla, softly, sadly, "this is that Council."

Samah shot her a displeased glance. Of the other Council members—four men and one more woman—two of the men and the woman frowned in agreement with Samah, the remaining two men nodded, apparently siding with Orla.

The rift in the Council gaped, chasm-like, at Alfred's feet, causing him to lose hold of his thoughts, that had never been grasped all that securely. He could only stare at his brethren, open-mouthed.

"We have answered your questions," Samah said, voice grating. "Have you any others?"

Alfred did, but he was having difficulty putting his questions in words proper to ask the head of the Council of Seven. At last he managed to say, lamely, "Why did you go to sleep?"

The question was simple. To his horror, Alfred heard echoing around it all the other questions that should have remained locked in his heart. They reverberated through the room in unspoken, anguished cries.

Why did you leave us? Why did you abandon those who needed you? Why did you shut your eyes to the chaos and destruction and misery?

Samah appeared grave and troubled. Alfred, appalled at what he'd done, could only stammer and flap his hands ineffectually in a vague effort to silence the voice of his own being.

"Questions begat questions, it seems," Samah said at last. "I see that I cannot easily answer yours unless you answer some of mine. You are not from Chelestra, are you?"

"No, Samah,[1] I am not. I am from Arianus, the world of air."

"And you came to this world through Death's Gate, I presume?"

Alfred hesitated. "It might be more correct to say I came by accident . . . or perhaps by dog," he added with a slight smile.

His words were creating pictures in the minds of those he addressed, pictures that they were obviously, from the bewilderment on their faces, having difficulty understanding.

Alfred could imagine their confusion. He could see in his mind Arianus, its various mensch races warring, its wonderful, marvelous machine doing absolutely nothing, its Sartan gone and forgotten. He could see in his mind his journey through Death's Gate, see Haplo's ship, see Haplo.

Alfred steeled himself for what he assumed must be Samah's

---

[1] You will note Alfred does not use a formal title, such as "sir" or "my lord" when speaking to the Head of the Council, which was the ruling body in Sartan society. Such distinctions of rank or class were supposedly unknown in Sartan society at the time of the Sundering. It would, however, have been more correct of Alfred to refer to Samah as Brother. The fact that Alfred does not indicates his continued distrust of his own people.

next question, but apparently the images were coming so fast
and furious that the Sartan had evidently shut them out completely in an attempt to concentrate on his own thoughts.

"You came accidentally, you say. You were not sent to wake
us?"

"No," said Alfred, sighing. "There was, to be honest, no one
to send me."

"Our people on Arianus did not receive our message? Our
plea for help?"

"I don't know." Alfred shook his head, stared down at his
shoes. "If they did, it was a long time ago. A long, long time
ago."

Samah was silent. Alfred knew what he was thinking. The
Councillor was wondering how best to ask a question he was
deeply reluctant to ask.

At length, the Councillor glanced at Orla.

"We have a son. He is in the other room. He is twenty-five
years of age, as counted at the time of the Sundering. If he had
continued on in his life and had not chosen the Sleep, how old
would he be?"

"He would not be alive," said Alfred.

Samah's lips trembled. He controlled himself, with an effort.
"We Sartan live long. Are you certain? If he grew to be an old,
old man?"

"He would not be alive, nor would his children be alive, nor
the children of his children."

Alfred did not add the worst, that it was very likely the
young man would have had no descendants at all. Alfred attempted to hide this fact, but he saw that the Councillor was
beginning to understand. He'd seen in Alfred's mind the rows
of crypts on Arianus, the dead Sartan walking the lava flows on
Abarrach.

"How long have we slept?" Samah asked.

Alfred ran a hand over his balding head. "I can't say for
certain, or give you numbers. The history, the time, differs from
world to world."

"Centuries?"

"Yes. I believe so."

Orla's mouth moved, as if she would speak, but she said
nothing. The Sartan appeared dazed, stunned. It must be a terri-

ble thing, Alfred thought, to wake and realize that eons have passed while you slept. Wake to the knowledge that the carefully crafted universe you imagined pillowed your slumbering head has fallen into ruin and chaos.

"It's all so . . . confused. The only ones who might have any accurate record at all, the only ones who truly remember what happened, are the—" Alfred stopped, the dread words on his lips. He hadn't meant to bring that up, not yet at least.

"The Patryns." Samah finished his sentence. "Yes, I saw the man, our ancient enemy, in your mind, Brother. He was free of the Labyrinth. You traveled with him."

Orla's forlorn expression brightened. She sat forward eagerly. "Can we find comfort in this? I disapproved of this plan"—a glance at her husband—"but I would like nothing better than to have been proven wrong. Are we to understand that our hopes for reform worked? That the Patryns, when they emerged from the prison, had learned their lesson, hard as it was, and that they have forsaken their evil dreams of conquest and despotic rule?"

Alfred did not immediately respond.

"No, Orla, you can find no comfort anywhere," Samah said coldly. "Of course, we should have known. Look at the image of the Patryn in this brother's mind! It is the Patryns who have brought this terrible destruction upon the worlds!" He slammed his hand down upon the arm of the chair, sent up a cloud of dust.

"No, Samah, you are wrong!" Alfred protested, startled at his own courage in defying the Councillor. "Most of the Patryns are still locked in that prison of yours. They have suffered cruelly. Countless numbers have fallen victim to hideous monsters that could only have been created by warped and evil minds!

"Those who have escaped are filled with hatred for us, hatred that has been bred into them for countless generations. A hatred that is in every way justifiable, as far as I'm concerned. I . . . I was there, you see, for a brief time . . . in another body."

His newfound courage was rapidly evaporating beneath the blazing glare of Samah's eyes. Alfred shriveled up, shrank back into himself. His hands plucked at the frayed lace on the sleeves of his shirt hanging limply beneath the worn velvet of his top coat.

"What are you talking about, Brother?" Samah demanded. "This is impossible! The Labyrinth was meant to teach, to instruct. It was a game—a hard game, a difficult game—but nothing more than that."

"It turned into a deadly game, I'm afraid," said Alfred, but he spoke to his shoes. "Still, there might be hope. You see, this Patryn I know is a most complex man. He has a dog—"

Samah's eyes narrowed. "You seem very sympathetic to the enemy, Brother."

"No, no!" Alfred babbled. "I really don't know the enemy. I only know Haplo. And he's—"

But Samah was not interested. He brushed aside Alfred's words as so much dust. "This Patryn I saw in your mind was free, traveling through Death's Gate. What is his purpose?"

"Ex-exploration—" Alfred stammered.

"No, not exploration!" Samah rose to his feet, stared hard at Alfred, who fell back before the penetrating gaze. "Not exploration. Reconnaissance!"

Samah glowered, glanced in grim triumph at the other Council members. "It seems we have, after all, awakened at a propitious time, Brethren. Once again, our ancient enemy intends to go to war."

CHAPTER ♦ 7

ADRIFT, SOMEWHERE

THE GOODSEA

♦

MORNING. ANOTHER MORNING OF DESPAIR, OF FEAR. THE MORN-ings are the worst time for me. I wake from terrible dreams and for a minute I pretend I'm back in my bed in my home and I tell myself that the dreams are nothing more than that. But I can't ignore the fact that the horror-filled dreams might, at any time, become reality. We have not seen any sign of the dragon-snakes, but we know Someone is watching us. We are none of us seaman, we have no idea how to steer this ship, yet Something is steering it. Something guides it. And we have no idea what.

Dread keeps us from even venturing on the upper deck. We have fled to the lower part of the ship, where the Something seems content to leave us alone.

Each morning, Alake, Devon, and I meet and try to swallow the food for which we have no appetite. And we look at each other and we ask ourselves silently if today will be the day, the last day.

The waiting is the most awful part. Our terror grows in us daily. Our nerves are ragged, taut. Devon—good-natured Devon—quarreled with Alake over some little offhand remark she made about elves that he took completely the wrong way. I can hear them now, still raving at each other. It's not anger that harries them, but fear. I think the fear will drive us mad.

In remembering, I can, for a while, forget. I will tell about our leave-taking.

It was bitter and grievous. As it turned out, making that

initial decision to give ourselves up to the dragon-snakes was the easy part. We composed ourselves, dried our tears, and talked over what we were going to say to our parents. We chose Alake as our speaker and went out to the terrace.

Our parents were not prepared for the sight of us. Eliason, having so recently lost his beloved wife to some elven malady, could not bear to look at Sabia, his only daughter and the very image of her lovely mother. He turned away, his eyes filled with tears.

At this, Sabia lost her courage. Going to him, she put her arms around him and her tears mingled with his. Of course, this said everything.

"You overheard!" Dumaka accused us, scowling. "You were listening again!"

I had never seen him so furious. Alake's carefully planned speech died on her trembling lips.

"Father, we mean to go. You cannot stop us . . ."

"No!" he roared in a fury, and began pounding on the coral with his clenched fist, beating it, smashing it until I saw the pink turn red with his blood. "No! I will die before I submit to this—"

"Yes, you will die!" Alake cried. "And our people will die! Is that what you want, Father?"

"Fight!" Dumaka's black eyes flashed fire, foam frothed on his lips. "We will fight them! The beasts are mortal, just as we are. They have a heart that can be slashed open, a head that can be cut off—"

"Yes," said my father stoutly. "We will do battle."

His beard was torn. I saw great clumps of it lying on the floor at his feet. That was the first time I fully understood what our decision meant. I don't think we had made it lightly, but we had made it considering only ourselves, thinking only of what *we* would suffer. Now I came to realize that though we might die and die horribly, we could only die once and it would be over and we would be safe with the One. Our parents (and those others who loved us) must suffer and die our deaths in their minds time and time again.

I was so ashamed, I couldn't face him.

He and Dumaka were ranting on about battle-axes and weapons they would manufacture and how the elves would enchant them. Eliason actually recovered enough to offer a few broken suggestions. I couldn't say a word. I began to think that maybe our people *did* have a chance, that we could fight the serpents and that our lives would be spared. And then I noticed Alake. She was strangely quiet, strangely calm.

"Mother," she said suddenly, coldly, "you have to tell them the truth."

Delu flinched. She cast her daughter a swift, smoldering glance that commanded silence, but it was too late. Her look made it worse, for we all saw plainly that she had something to hide.

"What truth?" demanded my mother sharply.

"I am not permitted to speak of it," Delu said thickly, keeping her eyes averted from us all. "As my daughter well knows," she added bitterly.

"You must, Mother," Alake persisted. "Or will you let them go blindly out to fight an enemy that cannot be defeated?"

"What does she mean, Delu?"

It was my mother again. She was the shortest person there. She is shorter even than I am. I can see her now, side whiskers quivering, chin jutted out, arms akimbo, feet planted firmly on the ground. Delu was tall and willowy; my mother came only to her waist. But, in my memory, it is my mother who stands tall to me that day, tall in her strength and courage.

Delu crumbled, a tree falling to my mother's blade. The human sorceress sank down onto a low bench, her hands clasping and unclasping in her lap, her head bowed.

"I can't go into detail," she said in a low voice, "I shouldn't be telling you this much, but . . . but . . ." She swallowed, drew a quivering breath. "I'll try to explain. When a murder has been committed . . ."

(I pause here to note that humans do actually kill their own kind. I know you might find it difficult to believe, but it is the truth. One would think that considering their short life span they would hold life sacred. But no. They kill for the most paltry of reasons, greed, vengeance, and lust being chief among them.)

"When a murder has been committed and the murderer cannot be found," Delu was saying, "the members of the Coven can—by use of a spell whose very existence I should not now be revealing—gather information about the person who has perpetrated the deed."

"They can even conjure up an image of the person," Alake added, "if they find a lock of hair or traces of the murderer's blood or skin."

"Hush, child. What are you saying?" her mother reprimanded, but her protest was weak, her spirit crushed.

Alake continued. "A single thread can tell the Coven what the murderer wore. If the crime is recent, the shock of the outrage lingers in the very air and we can draw from it—"

"No, Daughter!" Delu looked up. "That is enough. Suffice it to say that we can conjure an image not only of the murderer but also, for lack of a better term, the murderer's soul."

"And the Coven performed this spell in the village?"

"Yes, Husband. It was magic. I was forbidden to tell you."

Dumaka did not look pleased, but he said nothing. Humans revere magic, hold it in awe and fear. Elves take a more practical view of it, but that may be because elven magic deals with more practical things. We dwarves never saw much point in either. Oh, certainly it saves time and labor, but one has to give up freedom to pay for it. After all, who ever really trusts a wizard? Apparently, not even a spouse.

"And so, Delu, you cast this spell on the beast's droppings or whatever they left behind." My mother single-mindedly dragged us all back to the subject at hand. "And just what did you find out about their souls?"

"That they have none," said Delu.

My mother flung her hands in the air in exasperation, glanced at my father as much as to say they'd wasted their time for nothing. But I knew, from Alake's expression, that more was coming.

"They have no souls," Delu continued, fixing her stern gaze on my mother. "Can't you understand? All *mortal* beings have souls. Just as all *mortal* beings have bodies."

"And it's the bodies we're worried about," snapped my mother.

"What Delu is trying to say," Alake explained, "is that these serpents have no souls and are, therefore, not mortal."

"Which means they are immortal?" Eliason stared at the girl in shock. "They *can't* be killed?"

"We are not certain," Delu said wearily, rising to her feet. "That is why I thought it best not to bring it up. The Coven has never encountered any creatures like this. We simply do not know."

"But that is what you surmise?" Dumaka asked.

Delu would have preferred not to answer, it seemed, but after a moment, she concluded she had no choice.

"If what we have discovered is true, then they are not serpents. They are a creature of the genus known anciently as 'dragon.' The ancients held the dragon to be immortal, but that was probably only because the dragon was nearly impossible to kill. *Not* that it couldn't be killed." She was briefly defiant, but her defiance quickly faded. "The dragon is extremely powerful. Especially in magic."

"We cannot fight the beasts," said my father, "and have any hope of winning. Is that what you are saying? Because what I am saying is that it makes no difference to me! We will not voluntarily give up one dwarf—any dwarf—to them. And so will say my people."

I knew he was right. I knew we dwarves would see ourselves destroyed as a race before we would sacrifice one of our kind. I knew I was safe. I was filled with relief . . . and my shame deepened.

Dumaka looked around, his dark eyes fierce. "I agree with Yvngar. We must fight them."

"But, Father," Alake argued. "How can you doom all our people to death for my sake—"

"I do not do this for your sake, Daughter," Dumaka countered sternly. "I do this for the sake of our people. We give up one daughter to them and who knows but that next time these 'dragons' will demand all our daughters. And the time after that our sons. No!" He slammed his already bleeding hand on the coral. "We will fight. And so will say all our people!"

"I will not give up my precious child," Eliason whispered in a tear-choked voice.

He was holding onto Sabia as tightly as if he saw the coils winding around her already. Sabia clung to him, weeping for his grief more than for her own.

"Nor will my people ever agree to pay such a terrible price for their own well-being, even if, as Dumaka says, we could trust these snakes or dragons or whatever they be called.

"We will fight," Eliason continued, more resolutely. Then he sighed, and glanced around at us somewhat helplessly. "Though it has been many long, long epoches since elves went to battle. Still, I suppose the knowledge needed to make weapons is in our archives . . ."

My father snorted. "And you think these beasts will wait around for you elves to read the books and then dig the ore and build the smithies before you can set blade to hilt. Bah! We must make do with what we have. I will send battle-axes—"

"And I will provide you with spears and swords," Dumaka struck in, hard-edged, battle lust burning.

Delu and Eliason began to discuss and debate various military enchantments and mantras and cantrips. Unfortunately, elven magic and human were so dissimilar that neither could offer the other much assistance, but they both seemed to find comfort in at least the appearance of doing something constructive.

"Why don't you girls go back to Sabia's room," suggested my mother. "You've had a shock." Coming over, she hugged me to her breast. "But I will always honor and remember my brave daughter, offering her life for her people."

My mother left to join my father in a spirited argument with Dumaka over battle-axes versus pole-axes, and we girls were forgotten.

And so that was that. They'd made their decision. I felt that I should be rejoicing, but my heart—which had been strangely light after we'd chosen to sacrifice ourselves—felt as heavy as lead in my breast. It was all I could do to carry the burden; my feet dragged through the glistening, coral hallways. Alake was grim and thoughtful. Sabia was still occasionally shaken by sobs, and so we said nothing to each other until we reached the elf maid's room.

Even then, we did not speak, at least aloud. But our thoughts were like streams of water, all traveling the same direction, at last converging. I knew this because I looked suddenly at Alake and found her looking at me. We both turned, at the identical moment, to look at Sabia, whose eyes widened. She sank weakly down upon her bed, and shook her head.

"No, you can't be thinking that! You heard what my father said . . ."

"Sabia, listen to me." Alake's tone reminded me of times

when we'd try to get the elf maid to agree to play a trick on our
governess. "Are you going to be able to stand here in this room
and watch your people being slaughtered before your eyes and
say to yourself: 'I might have prevented this'?"

Sabia hung her head.

I went over to her, put my arm around her shoulders. Elves
are so thin, I thought. Their bones are so fragile you might break
them with a touch.

"Our parents will never permit us to go," I said. "And so
we must take matters into our own hands. If there is a chance,
even a tiny chance, that we could be the saviors of our people,
then we must take it."

"My father!" mourned Sabia, beginning to cry again. "It will
break my father's heart."

I thought of my father, of the clumps of beard lying on the
floor at his feet, of my mother hugging me, and my courage
almost failed me. Then I thought of the dwarves caught in the
dragon-snake's hideous, toothless mouths. I thought of Hartmut,
his battle-ax shining, but looking small and powerless compared
to the gigantic beasts.

I think of him now, as I write, and of my father and my
mother and my people, and I know that we did the right thing.
As Alake said, I could not have stood and watched my people
die and say to myself, *I might have prevented this!*

"Your father will have the elven people to think about, Sabia.
He will be strong, for your sake, you may be sure of that. Grundle"—Alake's black eyes shifted to me, her manner was brisk,
commanding—"what about the boat?"

"It's moored in the harbor," I said. "The captain and most
of the crew will be ashore during the rest hours, leaving only a
land-watch on board. We can handle them. I have a plan."

"Very well." Alake left that to me. "We'll sneak away in the
time of the deep sleep. Gather together whatever you think you
might need. I assume that there is food and water on board the
vessel?"

"And weapons," I added.

That was a mistake. Sabia looked as if she might faint, and
even Alake appeared dubious. I said no more. I didn't tell them
that I, for one, meant to die fighting.

"I will take what I need for my magic," said Alake.

Sabia gazed at us helplessly. "I could take my lute," she offered.

Poor girl. I think she had some vague idea of charming the dragon-snakes with her song. I almost laughed, caught Alake's eye, and sighed instead. Actually, once I thought about it, her lute and my ax would probably accomplish about the same thing.

"Very well. We part now, to put together what we need. Be circumspect. Be quiet. Be secret! We'll send a message to our parents telling them that we're too upset to come down to dinner. The fewer people we see the better. Do you understand? You tell no one." Alake fixed her stern gaze on Sabia.

"No one . . . except Devon," the elf maid replied.

"Devon! Absolutely not! He'd talk you out of it." Alake has a low opinion of men.

Sabia bristled. "He is my chosen husband-to-be. He has a right to know. We keep nothing from each other. It is a matter of honor between us. He won't say anything to anyone if I ask him not to."

Her small, pointed chin quivered in defiance, her slender shoulders squared. Trust an elf to develop a backbone at the worst possible time.

Alake didn't like it, but she could see as well as I that Sabia wouldn't be argued out of this.

"You'll resist all his pleadings and tears and arguments?" Alake said crossly.

"Yes," said Sabia, a pretty flush coming to her pale cheeks. "I know how important this is, Alake. I won't fail you. And Devon will understand. You'll see. He is a prince, remember. He knows what it means to have a responsibility to our people."

I poked Alake in the ribs. "I have things to do," I said gruffly. "And there's not much time."

The seasun was drifting beyond the far shore into the night. Already, the sea was dimming into deep purple; the servants were flitting about the palace, lighting the lamps.

Sabia rose from her bed and started to pack her lute in its case. Obviously, our conversation was at an end.

"We'll meet back here," I said.

Sabia nodded cool agreement. I managed to get Alake, who still seemed inclined to want to stay and argue, out of the bedroom and into the hall. Through the closed door, I could hear Sabia begin to sing an elven song called "Lady Dark," a song sad enough to break the heart.

"Devon will never let her go! He'll tell our parents!" Alake hissed at me.

"We'll come back early," I whispered, "and keep an eye on them. If he starts to leave, we'll stop him. You can do it with your magic, can't you?"

"Yes, of course." Alake's dark eyes flashed. "Excellent idea, Grundle. I should have thought of it myself. What time should we return?"

"Dinner's in a signe.[1] He's staying here in the palace. He'll be worried when she doesn't appear, and he'll come to see what's wrong. That gives us time."

"But what if she sends him a message to come earlier?"

"He can't risk insulting her father by missing a meal."

I knew quite a bit about elven etiquette, having been forced to endure it during my stay here. Alake had lived here, too, but—typical of humans—she'd always done exactly as she pleased. To give Alake her due, she probably would have starved to death before getting through one of the elven dinners, which could sometimes stretch into cycles, with several hours between courses. I figured that Eliason would have small appetite for his meal this day, however.

Alake and I separated, each returning to our own quarters. I bustled about, making up a small bundle of clothing, whisker brush, and other necessities, just as if I were packing to go visit Phondra on a holiday. The excitement and daring of our scheme kept me from thinking through to what must be its dreadful conclusion. It was only when it came time to write a farewell letter to my parents that my heart began to fail me.

Of course, my parents wouldn't be able to read what I had written, but I planned to enclose a note to the elven king, asking him to read it to them. I tore up many sheets before I was able

---

[1] Time on the seamoons is regulated by the passage of the seasun from under one shore to its rising on the opposite side. Human wizards determined this to be a 150-degree arc and split the day into two sextans of 75 degrees. Each sextan is divided into 5 signe; a signe is made up of 60 minutes.

to say what I wanted, and then left it so covered with tears I'm not sure anyone could decipher it. I hope and pray it brought some comfort to my parents.

When I was finished, I stuffed the letter in my father's beard-trimming kit, where he would find it in the morning and not before. I lingered, then, in my parent's guest quarters, looking lovingly at each little thing belonging to them and wishing with all my heart that I could see them one last time. But I knew quite well that I could never deceive my mother and so I left hastily, while they were still at dinner, and returned to the part of the palace where Sabia lived.

Finding a quiet niche, needing to be alone, I settled myself in it and asked the One for strength and guidance and help. I was greatly comforted and a peaceful feeling came over me, giving me to know that I was doing the right thing.

The One meant us to overhear that conversation. The One will not forsake us. These dragon-snakes may be evil, but the One is good. The One will guard us and keep us. No matter how powerful these creatures are, they are not more powerful than the One who, so we believe, made this world and all in it.

I was feeling much better, and was just beginning to wonder what had happened to Alake when I saw Devon dash past me, heading for Sabia's rooms. I crept out of my niche, hoping to see which antechamber he entered (for, of course, he wouldn't be allowed into Sabia's bedroom), and I bumped into Alake.

"What took you so long?" I asked irritably in a low tone. "Devon's already here!"

"Magic rites," she told me loftily. "I cannot explain."

I might have known. I heard Devon's worried voice and the voice of Sabia's duenna[2] answering him, telling him that Sabia was unwell, but would see him in the sitting room, if he wanted to wait.

He headed in that direction. Doors shut.

Alake darted into the hall, I trotted after her and we scuttled

---

[2] A duenna is a member of the royal court who acts as chaperon to unmarried women.

into the music room that adjoined the sitting room only a split instant ahead of Sabia and her duenna.

"Are you quite up to this, my dear?" The duenna was hovering over Sabia like a hen with one chick. "You don't look at all well."

"I do have a frightful headache," we heard Sabia say in a weak voice. "Could you fetch me some lavender water to bathe my temples?"

Alake placed her hand upon the coral wall, muttered several words, and it dissolved beneath her fingers, creating an opening big enough for her to peek through. She created another hole at my level. Fortunately, elves fill their rooms with furniture and vases and flowers and birdcages, so we were well-concealed, although I had to peer through the leaves of a palm and Alake was eye-to-eye with a singing phurah bird.

Sabia was standing near Devon, as close as was considered proper between betrothed couples. The duenna returned with woeful news.

"Poor Sabia. We are out of lavender water. I can't imagine how. I know the bottle was filled only yesterday."

"Could you please be a dear, Marabella, and fill it again? My head does throb most awfully." Sabia put her hand to her forehead. "There is some in my mother's old room, I believe."

"I'm afraid she is very ill," said Devon anxiously.

"But your mother's room is on the other side of the Grotto," said the duenna. "I shouldn't leave you two alone . . ."

"I only intend to stay a moment," said Devon.

"Please, Marabella?" pleaded Sabia.

The elven princess had never been refused anything in her life. The duenna fluttered her hands in indecision. Sabia gave a faint moan. The duenna left. Knowing that many new rooms had been opened and several old hallways overgrown between here and Sabia's mother's room, I didn't expect the duenna to find her way back much before morning.

Sabia, in her gentle voice, began to explain everything to Devon.

I can't describe the painful scene that followed between the two of them. They had grown up together and loved each other dearly since childhood. Devon listened in horrified shock that gave way to outrage, and he argued and protested vehemently. I was proud of Sabia, who remained calm and composed, though what I knew she was suffering over his agony brought tears to my eyes.

"Honor-bound, I have told you our secret, Beloved," she said, clasping her hands over his, looking straight into his eyes. "You have the power to stop us, to betray us. But you will not, I know, because you are a prince and you understand I make this sacrifice for the good of our people. And I know, my dearest, that your sacrifice will be far harder than mine, but I know you will be strong for my sake, as I am strong for yours."

Devon sank to his knees, overcome by grief. Sabia knelt beside him, put her arms around him. I drew away from my spyhole, bitterly ashamed of myself. Alake moved away from hers, covered both over with her hand and a word of magic. She generally scoffed at love. I noticed now that she had nothing to say on the subject and that she was blinking her eyes quite rapidly.

We sat in the music room in the dark, not daring to light a lamp. I whispered to her my plan to steal the boat, which she approved. When I mentioned, however, that I had very little idea how to operate it, her face grew grave.

"I don't believe that will be a problem," she said, and I guessed what she meant.

The dragon-snakes would be watching for us.

She spoke to me something of the magic spells she was studying at her level (she had recently moved up to Third House, whatever that means). I knew she wasn't really supposed to be talking much about her magic, and I must admit I wasn't all that interested and I understood nothing of what she was saying. But she was trying to distract us, keep us from thinking about our fear, and so I listened with pretended interest.

Then we heard a door shut. Devon must have left. Poor fellow, I thought, and wondered very much what he would do. Elves had been known to sicken and die of grief, and I had little doubt that Devon would not long outlive Sabia.

"We'll give her a few moments to compose herself," said Alake, with unusual consideration.

"Not too long," I cautioned. "The household must have been

in bed this past signe. We have to get out of this maze and through the streets and down to the wharf yet.''

Alake agreed and, after a few tense moments, we both decided that we could take no more waiting and headed for the door.

The hallway was dark and deserted. We had thought up a plausible story, in case we ran into Marabella, but there was no sign of her or her lavender water. Creeping over to Sabia's bedchamber, we tapped lightly on the door and softly pushed it open.

Sabia was moving around her bedroom in the darkness, gathering up her things. Hearing the door open, she jumped and swiftly flung a filmy scarf around her head, then turned to face us.

"Who is it?" she whispered in fear. "Marabella?"

"It's only us," I said. "Are you ready?"

"Yes, yes. Just a moment."

She was in a flutter, obviously, for she stumbled about the room in the darkness as if she'd never been inside it before. Her voice, too, had changed, I noticed, but concluded that she must be hoarse from sobbing. At length, falling over a chair, she made her way to us, clutching a silken bag out of which spilled lace and ribbons.

"I'm ready," she said in a muffled voice, keeping the scarf over her face, probably to hide her tear-swollen eyes and nose. Elves are so vain.

"What about the lute?" I asked.

"The what?"

"The lute. You were going to take your lute."

"Oh, uh. I . . . I decided . . . not to," she said lamely, coughed, and cleared her throat.

Alake had been keeping watch in the hall. She beckoned to us impatiently. "Come on before Marabella catches us!"

Sabia hastened after her. I was about to follow, when I heard what I thought was a sigh coming from the darkness, and a rustle in Sabia's bed. I looked back, saw an odd shadow, and was about to say something when Alake pounced on me.

"Come on, Grundle!" she insisted, digging her nails into my arm and dragging me out.

I thought no more of it.

We three made our way out of the Grotto safely. Sabia led us, and we only got lost once. Thank the One elves never feel the need, as do humans, to post guards over everything. The streets of the elven city were deserted, as would be any dwarven road at this time. It is only in human villages that you find people wandering about at all hours of the night.

We reached the boat. Alake cast her magical sleep over the dwarves on watch and they toppled to the decks snoring blissfully. Then we faced what would be our most difficult challenge during that entire night—hauling the slumbering dwarves out of the boat and back to shore, where we planned to hide them among some barrels.

The sleeping dwarves were so much deadweight, and I was certain I'd torn my arms out of their sockets after wrestling with the first. I asked Alake if she didn't know a flying spell we could cast on them, but she said she hadn't gone that far in her studies yet. Oddly, weak, fragile Sabia proved unusually strong and adept at dwarf-hauling. Again, I thought this strange. Was I truly blind? Or had the One commanded me to shut my eyes?

We manhandled the last dwarf off and slipped onto the boat, which was really just a much smaller version of the submersible I've already described. Our first task was to search the berths and the hold, gathering the various axes and pole arms the crew had left about. We carried these up to the open deck, located behind the observation room.

Alake and Sabia began to throw them overboard. I cringed at the splashing sounds the arms made, certain that it must be heard by everyone in the city.

"Wait!" I grabbed hold of Alake. "We don't have to get rid of all of them, do we? Couldn't we keep one or two?"

"No, we must convince the creatures that we are defenseless," said Alake firmly, and tossed the last few over the rail.

"There are eyes watching us, Grundle," Sabia whispered in awe. "Can't you feel them?"

I could, and that didn't make me any happier about handing over our weapons to the dolphins. I was glad that I'd had the foresight to slip an ax beneath my bed. What Alake doesn't know won't hurt her.

We trailed back to the observation room, none of us saying

anything, each wondering what would happen next. Once there, we stood staring at each other.

"I suppose I could try to run this thing," I offered.

But that wasn't necessary.

As Alake had foretold, the boat's hatches suddenly slammed shut, sealing us inside. The vessel, steered by no one that we could see, glided away from the pier and headed out into open sea.

The fevered excitement and thrill of our stealthy escape began to seep out of us, leaving us chilled; the full realization of what was likely to be our terrible fate was stark before us. Water swept over the deck and engulfed the windows. Our ship sank into the Goodsea.

Frightened and alone, we each reached out our hands to the others. And then, of course, we knew that Sabia wasn't Sabia.

It was Devon.

CHAPTER ♦ 8

THE HALL OF SLEEP

CHELESTRA

♦

IN THE COUNCIL CHAMBER, IN THE CITY OF THE SARTAN ON CHELES-tra, Samah's pronouncement that the Patryns must be going to war brought expressions of grim consternation to the faces of the Council members.

"Isn't this what they intend?" Samah demanded, rounding on Alfred.

"I . . . I suppose it might be," Alfred faltered, taken aback. "We never really discussed . . ." His voice peetered out.

Samah regarded him thoughtfully, intently. "A most fortunate circumstance, Brother, that you have arrived here *accidentally*, wakened us at this precise moment."

"I—I'm not certain what you mean, Councillor," answered Alfred hesitantly, not liking Samah's tone.

"Perhaps your arrival wasn't quite by accident?"

Alfred wondered suddenly if the Councillor could be referring to some higher power, if there could be One who would dare rely on such an unworthy, inept messenger as the bumbling Sartan.

"I—I suppose it might have been . . ."

"You suppose!" Samah leapt on the word. "You suppose this and you suppose that! What do you mean 'suppose'?"

Alfred didn't know what he meant. He hadn't known what he was saying, because he'd been trying to figure out what

Samah was saying. Alfred could only stutter and stare and look as guilty as if he'd come with the intent of murdering them all.

"I think you are being too hard on our poor brother, Samah," Orla intervened. "We should be offering him our grateful thanks, instead of doubting him, accusing him of being in league with the enemy."

Alfred stared, aghast. So *that's* what the Councillor had meant! He thinks the Patryns sent me! . . . But why? Why me?

A shadow passed over Samah's handsome face, a cloud of anger covering the sun's politic light. It was gone almost immediately, except for a lingering darkness in the smooth voice.

"I accuse you of nothing, Brother. I merely asked a question. Yet, if my wife believes I have wronged you, I ask you to forgive me. I am weary, undoubtedly a reaction from the stress of awakening and the shock of the news you have brought us."

Alfred felt called upon to say something in response. "I do assure you, Councillor, members of the Council"—he glanced at them pathetically—"that if you knew me, you would have no difficulty in believing my story. I came here accidentally. My entire life, you see, has been a sort of accident."

The other Council members appeared faintly embarrassed; this was no way for a Sartan, for a demigod, to talk or act.

Samah watched Alfred from beneath narrowed eyelids, not seeing the man, but seeing the images formed by his words.

"If there are no objections," the Councillor said abruptly, "I propose that we adjourn the Council until tomorrow, by which time, hopefully, we will have ascertained the true state of affairs. I suggest that teams be sent to the surface to reconnoiter. Are there any objections?"

There were none.

"Choose among the young men and women. Tell them to be wary and search for any traces of the enemy. Remind them to be particularly careful to avoid the seawater."

Alfred could see images, too, and he saw, as the Council members rose to their feet in apparent outward harmony and agreement, walls of bricks and thorns separating some from another. And no wall was higher or thicker than that dividing husband from wife.

There had been cracks in that wall, when they'd first heard the startling news of their long slumbering, and came to understand that the world had fallen apart around them. But the cracks were rapidly being filled in, Alfred saw, the walls fortified. He felt vastly unhappy and uncomfortable.

"Orla," Samah added, half-turning on his way out the door. The head of the Council always walked in the lead. "Perhaps you will be good enough to see to the needs and wants of our brother . . . Alfred." The mensch name came with difficulty to Sartan lips.

"I would be honored," said Orla, bowing in polite response. Brick by brick, the wall was growing, expanding.

Alfred heard the woman sigh softly. Her gaze, which followed after her husband, was wistful and sad. She, too, saw the wall, knew it was there. Perhaps she wanted to tear it down, but had no idea how to begin. As for Samah, he seemed content to let it be.

The Councillor walked out of the room, the others followed, three walking with him, two—after a glance at Orla, who only shook her head—removing themselves shortly afterward. Alfred remained where he was, ill at ease, not knowing what to do.

Cold fingers closed over his wrist. The woman's touch startled him. He nearly leapt out of his shoes, his feet slid in opposite directions, stirred up a cloud of choking dust. Alfred tottered and blinked, sneezed, and wished himself anywhere else, including the Labyrinth. Did she think he was in league with the enemy? He cringed and waited fearfully for her to speak.

"How nervous you are! Please, calm yourself." Orla regarded him thoughtfully. "I suppose, though, that this must have been as great a shock to you as to us. You must be hungry and thirsty. I know *I* am. Will you walk with me?"

There was nothing terrifying—even for Alfred—in being invited to dine. He was hungry. He'd had little time and less inclination for food on Abarrach. The thought of dining once more in peace and quiet, with his brothers and sisters, was blessed. For these were truly his people, truly like those he knew before he had himself taken his long sleep. Perhaps that's why Samah's doubts disturbed him so. Perhaps that's why his own doubts disturbed him.

"Yes, I'd like that. Thank you," Alfred said, glancing at Orla almost shyly.

She smiled at him. Her smile was tremulous, hesitant, as if

not often used. But it was a beautiful smile, and brought light to her eyes. Alfred stared at her in dumb admiration.

His spirits rose, flying so high that the walls and all thought of walls fell far down below him, out of sight, out of mind. He walked beside her, leaving the dusty chamber. Neither spoke, but moved together companionably, emerging onto a scene of quiet, efficient bustle. Alfred was thinking, and not being very careful with his thoughts, apparently.

"I am flattered at your regard for me, Brother," Orla said to him softly, a faint blush on her cheek. "But it would be more proper for you to keep such thoughts private."

"I . . . beg your pardon!" Alfred gasped, his face burning. "It's just . . . I'm not used to being around . . ."

He made a fluttering gesture with his hand, encompassing the Sartan, who were busily employed in restoring life to what had been dead for centuries. Alfred darted a swift and guilty glance around, fearing to see Samah glowering at him. But the Councillor was deeply engrossed in discussion with a younger man in perhaps his midtwenties, who, by his resemblance, must be the son Samah had mentioned.

"You fear he's jealous." Orla tried to laugh lightly, but her attempt failed, ended in a sigh. "Truly, Brother, you haven't been around many Sartan, if you are mindful of such a mensch weakness."

"I'm doing everything wrong." Alfred shook his head. "I'm a clumsy fool. And I can't blame it on living among mensch. It's just me."

"But matters would have been different had our people survived. You would not have been alone. And you have been very much alone, haven't you, Alfred?"

Her voice was tender, pitying, compassionate.

Alfred was very near to tears. He tried to respond cheerfully. "It hasn't been as bad as you suppose. I've had the mensch . . ."

Orla's look of pity increased.

Alfred, seeing it, protested. "No, it isn't the way you imagine. You underestimate the mensch. We all did, I believe.

"I remember what it was like before I slept. We hardly ever walked among the mensch, and when we did, it was only to come to them as parents, visiting the nursery. But I have lived long among them. I've shared their joys and sorrows, I've known their fears and ambitions. I've come to understand how helpless and powerless they feel. And, though they've done much that was wrong, I can't help but admire them for what they have accomplished."

"And yet," said Orla, frowning, "the mensch have, as I see in your mind, fallen to warring among themselves, slaughtering each other, elf battling human, human fighting dwarf."

"And who was it," asked Alfred, "who inflicted the most terrifying catastrophe ever known upon them? Who was it who killed millions in the name of good, who sundered a universe, who brought the living to strange worlds, then left them to fend for themselves?"

Two bright red spots blazed in Orla's cheeks. The dark line deepened in her forehead.

"I'm sorry," Alfred hastened to apologize. "I have no right . . . I wasn't there . . ."

"You *weren't* there, on that world that seems so near to me in my heart, and yet which my head tells me is long lost. You don't know our fear of the growing might of the Patryns. They meant to wipe us out completely, genocide. And then what would have been left for your mensch? A life of slavery beneath the iron-heeled boot of totalitarian rule. You don't know the agony the Council underwent, trying to determine how best to fight this dire threat. The sleepless nights, the days of bitter arguing. You don't know our own, our personal agony. Samah himself—" She broke off abruptly, biting her lip.

She was adept at concealing her thoughts, revealing only those she wanted. Alfred wondered what she would have said had she continued.

They had walked a long distance, far from the Hall of Sleep. Blue sigla ran along the bottom of the walls, guiding their way through a dusty corridor. Dark rooms branched off it, rooms that would soon become temporary Sartan living quarters. For now, however, the two stood alone in the rune-lit darkness.

"We should be turning back. I had not meant to come this far. We've passed the dining area." Orla started to retrace her steps.

"No, wait." Alfred put a hand on her arm, startled at his

own temerity in detaining her. "We may never have another chance to talk alone like this. And . . . I must understand! You didn't agree, did you? You and some of the other Council members."

"No. No, we didn't."

"What did *you* want to do?"

Orla drew a deep breath. She wasn't looking at him; she remained turned away. For a moment, Alfred thought she wasn't going to answer, and she apparently thought so, too, but then, with a shrug, she changed her mind.

"You will find out soon enough. The decision to make the Sundering was talked of, debated. It caused bitter disputes, split families." She sighed, shook her head. "What action did I counsel? None. I counseled that we do nothing, except take a defensive stand against the Patryns, should we be attacked. It was never certain they would, mind you. It was only what we feared . . ."

"And fear was victorious."

"No!" Orla snapped angrily. "Fear wasn't the reason we made the decision, at last. It was the longing to have the chance to create a perfect world. Four perfect worlds! Where all would live in peace and harmony. No more evil, no more war . . . That was Samah's dream. That was why I agreed to cast my vote with his over all other objections. That was why I didn't protest when Samah made the decision to send . . ."

Again, she stopped herself.

"Send?" Alfred prompted.

Orla's expression grew chill. She changed the subject. "Samah's plan should have worked. Why didn't it? What caused it to fail?" She glared at him, almost accusingly.

Not me! was Alfred's immediate protest. It wasn't *my* fault.

But, then again, maybe it was, he reflected uncomfortably. Certainly I've done nothing to make things better.

Orla walked back down the corridor, her steps brisk. "We've been away too long. The others will be worried about us."

The runelight began to fade.

"He is lying."

"But, Father, that's not possible. He's a Sartan—"

"A weak-minded Sartan, who has been traveling in the company of a Patryn, Ramu. He's obviously been corrupted, his mind taken over. We cannot blame him. He has had no Councillor to turn to, no one to help him in his time of trial."

"Is he lying about everything?"

"No, I don't believe so," Samah said, after a moment's profound thought. "The images of our people lying dead in their sleeping chambers on Arianus, the images of the Sartan practicing the forbidden art of necromancy on Abarrach, were too real, far too real. But those images were brief, fleeting. I'm not certain I understand. We must question him further to learn exactly what has happened. Mostly, though, I must know more about this Patryn."

"I understand. And what is it you would have me do, Father?"

"Be friendly to this Alfred, Son. Encourage him to talk, draw him out, agree with all he says, sympathize. The man is lonely, starved for those of his own kind. He hides in a shell he has built for his own defense. We will crack it with kindness and, once we have opened it, then we can set about his reclamation.

"I have, in fact, already started." Samah glanced complacently down the darkened corridor.

"Indeed?" His son's gaze followed.

"Yes. I've turned the wretched man over to your mother. He will be more likely to share his true thoughts with her than with us."

"But will she share her knowledge?" Ramu wondered. "It seems to me she has taken a liking to the man."

"She always did befriend every stray who came begging at our door." Samah shrugged. "But there is nothing more to it than that. She will tell us. She is loyal to her people. Just prior to the Sundering, she sided with me, supported me, abandoned all her objections. And so the rest of the Council was forced to go along. Yes, she'll tell me what I need to know. Especially once she understands that our goal is to help the poor man."

Ramu bowed to his father's wisdom, started to leave.

"All the same, Ramu." Samah stopped his son. "Keep your eyes open. I do not trust this . . . Alfred."

CHAPTER ♦ 9

ADRIFT, SOMEWHERE

THE GOODSEA

♦

SOMETHING EXCEEDINGLY STRANGE HAS OCCURRED AND I HAVE been (mercifully) so busy that I have had no time to write until now. But at last all is quiet, the excitement has subsided, and we are left only to wonder: What will happen to us now?

Where shall I start? Thinking back, I see it all began with Alake's magical attempt to summon the dolphins and speak to them. We wanted to find out, if possible, where we were headed and what we faced, even if our fate was a terrible one. It is the "not knowing" that is so difficult to bear.

I have said that we were adrift in the sea. That is not precisely accurate, as Devon pointed out to us during our midday meal. We are traveling in a specific direction, guided by the dragon-snakes. We have no control over the ship. We cannot even get near the steerage.

A terrible feeling comes over us when we walk in that direction. It saps the strength from our legs, leaves them wobbly and unable to move. It fills the heart and mind with images of death and dying. The one time we tried, we turned and fled in a panic, to hide, cowering, in our rooms. I dream of it still.

It was after that incident, when we'd recovered, that Alake decided to try to contact the dolphins.

"We haven't seen one since we embarked," she stated. "And that's very strange. I want to know what's going on, where we are headed."

Now that I thought of it, it was strange that we hadn't seen any fish. Dolphins are quite fond of company and are great gossips. They will generally flock around a ship, begging for news and passing along their own to anyone fool enough to listen.

"How do we . . . er . . . summon them?" I asked.

Alake seemed astonished that I didn't know. I don't understand why. No dwarf in his right mind would ever voluntarily summon fish! It was all we could do to get rid of the pesky things.

"I'll use my magic, of course," she said. "And I want you and Devon to be there with me."

I had to admit I was excited. I had lived among humans and elves, but had never seen any human magic, and I was surprised when Alake invited us. She said our "energies" would help her. I think, personally, she was lonely and afraid, but I kept my mouth shut.

Perhaps I should explain (as best I can) the Phondran and Elmas concept of magic. And the Gargan point of view.

Dwarves, elves, and humans all believe in the One, a powerful force that places us in this world, watches over us while we are here, and receives us when we leave. Each race takes a somewhat differing view of the One, however.

The basic dwarven credo is that all dwarves are in the One and the One is in all dwarves. Thus harm that befalls one dwarf befalls all dwarves and befalls the One as well—this is why a dwarf will never intentionally kill, cheat, or deceive another dwarf. (Not counting barroom brawls, of course. A sock on the jaw, delivered in a regular knock-'em-down, turn-'em-over, is generally considered beneficial to the health.)

In the old days, we dwarves believed the One to be interested mainly in ourselves. As for elves and humans, if they had been created by the One at all (and some held that they sprang up from the darkness, rather like fungi), it must have been an accident or else they were designed by a force opposing the One.

Long times of coexistence taught us to accept each other, however. We know now that the One has in care all living beings (although some old grandfathers maintain that the One loves dwarves, merely tolerates humans and elves).

Humans believe that the One rules all, but that—like any Phondran chieftain—the One is open to suggestion. Thus the humans are constantly badgering the One with supplications and demands. Phondrans also believe that the One has underlings, who perform certain menial tasks beneath the One's dignity. (That concept is *so* human!) These underlings are subject to human manipulation through magic, and the Phondrans are never happier than when altering the growing seasons, summoning winds, conjuring rain, and starting fires.

The Elmas take a far more relaxed view of the One. In their perspective, the One started everything off with a bang and now sits back lazily to watch it all go forward—like the bright, glittering, spinning toys Sabia used to play with as a child. The Elmas view magic not as something reverent and spiritual, but as entertainment or a labor-saving device.

Though only sixteen (no more than a babe to us, but humans mature rapidly), Alake was deemed quite skilled in magic already and I knew her mother's fondest wish was to hand her daughter the leadership of the Coven.

Devon and I watched Alake take her place before her altar, which she had set up in the empty cargo hold on deck two. It was, I must admit, a pleasure to watch her.

Alake is tall and well-made. (I have never, by the way, envied humans their height. An old dwarven proverb says, "The longer the stick, the easier to break." But I did admire Alake's graceful movements, like a frond bending in the water.) Her skin is a dark ebony. Her black hair is braided in countless tiny braids that hang down her back, each braid ending in beads of blue and orange (her tribal colors) and brass. If she lets her braids hang loose, the beads clash musically together when she walks, sounding like hundreds of tiny bells.

She wore the accepted dress of Phondra, a single piece of blue and orange cloth wound around the body, held in place by the cunning of the folds (a knack known only to Phondrans). The free end of the cloth is draped over the right shoulder (to show she is unmarried—married women place the fold over the left shoulder).

Silver ceremonial bracelets adorned her arms, silver bells hung from her ears.

"I've never seen you wear those bracelets, Alake," I said, making conversation to break the silence that was so terribly silent. "Are they yours or your mother's? Were they a gift?"

To my surprise, Alake, who is usually fond of showing off any new jewelry, made no reply and averted her face.

I thought she hadn't heard me. "Alake, I asked if—"

Devon jabbed me in the ribs with his sharp elbow. "Shush! Say nothing about her jewelry!"

"Why not?" I whispered back irritably. To be honest, I was getting sick and tired of tiptoeing around, fearful of offending someone.

"She wears her burial adornments," Devon returned.

I was shocked. Of course, I'd heard of the custom. At birth, Phondran girl-children are presented with silver bracelets and ear-jangles which, it is hoped, they will wear at their wedding and pass along to their own daughters. But, if a girl dies untimely, before her marriage, her bracelets and other jewelry are placed on the body when it is sent out to join the One in the Goodsea.

I felt miserable, tried to think of something to say to make everything all right, realized that nothing I said would help. So I sat, scuffing my heels against the floor and trying to take an interest in what Alake was doing.

Devon sat beside me. The furniture aboard the ship was built for dwarves. I felt sorry for the elf, who looked most uncomfortable, his long legs, encased in the silken folds of Sabia's skirt, spraddled out on either side of his short-legged stool.

Alake was taking an interminable length of time to set up the objects on the altar, stopping to pray over each one.

"If all humans pray like this over every little thing, my guess is that the One fell asleep long ago!" I spoke in what I thought was an undertone, but Alake must have heard me, because she looked shocked and frowned at me in reproof.

I decided I'd better change the subject and, glancing over at Devon wearing Sabia's clothes, I came up with something I'd long wondered.

"How did you manage to persuade Sabia to let you go in her place?" I asked the elf.

Of course, that was wrong, too. Devon, who had been keeping up a cheerful front, immediately grew sad, and turned *his* face away.

Alake darted over to me, pinched me, hard.

"Don't remind him of her!"

"Ouch! This does it!" I growled, losing patience. "I'm not to speak to Alake about her ear-jangles. I'm not to talk to Devon about Sabia, despite the fact that he's wearing her clothes and looks uncommonly silly in a dress. Well, in case you've both forgotten, it's my funeral, too, and Sabia was my friend. We've been trying to pretend we're on a holiday cruise. We're not. And it's not right to keep our words in our bellies, as we dwarves say. It poisons the food." I snorted. "No wonder we can't eat."

Alake stared at me in startled silence. Devon had the ghost of a smile on his pale face.

"You are right, Grundle," he admitted, casting his gaze down ruefully at the tight-bodiced, ribbon-bedecked, lace-covered, flower-ornamented gown. Elven males are nearly as slender as elven females, but they tend to be broader through the shoulders, and I noticed that here and there a seam had given way under the strain. "We *should* talk about Sabia. I've wanted to, but I was afraid of hurting you both by bringing up sad memories."

Impulsively, Alake knelt at Devon's side, took his hand in hers. "I honor you, my friend, for your courage and your sacrifice. I know of no man I hold in higher esteem."

Rare praise, from a human. Devon was pleased and touched. His cheeks flushed, he shook his head. "It was my own selfishness," he said softly. "How could I go on living, knowing she had died and . . . how she had died. My death will be so much easier, thinking of her safe and well."

I wondered grumpily how he thought she'd feel any better, knowing he was dead in her place. But then, that's a man: elf, human, dwarf—all the same.

"So how did you convince her to let you go?" I persisted. Knowing Sabia as I did, having seen her strong in her determination, I found it difficult to believe she had given in easily.

"I didn't," Devon said, the color in his cheeks deepening. "If you must know, this convinced her." He raised a clenched fist, showed bruised knuckles.

"You socked her!" I gasped.

"You hit her!" Alake echoed.

"I begged her to let me go in her place. She refused. There was no talking her around and I did the only thing I could do to prevent her from going. I knocked her out. What else *could* I do? I was desperate. Believe me, both of you, hurting Sabia was the hardest thing I ever had to do in my life!"

I could believe that. An Elmas will suffer pangs of guilt for days over accidentally stepping on a spider.

"As for my jewelry," Alake said, turning the silver bracelet on her arm with her hand, "these are mine, Grundle, given to me by my mother when I was born. I couldn't leave them any other message about where I was going or what I was doing. I tried, but it was too hard to put my feelings into words. When my mother finds that these are gone, she will know. She will understand."

Alake went back to her altar. Devon tugged at the tight sleeve of his gown, which must have been cutting off his circulation. I could have sat down and cried. The words had come out, but they were hard to hear and I didn't see how I had helped matters.

"So much for dwarven proverbs," I muttered into my side whiskers.

"I am ready to begin now," said Alake, and I breathed a sigh of relief.

Alake forbade me to write down the details of the ceremony, but I couldn't have done so, in any case, since I hadn't a clue as to what was going on. All I know is that it involved salted cod (a dolphin's favorite treat, if they can get it) and flute music and Alake chanting a lot of strange words and making fishlike noises. (Humans can speak the dolphin language. Dwarves could, I suppose, but why would we want to? Dolphins speak dwarven quite well.)

I dozed off, at one point, during the flute music, and was startled out of my nap when Alake spoke in normal words and voice.

"It is done. The dolphins should come to us now."

They might, I thought, if we threw the salt cod into the seawater. I couldn't see that it was doing much good where it was, lying in a silver dish on the altar. Perhaps she figured the stench would draw them.

As you may have guessed, I don't set much store by human or elf magic, and you can imagine my surprise when we all heard and felt a bump on the hull of the ship.

"They've come," said Alake complacently, and hastened off to the waterlock to greet them, her beads clashing, her bare feet (humans rarely wear shoes) padding swiftly over the deck.

I glanced at Devon, who shrugged and raised his eyebrows. He'd been planning to call them with a magical dolphin whistle, which made no noise at all that I could hear. Devon assured me, however, that dolphins could hear it quite clearly and considered the sound very pleasant.

We both hurried after Alake.

Our ship consists of four decks, numbered from the bottom to the top. Not a large craft, compared to the sun-chasers, but it was only used by the royal family on their occasional sinkings into the other realms.

Deck four is the topmost deck (if you don't count the outside). Here is the observation room and, beyond that, the pilot's house, which none of us had the courage to go near. A ladder extends down from the observation room, through a shaft that opens onto each other deck. At the aft end of the observation room, a huge set of windows provides a view of land or water, depending on where you are at the time. The seasun, shining through the water, fills this room with cheerful, blue-green light. Outside, you can see the open deck, surrounded by a railing. Only a human would be crazy enough to go out there when the ship is moving.

The cargo hold is located on deck three. Behind that is the common room, for eating, drinking, ax-throwing practice, or just visiting. This room has numerous small windows set in the sides. Behind the common room are the cabins for the royal family and the ship's crew, a tool room, then the impeller room, with its magical elven crystals that propel the ship.

Decks two and one were mostly more cargo space, plus the waterlock—an important feature. If you're not a dwarf, you're probably wondering what a waterlock is. As I've mentioned, no dwarf can (or wants to learn) to swim. A dwarf who falls into the sea would likely sink to the bottom of Chelestra unless he's caught and brought back to solid ground. Thus, all ships are built with a waterlock, which can be used to rescue any dwarf who happens to tumble into the sea.

We found Alake standing near the bottom of the waterlock, her face pressed against one of the portholes, staring out into the water. Hearing us approach, she turned. Her eyes were wide.

"It's not the dolphins. It's a human. At least, I think it's a human," she added dubiously.

"It is or it isn't," I said. "Can't you tell?"

"Look for yourself." Alake sounded shaken.

Devon and I crowded to the porthole, the elf being forced to nearly bend double to get down to my level.

Sure enough, the thing looked to be a human male. Or perhaps it would be better to say, he *didn't* look elven or dwarven. He was taller than a dwarf, his ears weren't pointed, and his eyes were round, not almond-shaped. But he was the wrong color for a human, his skin being a kind of bread-dough white. His lips were blue, his eyes circled with purple splotches, sunken in his head. He was half-naked, clad only in a pair of brown tight-fitting pants and the remnants of a white tattered shirt. He clung to a fragment of board and was, it seemed to me, about done for.

The bump we had heard was, presumably, this man running into the hull of the ship. He could see us through the porthole and made, as we watched, a feeble attempt to beat against the ships's side. He was weak, apparently, for his arm sank down as if he lacked energy to lift it. He slumped over the board, legs dangling limply beneath him in the water.

"Whatever he is, he's not going to be one for long," I said.

"Poor man," murmured Alake, her dark eyes soft with pity. "We must help him," she said briskly, and headed for the ladder that led to deck two. "We'll bring him on board. Warm him, give him food." She glanced back, saw neither of us moving. "Come on! He'll be heavy. I can't manage by myself."

Humans. Always racing to act, to do something. Never stopping to think. Fortunately, she had a dwarf along.

"Wait, Alake. Stop a moment. Consider where we're bound. Think what's going to happen to us."

Alake frowned at me, angered at having her way thwarted. "Well, what of it? The man is dying! We can't leave him."

"It might be the kindest thing we could do for him," Devon told her gently.

"If we rescue him now, we could be saving him only to doom him to a horrible fate later."

I was sorry to have to be so blunt, but sometimes it's the only way to get through to humans. Alake, realizing finally what we were saying, seemed to shrivel up. I'll swear she grew smaller as we watched. Her body sagged against the ladder.

Lowering her eyes, she ran her hand aimlessly up and down the smooth wooden rungs.

The ship was speeding on. Soon we'd leave the man far behind. He'd seen this, apparently, and was making a feeble attempt with the remainder of his flagging strength to paddle after us. The sight was heartrending. I turned away. But I might have known Alake couldn't stand it.

"The One sent him," she said, starting to climb the ladder. "The One sent him to us, in answer to my prayer. We have to save him!"

"You prayed for a dolphin," I pointed out irritably.

Alake said nothing, but gave me a reprimanding glance. "Don't be blasphemous, Grundle. Can you work this thing?"

"Yes, but I'll need Devon's help," I grumbled, following.

Actually, I could have done it by myself, being stronger than the elf prince, but I wanted to talk to Devon. I told Alake to keep an eye on the floating human, took Devon to deck two, the topmost part of the waterlock. I peered through a window into its sunlit interior, turned the crank on the hatch to make certain it was tightly closed and sealed. Devon started to assist me.

"What if the One didn't send this man?" I whispered urgently in the elf's ear. "What if he was sent by the dragon-snakes to spy on us?"

Devon looked considerably shocked. "Do you suppose that's a possibility?" he asked, doing his best to help and only getting in my way.

I shoved him to one side. "Don't you?"

"I guess. But why would they? They have us. We can't escape, even if we wanted to."

"Why are they doing any of this? All I know is that I wouldn't be too quick to trust this human, if that's what he is. And I think you better go back to being Sabia."

I turned to head down the ladder. Devon came after me, tripping over his skirts.

"Yes, perhaps you're right. But what about Alake? She'll have to go along with us. You have to tell her."

"Not me. She'll think I'm just making another excuse to get rid of him. You tell her. She'll listen to you. Go on. I'll manage this by myself."

We were on deck one again. Devon went over to Alake and
I was able, finally, to get on with the work undisturbed. I
couldn't hear any of their conversation, but I could tell that at
first Alake didn't agree with us, because I saw her shake her
head, causing her ear-jangles to ring wildly.

But Devon was patient with her, far more than I could have
been, and gradually argued her around. I saw her glance at me,
then out at the man, her face troubled and thoughtful. Finally,
she nodded unhappily.

Standing in front of the lower window that looks into the
waterlock, I took hold of the levers and yanked down on them,
hard. A panel located in the hull yawned open. Seawater, foaming and gurgling, poured into the waterlock, carrying with it
numerous indignant fish (no dolphins) and the human.

I waited for the water to reach the proper level and slammed
the panel shut.

"I've got him!" I cried.

We raced back up to deck two, the top of the waterlock. I
opened it, peered down. If he'd been a dwarf, he would have
been lying on the bottom and we would have had to use the
claws to drag him out. But, being human, he'd managed to swim
to the top of the water and floated there, only about an arm's
length away.

"Alake and I can handle him, Devon," I said to him softly.
"You go and put your scarf back on."

Devon left us. Alake came to help me, and between us we
managed to drag the human over to the side and hoist him out
onto the deck. I shut and sealed the waterlock, opened the bottom panel, let the irate fish swim out, and started the pumps to
work. Then I came back to look at our catch.

I must admit that I nearly revised my opinion when we got
the man on board and had a close look at him. If the dragon-
snakes were going to send a spy, it seemed to me they would
have chosen something better than this.

He was truly a pitiable sight, lying on the deck, shivering
from head to toe, coughing, convulsing, spitting up fluid, and
gasping like a fish out of water. Alake'd obviously never seen
anything like it. Fortunately, I had.

"What's wrong with him?" she asked anxiously.

"His body temperature's dropped too low and he's having

trouble making the adjustment from breathing water back to breathing air."

"How can you tell? What do we do for him?" Alake asked.

"Dwarves fall in the water sometimes, so I know what I'd do if he were a dwarf. Warm him up, inside and out. Put lots of blankets on him and give him all the brandywine he can drink."

"Are you certain?" Alake looked dubious. "I mean about the brandy?"

Drunk as a dwarf, so the saying is among the Phondrans. But who do you suppose buys most of our brandywine?

"You've got to fuddle his brain. That's what's causing him to gasp like that. His brain is telling his body it's supposed to be breathing water. Give his brain something else to think about and his body will go back to breathing air—as it was meant to," I added sternly.

"I see. Grundle, fetch me a bottle of the brandywine and my herb pouches. And, if you run into Dev— Sabia, tell him, I mean her, to bring me all the blankets he— she can find."

Well, we were certainly off to a great start. Fortunately, the human was so busy trying to stay alive that he didn't appear to have noticed Alake's confusion. I headed to the storeroom for the wine, blundered into Dev-Sabia on the way back. He was wound up in his scarf and veil, with a shawl over his shoulders to hide the ripped seams. I gave him Alake's instructions. He returned to his berth for the blankets.

I continued on my way, thinking about what Alake had said. It was odd that this human seemed so unused to being in the water. The Phondrans spend as much time in the Goodsea as they do on land and consequently never suffer from this condition, which we dwarves know as "water-poisoning." The man was obviously not a Phondran. Then, who was he and where had he come from?

It was more than one dwarf could figure out.

Arriving in the storeroom, I snagged one of the brandywine bottles, uncorked it, and took a mouthful just to make certain it was good.

It was. I blinked my eyes.

I took another mouthful or two, then popped the cork back on, wiped off my side whiskers, and hurried back to our passenger. Alake and Devon had lifted him into the bosun's chair—a chair attached to a rope that can be lowered up and down the shaft, used to handle the injured or those whose bulk made climbing ladders difficult. We hauled the man up to the crew's quarters on deck two, and helped him to a small cabin.

Fortunately, he was able to walk, though his legs were as wobbly as a newborn kitten's. Alake spread out a pile of blankets. He sank onto them weakly and we covered him with more. He was still gasping and looked to be in a considerable amount of pain.

I offered the brandy bottle. He seemed to understand, for he motioned me near. I put it to his lips, he took a gulp. His gasping changed to coughing, and I was afraid for a moment our cure was going to be the end of him, but he hung on. He managed to get down several more mouthfuls before he sank back weakly on the blankets. Already, his breathing had eased. He looked from one to the other of us, his eyes taking everything in, giving nothing back.

Suddenly, he tossed aside the blankets. Alake made a clucking sound, like a mother hen whose chick has wandered out from under her feathers.

The human ignored her. He was staring at his arms. He stared at his arms for the longest time, rubbing the skin almost frantically. He gazed at the back of his hands. Closing his eyes in what was obviously bitter despair, he sank back down on the blankets.

"What's the matter?" Alake asked, speaking human, coming over to kneel beside him. "Are you injured? What can we do to help?"

She started to touch his arm, but he drew away from her and snarled, like a wounded animal.

Alake persisted. "I'm not going to harm you. I only want to help."

He kept staring at her, and I saw his brow furrow in anger and frustration.

"Alake," I said quietly. "He can't understand you. He doesn't know what you're saying."

"But I'm speaking the human language . . ."

"Dev-Sabia, you try," I said, stuttering as badly as Alake. "Maybe he isn't human, after all."

The elf pulled the scarf down from around his mouth. "Where do you come from? What is your name?" he asked, speaking the musical Elmas language slowly and distinctly.

The stranger, frowning, shifted his eyes to Devon. The look of frustration changed to fury. Propping himself up on one arm, he shouted at us. We couldn't understand him, either, but we didn't need a translator.

"Get out!" he was yelling as plain as anything. "Get out and leave me alone!"

He collapsed back on the blankets, groaning. His eyes closed, he'd broken out in a sweat. But his lips continued to move, forming the words he no longer had the strength to utter.

"Poor man," said Alake softly. "He's lost and sick and afraid."

"That may be," I said, having my own opinion on the subject, "but I think we better do what he wants."

"Will . . . will he be all right?" Alake couldn't take her eyes off him.

"He'll be fine," I assured her, trying to edge her out the door. "If we stay, we'll only upset him."

"Grundle's right," Devon added. "We should leave him alone to rest."

"I think I should stay with him," Alake said.

Devon and I exchanged alarmed glances. The stranger's savage yell and his dark expression had unnerved us both. As if we didn't have trouble enough, it looked to me like we now had an insane human on our hands.

"Shh," I said, "you'll wake him. Let's talk out in the corridor."

We herded the reluctant Alake out of the room.

"One of us should keep an eye on him," Devon whispered in my ear.

I nodded, taking his meaning. One of us *shouldn't* be Alake.

"I'll bring my blanket out here . . ." She was already making plans to spend the night near him.

"No, no, you go to bed. I'll sit up with him. I'm experienced in this sickness." I cut off her protest. "He'll likely sleep for hours now, anyway. You should be well-rested and ready to tend him in the morning, when he wakes up."

She brightened at the prospect, but she still wavered, her gaze going to the door I had shut behind me. "I don't know . . ."

"I'll call you if there's any change," I promised. "You don't want him to see you in the morning all red-eyed and sleepy, do you?"

That clinched it. Alake bid us good-night, took one last peep at her patient, smiled softly to herself, and went off down the corridor.

"What do we do now?" Devon demanded, when she was gone.

"How should I know?" I snapped irritably.

"Well, you're a girl. You know about these things."

"What things?" I asked, though I knew well enough what he was talking about.

"It's obvious. She's attracted to him."

"Pooh! I remember when she rescued a wounded wolf cub once. She took it home and treated it the same way."

"That's no wolf cub," said Devon gravely. "He's young and strong and handsome and well-built, even for a human. It was all Alake and I could do to drag him down the corridor."

Which brought up another problem. If this man went berserk and decided to tear the ship apart, we three would be hard-pressed to stop him. But what about the dragon-snakes? It was obvious they were still in control; the ship continued to rush through the water. Did they know this stranger was aboard? Did they care?

I took a swig of the brandywine. "Go to bed," I told Devon crossly. "We're not going to figure anything out tonight. Maybe something'll happen by morning."

Something did.

I went back into the room with the man and settled myself in a dark corner near the door. If the human woke, I figured I could be up and out of there before he knew what was happening.

His sleep was restless, disturbed. He thrashed about on the blankets, muttering in his own language, whose words all seemed to me to be dark and sharp-edged and filled with hatred and anger. Sometimes he'd cry out, and once he gave a fearful scream and sat bolt upright, staring straight at me. I was on my feet and nearly out the door before I realized he wasn't seeing me at all.

He lay back down. I returned to my seat. He clutched at the blankets, kept saying one word over and over. It sounded like "dog." And sometimes he would groan and shake his head and cry, "Lord!"

Finally, from sheer exhaustion, I think, he fell into a heavy slumber.

I suppose I can admit that I'd been keeping the fire of courage burning in my heart by dousing it liberally with brandywine. I was no longer feeling afraid of him. (I wasn't feeling much of anything, to be honest.) Watching the man fall into this deep sleep, I decided to see what I could learn about him. Maybe go through his pockets, if he had any.

After some little trouble, I got to my feet. (The ship seemed to be rolling more than I recalled.) I made my way over to him and crouched down. What I saw sobered me faster than my mother's blackroot powder.

I don't remember what came after, except that I found myself running down the corridor, screaming like a banshee.

Alake, clutching her sleeping gown around her, stood in her doorway, staring at me in panic. Devon shot out of his room like it was on fire. He was forced to sleep in his dress. Poor fellow. Sabia's dress was all the clothes he'd thought to bring along.

"We heard you yell! What is it?" They both clutched at me. "What's the matter?"

"The strange human!" I was gulping for breath. "He's . . . turned blue!"

Alake gasped, "He's dying!" and raced back down the corridor, toward his room.

We ran after her, Devon remembering just in time to grab his veil and wind it around his head.

I suppose my shrieks must have wakened the man. (Devon told me later that he thought all the dragon-snakes in Chelestra were after me.) The human was sitting up in his bed, staring at his hands and arms, turning them over and over, as if he couldn't believe the limbs were his.

I don't blame him. If such a thing had happened to me, I would have stared, too. How can I describe it? I know you won't believe me. But I swear before the One that the man's arms and backs of his hands, his bare chest, and neck, were covered with blue picture-writing.

We had all run into the cabin before we realized the man was fully conscious. He raised his head, looked directly at us. We shrank back. Even Alake was somewhat daunted. The stranger's face was stern, grim.

But, as though he sensed our fear, he made some attempt to smile at us reassuringly.

His was a face, I remember thinking, that wasn't used to smiling.

"Don't be frightened. My name's Haplo," he said to Alake. "What do they call you?"

We couldn't answer. The man had spoken Phondran.

Perfect, fluent Phondran.

And next he . . .

But that will have to wait. Alake's calling me. Dinnertime. I'm actually feeling hungry.

CHAPTER ♦ 10

SURUNAN

CHELESTRA

♦

THE SARTAN, LED BY THE CAPABLE SAMAH, RETURNED TO LIFE WITH an energy that astounded and overwhelmed Alfred. The people went forth from the crypts out into a realm they had built for themselves long ago. Sartan magic soon brought life to their surroundings, which were so beautiful that Alfred often looked upon the landscape through a sheen of joyful tears.

Surunan. The word itself was derived from the root rune meaning center—the heart, the center of their civilization. At least that's what they'd intended it to be. Unfortunately, the heart had ceased beating.

But now it was alive once more.

Alfred walked its streets and marveled at its beauty. The buildings were made of rose and pearl marble, which had been brought with them from the old world. Shaped by magic, their tall spires soared into an emerald and turquoise sky. Boulevards and avenues and magnificent gardens, which had been sleeping as soundly as their makers, sprang into magical life and all led to the heart of Surunan—the Council Chamber.

Alfred had forgotten the pleasures of being with his own kind, of being able to share himself with others. He had hidden himself for so long, kept his true nature concealed, that it was a relief not to have to worry about revealing his own magical power. And yet even in this new and wonderful world, among his own people, he could not feel quite comfortable, or quite at ease.

There were two cities—an inner, central city, and an outer city that was much larger, if not as fine. The two were separated by high walls. Alfred, exploring the outer city, saw immediately that this was where mensch had once lived. But what had happened to them when the Sartan slept? The answer, from what he saw, might be a grim one. There was evidence, though the Sartan were doing their best to swiftly remove it, that devastating battles had been fought in this part of the city. Buildings had toppled, walls caved in, windows shattered. Signs, written in human, elven, dwarven, had been torn down, lay broken in the streets.

Alfred stared around sadly. Had the mensch done this to themselves? It seemed likely, from what he knew of their warlike natures. But why hadn't the Sartan stopped it? Then he remembered the images of horrible creatures he'd seen in Samah's thoughts. Who were they? Another question. Too many questions. Why had these Sartan gone back into hibernation? Why had they abandoned all responsibility to this world and to the others they had created?

He stood in the terraced garden of Samah's house one evening, thinking that there must be some terrible flaw within himself that kept bringing up such thoughts, some flaw that prevented him from being happy. He had, at last, everything he'd ever dreamed of possessing. He had found his people and they were all he'd hoped: strong, resolute, powerful. They were prepared to set right everything that had gone wrong. The crushing burdens that had been piled on top of him had been lifted. He had others to help him carry the load.

"What is wrong with me?" he asked himself sadly.

"I heard once," came a voice in answer, "of a human who had been locked up in a prison cell for years and years. When at last they opened the cell doors and offered the man his freedom, he refused to go out. He was frightened by freedom, by light and fresh air. He wanted to stay in his dark cell, because he knew it. He was safe there, and secure."

Alfred turned to see Orla. She was smiling at him; her words and tone were pleasant. But Alfred saw that she was truly concerned about his confused and unsettled state.

He blushed, sighed, and lowered his eyes.

"You have not left your cell, Alfred." Orla came to stand

beside him, placed her hand on his arm. "You persist in wearing mensch clothes." This subject called to mind, perhaps, by the fact that Alfred was gazing intently at the shoes that housed his overlarge feet. "You will not tell us your Sartan name. You will not open your heart to us."

"And have you opened your hearts to me?" Alfred asked quietly, looking up at her. "What terrible tragedy occurred here? What happened to the mensch that used to live here? Everywhere I look, I see images of destruction, blood on the stones. Yet no one speaks of it. No one refers to it."

Orla paled, her lips tightened.

"I'm sorry." Alfred sighed. "It's none of my business. You have all been wonderful to me. So patient and kind. The fault is mine. I'm working to overcome it. But, as you said, I've been shut in the darkness so long. The light . . . hurts my eyes. I don't suppose you can understand."

"Tell me about it, Brother," Orla said gently. "Help me understand."

Again she was avoiding the subject, turning the conversation away from her and her people, sending it straight back to him. Why the reluctance to talk about it? Except that every time he mentioned it, he sensed fear, shame.

Our plea for help . . . Samah had said.

Why? Unless this was a battle the Sartan had been losing. And how was that possible? The only enemy capable of fighting them on their level was locked away in the Labyrinth.

Alfred was, without realizing what he was doing, pulling the leaves off of a flowering vinil. One by one, he tore them loose, stared at them, not seeing them, then dropped them to the ground.

Orla's hand closed over his. "The plant cries out in pain."

"I'm sorry!" Alfred dropped the flower, looked in horror at the ravages he'd committed. "I . . . wasn't thinking. . . ."

"But your pain is the greater," Orla continued. "Please, share it with me."

Her gentle smile warmed him like spiced wine. Alfred, intoxicated, forgot his doubts and questions. He found himself pouring out thoughts and feelings he'd kept locked up so long, he wasn't fully aware of them himself.

"When I awoke, and discovered that the others were dead,

I refused to admit the truth to myself. I refused to admit I was alone. I don't know how long I lived in the mausoleum on Arianus . . . months, maybe years. I lived in the past, remembering what life had been like when I was among my brethren. And soon, the past became more real to me than the present.

"Every night, I would go to sleep and tell myself that when I woke the next morning, I would find them all awake, too. I wouldn't be alone anymore. That morning, of course, never came."

"Now it has!" said Orla, closing her hand over his once again.

He looked at her, saw her eyes glimmer with tears, and came very near weeping himself. Clearing his throat, he swallowed hard.

"If so, the morning has been long in coming," he said huskily. "And the night that preceded it was very dark. I shouldn't be troubling you—"

"No, I'm sorry," she said hurriedly. "I shouldn't have interrupted you. Please, go on."

She continued to hold his hand. Her touch was warm, firm, comforting. Unconsciously, he moved nearer to her.

"One day, I found myself standing in front of the crypts of my friends. My own was empty and I remember thinking, 'I have only to climb back in, shut my eyes, and this pain will end.' Yes, suicide," Alfred said calmly, seeing Orla stare at him in horror and shock. "I had come to a turning point, as the mensch say. I finally admitted to myself that I was alone in the world. I could either go forth and be part of life, or abandon it. My struggle was bitter. In the end, I left behind all I had known and loved and went out into the world.

"The experience was dreadful, terrifying. More than once, I thought of running back, hiding myself forever in the tombs. I lived in constant fear that the mensch would discover my true powers and try to use me. Where before I had lived in the past and found comfort in my memories, I saw now that those memories were a danger. I had to put all thoughts of my former life out of my head, or be constantly tempted to use it, to draw on it. I had to adapt to the mensch way of life. I had to become one of them."

Alfred ceased talking, stared out into the night sky that was deep blue, streaked by lighter blue clouds.

"You cannot believe the loneliness," he said at last, so softly that Orla was forced to move closer to him to hear. "The mensch are so very, very lonely. The only means they have of communicating are physical. They must rely on words or a look or a gesture to describe what they feel, and their languages are so limited. Most of the time, they are unable to express what they truly mean, and so they live their lives and die without ever knowing the truth, about themselves or others."

"A terrible tragedy," murmured Orla.

"So I thought, at first," Alfred answered. "But then I came to realize that many of the virtues which the mensch possess have grown out of this inability to see into each other's souls, the way we Sartan do. They have words in their languages like faith, trust, honor. One human says to another, 'I have faith in you. I trust you.' He doesn't know what's in his friend's heart. He can't see inside. But he has faith in him."

"And they have other words we Sartan do not," said Orla, more sternly. She let go his hand, drew away from him. "Words such as deceit, lie, betray, treachery."

"Yes," Alfred agreed meekly. "But, I found that it all balanced itself out, somehow."

He heard a whine, felt a cold nose press itself against his leg. Reaching down his hand, Alfred absently fondled the dog's soft ears, patted it on the head to keep it quiet.

"I'm afraid you're right. I *don't* understand," said Orla. "What do you mean by *balance*?"

Alfred seemed to have a menschlike difficulty putting his thoughts into words. "It's just . . . I'd see one mensch betray another and I'd be shocked and sickened. But, almost immediately after that, I'd come across an act of true selfless love, of faith, sacrifice. And I'd feel humbled and ashamed of myself for judging them.

"Orla." He turned to face her. The dog pressed closer and he scratched the animal behind its ear. "What gives us the right to judge them? What gives us the right to say that our way of life is the right way of life and that theirs is wrong? What gives us the right to impose our will on them?"

"The very fact that the mensch do have such words as murder and betrayal!" she replied. "We must, by guiding them with a firm hand, train them out of these debilitating weaknesses, lead them to rely solely on their strengths."

"But might we not," Alfred argued, "inadvertently train them out of everything—strengths and weaknesses both? It seems to me that the world we wanted to create for the mensch was a world where the mensch were totally subservient to our will. I'm sure I'm wrong," he continued humbly, "but I don't understand the difference between that and what the Patryns intended."

"Of course there's a difference!" Orla flared. "How can you even think of comparing the two?"

"I'm sorry," said Alfred in remorse. "I've offended you. And after all your kindness to me. Don't pay any attention to me. I— What's the matter?"

Orla was staring, not him, but at his feet. "Whose dog is that?"

"Dog?" Alfred glanced down.

The dog looked up, and wagged its plumy tail.

Alfred staggered back against the rock wall.

"Blessed Sartan!" he gasped. "Where did *you* come from?"

The dog, pleased that it now had everyone's attention, pricked its ears, cocked its head expectantly, and barked once.

Alfred went deathly pale. "Haplo!" he cried. "Where are you?" He searched around wildly.

At the sound of the name, the dog began to whine eagerly, barked again loudly.

But no one answered.

The dog's ears drooped. The tail ceased to wave back and forth. The animal sank to the ground, put its nose between its paws, sighed, and looked up at Alfred dejectedly.

Alfred, recovering his composure, stared at the animal.

"Haplo's not here, is he?"

The dog reacted to the name again, lifted its head, gazed about wistfully.

"Dear, dear," Alfred murmured.

"Haplo!" Orla spoke the name with reluctance, it might have been coated with poison. "Haplo! That is a Patryn word."

"What? Oh, yes, I believe it is," Alfred said, preoccupied.

"Means 'single.' The dog doesn't have a name. Haplo never gave it one. An interesting point, don't you think?" He knelt down beside the animal, stroked its head with a gentle, trembling hand. "But why are you here?" he asked. "Not sick, are we? No. I didn't think so. Not sick. Perhaps Haplo sent you to spy on me? That's it, isn't it?"

The dog gave Alfred a reproachful glance. *I expected better from you than this*, it seemed to say.

"The animal belongs to the Patryn," Orla said.

Alfred looked up at her, hesitated. "You might say that. And then again . . ."

"It could be spying on us for him, right now."

"It could be," Alfred conceded the point. "But I don't think so. Not that we haven't used the animal for such purposes before—"

"We!" Orla drew back, away from him.

"I . . . That is . . . Haplo told it . . . In Abarrach . . . The prince and Baltazar, a necromancer. I didn't really want to spy on them but I didn't have much choice . . ."

Alfred saw he wasn't helping matters. He began again. "Haplo and I were lost in Abarrach—"

"Please!" Orla interrupted faintly. "Please quit saying that name. I—" She covered her eyes. "I see horrible things! Hideous monsters! Brutal death . . ."

"You see the Labyrinth. You see where you . . . where the Patryns have been imprisoned all these centuries."

"Where *we* imprisoned them, you were about to say. But, it's so real in your mind. As if you've been there . . ."

"I have been there, Orla."

To his vast astonishment, she turned pale, stared at him in fright.

Alfred was quick to reassure her. "I didn't actually mean I'd been there—"

"Of course," she said faintly. "It . . . it's impossible. Don't say such things, then, if you don't mean them."

"I'm sorry. I hadn't intended to upset you." Although Alfred was completely at a loss to know why she was upset. And frightened. Why frightened? More questions.

"I think perhaps you had better explain yourself," she said.

"Yes, I'll try. I was in the Labyrinth, but it was in Haplo's body. I traded minds with him, one might say. It was when we were going through Death's Gate."

"And did he trade places with you?"

"I think so. He never said anything, you see, but, then, he wouldn't. It was even difficult for him to call me by name. He used to call me Sartan. Just like that. With a sneer. I can't blame him. He has little cause to love us . . ."

Orla was frowning. "You fell into a Patryn's consciousness. I don't believe anything like that has ever happened to a Sartan."

"Probably not," Alfred agreed sadly. "I seem to be always falling into something—"

"You must tell Samah."

Alfred flushed, lowered his eyes. "I'd really rather not . . ." He began petting the dog.

"But this could be extremely important! Don't you see? You've been inside one. You can tell us how they think and why they react as they do. You can give us insight that may yet help us defeat them."

"The war is over," he reminded her, gently.

"But another one may come!" she said, fist clenching, driving into her palm.

"That's what Samah believes. Is that your belief, as well?"

"Samah and I have had our differences," Orla said briskly. "All know it. We have never hidden it. But he is wise, Alfred. I respect him. He is head of the Council. And he wants what we all want. To live in peace."

"Is that what he wants, do you think?"

"Well, of course!" Orla snapped. "What did you suppose?"

"I don't know. I wasn't certain."

Alfred recalled the expression on Samah's face when he said, *It seems we have, after all, awakened at a propitious time, Brethren. Once again, our ancient enemy plans to go to war.* His mind conjured up the image. Orla shared it with him. Her face softened.

"Talk to Samah. Be honest with him. And"—she sighed— "he will be honest with you. He will answer your questions. He will tell you what happened to us in Chelestra. And why we, as you think, abandoned our responsibilities."

Alfred's face burned. "I didn't mean—"

"No. In a way, you are right. But you should know the truth

before you judge us. Just as we should know the truth before
we judge you."

Alfred didn't know what to say. He could come up with no
more arguments.

"And now," said Orla, folding her hands together in front
of her, "what about the dog?"

"What about the dog?" Alfred looked uneasy.

"If this dog belongs to the Patryn, why is it here? Why has
it come to you?"

"I'm not sure," Alfred began hesitantly, "but I think it's
lost."

"Lost?"

"Yes. I think the dog has lost Haplo. The animal wants me
to help it find its master."

"But that's nonsense! You're talking like a child's storybook.
This creature may be intelligent enough for its kind, but it is still
nothing more than a dumb animal—"

"Oh, no. This is a very extraordinary dog," Alfred said solemnly. "And if it is here in Chelestra, you may be certain that
Haplo is here . . . somewhere."

The dog, assuming that with all this talk they must be making progress, lifted its head and wagged its tail.

Orla frowned. "You believe the Patryn is here, on
Chelestra?"

"It certainly makes sense. This is the fourth world, the last
world he was to visit before—" He stopped.

"—before the Patryns launch their attack."

Alfred nodded silently.

"I can understand why this knowledge that our enemy may
be in this world disturbs you. Yet you seem more sad than
upset." Orla stared down at the animal in perplexity. "Why are
you so worried over a lost dog?"

"Because," Alfred replied gravely, "if the dog has lost Haplo,
then I fear Haplo may have lost himself."

CHAPTER ♦ 11

ADRIFT SOMEWHERE

THE GOODSEA

♦

HAPLO LAY ON HIS PALLET ON BOARD THE STRANGE VESSEL, DOING nothing but resting and staring at his arms and his hands. The sigla were as yet only faintly visible—a blue as pale and weak as the eyes of that fool Sartan, Alfred. But the runes were there! They'd come back! And with them, his magic. Haplo closed his eyes, breathed deeply, a sigh of relief.

He recalled those terrible moments when he'd regained consciousness on board this ship, discovered himself surrounded by mensch, and known himself to be helpless, defenseless. He couldn't even understand what they were saying!

It hadn't mattered that they were females, barely old enough to be out of the nursery. It hadn't mattered that they had been gentle and kind, that they had regarded him with awe, sympathy, pity. What mattered was that they had been in control of the situation. Haplo, weak from exhaustion, hunger, bereft of his magic, had been at their mercy. For a moment, he had bitterly regretted seeking their help. Better he should have perished.

But, now, the magic was returning. His power was coming back. Like the sigla, the magic was weak still. He couldn't do much beyond the most rudimentary rune structures; he'd regressed back to his childhood magical abilities. He could understand languages, speak them. He could probably provide himself with food, if necessary. He could heal any minor hurts. And that was about it.

Thinking what he lacked, Haplo was suddenly angry, frustrated. He forced himself to calm down. To give way to his anger was to lose control again.

"Patience," he said to himself, lying back on his bed. "You learned it the hard way in the Labyrinth. Be calm and be patient."

He didn't appear to be in any danger. Though just exactly what the situation was wasn't clear. He'd tried to talk to the three mensch girls, but they'd been so astounded at his sudden use of their language—and the startling appearance of the runes on his skin—that they'd fled before he could question them further.

Haplo had waited, tensely, for some older mensch to enter and demand to know what was going on. But no one came. Lying still, straining to listen, Haplo heard nothing except the creaking of the ship's timbers. He would have almost supposed, if it hadn't seemed too improbable, that he and these girls were the only ones on board.

"I was too hard on them," Haplo counseled himself. "I'll have to take it easy, be careful not to startle them again. They could be of use to me." He looked around in satisfaction. "It seems likely that I've got myself another ship."

He was feeling stronger every moment, and had just about decided he would risk leaving his cabin to go in search of someone, when he heard a soft tapping on his door. Quickly, Haplo lay back down, pulled the blanket up around him, and pretended to be asleep.

The tapping repeated. He heard voices—three voices—debating what to do. The door creaked. It was being opened slowly. He could imagine eyes peering in at him.

"Go on, Alake!" That was the dwarf, her voice low and gruff.

"But he's asleep! I'm afraid I'll wake him."

"Just set the food down and go." An elf maid. Her voice was light and high-pitched, but Haplo caught himself thinking there was something not quite right about it.

Haplo heard the sound of bare feet padding into his room. He deemed it time to wake up now, slowly, careful not to frighten anyone. He drew a deep breath, stirred, and groaned. The footsteps came to an abrupt halt. He heard the girl suck in her breath.

Opening his eyes, Haplo looked up at her and smiled.

"Hullo," he said in her language. "Alake, isn't it?"

The girl was human and one of the most attractive human females Haplo'd ever seen. She'll be a beauty, he thought, when she grows up. Her skin was soft, velvet black; her hair was so black as to be almost blue and shone as brightly as a raven's wing. Her eyes were large and melting brown. Despite a very understandable amount of alarm, she remained where she was, didn't run away.

"That smells good," he continued, reaching out his hands for the food. "I don't know how long I drifted in the sea, without anything to eat. Days maybe. Alake, that's your name. Right?" he repeated.

The girl placed the dish in his hands. Her eyes were lowered. "Yes," she said shyly. "My name is Alake. How did you know?"

"A lovely name," he said. "Almost as lovely as the woman it graces."

He was rewarded with a smile and a flutter of long lashes. Haplo began to eat, some sort of stew and a loaf of slightly stale bread.

"Don't leave," he mumbled, his mouth full. He hadn't realized just how hungry he was. "Come in. Let's talk."

"We're afraid we're disturbing your rest," began Alake, glancing at her two companions, who had remained standing by the door.

Haplo shook his head, gestured with a hunk of bread. Alake sat down nearest him, but not close enough to be considered immodest. The elf maid crept inside the door and found a seat in a chair in the shadows. She moved awkwardly, lacking the grace Haplo normally associated with elves. But perhaps that was because she was wearing a dress that appeared to be too small for her. A shawl covered her arms. A long silken veil was wrapped around her head and face, leaving nothing showing except her almond-shaped eyes.

The dwarf stumped in on short, thick legs, squatted down comfortably on the floor, folded her arms across her chest, and regarded Haplo with deep suspicion.

"Where do you come from?" she demanded, speaking dwarven.

"Grundle!" Alake reprimanded. "Let him eat his dinner."

The dwarf ignored her. "Where do you come from? Who sent you? Was it the dragon-snakes?"

Haplo took his time answering. He cleaned his bowl out with the bread, asked for something to drink. The dwarf wordlessly passed over a bottle of some strong-smelling liquor.

"Would you rather have water?" Alake inquired anxiously.

Haplo thought privately that he'd had water enough to last him a lifetime, but he didn't want to lose his faculties in the bottom of a brandy bottle, and so he nodded.

"Grundle—" Alake began.

"I'll go," murmured the elf maid, and left the small room.

"My name is Haplo," he began.

"You told us that last night," Grundle stated.

"Don't interrupt!" Alake said, flashing her friend an angry glance.

Grundle muttered something and leaned back against the wall, her small feet propped out in front of her.

"The ship in which I sailed broke apart. I managed to escape, and drifted about in the water until you found me and were kind enough to take me on board." Haplo smiled again at Alake, who lowered her eyes and toyed with the brass beads in her hair. "As for where I'm from, you've probably never heard of the name, but it's a world much like your own."

That was a safe enough answer. He might have known it wouldn't satisfy the dwarf.

"A seamoon like ours?"

"Something similar."

"How do you know what our seamoon is like?"

"All know that the . . . um . . . seamoons of Chelestra are the same," Haplo answered.

Grundle jabbed a finger at him. "Why do you draw pictures on your skin?"

"Why do dwarves wear beards?" Haplo countered.

"That's enough, Grundle!" Alake snapped. "What he says makes perfect sense."

"Oh, he can talk well enough," the dwarf returned. "Not that he said much of anything, if you'll notice. But I'd like to hear what he's got to say about the dragon-snakes."

The elf maid had returned with the water. Handing the

pitcher to Alake, the elf said, in a low voice, "Grundle is right. We need to know about the dragon-snakes."

Alake gave Haplo an apologetic glance. "Sabia and Grundle fear that you have been sent by the dragon-snakes to spy on us. I have no idea why, since we are their captives and we go to meet our doom willingly—"

"Wait! Slow down." Haplo raised a hand to halt the flood. He eyed the young women. "I'm not sure I understand what you're saying. But, before you explain, let me tell you that the person who sent me is my liege lord. He is a man, not a dragon. And from what I've seen of dragons in my world, I wouldn't do a damn thing for one except kill it."

Haplo spoke quietly, his tone and manner convincing. And, in this, he spoke the truth. Dragons in the Labyrinth are highly intelligent, fearsome beings. He'd seen other dragons during his travels. Some were evil, others purportedly good, but he'd found nothing in any of the creatures he trusted.

"Now," continued Haplo, seeing the dwarf opening her mouth, "suppose you tell me what you three are doing on board this ship all alone."

"Who says we're alone?" Grundle struck in, but her protest was faint and halfhearted.

It wasn't so much that the three girls believed him, Haplo realized, but that they wanted to believe him. After Haplo'd heard their story, he understood why.

He listened with outward composure to Alake tell their tale. Inwardly, he was fuming. If he had believed in a Higher Power controlling his destiny, which he most assuredly did not, despite Alfred's tricks to convince him otherwise,[1] then he would have thought the Higher Power was laughing heartily. Weakened in his own magic, weaker than he'd ever been in his life, Haplo'd managed to get himself rescued by three sacrificial lambs trotting meekly to their deaths!

"You can't be serious!"

"We are," said Alake. "It is for the sake of our people."

"You chose to do this? You haven't tried to escape? To get away?"

---

[1] As related in *Fire Sea*, vol. 3 of *The Death Gate Cycle*.

"No, and we won't, either," said Grundle resolutely. "This was our decision. Our parents didn't even know we were leaving. They would have tried to stop us."

"And they would have been right!" Haplo glared at the three. Trotting along to their deaths . . . and taking him with them!

Alake's voice sank to a whisper. "You think we're fools, don't you?"

"Yes," Haplo answered bluntly. "These dragon-snakes, from what you've told me, have tortured and murdered people. And you think they're going to keep their word, accept three sacrifices, then meekly slither away?"

Grundle cleared her throat loudly, drummed her heels on the deck. "Then why make the bargain at all? What do the dragon-snakes get out of it? Why not just murder us and be done with it?"

"What do the dragon-snakes get out of it? I'll tell you what they get. Fear. Anguish. Chaos. In my land, we have creatures that live off fear, thrive off it. Think about it. These dragon-snakes, if they're as powerful as you say, could have come in the night and attacked your seamoons. But, no. What do they do? They come by day. They wreak havoc on small numbers of your people. They give messages, demand sacrifices. And look at the results!

"Your people are far more terrified now than they would have been if they'd had to beat off a sudden attack. And the three of you running off like this has only made things worse for your people, not better."

Alake wilted beneath Haplo's glowering gaze. Even the stubborn Grundle appeared to lose her defiant attitude, and began to tug uneasily at her side whiskers. Only Sabia, the elf maid, remained cool and calm. She sat on her stool, straight-backed, upright, looking distant and aloof, as if she alone were content with her decision. Nothing he said had made a difference to her.

Odd. But then the elf maid was odd. Haplo couldn't figure out why. There was something about her . . .

Her.

Haplo noticed, suddenly, the way Sabia was sitting. When she'd first sat down, she kept her knees close together, ankles

demurely crossed beneath the long skirt. But during Alake's long
retelling of their woeful tale, the elf maid had relaxed, forgotten
herself. Now she was sitting spraddle-legged on the short stool,
her knees akimbo, her hands resting on her knees, her feet
tucked behind.

If I'm right, Haplo thought, this is certain to clinch it. They'll
have no choice but to go along with me.

"What do you think's happening right now in your family?"
Haplo demanded of Alake. "Instead of preparing for war, as he
should be doing, your father is now afraid to do anything! He
doesn't dare attack the dragon-snakes while they have you captive. He's gnawed by remorse, grows weaker with despair every
day."

Alake was weeping silently. Sabia reached out, took hold
of her hand. Haplo rose to his feet, began to pace the small
cabin.

"And you." He rounded on the dwarf. "Your people?
What are they doing? Arming themselves, or mourning the
loss of their princess? All of them, waiting. Waiting in hope
and in dread. And the longer they wait, the larger their fear
grows."

"They'll fight!" Grundle insisted, but her voice quivered.

Haplo ignored her, continued to pace, ten steps each direction, every turn bringing him nearer Sabia, who was busy trying
to comfort Alake.

Grundle sprang up suddenly from her stool, stood facing
Haplo defiantly, small hands on her hips.

"We knew that our sacrifice might be for nothing. But it
seemed to us that if there was the tiniest chance that the dragon-
snakes would keep their part of the bargain, then it was worth
it to save our people. And I still say so. What about you Alake?
Sabia?"

Alake's brown eyes shimmered with tears, but she managed
to nod emphatically.

"I agree," said Sabia, her voice muffled by the scarf. "We
must go through with it. For the sake of our people."

"The dragon-snakes keep *their* part of the bargain, eh?"
Haplo eyed them in grim amusement. "And how about you?
What about you keeping your part of the bargain? If these
beasts are, by some remote chance, fair and honorable, how

do you think they'll react when they find out they've been cheated?''

Reaching out his hand, Haplo caught hold of Sabia's veil and yanked it off.

Sabia snatched futilely at the scarf. When that failed, she averted her face, lowered her head. "Really, sir, what are you doing?'' Too late, she brought her knees together, crossed her ankles.

"Three royal daughters." Haplo raised an eyebrow. "What were you planning to tell the dragon-snakes? That elf maids all look like they've got an apple stuck in their throats? That all elf maids have strong jawlines and well-developed, muscular shoulders? That this is why their chests are flat? Not to mention other accoutrements not generally found on maidens." Haplo shifted his gaze meaningfully to the elf's groin.

Sabia blushed as deeply as if he *had* been a she. He stole a glance at Alake, who was staring at him, stricken, then at Grundle, who sighed and shook her head.

The young elf stood up, faced Haplo defiantly.

"You are right, sir. I thought only to save the girl I loved and was to have married. It never occurred to me that this deception would give the dragon-snakes the chance to claim that *we'd* broken faith with them."

"We never thought about that!" Alake clasped her hands together, fingers twisting nervously. "The dragon-snakes will be furious . . ."

"Maybe it won't matter."

That was the dwarf, Grundle, causing trouble again. Haplo could have cheerfully strangled her.

"Devon's not a princess, but he's a prince. As long as the dragon-snakes have three people from royal households, what do they care if we're male or female?"

"They did say three daughters," Alake murmured, looking pathetically hopeful. "But perhaps Grundle's right . . ."

Haplo decided that it was time to end this once and for all. "Did it ever occur to you that the dragons may not intend to kill you? They may have other plans for you, plans that require females. Breeding, for example?"

Alake moaned, covered her mouth with her hands. The elf put his arm around her comfortingly, said something to her in a low voice. Grundle was as pale as the dwarf's nut-brown skin would allow. She collapsed back onto a stool, stared unhappily at the deck beneath her feet.

I meant to frighten them. I succeeded, and that's all that matters, Haplo told himself coldly. Now they'll go along with me. No more arguments. I'll take over this ship, ditch these three mensch somewhere, and get on about my business.

"What do you want us to do, sir?" asked the elf.

"First, what's your real name?" Haplo growled.

"Devon of the House of—"

"Devon will do. What or who's steering this ship? Not you, I take it. Who else is on board?"

"We . . . don't know, sir." Devon said helplessly. "We assume it's the dragon-snakes. Their magic . . ."

"You haven't tried to change course? Stop the ship?"

"We can't even get close to the steerage. There's something horrible in there."

"What is it? Can you see it?"

"No," Devon admitted, ashamed. "We . . . couldn't get close enough to see anything."

"It's a terrible feeling, I tell you!" stated Grundle sullenly, defiantly. "Like walking into death."

"Which is exactly what you're doing now," Haplo snapped.

The three glanced at each other, lowered their heads. Children, lost and alone, facing a dreadful fate. Haplo regretted his harsh comment.

You don't want to frighten them too much, he cautioned. You're going to need their help.

"I'm sorry I upset you," he apologized gruffly. "But we have a saying in my world: The dragon is always smaller in the eye than in the mind."

"Meaning it's better to know the truth," said Alake, wiping away her tears. "You're right. I'm not nearly as frightened as I was. Though, if what you say is true, I have more reason to be."

"It's like having a tooth pulled," said Grundle. "You always suffer more thinking about it than having it done." She cocked a bright eye at Haplo. "You're pretty smart . . . for a human. Where did you say you came from?"

Haplo looked sharply at the dwarf. A shrewd thinker, that

one. He would have to keep an eye on her. Right now, though, he didn't have time to waste fending off her needling jabs.

"You shouldn't be as concerned about where I've been as where you're going unless we can get this ship turned around. Which way's the steerage from here?"

"But how will you do that?" Alake asked him, drawing near. Her eyes, when she looked at him, were warm and soft. "It's obviously being controlled by powerful magic."

"I have some knowledge of magic, myself," said Haplo.

Ordinarily, he preferred to keep such knowledge to himself, but in this case, the mensch would see him using his magic. Better to prepare them in advance.

"Do you?" Alake drew a deep breath. "So do I. I've been admitted to the Third House. What House are you?"

Haplo recalled what little he knew of the human's crude talent for the arcane, remembered that they loved nothing more than to shroud even the most rudimentary magical spells in mystery.

"If you are that high in the ranking, you must know that I am not permitted to speak of it," he said.

His mild rebuke did him no harm with the human girl. By her shining eyes, her admiration for him increased.

"Forgive me," she said immediately. "It was wrong of me to ask. We'll show you the way."

The dwarf cast him another shrewd glance, tugged at her side whiskers.

Alake guided him through the small, narrow corridors of the ship. Grundle and Devon came along, the dwarf pointing out to him the various mechanical devices that powered the vessel, which she called a "submersible." Haplo, glancing out the portholes, could seeing nothing but water, lit by a soft, blue-green light, above, below, and all around.

He was beginning to think that this so-called world of water was, in truth, a world made of nothing but water. There must be land somewhere. Obviously, people who built boats to sail the seas didn't live in those seas like fish. He was intensely curious to know about the seamoons the dwarf had mentioned, must try to think of a way to find out that wouldn't start the wheels turning in the heads of these mensch. He also needed to know more about the seawater itself, whether his growing misgivings about it were true.

Grundle and Devon were, between them, explaining how the submersible operated. Built by dwarves, it was powered by a combination of dwarven mechanical ingenuity and elven mechanical magic.

It seemed, from what Haplo could piece together out of the somewhat confused explanation given him by the dwarf, that the main difficulty in sinking (sailing) a vessel was to get it away from the influence of the seamoons. Due to the gravitational push (not pull) of the moons, the submersibles, which were filled with air, were naturally less dense than the water around them and tended to float toward the worlds as though being drawn by a rope. In order to cause the submersible to sink, it was necessary to increase the density of the ship without flooding it full of water.

Here, Devon explained, was where the elven magic came in. Special magical crystals, engineered by the elven wizards, could increase or decrease their own mass on command. Called mass displacers, these crystals actually solved two problems for ships. First, by increasing the mass in the keel, the ships could sink into the sea as their density became greater than that of the water around them. Second, as the ship sank away from the influence of the outward-pressing gravity of the worlds, the mass displacers provided an artificial gravity for the occupants of the submersible.

Haplo only vaguely understood the concept, understood nothing of "outward-pressing gravity" and "mass displacers." Understood nothing, except that they were magic.

"But," said Haplo casually, appearing to be intensely interested in a rat's tangle of ropes, pulleys, and gears, "I didn't think magic worked in the seawater."

Alake looked startled, at first, then she smiled. "Of course. You are testing me. I would give you the correct response, but not in front of the uninitiated." She nodded at Grundle and Devon.

"Humpf!" grunted the dwarf, unimpressed. "This way to the pilot's house." She began to climb the ladder leading to the topmost deck. Devon and Alake went up after her.

Haplo followed, said nothing more. He hadn't missed Alake's surprised expression. Apparently, human and elven magic worked in the sea. And, since something was guiding the boat, dragon magic worked in the seawater, as well. Seawater that had, so to speak, washed away Haplo's magic. Or had it? Maybe his debilitation had been caused by the passage through Death's Gate. Perhaps . . .

A tingling sensation on Haplo's skin interrupted his ruminations. It was slight, barely felt, as if silken threads of cobwebs were brushing across his flesh. He recognized it, wished he'd thought to wrap the blanket around him. A quick glance confirmed his fears. The sigla on his skin were beginning to glow, a sign of danger. The light was faint, faint as the runes themselves, but his magic was warning him as best it could in his weakened state.

The mensch pulled themselves up over the top, but did not proceed farther. Devon's lips tightened. Grundle gave a sudden, loud, nervous "hem!" that made everyone jump. Alake began to whisper to herself, probably some sort of charm.

The tingling on Haplo's arms became almost maddening, like the tiny feet of myriad spiders crawling over him. His body was instinctively preparing itself to face danger. Adrenaline pumped, his mouth dried, his stomach muscles tightened. He tensed, searched every shadow, cursed the faint light of the sigla, cursed the fact that he was weak.

The dwarf lifted a quivering hand, pointed ahead, at a darkened doorway located at the end of the corridor.

"That's . . . the steerage."

Fear flowed from out that doorway like a dark river, threatening to drown them in its suffocating tide. The mensch huddled together, staring with horrible fascination down the corridor. None of them had noticed his alteration yet.

Alake shivered. Grundle was panting like a dog. Devon leaned weakly against the bulkheads. It was obvious the mensch could not go on. Haplo wasn't certain he could.

Sweat trickled down his face. He was having difficulty breathing. And still no sign of anything! But he knew, now, where the danger was centered, and he was walking right toward it. He had never experienced fear like this, not in the darkest, most horrible cave in the Labyrinth. Every fiber of his being was urging him to run away as fast as he could. It took a concerted effort on his part to keep moving forward.

And, suddenly, he couldn't. He came to a halt, near the mensch. Grundle looked around at him. Her eyes widened, she let out a crowing gasp. Alake and Devon shuddered, turned to stare.

Haplo saw himself reflected in three pair of astounded, frightened eyes, saw his body glowing a faint, iridescent blue, saw his face strained and drawn, glistening with sweat.

"What's ahead of us?" he said, pointing. "What's beyond that door?" It took him three breaths to squeeze the words past the tightness in his chest.

"What's wrong with your skin?" Grundle cried shrilly. "You're lit up—"

"What's in there?" Haplo hissed through clenched teeth, glaring fiercely at the dwarf.

She gulped. "The . . . the pilot's house. You see?" she added, growing bolder. "I was right. Like walking into death."

"Yeah, you were right." Haplo took a step forward.

Alake clutched at him. "Wait! You can't go! Don't leave us!"

Haplo turned. "Wherever it is they're taking you—will it be any better?"

The three stared at him, silently begging him to say he'd been wrong, to tell them everything was going to be all right. But he couldn't. Truth, harsh and bitter, like a cold wind, blew out hope's faint, flickering light.

"Then we'll come with you," said Devon, pale but resolute.

"No, you won't. You're going to stay right here, all three of you."

Haplo looked down the corridor, glanced again at his arms. The sigla's glow was faint, the runes on his body barely visible. He cursed softly, beneath his breath. A child in the Labyrinth could defend itself better than he could, at this moment.

"Do any of you have a weapon? You, elf? A sword, a knife?"

"N-no," Devon stammered.

"We were told not to bring any weapons," Alake whispered fearfully.

"I have an ax," Grundle said, tone defiant. "A battle-ax."

Alake stared at her, shocked.

"Bring it to me," Haplo ordered, hoping it wasn't some puny toy.

The dwarf looked at him long and hard, then ran off. She returned, puffing, carrying what Haplo was relieved to see was a sturdy, well-made weapon.

"Grundle!" said Alake reprovingly. "You know what they told us!"

"As if I'd listen to a bunch of snakes!" Grundle scoffed. "Will this do?"

She handed the ax to Haplo.

He grasped it, hefted it experimentally. Too bad he didn't have time to inscribe runes on it, enhance it with magical power. Too bad he didn't have the strength to do it, he reminded himself ruefully. Well, it was better than nothing.

Haplo started to creep forward. Hearing footsteps shuffling along behind him, he whirled around, glared at the mensch.

"You stay there! Understand?"

The three wavered, looked at each other, then at Haplo. Devon began to shake his head.

"Damn it!" Haplo swore. "What can three terrified kids do to help me? You'll only get in my way. Now keep back!"

They did as he told them, huddling against the walls, watching him with wide, frightened eyes. He had the feeling, though, that the minute he turned his back, they'd be creeping up behind.

"Let them take care of themselves," he muttered.

Ax in hand, he started down the corridor.

The sigla on his skin itched and burned. Despair closed in on him, the despair of the Labyrinth. You slept out of exhaustion, never to find easeful rest. You woke every day to fear and pain and death.

And anger.

Haplo concentrated on the anger. Anger had kept the Patryns alive in the Labyrinth. Anger carried him forward. He would not rush meekly to his fate like the mensch. He would fight. He . . .

Haplo reached the door that led into the steerage, the door that threatened—guaranteed—death. Pausing, he looked, listened. He saw nothing but deep, impenetrable darkness, heard nothing but the beating of his own heart, his own short and shallow breathing. His grip on the ax was so tight his hand ached. He drew a breath, bounded inside.

Darkness closed over him, fell down on him like the nets the gibbering monkkers of the Labyrinth use to snare the unwary. The faint glow of his sigla disappeared. He knew himself to be completely helpless, completely at the mercy of whatever was in here. He stumbled about in a blind panic, fighting to free himself. The ax slid from his sweat-damp hand.

Two eyes, slits of red-green flame, slowly opened. The darkness took shape and form around the eyes, and Haplo was aware of a gigantic serpentine head. He was aware, too, of a ripple in the darkness, a shimmer of doubt, astonishment.

"A Patryn?" The voice was soft, sibilant.

"Yes," Haplo answered, tense, wary. "I am a Patryn. What are you?"

The eyes closed. The darkness returned, strong, intense, guarding. Haplo stretched out a groping hand, hoping to find the steering mechanism. His fingers brushed against cold, scaly flesh. A viscous liquid clung to his skin, chilled his blood, began to burn his skin. His stomach wrenched in revulsion. Shuddering, he tried to wipe the slime off on his trousers.

The eyes opened again, their light eerie. The eyes were huge. It seemed he could have walked into the black, slit pupils without ducking.

"The Royal One bids me give you welcome and say to you, 'The time is at hand. Your enemy is awake.' "

"I don't know what you mean, what you're talking about," Haplo said warily. "What enemy?"

"The Royal One will explain everything if you will honor him with your presence. However, I am permitted to speak one word that may quicken your interest. I am to say, 'Samah.' "

"Samah!" Haplo breathed. "Samah!"

He couldn't believe what he'd heard. It didn't make sense. He wanted to question the creature, but, suddenly, his heart began to pound. The blood rushed to his head, fire filled his brain. He took a step, staggered, and pitched forward onto his face to lie still and unmoving.

The green-red eyes glittered, slowly shut.

CHAPTER ♦ 12

ADRIFT SOMEWHERE

THE GOODSEA

♦

So NOW WE'VE GOT THIS HUMAN, THIS HAPLO. I WANT VERY MUCH to trust him, and yet I don't. Is it just the prejudice of a dwarf against any of another race? That might have been so, back in the old days. But I would trust Alake with my life, the same with Devon. Unfortunately, my life appears to be not in their care, but in Haplo's.

It will be a relief to write down how I really feel about him. I can't say a word against him to Alake, who has fallen for this man deeper than a dwarf in his ale mug. As for Devon . . . he was suspicious of him at the beginning, but after what happened with the dragon-snakes . . . well, you might have thought an elven warrior of ancient days had come to call him to arms.

Alake says that I am only chewing sour grapes because Haplo made me see that we acted like fools, running off to give ourselves to be sacrificed. But we dwarves are naturally skeptical and suspicious of strangers. We tend not to trust anyone until we get to know them several hundred cycles.

This Haplo has yet to say anything about where he comes from and who he is, and, beyond that, he's made one or two extremely curious statements and has behaved most peculiarly in regard to the dragon-snakes.

I admit I was wrong about one thing—Haplo is obviously not a spy sent by the dragons. It is difficult to see inside the man. A shadow covers him and his words. He walks in a darkness of his own creation, using it, I would guess, for protection and defense. Yet, sometimes, despite himself, the clouds are rent by a flash of lightning, both frightening and illuminating. Such a flash came from Haplo when we told him about the dragon-snakes.

In fact, thinking back on his reaction, I begin to see that he went out of his way to convince us we should try to seize control of the ship and flee to safety. Which makes what happened later all the more strange.

And I must give credit where it is due. Haplo is the bravest man I've ever met. I know of no dwarf, not even Hartmut, who could have walked down the dread corridor and into the steerage.

We kept behind, waiting for him, as he ordered.

"We should go with him," Devon said.

"Yes," agreed Alake faintly, but I noticed that neither of them moved a muscle. "I wish we had some no-fear weed. Then we wouldn't be afraid."

"Well, we don't. Whatever it is," I whispered. "As for wishes, I wish I was back home!"

Devon was that faint color of blue-green elves turn when they're sick or afraid. Sweat glistened on Alake's black skin, and she shivered like a leaf. I'm not ashamed to say that my shoes were as good as nailed to the deck. Otherwise I would have done the sensible thing and run for dear life.

We watched Haplo enter the steerage. Blackness covered him, swallowed him up whole. Alake gave a little cry and hid her face in her hands. Then we heard voices . . . Haplo's voice talking and another answering.

"At least nothing's killed him yet," I muttered.

Alake perked up, lifted her head. We all strained to hear what was being said.

The words were gibberish. We looked at each other questioningly. None of us understood.

"It's that same language he talked when he was out of his head," I whispered. "And whatever's in there understands it!"

Which was something I didn't like one bit, as I was just about to say, when Haplo suddenly gave a great cry that stopped my breathing. And then Alake gave a cry as if someone had torn out her heart. She darted down the passage, heading straight for the steerage!

Devon ran after Alake, leaving me to reflect on the brainless

natures of elves and humans (and dwarves). I had no choice, of
course, but to run after them.

I arrived in the steerage to find Alake bent over Haplo, who
was lying unconscious on the deck. Devon, with more presence
of mind than I would have given an elf, had picked up the battle
ax and was standing over the two protectively.

I looked quickly about the steerage. It was darker than the
inside of our mountain and smelled awful. The stench made me
gag. It was horribly cold, but the strange, paralyzing feeling of
terror that had kept us out of here before was gone.

"Is he dead?" I asked.

"No!" Alake was stroking back his hair. "He's fainted. He
drove it away! Don't you see, Grundle?"

I saw the love and admiration in her eyes and my heart sank.

"He fought it and drove it away! He's saved us."

"He did. He truly did!" Devon said, gazing down at Haplo
in awe.

"Give me that!" I said grumpily, and snatched the ax away
from the elf, "before you cut off something valuable and really
turn yourself into a girl! And what do you mean, he drove it
away? That scream of his didn't sound like any battle cry to me."

But, of course, neither Alake nor Devon was paying the
slightest attention to me. Their concern was for their hero. And,
I had to admit, whatever had been in the steerage seemed to be
gone now. But had Haplo driven it away? Or had the two of
them reached a friendly agreement?

"We can't stay here," I pointed out, propping the ax up in
a corner, as far from the elf (and Haplo) as possible.

"No, you're right," Alake agreed, looking around with a
shudder.

"We could make a litter out of blankets," Devon suggested.

Haplo opened his eyes, found Alake hanging over him, her
hand on his head. I never saw anyone move so swiftly. His
actions were a blur. He struck out at Alake, flung her away from
him, and was on his feet, crouched, ready to spring.

Alake lay on the deck, staring at him in shock. None of us
moved or said a word. I was almost as frightened as I'd been
before.

Haplo glanced around, saw only us, and seemed to come to
his senses. But he was furious.

"Don't touch me!" he snarled in a voice colder and darker than the darkness in the steerage. "Don't ever touch me!"

Alake's eyes filled with tears. "I'm sorry," she whispered. "I didn't mean any harm. I feared you were hurt . . ."

Haplo bit off whatever else he'd been going to say, stared at poor Alake grimly. Then, with a sigh, he straightened, shook his head. His anger died. For an instant, the darkness over him seemed to lift.

"Here, don't cry anymore. I'm the one who's sorry," he said tiredly. "I shouldn't have yelled at you like that. I was . . . somewhere else. In a dream. A terrible place."

He frowned, and the darkness returned to cover him. "I react like that out of instinct. I can't help myself, and I might accidentally hurt one of you. So just . . . don't ever come near me when I'm asleep. All right?"

Alake gulped and nodded and even managed to smile. She would have forgiven him if he'd jumped up and down on her. I saw that plain enough and I think Haplo was beginning to see how it was with her. He looked kind of startled and confused and, for an instant, almost helpless. It was enough to make me laugh, except I felt like crying.

I thought he was going to say something and he thought so, too, but then he must have seen that it would only make things worse. He kept quiet, turned to examine the steerage.

Devon helped Alake to her feet. She smoothed her gown.

"You all right?" Haplo said gruffly, not looking at her.

"Yes," she answered shakily.

He nodded.

"So," I said, "did you drive the dragon-snake or whatever it was off? Can you take control of the ship?"

He looked at me. His eyes are like no one's eyes I've seen before. They run through you like needles.

"No. I didn't drive the dragon-snake off. And, no, we can't take over the ship."

"But the beast's not here!" I pointed out. "I can feel the difference. We all can. I'm going to try. I know something about steering a boat. . . ."

I didn't, but I wanted to see what would happen. I put my hands on the wheel. Sure enough, he was there beside me. His hand closed over my arm and his grip was like iron.

"Don't try it, Grundle." He wasn't threatening. He was very quiet, very calm. I felt my stomach twist into a knot. "I don't think it would be wise. The dragon-snake isn't gone. It was never really here. But that doesn't mean they're not watching, listening to us right now. Their magic is powerful. I wouldn't want you to get hurt."

He was implying that he wouldn't want the dragon-snakes to hurt me. But, looking into those eyes, I wasn't so sure that was what he truly meant. His grip on my arm tightened. Slowly, I let go of the wheel, and he let go of me.

"And now, I think we should all return to our cabins," Haplo said.

We didn't move. Alake and Devon looked stricken, their last hope gone. I could still feel his hand on my arm, see the marks of his fingers.

"You talked to them!" I blurted out. "I heard you! In your language! Or is it *their* language? I think you're in league with them!"

"Grundle!" Alake cried. "How could you!"

"It's all right." Haplo shrugged, smiled out of one corner of his mouth. "Grundle doesn't trust me, do you?"

"No," I said bluntly.

Alake frowned, clicked her tongue against the roof of her mouth. Devon shook his head at me.

Haplo continued to regard me with that strange half-smile. "If it's any comfort to you, Grundle, I don't trust you, either. Elves, dwarves, humans. You're all friends, you tell me. Your races live together in peace. You expect me to believe that, after what I've seen? Or is this all some elaborate hoax, laid by my enemies?"

We were all silent. Alake looked unhappy, Devon uncomfortable. They had wanted so much to believe . . .

I pointed at Haplo's skin, at the blue markings I'd seen glow with an eerie, radiant light.

"You're a warlock," I said, using the human term. "Your magic is powerful. I felt it. We all felt it. Could you turn this ship around, take us back home?"

He was quiet a moment, eyeing me with a cold and narrow gaze. Then he said, "No."

"Can't or won't?" I demanded.

He didn't answer.

I cast Alake and Devon a glance of bitter triumph. "Come on. We better decide what we can do to help ourselves. Maybe we could swim for it—"

"Grundle, you can't swim," Alake said, sighing. She was on the verge of tears. Her shoulders sagged.

"There's no land near anyway," argued Devon. "We'd end up exhausted, half-starved. Or worse."

"Wouldn't that be better than the dragon-snakes?"

They finally realized what I was saying. They looked at each other, wavering, hesitating.

"Come on," I repeated.

I was near the door. Alake, drooping, started to come after. Devon had his arm around her. With what sounded like a curse, Haplo shoved roughly past us. Reaching the door, he blocked it with an outstretched arm.

"No one's going anywhere, except back to his or her room."

Alake stood tall, faced him with dignity. "Let us pass." She was trying hard to keep her voice from trembling.

"Stand aside, sir," said Devon in low tones.

I took a step forward.

"Damn it!" Haplo glared at us. "These dragon-snakes won't let you go. Try some fool stunt like jumping ship and you'll only end up getting hurt. Listen to me. Grundle was right. I can talk to these dragon-snakes. We . . . understand each other. And I promise you this. As far as it's in my power to prevent it, I won't let harm come to you." He looked at Alake and Devon and at me. "I swear it."

"By what?" I asked.

"What would you have me swear by?"

"The One, of course," Alake said.

Haplo appeared perplexed. "What One? Is it a human god?"

"The One is the One," Devon answered, at a loss to explain. Everyone knew about the One.

"The highest power," Alake replied. "Creator, Mover, Shaper, Finisher."

"Highest power, huh?" Haplo repeated, and I could see he didn't much like that idea. "You all believe in this One? Elves, humans, dwarves?"

"It's not a matter of believing," Devon said. "The One is."

Haplo eyed us narrowly. "Will you go to your rooms and stay there? No more talk of throwing yourselves into the sea?"

"If you swear by the One," I said. "That's an oath you can't break."

He smiled quietly, as if he knew better. Then, shrugging, he said. "I swear by the One. If it lies in my power to prevent it, no harm will come to you."

I looked at Alake and Devon. They both nodded their heads, satisfied.

"Very well," I growled, though I had seen his mouth twist when he spoke the words.

"I'll cook something," offered Alake, faintly, and she hurried away.

Devon—before I could stop him—picked up the ax. I could see battle-lust, the gleam of swords and armor, shining in the elf's eyes.

"Do you think, sir, you could teach me how to use this?"

"Not in a dress!" I told him, then stomped off to my room.

I wanted to be alone to think, to try to figure out what was going on. Especially, to try to figure out Haplo.

There was a knock on my door.

"I'm not hungry!" I called out irritably, thinking it was Alake.

"It's me, Haplo."

Startled, I opened the door a crack, peered out. "What do you want?"

"Seawater."

"Seawater?" Gone mad again, I thought.

"I need seawater. For an experiment. Alake told me you knew how to open the hatch."

"What do you want seawater for?"

"Forget it." Haplo turned away. "I'll ask Devon—"

"The elf!" I snorted in disgust. "He'd flood the ship. Come with me."

Which wasn't exactly the truth. Devon could probably have managed about the seawater, but I wanted to find out what this Haplo was up to now.

We went back through the submersible, heading toward the rear. I fetched a bucket from the galley.

"This be enough?" I asked.

Haplo nodded. Alake said something about dinner being ready in a short while.

"We won't be long," he said.

We continued on, passed Devon doing what he must have thought were some sort of exercises with the battle-ax.

"He'll slice off his foot!" I grumbled, cringing at the wild way he was swinging the ax around.

"Don't underestimate him," said Haplo. "I've traveled in lands where elves are quite adept at warfare. I suppose they could learn again. If they had someone to lead them."

"And someone to fight," I pointed out.

"But your people were ready to band together and fight these dragon-snakes. What if I could prove to you that the dragons aren't the real enemy? What if I could show you that the real enemy is far more subtle, his intentions far more terrible? What if I brought you a leader of great wisdom and power to fight against this foe? Would your people and the humans and the elves fight together?"

I sniffed. "You're saying that these dragon-snakes have wrecked our sun-chaser, murdered and tortured our people, just to prove to us that we have a more dangerous enemy?"

"Stranger things have happened," Haplo replied coolly. "Maybe it's all been a misunderstanding. Maybe they think you're aligned with the enemy."

His eyes were suddenly sharp needles again, piercing right through me. That was the second time he'd said something like that. I could see no sense in arguing, especially since I had no idea what he was talking about. I said nothing, therefore, and he dropped the subject.

We had reached the waterlock by this time anyway. I opened the panel just long enough to let water inside—about ankle deep—before shutting it again. I lifted the access hatch, grabbed my bucket, tied it to a rope, dropped it down into the water, filled it, and hauled it back up.

I held out the full bucket to Haplo. To my astonishment, he drew back, refused to touch it.

"Take it in there," he said, pointing to the hold.

I did as he said, growing more and more curious. The bucket was heavy and awkward to carry, water sloshed out, spilled on my shoes and the deck. Haplo was extremely careful to avoid stepping in even the smallest puddle.

"Set it down," he ordered, indicating a far corner.

I put the bucket down, rubbed my palms where the handle had bit into them.

"Thank you," he said, standing, waiting.

"You're welcome." Pulling up a stool, I seated myself comfortably.

"You can leave anytime now."

"I've got nothing better to do," I said.

He was angry, and I thought for a moment he was going to pick me up and throw me out. (Or try to, at any rate. Dwarves aren't easy to budge, once they've decided to stay put.) He glared at me. I glared right back, crossed my arms over my chest, and settled myself more firmly on the stool.

Then, a thought seemed to occur to him. "You might be useful, after all," he muttered, and let me be.

As for what happened next, I'm not certain I believe it myself, though I saw it with my own eyes.

Haplo knelt down on the deck and began to write on one of the wooden planks, using nothing but his fingertip!

I started to laugh, ended up almost choking to death.

When his finger touched the wood, a thin wisp of smoke curled up into the air. He drew a straight line, left a trail of flame behind. The fire died in an instant, leaving a brown, scorched mark, as if he'd been writing on the planks with a red-hot poker. But he wasn't. He was only using his own flesh, and it was setting the wood ablaze.

He worked rapidly, making strange marks on the deck, marks that looked similar—I thought—to those blue lines and swirls on his arms and the backs of his hands. He drew maybe ten of these in a circle, taking care to make certain that they were all connected. The smell of burning wood was strong. I sneezed.

Finally, he was finished. The circle was complete. He sat back, studied it a moment, and then nodded to himself in satisfaction. I stared hard at his fingers, could see no sign of any scorch marks.

Haplo rose to his feet and stepped onto the circle he'd drawn.

Blue light began to radiate up from the markings he'd burned on the deck and suddenly Haplo wasn't standing on the deck. He floated up in the air, seemingly supported by nothing except the blue light.

I gasped and jumped up so fast I upset my stool.

"Grundle! Don't leave," he said hastily. He moved, and the next thing I knew he was standing on the deck again. The blue light, however, continued to glow. "I want you to do something for me."

"What?" I asked, keeping as far from the weird light as I could.

"Bring the bucket over and pour water on the circle."

I stared at him suspiciously. "That's all?"

"That's all."

"What will happen?"

"I'm not sure. Maybe nothing."

"Why don't you do it, then?"

He smiled, trying to be pleasant. But his eyes were cold and hard. "I don't think the water agrees with me."

I thought it over. Dumping a pailful of water on some scorched planks wasn't liable to hurt me. And, I have to admit, I was extremely curious to see what would happen next.

He wasn't kidding about being worried about the water. The minute I picked up the bucket, Haplo backed into a corner, crouched behind a barrel, to keep from getting splashed.

I tossed the water onto the circle of strange marks that glowed with a blue light.

The light vanished instantly. And, as I watched, amazed, I saw the burn marks on the plank start to fade away.

"But, that's impossible!" I cried, dropping the bucket and backing off.

Haplo came out from behind the barrel. He walked across the deck, came to stand in front of the rapidly disappearing circle.

"You're getting your boots wet," I pointed out.

By the grim expression on his face, he didn't seem to care anymore. He lifted one foot, held it over the place where the circle had supported him. Nothing happened. His boot slammed down on the deck.

"In all my life, I've never seen or heard of anything—" He

broke off, started some new thought. "Why? What can it mean?" His face darkened, he clenched his fist. "The Sartan."

Turning, without a word or a glance at me, he stormed out of the cabin. I heard his footfalls in the passageway, the slamming of his door. I crept over, stared down at the wet deck. The burn marks were almost completely gone. The wooden planks were wet, but unscarred.

The three of us, Alake, Devon, and I, ate dinner alone. Alake tapped on Haplo's door and called, but there was no answer. She returned, disappointed and downcast.

I didn't say anything to her or to Devon. To be honest, I wasn't certain they'd believe me and I didn't want to start an argument. After all, I have no proof of anything I saw except a couple of wet boards.

But at least I know the truth.

Whatever that truth may be.

More later. I'm so sleepy I can't hold the pen any longer.

CHAPTER ♦ 13

SURUNAN

CHELESTRA

♦

Alfred spent many pleasant hours walking the streets of Surunan. Like its inhabitants, the city had awakened from its long, enforced slumber and returned swiftly to life. There were far more people than Alfred had first supposed. He must have discovered only one of many Sleeping chambers.

Guided by the Council, the Sartan worked to restore their city to its original beauty. Sartan magic made dead plants green, repaired crumbling buildings, wiped away all traces of destruction. Their city restored to beauty, harmony, peace, and order, the Sartan began to discuss how to do the same to the other three worlds.

Alfred reveled in the tranquility, the beauty his soul remembered. He delighted in the Sartan conversation, the multiplicity of wonderous images created by the magic of the rune language. He heard the music of the runes and wondered, his eyes moist with pleasure, how he could have ever forgotten such beauty. He basked in the friendly smiles of his brothers and sisters.

"I could live here and be happy," he said to Orla.

They were walking through the city, on their way to a meeting of the Council of Seven. The dog, who had not left Alfred's side since the night before, accompanied them. The beauty of Surunan was food to Alfred's soul, which, he realized now, had nearly withered up and died of starvation.

He could, he noted wistfully, actually walk the streets without falling over his feet or anyone else's.

"I understand how you feel," said Orla, looking about with

pleasure. "It is as it used to be. It seems as if no time has passed at all."

The dog, feeling itself forgotten, whined and shoved its head into Alfred's dangling hand.

The touch of the cold nose made Alfred jump. Startled, he looked down at the dog, forgot to watch where he was going, and tumbled into a marble bench.

"Are you all right?" Orla asked in concern.

"Yes, thank you," Alfred mumbled, picking himself up and endeavoring to put himself back together.

He looked at Orla in her soft white robes, at all the other Sartan dressed alike in their white robes. And he looked down at himself, still wearing the faded purple velvet suit of the mensch court of King Stephen of Arianus. Frayed lace cuffs were too short for his long, gangly arms; the hose covering his ungainly legs were wrinkled and sagging. He ran his hand over his balding head. It seemed to him that the smiles of his brothers and sisters were no longer friendly, but patronizing, pitying.

Alfred wanted, suddenly, to grab his brethren by the collars of their long, white robes and shake them until their teeth rattled.

Time *has* passed! he wanted to shout. Eons. Centuries. Worlds that were young and newly born out of fire have cooled and grown old. While you slept, generations have lived and suffered and been happy and died. But what does that mean to you? Nothing more than the thick layers of dust covering your perfect white marble. You sweep it away and prepare to go on. But you can't. No one remembers you. No one wants you. Your children have grown and left home. They may not be doing that well on their own, but at least they're free to try.

"Something *is* the matter," said Orla solicitously. "If you're hurt, the Council can wait . . ."

Alfred was startled to find himself trembling; his unspoken words churned inside him. Why not say them? Why not let them out? Because I may be wrong. Most probably I am wrong. Who am I, after all? Not very wise. Not nearly as wise as Samah and Orla.

The dog, accustomed to Alfred's sudden and erratic tumbles, had leapt lightly out of the way when he fell. It returned to gaze up at him with a certain amount of reproach.

I have four feet to worry about and you only have two, the dog advised him. *One would think you could manage better.*

Alfred was reminded of Haplo, of the Patryn's irritation whenever the Sartan stumbled over himself.

"I think," said Orla, eyeing the dog severely, "we should have left the animal behind."

"He wouldn't have stayed," said Alfred.

Samah appeared to be of the same opinion. He eyed the dog, sitting at Alfred's feet, suspiciously.

"You say that this dog belongs to a Patryn. You have said yourself that this Patryn uses the animal to spy on others. It shouldn't be in a Council meeting. Remove it. Ramu"—he gestured to his son, who was acting as Council Servitor[1]—"remove the animal."

Alfred made no protest. The dog growled at Ramu, but—at a soft word from Alfred—suffered itself to be led out of the Council Chamber. Ramu returned, shutting the door behind him and taking up his proper place before it. Samah took his place behind the long, white, marble table. The six Council members took their places, three on his left and three on his right. All sat down simultaneously.

The Sartan, in their white robes, faces alight with wisdom and intelligence, were beautiful, majestic, radiant.

Alfred, seated on the Supplicant's Bench, saw himself by contrast—huddled, faded, and bald. The dog, tongue lolling, lay at his feet.

Samah's eyes skipped over Alfred, fixed on the dog. The head of the Council frowned, glanced at his son.

Ramu was astonished. "I put him out, Father, and"—he glanced behind him—"I shut the door! I swear!"

---

[1] A position of honor, granted to those deemed most likely to be full members of the Council at some future date. The post is often hereditary, but is open to all Sartan. Applicants come before the Council and must pass certain secret tests, pertaining not only to their abilities in magic, which must be superior, but to their general knowledge. Servitors act as pages, runners, and must be prepared to defend the Council members in the unlikely event that they are ever attacked. There are seven Servitors, but only two attend regular Council sessions.

Samah motioned Alfred to stand and come forward, into the Supplicant's Circle.

Alfred did so, feet shuffling.

"I ask you to put the animal outside, Brother."

Alfred sighed, shook his head. "He'll just come right back in. But I don't think you need worry about him spying on us for his master. He's lost his master. That's why he's here."

"He wants you to look for his master, for a Patryn?"

"I believe so," said Alfred meekly.

Samah's frown darkened. "And this doesn't seem strange to you? A dog belonging to a Patryn, coming to you, a Sartan, for help?"

"Well, no," said Alfred, after a moment's reflection. "Not considering what the dog is. That is, what I think it is. Or might be." He was somewhat flustered.

"What is this dog, then?"

"I'd rather not say, Councillor."

"You refuse a direct request of the head of the Council?"

Alfred hunched his head into his shoulders, like a threatened turtle. "I'm probably wrong. I've been wrong about a great many things. I wouldn't want to give the Council misinformation," he concluded lamely.

"I do not like this, Brother!" Samah's tone was a whiplash. Alfred flinched beneath it. "I have tried to make allowances for you, because you have lived so long among mensch, bereft of the companionship, counsel, and advice of your own kind. But now you have walked among us, lived among us, eaten our bread, and yet you willfully persist in refusing to answer our questions. You will not even tell us your real name. One might think you distrusted us—your own people!"

Alfred felt the justness of this accusation. He knew Samah was right, knew the flaw to be in himself, knew he was unworthy to stand here, to be among his people. He wanted desperately to tell them all he knew, to fling himself prostrate at their feet, to hide beneath the hems of their white robes.

Hide. Yes, that's what I'd be doing. Hide from myself. Hide from the dog. Hide from despair. Hide from hope . . .

He sighed. "I trust you, Samah, members of the Council. It's myself that I don't trust. Is it wrong to refuse to answer questions to which I don't know the answer?"

"Sharing information, sharing your speculations, might benefit us all."

"Perhaps," said Alfred. "Or perhaps not. I must be the judge."

"Samah," Orla said gently, "this arguing is pointless. As you said, we must make allowances."

If Samah had been a mensch king, he would have ordered his son to take Alfred and wring the information out of him. And it seemed, for a moment, as if the Councillor was regretting he *wasn't* such a king. His hand clenched in frustration, his brow furrowed. But he mastered himself, continued on.

"I am going to ask you a question and I trust you will find it in your heart to answer."

"If I can do so, I will," Alfred replied humbly.

"We have urgent need to contact our brethren in the other three worlds. Is such contact possible?"

Alfred looked up, amazed. "But, I thought you understood! You *have* no brethren in the other worlds! That is," he added, shuddering, "'unless you count the necromancers on Abarrach.'"

"Even these necromancers, as you term them, are Sartan," said Samah. "If they have fallen into evil, all the more reason to try to reach them. And you yourself have admitted that you have not traveled to Pryan. You don't know for certain that our people are no longer on the world."

"But I have talked to one who has been there," Alfred protested. "He found a Sartan city, but no trace of any Sartan. Only terrible beings, that *we* created—"

"And where did you get this information?" Samah thundered. "From a Patryn! I see his image in your mind! And you would have us believe it?"

Alfred shrank into himself. "He would have no reason to lie—"

"He would have every reason! He and this lord who plans to conquer and enslave us!" Samah fell silent, glaring at Alfred. "Now, answer my question!"

"Yes, Councillor. I suppose you could go through Death's Gate." Alfred wasn't being very helpful, but he couldn't think of anything else to say.

"And alert this Patryn tyrant to our presence. No, not yet. We are not strong enough to face him."

"And yet," said Orla, "we may not have any choice. Tell Alfred the rest."

"We must trust him," said Samah bitterly, "although *he* does not trust us."

Alfred flushed, stared down at his shoes.

"After the Sundering came a time of chaos. It was a dreadful time," Samah said, frowning. "We knew there would be suffering and loss of life. We regretted it, but we believed that the greater good to come would make up for it."

"That is the excuse of all who wage war," said Alfred in a low voice.

Samah paled in anger.

Orla intervened. "What you say is true, Brother. And there were those who argued against it."

"But what is done is done and that time is long past," Samah said in stern tones, seeing several of the Council members shift restlessly in their seats. "The magical forces we unleashed proved far more destructive than we had anticipated. We found, too late, that we could not bring them under control. Many of our people sacrificed their own lives in an attempt to stop the holocaust that swept over the world. To no avail. We could only watch in helpless horror and, when all was ended, do what we could to save those who had managed to survive.

"The creation of the four worlds was successful, as was the imprisonment of our enemies. We took the mensch and brought them to havens of peace and safety. Such a world was Chelestra.

"This world was the one of which we were the proudest. It hangs in the darkness of the universe like a beautiful blue-white jewel. Chelestra is made completely of water. On the outside, it is ice; the chill of the space around it freezes the water solid. Within Chelestra's heart, we placed a seastar, which warms the water and warms as well the durnai, hibernating, living beings that drift around the seasun. The mensch call them seamoons. It was our intent, after the mensch had lived here many generations and become accustomed to it, that they should move onto these seamoons. We would remain here, on this continent."

"This isn't a seamoon?" Alfred looked confused.

"No, we needed something more solid, more stable. Something that more closely resembled the world we left behind. Sky, sun, trees, clouds. This realm rests on a huge formation of solid rock formed in the shape of a chalice. Runes cover its surface with intricate patterns of force both outside the stone and within.

"Inside the cup is a mantle of molten rock, covered by a surface crust not unlike our original world. Here we formed clouds, rivers and valleys, lakes and fertile land. Above all arches the dome of the sky that keeps the sea at bay while letting in the light of the seasun."

"You mean," said Alfred, awed, "that we are now surrounded by water?"

"The turquoise blue you see above you that you call sky is not sky as you know it, but water," said Orla, smiling. "Water that we could share with other worlds, worlds such as Abarrach." Her smile faded. "We came here, out of despair, hoping to find peace. We found instead death, destruction."

"We built this city with our magic," Samah continued. "We brought the mensch to live here. For a time, all went well. Then, creatures appeared, coming up out of the deep. We couldn't believe what we saw. We, who had made all the animals of all the new worlds, had not made these. They were ugly, horrible to look on. They smelled foul, of decay and putrefaction. The mensch called them dragons, naming them after a mythical beast of the Old World."

Samah's words created images in the mind. Alfred listened and saw and was carried back with the head of the Council to a far distant time. . . .

. . . Samah stood outside, upon the steps of the Council Chamber, and gazed in anger and frustration down upon the newly made city of Surunan. All around him was beauty, but he took no comfort in it. The beauty, instead, seemed a mockery. Beyond the high, glistening, flower-covered city walls, he heard the voices of the mensch beat against the marble like the pounding of a storm-tossed sea.

"Tell them to return to their homes," Samah ordered his son, Ramu. "Tell them all will be well."

"We told them, Father," Ramu replied. "They refuse."

"They are frightened," Orla explained, seeing her husband's face harden. "Panicked. You can't blame them. After all they've been through, all they've suffered."

"And what about all *we've* suffered. They never think of that!" Samah returned bitterly.

He was silent long moments, listening to the voices. He could distinguish the races among them: the raucous blaring of the humans, the flutelike laments of the elves, the booming bass of the dwarves. A terrible orchestra that, for the first time in its existence, was playing in concert, instead of each section trying to drown out the other.

"What do they want?" he asked finally.

"They are terrified of these so-called dragons. The people want us to open the gates to our part of the city," Ramu told him. "They think they will be safer inside our walls."

"They are just as safe in their own homes!" Samah said. "The same magic protects them."

"You can't blame them for not understanding, Father," Ramu replied scornfully. "They are like children, frightened by the thunder, who seek the safety of the parents' bed."

"Open the gates, then. Let them in. Make room for them where you can and do what you can to keep the damage they cause to a minimum. Make it clear to them that it is only temporary. Tell them that the Council is going out to destroy the monsters and, when this is done, we expect the mensch to return peacefully to their homes. Or as peacefully as can be expected of them," he added in acerbic tones.

Ramu bowed and went to do his father's bidding, taking with him the other servitors to assist.

"The dragons have done no great harm," said Orla. "I am sick of killing. I entreat you, again, Samah, to try to talk with them, find out something about them and what they want. Perhaps we can negotiate—"

"All this you said before the Council, Wife," Samah interrupted her impatiently. "The Council voted and the decision was made. We did not create these creatures. We have no control over them . . ."

"And so they must be destroyed," Orla concluded coldly.

"The Council has spoken."

"The vote was not unanimous."

"I know." Samah was cold, still angry. "And to keep peace in the Council and in my home, I will talk to these serpents, learn what I can about them. Believe it or not, Wife, I, too, am sick of killing."

"Thank you, Husband," Orla said, attempting to slide her arm through his.

Samah stiffened, held himself away from her touch.

The Sartan Council of Seven left their walled city for the first time since they had arrived in this new world of their own creation. Joining hands, performing a solemn and graceful dance, the seven sang the runes and called upon the winds of ever-shifting possibility to carry them over the walls of the center city, over the heads of the wailing mensch, to the nearby shores of the sea.

Out in the water, the dragons awaited them. The Sartan looked on them and were appalled. The serpents were huge, their skin wrinkled. They were toothless and old, older than time itself. And they were evil. Fear emanated from the dragons, hatred gleamed in their red-green eyes like angry suns, and shriveled the very hearts of the Sartan, who had seen nothing like it, not even in the eyes of the Patryns, their most bitter enemy.

The sand, which had once been as white and gleaming as crushed marble, was now gray-green, coated by trails of foul-smelling slime. The water, covered with a thick film of oil, washed sluggishly up on the polluted shore.

Led by Samah, the Council members formed a line upon the sand.

The dragons began to slither and leap and writhe. Churning the seawater, the serpents stirred up great waves, sent them crashing to shore. The spray from the waves fell on the Sartan. The smell was putrid, brought a horrid image. They seemed to be looking into a grave in which lay moldering all the hastily buried victims of sinister crimes, all the rotting corpses of the battlefield, the dead of centuries of violence.

Samah, raising his hand, called out, "I am head of the Council, the governing body of the Sartan. Send one of your kind forward to talk with us."

One of the dragons, larger and more powerful than the rest, reared its head out of the water. A huge wave surged to shore. The Sartan could not escape it, and were drenched to the skin, their clothes and hair wringing wet. The water was cold, chilled them to the bone.

Orla, shivering, hastened to her husband's side. "I am convinced. You are right. These creatures are evil and must be destroyed. Let's do what we have to, quickly, and leave."

Samah wiped seawater from his face, looking at it, looking at his hand in awe and perplexity. "Why do I feel so strange? What is happening? As if my body were suddenly made of lead, heavy and clumsy. My hands don't seem to belong to me. My feet cannot move—"

"I feel it, too," cried Orla. "We must work the magic swiftly—"

"I am the Royal One, king of my people," called the serpent, and its voice was soft and barely heard and seemed to come from a far distance. "I will speak with you."

"Why have you come? What do you want?" Samah shouted above the crashing of the waves.

"Your destruction."

The words twisted and writhed in Samah's mind as the dragons twisted in the water, dipping their serpent heads in and flinging them back out, flailing and lashing their bodies and tails. The seawater foamed and boiled and surged erratically over the shore. Samah had never faced any threat as dire as this one and he was uncertain, uneasy. The water chilled him, numbing limbs, freezing feet. His magic could not warm him.

Samah raised his hands to draw the runes in the air. He began to move his feet in the dance that would paint the runes with his body. He lifted his voice to sing the runes to the wind and the water. But his voice sounded flat and raucous. His hands were like claws, tearing the air. His feet moved in opposing directions. Samah stumbled, clumsy, inept. The magic washed away.

Orla tried to come to her husband's aid, but her body unaccountably failed her. She wandered across the shore, her feet reacting to a will that was no longer under her control. The remaining members of the Council staggered along the shore or tumbled into the water, like drunken revelers.

Samah crouched in the sand, battling fear. He faced, he guessed, a terrible death.

"Where did you come from?" he cried in bitter frustration, watching the dragons surge into shore. "Who created you?"

"You did," came the reply.

♦

The horrible images faded, leaving Alfred weak and shaken. And he had only been a witness. He could not imagine what it must have been like to have lived through the incident.

"But the dragon-snakes did not kill us that day, as you may have surmised," Samah concluded dryly.

He had related his tale calmly enough, but the usually firm, confident smile was thin and tight. The hand that rested upon the marble table shook slightly. Orla had gone extremely pale. Several of the other Council members shuddered, one let his head sink into his hands.

"There came a time when we longed for death," Samah continued, his voice soft, as if he spoke to himself. "The dragons made sport of us, drove us up and down the beach until we were faint and exhausted. When one of us fell, the great toothless mouth closed over the body, dragged the person to his feet. Terror alone put life in our bodies. And, at last, when we could run no more, when our hearts seemed as if they must burst and our limbs would no longer support us, we lay in the wet sand and waited to die. The dragons left us, then."

"But they came back, in greater numbers," Orla said. Her hands rubbed the marble table, as if she would smooth out its already smooth surface. "They attacked the city, their huge bodies battering into walls, killing and torturing and maiming any living thing they found. Our magic worked against them and we held them off for a long time. But we could see that the magic was starting to crumble, just as did the rune-covered walls surrounding our city."

"But why?" Alfred gazed from one to the other in shocked perplexity. "What power do these dragons have over our magic?"

"None. They can fight it, certainly, and they resist it better than any other living beings we have faced, but it was not, we soon discovered, the power of the dragons that left us helpless and defenseless on the beach. It was the seawater."

Alfred gaped, astonished. The dog lifted its head, its ears pricked. It had fallen asleep, nose on paws, during the recital of the battle with the dragons. Now it sat up, looked interested.

"But you created the seawater," said Alfred.

"As we—supposedly—created these dragon-snakes?" Samah gave a bitter laugh. He eyed Alfred shrewdly. "You have not come across anything like them in other worlds?"

"N-no. Dragons, yes, certainly, but they could always be controlled by magic, by mensch magic even. Or seemed to be," he added suddenly, thoughtfully.

"The water of the sea, this ocean that we named 'Goodsea' "—Samah spoke the word with irony—"has the effect of completely destroying our magic. We don't know how or why. All we know is that one drop of the seawater on our skin begins a cycle that breaks down the rune structure, until we are helpless—more helpless, in fact—than mensch.

"And that is why, in the end, we ordered the mensch out into the Goodsea. The seasun was drifting away. We lacked the magical energy to stop it; all our power had to be conserved to fight the dragons. We sent the mensch to follow the seasun, to find other seamoons, where they could live. The creatures of the deep, whales and dolphins and others the mensch had befriended, went with them, to help guard and defend them from the dragons.

"We have no idea whether the mensch made it safely or not. Certainly, they stood a better chance than we did. The seawater has no effect on them or their magic. In fact, they seem to thrive on it. We stayed behind, waiting for the seasun to leave us, waiting for the ice to close over us . . . and over our enemy. We were fairly certain, you see, that the dragons wanted us. They cared little for the mensch."

"And we were right. The dragons kept up the attack on our city," Orla continued, "but never in numbers sufficient to win. Victory did not seem to be their goal. Pain, suffering, anguish— that is what they wanted. Our hope was to wait, buy time. Each day the sun's warmth lessened, the darkness gathered around us. Perhaps the dragons, intent on their hatred for us, did not notice. Or perhaps they thought their magic could overcome it. Or, perhaps, at the end, they fled. All we know is that one day the sea froze and on that day the dragons did not appear. On that day, we sent a final message to our people in the worlds beyond, asking that in a hundred years they come to wake us. And we went to sleep."

"I doubt if they ever got your message," said Alfred. "Or if

they did, they couldn't have come. Each world had its own problems, it seems." He sighed, then blinked. "Thank you for telling
me. I understand better now and I . . . I'm sorry for the way
I've been acting. I thought . . ." He stared at his shoes, shuffled
his feet uncomfortably.

"You thought we had abandoned our responsibility," Samah
said grimly.

"I've seen it before. On Abarrach . . ." Alfred gulped.

The Councillor said nothing, looked at him expectantly. All
the Council members were looking at him expectantly.

Now you understand, they were telling him. Now you know
what to do.

Except that he didn't. Alfred spread trembling hands.

"What is it you want of me? Do you want me to help
fight the dragons? I know something about the creatures, those
we have on Arianus. But they seem to me to be very weak
and ineffectual dragons, compared to these serpents you've
described. And as for experimenting with seawater, I'm
afraid—"

"No, Brother," Samah interrupted. "Nothing so difficult. You
told Orla that the arrival of this dog on Chelestra meant that the
dog's master was also on Chelestra. You have the animal. We
want you to find the master and bring him to us."

"No," said Alfred, flustered, nervous. "I couldn't . . . He let
me go, you see, when he could have taken me prisoner to the
Labyrinth—"

"We have no intention of harming this Patryn." Samah's tone
was soothing. "We only want to ask him questions, discover the
truth about the Labyrinth, his people's suffering. Who knows,
Brother, but that this could be the beginning of peace negotiations between our people? If you refuse, and war breaks out,
how could you live with yourself, knowing that it had once been
in your power to prevent it?"

"But I don't know where to look," Alfred protested. "And I
wouldn't know what to say. He wouldn't come—"

"Wouldn't he? To face the enemy he has longed to challenge?
Consider it," Samah added before the flustered Alfred had time
to think up another argument. "Perhaps you can use the dog as
your means of getting him to return."

"Surely, you aren't going to refuse a request of the Council?"

asked Orla softly. "A request that is so reasonable? One that affects the safety of us all?"

"No, of . . . of course not," Alfred said unhappily.

He looked down at the dog.

The animal cocked its head, thumped its plumy tail on the floor, and grinned.

CHAPTER ♦ 14

THE GOODSEA

CHELESTRA

♦

HAPLO LAY FLAT ON HIS BED, STARING AT THE BACKS OF HIS HANDS. The sigla tattooed on the skin were a deeper, darker blue; his magic was growing stronger every moment. And the runes were beginning to glow faintly, the prickling sensation tingled over his body—the warning signal of danger, far away still, yet rapidly approaching.

The dragon-snakes. Without a doubt.

It seemed to Haplo that the ship had picked up speed. The vessel's motion was less smooth, more erratic, and he sensed an increased vibration in the deck beneath his feet.

"I could always ask the dwarf. She would know," Haplo muttered.

And, of course, he should tell the mensch that they were nearing the lair of the dragon-snakes. Warn them to make themselves ready . . .

To do what? Die?

Devon, the slender, delicate elf, had nearly decapitated himself with the battle-ax.

Alake had her magic spells, but hers were cantrips that any child in the Labyrinth could perform by the time it was past its second Gate. Against the awesome power of the dragon-snakes, it would be like pitting that child against an army of snogs.

Grundle. Haplo smiled, shook his head. If any one of those mensch could deal with the dragon-snakes, it would be the dwarf maid. If nothing else, she'd be too stubborn to die.

He ought to go tell them, do what he could to prepare them. He sat up.

"No," he said suddenly, and flung himself back on the bed. "I've had enough dealings with the mensch for one day."

What in the name of the Labyrinth had possessed him to make that promise to them? Not letting them come to harm! He'd be damn lucky if he could keep himself alive.

He clenched his hands to fists, studied the sigla drawn taut over bones and tendons. Raising his arms, he looked at the sharp, clean outline of the muscles beneath the tattooed skin.

"Instinct. The same instinct that led my parents to hide me in the bushes and lead the snogs away from me. The instinct to protect those weaker than ourselves, the instinct that allowed our people to survive the Labyrinth!"

He sprang to his feet, began pacing his small cabin. "My lord would understand," he reassured himself. "My lord feels the same. Every day of his life, he returns to the Labyrinth, returns to fight and defend and protect his children, his people. It's a natural emotion . . ." Haplo sighed, swore softly. "But it's damn inconvenient!"

He had other, more urgent matters to think about than keeping three mensch kids alive. The foul seawater that washed away his rune magic faster than ordinary water washed away dirt. And the dragon-snakes' promise.

At least, he assumed it was a promise.

Samah. The great Samah. Head of the Council of Seven. The Councillor who had engineered the Sundering, the Councillor who had brought about the Patryn's downfall, imprisonment, and eons of suffering.

Councillor Samah. Many things had died in the Labyrinth, but not that name. It had been handed down from generation to generation, breathed with the last dying breath of father to son, spoken with a curse from mother to daughter. Samah had never been forgotten by his enemies, and the thought that Samah might be discovered alive filled Haplo with unspeakable joy. He didn't even think to ask how it was possible.

"I'll capture Samah and take him to my lord—a gift to make up for my past failures. My lord will see to it that Samah pays and pays dearly for every tear shed by my people, for every drop of blood. Samah will spend his lifetime paying. His days will be filled with pain, torment, fear. His nights with horror, agony, terror. No rest. No sleep. No peace, except in death. And soon, very soon, Samah will be begging to die."

But the Lord of the Nexus would see to it that Samah lived. Lived a very long life . . .

A violent pounding on the door brought Haplo out of a blood-gilded reverie. The pounding had been going on for some time, but he'd been hearing thunder in his waking dreams of vengeance and hadn't noticed.

"Perhaps we shouldn't bother him, Grundle," came Devon's soft voice through the door, "He might be asleep . . ."

"Then he jolly well better wake up!" answered the dwarf.

Haplo rebuked himself for his lapse; such a slip would have cost him his life in the Labyrinth. Stalking over to the door, he yanked it open so suddenly that the dwarf, who had been beating on it with the handle of the battle-ax, tumbled inside.

"Well? What do you want?" Haplo snapped.

"We . . . we've wakened you," said Alake, her gaze shifting nervously from him to the rumpled bed.

Devon stammered. "W-we're sorry. We didn't mean—"

"The ship's picking up speed," stated Grundle. Her own gaze rested suspiciously on Haplo's skin. "And you're glowing again."

Haplo said nothing, glared at her, trusting she'd take the hint and go away. Alake and Devon were already sidling backward.

But Grundle was not to be intimidated. She rested the battle-ax on her shoulder, planted her feet firmly on the swaying deck, and looked Haplo in the face. "We're getting close to the dragon-snakes, aren't we?"

"Probably," he said, and started to close the door.

Grundle's stocky body blocked it.

"We want you to tell us what to do."

How the hell should I know? Haplo felt like shouting back at her in exasperation. I've come near a magical power like this in the Labyrinth, but nothing this strong. And all these dragon-snakes have to do is toss a bucket of seawater on me and I'm finished!

The mensch stood quietly, looking at him, trusting him (well, two of them trusted him), all of them silently pleading, hoping.

Who had given them that hope? And did he have the right to destroy it?

Besides, he told himself coldly, they might be useful. In the back of his mind was a plan . . .

"Come in," he said grudgingly, holding the door open wide.

The mensch trooped inside.

"Sit down," Haplo told them.

There was only the bed. Alake looked at it—rumpled, still warm from Haplo's body. Her lashes fluttered, brushed against her cheeks. She shook her head.

"No, thank you. I will stand. I do not mind. . . ."

"Sit!" Haplo ordered grimly.

She sat, perched on the very edge of the bed. Devon took his place beside her, long legs spraddled uncomfortably. (Dwarven beds are built low to the floor.) Grundle plopped herself down near the head of the bed, her short legs swinging back and forth, heels scuffing against the deck. All three looked up at him, faces serious, solemn.

"Let's get one thing straight. I don't know any more about these dragon-snakes than you do. Less, maybe."

"They spoke to you," Grundle informed him.

Haplo ignored her.

"Shush, Grundle," whispered Alake.

"What we do to protect ourselves is mostly common sense. You"—Haplo shifted his gaze to the elf—"better keep pretending to be a girl. Cover your face and head and don't take the scarf off, no matter what. And keep your mouth shut. Keep quiet and let me do the talking. That goes for all of you," Haplo added with a meaningful glare at the dwarf.

Grundle snorted and tossed her head. She had placed the battle-ax between her legs and was nervously rapping the haft on the deck. The ax reminded Haplo of something.

"Are there any more weapons aboard? Small ones. Like knives?"

Grundle sniffed in scorn. "Knives are for elves. Dwarves don't use such puny weapons."

"But there are knives on board," offered Alake. "In the galley."

"Cooking knives," muttered Haplo. "Are they sharp, small?

Could Devon hide one in his belt? Could you hide one . . . somewhere." He gestured at Alake's tight, form-fitting clothes.

"Of course they're sharp!" stated Grundle indignantly. "I'd like to see the day a dwarf would craft a dull knife! But they could be sharp as this ax and still not penetrate the hide of those foul beasts."

Haplo was silent, trying to think of the easiest, gentlest way to say what he had in mind. There was, he decided at last, no easy, gentle way. "I wasn't thinking about using them on the dragon-snakes." He said nothing more, hoping they'd get the idea.

They did . . . after a moment.

"You mean," said Alake, her black eyes large and wide, "that we're to use them . . . on . . . on . . ." She swallowed.

"Yourselves," said Haplo, deciding to be brisk, matter-of-fact. "Death can sometimes come as a friend."

"I know," said Alake, shivering. "I saw how my people died."

"And I saw the elf the dragon-snakes tortured," Devon added.

Grundle said nothing, for a change. Even the feisty dwarf looked subdued.

Devon drew a deep breath. "We understand what you are saying and we're grateful, but I'm not sure we could . . ."

You could, Haplo told him silently. When the horror and the agony and the torment become more than you can bear, you'll be desperate to end it.

But how can I say that to them? Haplo wondered bitterly. They're children. Beyond a splinter in the foot or a fall and a bump on the head, what do they know of pain and suffering?

"Could you . . ." Devon licked his lips. He was trying very hard to be brave. "Could you . . . show us how?" He flicked a glance to the girls on either side of him. "I don't know about Alake and Grundle, but I never had to . . . do anything like this." He smiled ruefully. "I'm pretty certain I'd botch it up."

"We don't need knives," said Alake. "I wasn't going to say anything, but I have certain herbs with me. A small amount is used to ease pain, but if you chew a whole leaf—"

"—it eases you right into the next life," Grundle concluded. She regarded the human with grudging admiration. "I didn't know you had it in you, Alake." A thought seemed to occur to her, however. "But what do you mean, you weren't going to tell us?"

"I would have," Alake replied. "I would have given you the choice. As I said," she added softly, lifting her black eyes to Haplo, "I saw how my people died."

He realized, then, that she was in love with him.

The knowledge did nothing to make him feel any better. In fact, it made him feel worse. It was just one more damn thing he had to worry about. But why should he? What difference did it make to him whether he broke the heart of this wretched human or not? She was, after all, only a mensch. But he could tell by the way she looked at him that he'd have to revise his notion of her being a child.

"Good. Good for you, Alake," he said, sounding as cold and dispassionate as possible. "You've got these herbs hidden where the dragon-snakes won't find them."

"Yes, they're in my—"

"Don't!" He raised his hand. "Don't say. What none of the rest of us know, the creatures can't wring out of us. Keep the poison safe and keep it secret."

Alake nodded solemnly. She continued to gaze at him, her eyes warm and liquid.

Don't do this to yourself. It's impossible, Haplo wanted to tell her.

Perhaps I should tell her. Perhaps that would be best. But how can I explain? How can I explain that to fall in love in the Labyrinth is to inflict a deliberate wound on yourself? Nothing good can come of love. Nothing but death and bitter sorrow and empty loneliness.

And how can I explain that a Patryn could never seriously love a mensch? There were instances, according to what Haplo knew about the pre-Sundering days, when Patryns, men and women both, had found pleasure among the mensch. Such liaisons were safe[1] and amusing. But that had been long ago. His people took life more seriously now.

---

[1] By safe, Haplo means that no children could come of such a dalliance, since the various races are not genetically compatible.

Alake lowered her eyes, her lips were parted in a shy smile. Haplo realized that he had been staring at her and, undoubtedly, she was getting the wrong impression.

"Go on, now. Clear out," he said gruffly. "Go back to your cabins and make yourself ready. I don't think we have long to wait. Devon, you might take one of those knives, just to be on the safe side. You, too, Grundle."

"I'll show you where to find them," Alake offered.

She smiled at Haplo as she left, cast him a sidelong glance from beneath her long eyelashes, then led the way out the door.

Devon followed after her. The elf studied Haplo on the way out, and the elf's eyes were suddenly cool and shadowed. He said nothing, however. It was Grundle who stopped on the threshold, jaw outthrust, side whiskers bristling.

"You hurt her"—the dwarf raised a small, threatening fist—"and, snakes or no snakes, I'll kill you."

"I think you have other matters to concern you," said Haplo quietly.

"Humpf!" Grundle snorted, and shook her whiskers at him.

Turning her small back, she stumped off, battle-ax bouncing on her shoulder.

"Damn!" Haplo slammed shut the door.

The Patryn paced his small cabin, making plans, discarding them, making others. He had just come to the point of admitting to himself that this was all nonsense, that he was trying futilely to control what he had no control over, when his room was suddenly plunged into darkness.

Haplo stopped in his tracks, blind, disoriented. The submersible hit something, the jolt sent him flying. He crashed up against one of the walls. A grinding sound coming from below led him to guess the ship had run aground.

The vessel rocked, shifted, listed to one side, then seemed to settle itself. All movement, all sound, ceased.

Haplo stood absolutely still, holding his breath, listening.

His cabin was no longer dark. The sigla on his skin glowed a bright blue, bathing himself and every object in the small cabin with an eerie, shimmering light. Haplo had only once before seen the runes react this strongly to danger and that had been in the Labyrinth, when he'd accidentally stumbled upon the cave

of a blood dragon, the most feared of all the fearsome creatures
in that hellish place.

He'd turned tail and run then, run until his leg muscles
burned and cramped and his lungs ached, run until he'd
been literally sobbing with pain and exhaustion, and then he'd
run some more. His body was telling him to run for it
now. . . .

He stared at the glowing sigla, felt the almost-maddening
tingling sensation pricking him to action. But the dragon-snakes
had not threatened him. They had done just the reverse, promising him—or seeming to promise him—revenge on an ancient
enemy.

"It could be a trick," he reasoned. "A trick to lure me here.
A trap? But why?"

He looked again at the runes on his skin, was reassured. He
was strong, his magic was strong, back to normal. If it was a
trap, these dragon-snakes were going to discover they'd caught
more than they'd bargained for—

Cries, shouts, footsteps, jarred Haplo from his thoughts.

"Haplo!" It was Grundle, howling.

He flung open his door. The mensch came running toward
him, racing down the corridor. Alake lit their way, holding in
her hand a lantern containing some sort of spongelike creature
that gave off a bright, white light.[2] The mensch appeared considerably startled to see Haplo, whose skin was glowing as brightly
as their lantern. They stumbled to a halt, huddled together,
stared at him in awe.

In the darkness, the sigla shining brilliantly, he must be a
marvelous spectacle.

"I . . . I guess we don't need this," said Alake faintly, and
dropped the lantern.

It fell to the deck with a clatter that went through Haplo like
sharp knives.

"Shut up!" he hissed.

---

[2]The pricklebulb fish. Spherical with long razor-edged fronds, it emits a
bright light that serves as a lure for its victims. If it feels threatened, its
light glows even brighter, until it blinds the potential predator and drives
it away. For this reason, it is wise to keep the lantern well fed and
comfortable.

The three gulped, nodded, exchanged frightened glances.

They must think the dragon-snakes are spying on us. Well, perhaps they are, Haplo thought grimly. Every trained and inbred instinct warned him to tread softly, walk warily.

He motioned, with his hand, for them to come closer. They moved down the passageway, trying their best to be quiet. Alake's beads jangled, Grundle's heavy boots thumped on the deck with a hollow sound, Devon got tangled up in his skirts, tripped, stumbled into a wall.

"Hush!" Haplo commanded softly, furiously. "Don't move!"

The mensch froze. Making less noise than the darkness, Haplo crept over to Grundle, knelt beside her.

"What's happened? Do you know?"

The dwarf nodded, opened her mouth.

Haplo drew her near him, pointed to his ear. Her whiskers tickled his cheek.

"I think we've sailed into a cave."

Haplo considered. Yes, that made sense. It would explain the sudden darkness.

"Is this place where the dragon-snakes live, do you think?" asked Alake.

She had moved over to stand beside Haplo. He could feel her slender body trembling, but her voice was firm.

"Yes, the dragon-snakes are here," Haplo said, looking at the glowing sigla on his hands.

Alake edged closer. Devon drew a deep, shivering breath, pressed his lips tightly together. Grundle humpfed and frowned.

No screams, no tears, no panic. Haplo was forced to give the mensch grudging credit for that much courage.

"What do we do?" asked Devon, trying very hard to keep his voice from cracking.

"We stay here," said Haplo. "We don't go anywhere or do anything. We wait."

"We're not going to be waiting very long," Grundle observed.

"What? Why not?" Haplo demanded.

In answer, she pointed above his head. Haplo looked up. The light shining from his skin illuminated the wooden planks

above them. They were wet, shining. A drop of water fell to the
floor at Haplo's feet. Another followed, and another.

Haplo sprang back, flattened himself against the wall. He
stared at the water on the deck, looked up at the drops that
were falling from the overhead. The drops had merged into a
trickle, the trickle was rapidly becoming a stream.

"The ship's breaking apart," stated Grundle, then frowned.
"Dwarven submersibles don't break apart, though. It must be
the snakes."

"They're driving us out. We'll have to swim," said Alake.
"Don't worry, Grundle. Devon and I will help you."

"*I'm* not worried," said the dwarf. Her gaze slid to Haplo.

For the first time in his life, he knew stark terror—weakening, debilitating. His fear robbed him of his ability to think, to
reason. He could do nothing except stare with a terrible fascination at the water that was creeping nearer and nearer his feet.

Swim! He almost laughed. So it *is* a trap! They lure me here,
then see to it that I'm helpless.

Water splashed on his arm. Haplo flinched, wiped it off hastily. Too late. Where the seawater touched the skin, the sigla's
glow darkened. The water was rising, it sloshed over the toes of
his boots. He could feel the circle of his magic slowly begin to
crack and crumble.

"Haplo! What's wrong!" Alake cried.

A section of the hull gave way. Wood snapped and splintered. Water cascaded in through the gaping hole. The elf lost
his footing, slid beneath the torrent. Alake, clinging to an upright beam, caught hold of Devon's wrist, saved him from being
washed down the corridor. He staggered to his feet.

"We can't stay here!" he shouted.

The water was level with Grundle's waist and the dwarf maid
was starting to panic. Her nut-brown complexion had gone sal-
low. Her eyes were round, her chin beginning to quiver.
Dwarves can breathe the seawater, in the same manner as elves
and humans, but—probably because their solid bodies are so
ungainly in the water—they don't like the sea, don't trust it.

Grundle had never been in water up over her ankles. Now
it was rising to her chest.

"Help! Alake, Devon! help m-me!" she shrieked, flailing
about with her arms, splashing wildly. "Alakeeeee!"

"Grundle! It's all right!"

"Here, catch hold of my hand. Ouch! Don't pinch. I've got you. Let loose a bit. There, take Alake's hand, too."

"I have you, Grundle. You're going to be fine. Relax. No, don't swallow the water. Duck your head down and take a breath just as you would the air. No! Don't! You'll choke! She's choking. Grundle . . ."

The dwarf sank beneath the water, came up coughing and sputtering, increasing her panic.

"We better get her to the surface!" cried Devon.

Alake cast a worried look in Haplo's direction.

He had neither moved nor spoken. The water was up to his thighs. The light from his skin had all but died out.

Haplo saw her look, saw that *she* was concerned about him. He almost laughed out loud.

"Go on!" he snarled.

More planks were giving way, the water was almost to Grundle's nose. The dwarf maid fought to keep her head above it, panted and gurgled.

Devon winced in pain. "She's tearing my hand off, Alake! Come on!"

"Go!" Haplo commanded angrily.

The hull gave way with a shattering crash. Water surged inside the ship, closed over Haplo's head. He lost sight of the mensch, lost sight of everything. It was as if night had taken on liquid shape and form. He knew a moment's panic equal to the dwarf's. He held his breath until it hurt, not wanting to breathe the darkness. A part of his despairing mind told him it would be far easier to drown. His body refused to let him, however.

He gasped, began to breathe water. After a few moments, his head cleared. He couldn't see, and groped his way among the wreckage. Shoving broken timbers to one side, he managed to free himself.

He swam aimlessly, wondering if he was going to be doomed to flounder about in this watery night until he collapsed from exhaustion. But even as the thought took shape in his mind, his head popped up out of the water. Gratefully, he sucked in air.

Floating on the surface, he trod water quietly, and looked around him.

A large campfire had been built on the shore. Wood crackled and burned, offering comforting warmth and light. Its ruddy glow was reflected off the cavern's rock ceiling and walls.

Haplo sensed fear, coming from outside him. Overwhelming terror surrounded him. The walls were covered with some sort of sticky green-brown substance that seemed to ooze from the rock like blood. He had the strange impression that the cave itself was wounded, that it lived in fear. Fear and horrible pain.

Ridiculous.

Haplo glanced swiftly behind him, to either side, but could see little. Here and there, a gleam of firelight played on wet rock.

The sound of splashing drew his attention. Three figures—black shadows against the orange firelight—emerged from the water. Two of the figures were helping the third, who could not walk. By this, the musical sound of clashing beads, and a muffled groan from the third figure, Haplo judged them to be his mensch.

He saw no sign of the dragon-snakes.

Alake and Devon managed to drag Grundle partway up the shore. Once there, obviously exhausted, they let loose of her hands. All sank down to rest. But Alake had only taken a few deep breaths before she was back on her feet, heading again for the water.

"Where are you going?" The elf's clear voice echoed in the cavern.

"I've got to find him, Devon! He may need help. Did you see his face—"

Haplo, muttering imprecations beneath his breath, swam for the shore. Alake heard the sound of his splashing. Unable to see what or who was making the noise, she froze. Devon hurried to her side. Metal glinted in his hand.

"It's me!" Haplo called to them. His stomach scraped against solid ground. He stood up, walked, dripping, out of the water.

"Are . . . are you all right?" Alake reached out a timid hand, withdrew it at the sight of the scowl on Haplo's face.

No, he wasn't all right. He was all wrong.

Ignoring both the human and the elf, he stomped past them, strode swiftly to the fire. The sooner he dried off, the sooner his magic would return. The dwarf lay in a sodden heap on the sand. He wondered if she was dead. A muffled groan reassured him.

"She hurt?" he asked, reaching the fire.

"No," answered Devon, coming up from behind.

"She's scared, more than anything," Alake added. "She'll come around. What . . . what are you doing?"

"Taking off my clothes," Haplo grunted. He had stripped off his shirt and his boots, was now unlacing his leather trousers.

Alake gave a strangled cry. She hastily averted her face, covered her eyes with her hands. Haplo grunted again. If the girl had never seen a naked man before, she was going to see one now. He had neither the time nor the patience to indulge a human female's sensibilities. Though his warning magic was gone, the sigla washed away, he had the distinct feeling that they weren't alone in this cave. They were being watched.

Flinging his trousers to the sand, Haplo crouched by the blaze, held out his hands and arms to the warming fire. In satisfaction, he watched the droplets of water evaporate, begin to dry. He glanced around.

"Pull your scarf over your head," he ordered Devon. "Sit by the fire. It'd look suspicious if you didn't. But keep your face out of the light. And put that damn knife away!"

Devon did as he was told. He thrust the knife in his breast, dragged a strip of wet cloth up over his head and face. Shivering, he crept near the fire, started to squat down, legs crossed.

"Don't sit like a man!" Haplo hissed. "On your knees. That's it. Alake, bring Grundle over here. And wake her up. I want everyone conscious and alert."

Alake nodded, not taking time to reply. She hastened over to the prostrate dwarf.

"Grundle, you've got to get up. Haplo says so. Grundle"— Alake's voice lowered—"I can feel the evil. The dragon-snakes are here, Grundle. They're watching us. Please, you've got to be brave!"

The dwarf groaned again, but she sat up, huffing and wheezing and blinking water out of her eyes. Alake helped her to her feet. The two started walking toward the fire.

"Wait!" Haplo breathed.

Slowly, he rose.

Behind him, he heard Alake draw in her breath sharply, heard Grundle mutter something in dwarven, then fall silent. Devon melted back into the shadows.

Red-green eyes appeared out of the darkness, made the light of the fire seem dim by contrast. The eyes were slanted, snake eyes and there were many of them, innumerable, far more than Haplo could count. They towered over him, their height unbelievable. A sound came of giant, heavy bodies undulating over sand and rock. A stench, foul and putrid, seemed to coat his nose and mouth with the flavor of death, decay. His stomach clenched. Behind him, he heard the mensch whimper in terror. One of them was retching.

Haplo didn't turn around. He couldn't turn around. The dragon-snakes slithered into the firelight. Flames shone on huge, scaled, shining bodies. He was overwhelmed by the enormity of the creatures that loomed before him. Enormous not only in size, but in power. He was awed, humbled. He no longer regretted the loss of his magic, for it would have been of no use. These beings could crush him with a breath. A whisper would hammer him into the ground.

Hands clenched at his side, Haplo waited calmly for death.

The largest among the dragon-snakes suddenly reared its head. The green-red eyes burned, seemed to bathe the cavern in an unholy radiance. Then the eyes closed, the head sank to the sand before Haplo, who stood naked in the firelight.

"Patryn," it said reverently. "Master."

CHAPTER ♦ 15

DRAKNOR

CHELESTRA

♦

"WELL, TEAR OUT MY WHISKERS BY THE ROOTS!"

Haplo heard the dwarf's awed murmur, felt something of the same himself. The gigantic dragon-snake prostrated its head on the ground before the Patryn. Its fellows had drawn back a respectful distance, their scaled necks arched, heads bowed, slit-eyes closed.

Haplo remained tense, wary, alert. Dragons were intelligent, tricky creatures, not to be trusted.

The dragon-snake lifted its head, reared its body almost to the cavern's high ceiling. The mensch gasped and cried out. Haplo raised a hand.

"Be quiet," he ordered.

The dragon-snake was, apparently, merely shifting to a more comfortable position. It wound its body round and round, looping in upon itself, and came to rest with its head pillowed on its own coils.

"Now, we can speak together more comfortably. Please, Patryn, be seated. Welcome to Draknor."[1]

The dragon-snake spoke the Patryn language, a rune-based language that should have presented images to Haplo's mind, as well as words. But he saw nothing, heard only the sound, and it was flat and lifeless. A shiver crawled over the Patryn's

[1] Human translation: the Dark Place.

skin. It was as if the dragons had reduced the power of the runes to nothing more than shapes and figures, to be manipulated at will.

"Thank you, Royal One." Haplo seated himself again, never taking his eyes from the dragon-snake.

The snake's own slit-eyed gaze slid to the mensch, who had not moved. "But why do our young guests keep from drying themselves at the fire? Is the blaze too hot? Perhaps not hot enough. We know so little of you frail beings, we cannot judge properly . . ."

Haplo shook his head. "They're afraid of you, Royal One. After what you did to their people, I can hardly blame them."

The dragon-snake shifted its coils. Its eyelids closed, a soft, sibilant sigh escaped its toothless mouth. "Ah, I fear we've made a terrible mistake. But we will make it up to them."

The red eyes opened, the snake's tone was anxious. "You have influence over them? They trust you? Yes, of course. Assure them that we mean them no harm. We will do everything in our power to make their stay among us comfortable. A warm place to sleep? Food, dry clothing? Precious jewels, gold, silver? Will all this make them happy, soothe their fright?"

The ground in front of Haplo was suddenly littered with bowls and baskets and dishes and trays containing every type of luscious food imaginable: mounds of fragrant fruit, plates of steaming meat, bottles of wine, casks of foaming ale.

Clothing of all make and description billowed in the air like multicolored, silken birds, fluttered down to land at Alake's feet, draped over Devon's nerveless arms, sparkled in Grundle's startled eyes. Caskets of emeralds and sapphires and pearls spilled their shining contents into the sand. Mounds of golden coins gleamed in the fire's light.

Another fire sprang up in the distance, revealing a cave within a cave.

"It is warm and dry," said the dragon-snake. Speaking to the mensch, it had switched to the human language. "We have filled it with sweet grasses for your beds. You must be exhausted and hungry." It spoke in elven. "Please, take our gifts, retire for the night." It concluded in dwarven. "You need have no fear. Your slumber will be safe, blessed. My people will guard it."

The other dragon-snakes wove their bodies in a sinuous

dance, the words "safe . . . blessed" hissed through the echoing cave.

The mensch, having expected death, torture, torment, were completely disarmed and bewildered by the lavish gifts. They stood staring, dazed and, if anything, more frightened.

Grundle was the first to recover her tongue. A circlet of silver had dropped out of the air, onto her head, over one eye. Floundering through a heap of cloth and mounds of food, she stomped over to Haplo.

Hands on her hips, she pointedly ignored the dragon-snakes, spoke to the Patryn as if no one else was on the beach except the two of them.

"What is all this? What's going on? What are you two talking about in that dark language of yours?"

"The dragon-snake says there's been a mistake. It's trying to make amends. I think—" Haplo began, but he didn't get far.

"Amends!" Grundle raised a clenched fist, whipped around to face the dragon-snake. "For destroying the sun-chasers, for butchering Alake's people, for torturing that poor elf! I'll give the beast amends. I'll—"

Haplo caught hold of her, dragged her down, squirming and kicking. "Stop it, you little fool! You want to get us all killed?"

Panting, Grundle glared up at him. He held her fast until he felt the sturdy body relax in his grip.

"I'm all right now," she told him sullenly.

He let her up. She crouched at his side, rubbing her bruised wrists. Haplo motioned to the other two to come join them.

"Listen to me, all of you!" he said. "I'm going to try to find out what's going on. But in the meantime, you three will accept the dragon's hospitality with a good grace. We might yet come out alive—you *and* your people. That's why you came, wasn't it?"

"Yes, Haplo," said Alake. "We'll do what you say."

"I don't suppose we have much choice, do we?" Devon asked, his words muffled by the wet scarf around his head.

Grundle nodded grudgingly. "But I still don't trust them!" she added, shaking her whiskers at the snakes in defiance.

"Good." Haplo smiled. "I don't either. Keep your eyes and ears open, your mouths shut. Now, do as the dragon-snake suggests. Go to that cave. You and Alake and . . . uh—"

"Sabia."

"Sabia. You three go into that cave and try to get some sleep. Take dry clothes with you and some wine and whatever else you want. Food, maybe."

Grundle sniffed. "It's probably poisoned."

Haplo checked an exasperated sigh. "If they wanted to kill you, they could have dropped an ax on your head, instead of that." He pointed to the silver crown, which had once more slipped down over one eye.

Removing the circlet, the dwarf regarded it suspiciously, then she shrugged.

"You make sense," she said, sounding surprised.

Tossing the silver to the sand, she grabbed a basket of bread in one hand, hefted a small barrel of ale with the other, and trudged off toward the cave.

"Go with her," Haplo told Alake, who was lingering near him. "You'll be fine. Don't worry."

"Yes, I know. I . . . I will take your clothes and dry them for you," Alake offered.

She darted Haplo a sidelong glance, then swiftly averted her gaze and started to pick up his wet trousers.

"No need," Haplo said, laying a gentle hand on her arm. "Thank you, but the dragon-snakes have provided clothing for me, as well. However, you might want to pick out something for . . . her . . . Sabia. Something that fits better."

"Yes, you're right." Alake seemed relieved to have a task to perform.

She began to sort among the vast amount of raiments scattered about the sand. Finding what she wanted, she looked back at Haplo with a smile, cast a cool, defiant glance at the dragon-snakes, then hurried off after Grundle.

Devon, still keeping to the shadows, was gathering up food and wine. He was about to follow the others to the cave, when Haplo beckoned.

"Two of you sleep. One stays awake. Understand?" He spoke softly, in elven.

Devon made no response, merely nodded and went on his way.

Haplo turned back to the dragon-snake, who had rested quietly the entire time, its head on its coiled body, its eyes blinking lazily in the firelight.

"Truly," it said, when the three had disappeared into the cave, "you Patryns have a way with the mensch. If your people had been free to help them, all these centuries, what marvelous things might they have accomplished. Alas, it was not to be."

The dragon-snake sadly mused to itself long moments, then shifted its great bulk.

"However, now that you have escaped your unjust incarceration, you will, no doubt, make up for wasted time and opportunity. Tell me about your people and your plans."

Haplo shrugged. "Our story is long, Royal One, and, though it is bitter to us, would probably be boring to others." He had no intention of telling these creatures anything about his people. His body was dry; he could see the faint outlines of the sigla returning to his skin. "Do you mind if I get dressed?"

He had noticed, suddenly, a number of weapons, lying among the piles of jewels and clothing. He wanted a closer look.

"Please. By all means. How thoughtless of me not to have suggested it. But then"—the snake glanced complacently at its own scaled skin—"we tend not to think in such terms."

Haplo rummaged among the mass of clothing, found what he needed, and dressed himself. All the while his eyes were on a sword. He wondered how he could manage to pick it up without arousing the snake's ire.

"But the sword is yours, Master," said the dragon-snake calmly.

Haplo looked at it in wary astonishment.

"It is not wise to go unarmed in the presence of your enemy," the dragon-snake remarked.

Haplo lifted the sword, hefted it experimentally, liked the way it felt. Almost as if it had been made for his hand. He found a swordbelt, buckled it on, slid the weapon in its sheath. "By enemy, I take it you mean the Sartan, Royal One."

"Who else?" The dragon-snake appeared confused. Then, suddenly, it understood. "Ah, you refer to us. I should have known. You formed your opinion of us after talking to *them*." It glanced at the cave.

"Provided they told me the truth," Haplo said.

"Oh, they did. I'm certain." The dragon-snake sighed again and its sigh was echoed by its fellows. "We acted hastily and perhaps were, shall we say, overzealous in our efforts to intimidate them. But all creatures have a right to defend themselves. Is the wolf called cruel when he goes for the throat of the lion?"

Haplo grunted, glanced at the display of magical power that was manifest on the ground all around him. "You want me to believe you're frightened of a handful of elves, humans, and dwarves?"

"Not the mensch," hissed the dragon-snake. "Those who stand behind the mensch! Those who brought them here!"

"The Sartan."

"Yes! Your ancient enemy and ours."

"You're saying that the Sartan are here, on Chelestra."

"An entire city of them. Led by one whose name is not unfamiliar to you."

"Samah?" Haplo frowned. "So you said to me on board the ship, Royal One. But it can't be the same Samah, the Councillor responsible for imprisoning us—"

"The one! The same!" The dragon-snake reared up from among its coils, its red-green eyes flared. Whispering to itself, seething, it slowly calmed, settled back down. "By the way, what are you called, Patryn?"

"Haplo."

"Haplo." The snake seemed to taste the word, found it to its liking. "Then, Haplo, I will tell you how it is that this Samah has returned again to a universe he and those of his accursed race nearly destroyed.

"After the Sundering, Samah and his Council of Seven looked over the four new worlds they had created and chose the most beautiful among them on which to make their home. They brought with them their favorites among the mensch, to serve as their slaves, and founded their city of Surunan on a magically created landmass which they call the Chalice.

"Imagine their surprise when they discovered that their beautiful world was already inhabited."

"Your people, Royal One?"

The dragon-snake modestly lowered its head in acquiescence.

"But where did you come from? Who created you?"

"You did, Patryn," said the dragon-snake softly.

Haplo frowned, puzzled. But before he could question further, the dragon-snake had continued on.

"At first, we welcomed these newcomers to our world. We hoped for prosperous, peaceful interaction with them. But

Samah hated us, because he could not enslave us, as he enslaved the wretched mensch. He and the other Council members attacked us, completely without provocation. Naturally, we defended ourselves. We did not kill them, however, but sent them running back to their city in disgrace."

"You defeated Samah?" Haplo asked, dubious. "The most powerful of all the Sartan who ever lived?"

"You may have noticed a certain odd property of this seawater . . ." said the dragon snake suggestively.

"I didn't drown in it, if that's what you mean, Royal One. I can breathe it the same as air."

"I wasn't referring to that."

Haplo shook his head. "I can't think of anything else."

"Indeed?" The snake shifted its bulk slightly, almost as if it were laughing. "I would have guessed the seawater to have the same effect on the magic of both races—Sartan and Patryns. Most peculiar."

Haplo could scarcely breathe. The terrible joy that filled his being produced an actual, physical pain in his chest. He needed an outlet for his emotion, reached for some food, though he wasn't hungry.

The seawater in this world destroyed Sartan magic! And on this world, surrounded by seawater, was the Patryn's most hated enemy. Haplo lifted a wineskin, nearly dropped it. His hands shook with elation. Carefully, he laid the wineskin back down. Be calm. Be wary. Don't trust these creatures.

He tried to appear casual. He took a bite of something, not knowing or caring what. "But all this you describe must have happened many generations ago. How is it possible that Samah is alive, Royal One? Perhaps you've made a mistake."

"No mistake," said the dragon-snake. "But . . . the food. Is it to your liking? Will you have more of anything?"

Haplo hadn't tasted what he put in his mouth. "No, thank you. Please go on."

The snake obliged. "We hoped that, after we had chastised them, the Sartan would leave us alone, allow us to pursue our lives in peace. But Samah was furious at us. We had made him look the fool in the eyes of the mensch, who, seeing these god-like creatures brought so low, began to talk openly of revolt. He vowed revenge on us, no matter what the cost to his people or to the innocent mensch.

"Using their magical powers—you may guess, by the way, that the Sartan had now an extreme aversion to seawater— Samah and the Council wrenched loose the seastar from its stationary position in the center of this world. The seasun began drifting away. The water grew colder, the temperature in both their Chalice and in our seamoon began to drop. Thus, though it meant that they themselves would be forced to abandon the world, fleeing through Death's Gate, the Sartan hoped to freeze us to death.

"Of course they would have, in the process, frozen the mensch, as well. But what were a few thousand humans, dwarves, and elves, compared to the vast numbers already sacrificed to Sartan ambition during the Sundering? The mensch discovered this evil plot, however, and rebelled against their masters. They built ships and fled into the Goodsea, chasing after the seasun.

"The mensch exodus appalled and alarmed the Sartan. They didn't want this world for themselves any longer, but neither did they intend to leave it to the mensch. They swore that not one mensch should survive. At this point, we had a choice to make."

The dragon-snake sighed, raised its head, looked at its fellows with pride. "We could have gone with the mensch. They begged us to go, to protect them from whales and other fearsome creatures of the deep brought here by the Sartan to keep the mensch in line. But we knew that we were the only ones who could stand between the mensch and the fury of the Sartan. We chose to stay behind, though it meant that we must suffer.

"We saved the mensch and prevented the Sartan from fleeing through Death's Gate. The ice closed in on them and on us. They had no choice but to seek refuge in the Sleep. We hibernated, knowing that someday the seastar would drift this direction again. Our enemies would awake, and so would we."

"But why, then, Royal One, did you attack the mensch? You were once their saviors."

"Yes, but that was long, long ago. They have forgotten all about us and the sacrifice we made." The dragon-snake sighed heavily, sank back down on its coils. "I suppose that we should have taken the passage of time into account and made allowances, but we were thrilled over returning to this beautiful world and eager to make the acquaintance of the descendants of those for whom we had risked all to save.

"We came upon the mensch too suddenly, without warning. Admittedly, we are not lovely to look upon. Our smell, I am told, offends the nostrils. Our size intimidates. The mensch were horribly frightened and attacked us. Hurt by such ingratitude, we, I regret to say, fought back. Sometimes we do not know our own strength."

The dragon-snake sighed again. Its fellows, deeply affected, whispered in grief, lowered their heads into the sand.

"When we were able to view the matter in a calmer light, we at once acknowledged that much of the blame lay with us. But how could we rectify it? If we came upon the mensch again, they would only redouble their efforts to kill us. And so we decided to bring the mensch to us. One of each race, a daughter of each of the royal households. If we could convince these gentle damsels that we meant no harm, then they would return to their people, offer our apologies, and all would be well. We would all live in peace and harmony."

Gentle damsel. Grundle? Haplo chuckled to himself at the thought. But he said nothing, brushed it aside, brushed aside any doubts he might have had over the dragon-snake's veracity.

Parts of the snake's story didn't exactly fit the facts as he'd heard them from the mensch, but that didn't matter now. What mattered was a chance to strike a blow, a telling blow, at the Sartan.

"Peace and harmony are all very well, Royal One," Haplo said, watching the snake closely, feeling his way, "but the Sartan will never allow it. Once they know you have returned, they'll do their best to destroy you."

"Too true," agreed the dragon-snake. "Destroy us and enslave the mensch. But what can be done? Our numbers are few; many of us did not survive the hibernation. And the Sartan, or so we hear from our spies, the gushni,[2] are stronger than ever. They've received reinforcements through Death's Gate."

"Reinforcements." Haplo shook his head. "That's not possible . . ."

"One has come, at least." The dragon-snake spoke with conviction. "A Sartan who travels freely through Death's Gate, visiting other worlds. He disguises himself as a mensch, calls himself by a mensch name. He pretends to be bumbling and clumsy, but we know him for what he is. He is the one we call Serpent Mage. And he is far more powerful than Samah himself."

The dragon-snake's eyes narrowed. "Why do you laugh, Patryn?"

"I'm sorry, Royal One," said Haplo, grinning, "but I know this Sartan. And you don't need to worry about him. He doesn't pretend to be bumbling and clumsy. He *is* bumbling and clumsy. And he doesn't travel through Death's Gate. More likely he fell through it, by accident."

"He's not powerful?"

Haplo jerked a thumb toward the cave. "Those mensch in there are more powerful."

"You astonish me," stated the dragon-snake, and it did truly seem surprised. It cast a slit-eyed, red-green glance at its fellows. "All our information led us to believe quite the opposite. He is the Serpent Mage."

"Your information's wrong," said Haplo, shaking his head, unable to keep from laughing again at the thought. Alfred, a Serpent Mage! Whatever that was, he wasn't.

"Well, well, well. My, my, my," mused the dragon-snake. "This does require some rethinking. But, we seem to have strayed from your original point. I asked what could be done about the Sartan. You, I think, have the answer."

Haplo took several steps nearer the dragon-snake, ignoring the faint warning glow of the sigla on his skin.

---

[2] Similar in appearance to jellyfish, each has a shared intelligence with all the others, each one contains all the knowledge of the entire group. They make excellent spies, since what one learns is instantly passed on to every other gushni in Chelestra. They cannot speak and are probably linked to the dragon-snakes telepathically.

"These three races of mensch get along well together. They were, in fact, preparing to unite to go to war against you. What if we convinced them that they had a more dangerous foe?"

The dragon-snake's eyes opened wide, the red-green glow turned completely red, was blinding in its intensity. Haplo squinted against it, was forced to shield his eyes from the glare with an upraised hand.

"But these mensch are peace-loving. They won't fight."

"I have a plan, Royal One. Believe me, if it comes to their survival, they'll fight."

"I see the shape of your plan in your mind and you are right, it will work." The dragon-snake closed its eyes, lowered its head. "Truly, Haplo, you Patryns deserve to be the masters of this world. We bow before you."

The dragon-snakes all prostrated their heads in the dust, gigantic bodies writhed in homage. Haplo felt suddenly exhausted, so weary that he staggered where he stood, almost fell.

"Go, now, to your well-deserved rest," whispered the dragon-snake.

Haplo stumbled off across the sand, heading for the cave where the mensch sheltered. He could not remember ever feeling this tired before, assumed it must be a reaction to the loss of his magic. He entered the cave, cast one glance around at the mensch, assured them they were safe, then slumped to the ground, sank into a deep and dreamless sleep.

The king dragon-snake rested its head comfortably once again on its coils, red-green eyes gleamed.

CHAPTER ♦ 16

SURUNAN

CHELESTRA

♦

ALFRED, ACCOMPANIED BY THE DOG, LEFT THE COUNCIL MEETING as soon as he possibly could and began to roam about Surunan. His joy in his newfound realm had been destroyed. He looked at beauty that could no longer touch him; listened to a language that was his own, yet sounded foreign to him; felt himself a stranger in what should have been his home.

"Find Haplo," he muttered to the dog, who, hearing the beloved name, began to whine eagerly. "How do they expect me to find Haplo? And what am I to do with him if I find him?"

Distraught and confused, he wandered the streets aimlessly.

"How can I find Haplo when even you can't find your master?" he demanded of the dog, who gazed up sympathetically but was unable to supply an answer.

Alfred groaned. "Why don't they understand? Why can't they just let me alone?"

He stopped, suddenly, looked around. He had traveled farther than he had intended, farther than he'd ever been before. He wondered bleakly if his body—as usual—had decided to run away and had not bothered to inform his brain of the decision.

" 'We only want to ask the Patryn questions.' Samah's words, and the Councillor wouldn't lie to me. He *couldn't* lie. One Sartan can never lie to another.

"Why, then," Alfred asked the dog unhappily, "don't I trust Samah? Why do I trust him less than I trust Haplo?"

The dog was unable to say.

"Perhaps Samah's right." Alfred continued, a prey to misery. "Perhaps the Patryn *has* corrupted me. I wonder if they have the power to do that? I never heard of a Sartan falling under a Patryn's enchantment, but I suppose it's possible." He sighed, passed his hand over his bald head. "Especially with me."

The dog saw that Alfred was not, after all, going to produce Haplo on the spot. Panting in the heat, it flopped down at the Sartan's feet.

Alfred was tired and hot himself. He looked about wearily for a place to rest. Not too distant stood a smallish square building made of the eternal white marble that the Sartan loved and which Alfred was beginning to find a trifle boring. A covered porch, supported by innumerable white marble columns, surrounded it, gave it the stolid, formal look of a public building, not the more relaxed air of a private residence.

Strange that it should stand so far from the other public buildings, located in the heart of the city, Alfred thought as he approached it. The cool shadowy portico offered a welcome respite from the bright sunlight that shone interminably on the Sartan city. The dog trotted along after him.

Reaching the porch, Alfred was disappointed to find no benches where he could sit and rest. Assuming that there must be some inside, he waited until his eyes had adjusted to the shadowy interior, then read the runes inscribed upon the large, bronze double doors.

He was puzzled and considerably startled to find runes of warding. The sigla weren't very strong, nothing like the ones that had tried to bar their way into the Chamber of the Damned on Abarrach.[1] These runes were far milder, advised Alfred in a friendly fashion that the nice, polite, and proper thing for him to do would be to leave. If he had business inside, he was told to seek permission to enter from the Council.

Any other Sartan—Samah, for example, or Orla—would have smiled, nodded, and immediately turned around and left. Alfred started to do just that. He fully intended to do just that—turn around and leave.

In fact, half of him did turn around. The other half, unfortu-

[1] *Fire Sea*, vol. 3 of *The Death Gate Cycle*.

nately, chose that moment to decide to open the door a crack and take a peep inside, with the result that Alfred stumbled over himself, fell through the door, and landed flat on his face in the dust.

A game, thought the dog, and bounded in after the Sartan. The animal began licking Alfred's face and biting playfully at his ears.

Alfred endeavored to induce the playful animal to remove itself from his person. Kicking and flailing on the dust-covered floor, he accidentally struck the door with his foot. The door swung shut, closing with a boom that sent dust flying into the air. Both Alfred and the dog began to sneeze.

Alfred took advantage of the dog's preoccupation with the dust up its nose to rise hurriedly to his feet. He was uneasy without quite knowing why. Perhaps it was the absence of light. The building's interior wasn't cloaked with the absolute blackness of night, but it was shrouded in a murky duskiness that distorted shapes, made the ordinary seem strange and consequently ominous.

"We'd better leave," said Alfred to the dog, who, rubbing its nose with its paws, sneezed again and seemed to think this an excellent idea.

The Sartan groped his way through the gloom to the double doors, started to open them, discovered that there was no handle. He stared at the entrance, scratching his head.

The doors had shut completely, not a crack remained. It was as if they had become part of the wall. Alfred was quite perplexed. No building had ever done this to him before. He peered intently at where the doors had been, expecting sigla to light up, advising him that he was wrongfully attempting to enter an egress and suggesting that he take the back stairs.

Nothing of the sort appeared. Nothing of any sort appeared.

Alfred, uneasiness growing, sang a few runes in a quavering voice, runes that should have opened the door, provided a way out.

The runes shimmered, then faded. Negating magic at work on the door. Whatever spell he cast would instantly be countered by a negative spell of the same power.

Alfred groped about in the dusky shadows, searching for a way out. He stepped on the dog's tail, bruised his shin on a marble bench, and scraped the flesh off his fingers trying to open a crack that he thought might be another door, but turned out to be a flaw in one of the marble blocks.

Apparently whoever came into this building was meant to stay in this building. Odd. Extremely odd. He sat down on the bench to consider the matter.

Admittedly, the sigla on the outside had requested that he not go in, but it had been a request, not a prohibition. Also admittedly, he had no business inside here, nor had he obtained permission from the Council to enter.

"Yes, I'm in the wrong," he said to the dog, petting it to keep it near him, finding comfort in its presence, "but I can't be too wrong, otherwise they would have laid far stronger warding spells on the door that would definitely keep people out. And obviously people come in here, or at least they did once long ago.

"And because it doesn't say anything about there being another way out," he continued, thinking, "that must mean that there is another way out and everyone who came in knew about it. The way out was common knowledge and therefore they didn't bother to put up directions. I don't know about it, of course, because I'm a stranger, but I should be able to find it. Perhaps there's a door on the side or around back."

Feeling more cheerful, Alfred sang a light-shedding rune that appeared in the air over his head (absolutely fascinating the dog) and headed for the building's interior.

Now that he could see clearly, Alfred was able to get a much better picture of his surroundings. He was in a hallway that ran the length of the building's front and, from what he could tell by advancing to the end, then turned a sharp right angle, continued on down the side. Dim light filtered in through several skylights in the ceiling—skylights that, observed Alfred, could use a good cleaning.

He was reminded of one of Bane's toys—a box that had another, smaller box nesting inside it, and another smaller box inside that.

A door in the center of the wall opposite the doors through which he had come offered entry into the next smaller of the boxes. Alfred studied this door and the walls around it carefully, telling himself that if there were runes of warding upon it, he would heed their warning. The door was smooth, however, had no advice or help to offer.

Alfred pushed on it gingerly.

The door opened, swinging easily on silent hinges. He entered, keeping the dog close at hand, and propped the door open with his shoe, when it seemed likely to shut behind him. Hobbling, one shoe on and one off, he entered the room and stood looking around in amazement.

"A library," he said to himself. "Why, it's nothing more than a library."

Alfred wasn't quite sure what he'd expected (vague thoughts of nasty beasts with long, sharp teeth had been lurking in the back of his mind), but it wasn't this. The room was huge, open, airy. A large skylight of frosted glass softened the glare of the sun, provided light to read by that was also easy on the eyes. Wooden tables and chairs filled the central portion of the room. The walls were honeycombed with large holes bored into the marble, and in each of these holes was housed neat stacks of gold scroll tubes.

There was no dust at all in this room; strong runes of preserving and protection adorned the walls, to prevent the scrolls from deteriorating.

Alfred spotted a door on the far wall.

"Ah, the way out."

He headed for it, moving slowly in order to make his way through the maze of tables and do as little damage to them and himself as possible. This proved difficult, for he discovered, as he traversed the room, that the various scroll compartments were labeled and catalogued for ease of access, and his attention kept wandering.

The Ancient World. He read the various categories: Art . . . Architecture . . . Entomology . . . Dinosaurs . . . Fossils . . . Machines . . . Psychology . . . Religion . . . Space Program (Space? What did that mean? Empty space? Open space?) . . . Technology . . . War . . .

Alfred's footsteps lagged, came to a stumbling halt. He gazed about him in ever-increasing awe. *Nothing more than a library,* he'd said to himself. What a fool! This was *the* library. The Great Library of the Sartan. His people on Arianus had assumed it was lost in the Sundering. Alfred looked to another wall: *The History of the Sartan.* And, below that, much less extensive, though with numerous subcategories: *The History of the Patryns.*

Alfred sat down rather suddenly. Fortunately, a chair happened to be in the vicinity or he would have fallen to the floor. All thoughts of leaving vanished from his head. What wealth! What richness! What fabulous treasure! The story of a world he knew only in his dreams, a world that had been whole, then was wrenched violently apart. The story of his people and that of their enemy. Undoubtedly, the events that led up to the Sundering, Council meetings, discussions . . .

"I could spend days here," Alfred said to himself, dazed and happy, happier than he could remember being in vast eons of time. "Days! Years!"

He felt moved to express his homage for this vault of knowledge, for those who had kept it safe, perhaps sacrificed objects precious to them personally to save what would be of immense value to future generations. Rising to his feet, he was about to perform a solemn dance (much to the dog's amusement) when a voice, dry and brittle, shattered his euphoria.

"I might have known. What are you doing here?"

The dog leapt up, hackles bristling, began barking frantically at nothing.

Alfred, the very breath scared out of him, clutched weakly at a table and stared around him, eyes bulging.

"Who . . . who's there? . . ." he gasped.

One figure, then two, materialized, in front of him.

"Samah!" Alfred heaved a sigh of relief, collapsed into a chair. "Ramu . . ." Removing a handkerchief from a shabby pocket, Alfred mopped his head.

The head of the Council and his son, faces grim and accusing, came to stand in front of Alfred.

"I repeat—what are you doing here?"

Alfred looked up, began to tremble in every limb. The sweat chilled on his body. Samah was obviously, dangerously, angry.

"I . . . I was looking for the way out . . ." replied Alfred, meekly.

"Yes, I imagine you were." The Councillor's tone was cold, biting. Alfred shrank away from it. "What else were you looking for?"

"N-nothing . . . I—"

"Then why come here, to the library? Shut that beast up!" Samah snapped.

Alfred reached out a shaking hand, grabbed hold of the dog by the scruff of its neck, and pulled it near. "It's all right, boy," he said in a low voice, though he wondered why the dog should believe him when he didn't believe himself.

The dog quieted, at Alfred's touch; its barking changed to a rumbling growl, deep in its chest. But it never took its eyes off Samah and, occasionally, when it thought it could get away with it, its lip curled, showing a fine set of sharp teeth.

"Why did you come to the library? What were you looking for?" Samah demanded again. He emphasized his words with a blow of his hand upon the table, causing both it and Alfred to shiver.

"It was an accident! I . . . I came here by accident. That is," Alfred amended, withering beneath Samah's burning gaze, "I came to this building on purpose. I was hot . . . you see . . . and the shade . . . I mean, I didn't know it was a library . . . and I didn't know I wasn't supposed to be here . . ."

"There are runes of prohibition on the door. Or at least there were, the last time I looked," Samah stated. "Has something happened to them?"

"N-no," Alfred admitted, gulping. "I saw them. I only meant to take a quick peep inside. Curiosity. It's a terrible failing of mine. But . . . well . . . I tripped, you see, and fell through the door. Then the dog jumped on me and my feet must have . . . that is, I think I probably . . . I'm not sure how, but I guess I . . . kicked the door shut," he finished miserably.

"Accidentally?"

"Oh, yes, of course!" Alfred babbled. "Quite . . . by accident." His mouth was drying up. He was drying up. He coughed. "And . . . and then, you see, I couldn't find the way out. So I came in here, searching for it—"

"There is no way out," Samah said.

"There isn't?" Alfred blinked like a startled owl.

"No. Not unless one has the key-sigil. And I am the only one with the key. You obtain it from me."

"I—I'm sorry," Alfred stammered. "I was just curious. I didn't mean any harm."

"Curiosity—a mensch failing. I might have known you would

be afflicted by it. Ramu, check to see that nothing has been disturbed."

Ramu hastened off. Alfred kept his head lowered, his eyes looking anywhere, at anything, to avoid meeting Samah's. He glanced at the dog, still growling. He glanced at Ramu, noted absently that he went straight for one certain compartment under *History of the Sartan* and examined it carefully, even going to the trouble of magically checking to find out if any of Alfred's presence lingered in the vicinity.

Acutely wretched and unhappy, Alfred thought nothing of this at the time, though he did note that Ramu spent far less time checking the other compartments, barely giving most of them a glance, until he came to the ones marked *Patryns*. These, too, he inspected thoroughly.

"He hasn't been near them," he reported to Samah. "He probably didn't have time to do much."

"I wasn't going to do anything!" Alfred protested. He was beginning to lose his fear. The more he thought about it, he decided he had a right to be angry at this treatment. He drew himself up, faced Samah with dignity. "What do you think I was going to do? I entered a library! And since when is the collected knowledge and wisdom of my people forbidden to me? And why is it forbidden to others?"

A thought occurred to him. "And what are *you* doing here? Why did *you* come, unless you knew I was here . . . You *did* know I was here! You have some sort of alarm—"

"Please, calm yourself, Brother," Samah said soothingly, his anger seeming to suddenly evaporate, like rain when the sun comes out. He went so far as to start to lay a conciliatory hand on Alfred's arm—a move the dog didn't like, apparently, for it thrust its body protectively between Alfred and the head of the Council.

Samah cast the dog a cold glance, withdrew his hand. "You have a bodyguard, it seems."

Alfred, flushing, attempted to shove the animal to one side. "I'm sorry. He—"

"No, no, Brother. It is I who should be making the apology." Samah shook his head, sighed ruefully. "Orla tells me I am working too hard. My nerves are frayed. I overreacted. I forgot that, being a stranger, you had no way of knowing our rules concerning the library. It is, of course, open to all Sartan.

"But, as you can judge"—he waved his hand toward the ancient-history section—"some of these scrolls are old and very fragile. It would never do, for example, to permit small children to get hold of them. Or those who might be browsing through out of idle curiosity. Such people, inadvertently, of course, and meaning no harm, might yet do irreparable damage. I don't think you can blame us, if we like to know who enters our library?"

No, Alfred had to admit, that sounded reasonable enough. But Samah wasn't the type of man to rush here because he feared children were smearing grape jelly on his precious manuscripts. And he *had* been afraid. Angry and afraid, his anger covering his fear. Alfred's eyes, of their own accord, strayed to that compartment, the first compartment Ramu had checked.

"Serious scholars are welcome, certainly," Samah was continuing. "They have only to come before the Council and request the key."

Samah was watching him closely. Alfred tried to stop his eyes from looking at the compartment, tried to keep them focused on Samah, but it was a struggle. They kept wanting to dart in that direction. Alfred wrenched them back. The strain was too much. His eyelids began to twitch, he started to blink uncontrollably.

Samah stopped talking, stared at him. "Are you well?"

"Forgive me," Alfred murmured, shading his eyes with his hand. "A nervous disorder."

The Councillor frowned. Sartan did not suffer from nervous disorders. "Do you understand, Brother, why we like to monitor the comings and goings of all who enter?" he asked somewhat tightly. It was obvious his patience was wearing thin.

Do I understand why a library turns into a trap, sounds an alarm, and holds those who enter hostage until the head of the Council comes to interrogate them? No, thought Alfred, I really don't understand that at all.

But he only nodded and mumbled something that might have been certainly he understood.

"Come, come!" Samah said, with a forced smile. "An accident, as you say. No harm done. I am certain you are sorry for what you did. And Ramu and I are sorry for nearly scaring you to death. And now, it is dinnertime. We will tell our tale to Orla. I'm afraid, Ramu, your mother will have a laugh over this mistake at our expense."

Ramu gave a sickly chuckle, looked anything but jocular.

"Please, be seated, Brother," Samah said, gesturing to a chair. "I will go and open the way out. The runes are complex. It takes some time to render them and you appear to be fatigued. No need to stand around waiting. Ramu will remain here to keep you company in my absence."

Ramu will remain to make certain I don't spy on you, discover the way out. Alfred sank down into the chair, placed his hand on the dog's head, stroked the silky ears. I might be doing more harm than good, he considered, but it seems to me that I have a right to ask.

"Samah," he called, halting the head of the Council on his way to the far door. "Now that I know the rules of the library, could I have your permission to enter? The mensch are somewhat a hobby of mine, you see. I once did a study on the dwarves of Arianus. I note that you have several texts . . ."

He knew the answer, saw it in Samah's eyes.

Alfred's voice dried up. His mouth opened and closed several times, but nothing more followed.

Samah waited patiently until he was certain Alfred was finished.

"Certainly you may study here, Brother. We would be most happy to make any and all documents relative to your work available to you. But not now."

"Not now," Alfred repeated.

"No, I'm afraid not. The Council wants to inspect the library and make certain that no damage was done during the long Sleep. Until we have time to devote to this task, I recommended to the Council that the library be closed. And we must take care that, from now on, no one enters 'by accident.' "

The Councillor turned upon his heel and left, disappearing out the door on the far wall that opened to a spoken sigil, a rune uttered in a voice soft and low. The door shut behind him.

Alfred heard, beyond it, the sound of chanting, but he was unable to distinguish any of the words.

Ramu sat down across from Alfred and began to make friendly overtures to the dog; overtures that were coldly rebuffed.

Alfred's eyes slid, once more, to the forbidden scroll compartment.

CHAPTER ♦ 17

GARGAN

CHELESTRA

♦

WE ARE HOME. HOME!

I am torn between joy and sadness, for a terrible tragedy occurred while we were gone . . . But I'll write down all, everything in its proper time and place.

As I work on this, I'm sitting in my room. Around me are all my dear possessions, just the way I left them. This astonished me beyond words. Dwarves are very practical-minded about death, unlike two other races I could mention. When a dwarf dies, his family and friends hold a night of mourning for their loss and a day of celebration for the dead one's gain in now being a part of the One. Following that, all the dwarf's possessions are distributed among family and friends. His room is cleaned out and another dwarf moves in.[1]

I had assumed that the custom would have been followed in my case and was prepared for the fact that Cousin Fricka would, by now, be ensconced in my room. In fact, I don't mind admitting that I was looking forward to bouncing my obnoxious relative and her curly side whiskers out the door and down the stairs.

---

[1]Living space is a problem for dwarves on the seamoons. Since dwarves prefer to dwell below ground level, they build their homes in tunnels beneath the seamoon's landmass. Unfortunately, due to the fact that the inner core of the moon is, in reality, a living being, the dwarves found themselves unable to go beyond a certain point. The dwarves don't know the moon is alive; they struck a protective mass through which they could not penetrate.

However, it seems that my mother could not get it into her head that I was truly dead. She steadfastly refused to believe it, although Aunt Gertrude (so my father told me) actually went so far as to hint that my mother had lost her mind. At which point, according to my father, my mother decided to demonstrate her skill in ax-throwing, offering in a rather vigorous and alarming fashion to "part Gertrude's hair" or words to that effect.

While my mother was hauling the battle-ax down from its place on the wall, my father mentioned casually to my aunt that while my mother's throwing arm was still strong, her aim was not what it had been in their youth. Aunt Gertrude remembered suddenly that she had business elsewhere. She pried Fricka out of my room (probably with a winch) and they flounced off.

But I've wandered down a side tunnel, as the saying goes. The last I wrote, we were heading in our ship toward certain death and now we're home safe and sound, and I really have no idea how or why.

No heroic battles in the dragon-snake cave. Just a lot of talk in a language none of us understood. Our ship broke up. We had to swim to the surface. The dragon-snakes found us, and instead of murdering us, they gave us presents and sent us into a cave. Then Haplo stayed up all night talking to them. When he finally came back, he said he was tired and didn't want to talk and he'd explain everything some other time. But he assured us that we were safe and told us we could sleep securely and that in the morning we'd be going home!

We were astounded and discussed it quietly (Alake made us whisper so as not to disturb Haplo). We couldn't unravel the tangle, however, and finally, being exhausted ourselves, we fell asleep.

The next morning, more food appeared, along with more presents. And, peeping out of the cave, I saw to my astonishment that our submersible, good as new, was moored on the shore. There was no sign of the dragon-snakes.

"The dragons fixed your ship," said Haplo, between mouthfuls of food. "We'll use it to sail back home."

He was eating something Alake had cooked and she was sitting beside him, watching him with adoring eyes.

"They did it for you," she said softly. "You saved us, as you promised. And now you're taking us home. You will be a hero to our people. Whatever you want will be yours. Whatever you ask for will be granted."

She was hoping, of course, that he'd ask to marry the chieftain's daughter—meaning her.

Haplo shrugged and said he hadn't done all that much. But I could tell he was pleased with himself. I noted that the blue marks had started coming back on his skin. Also that he took extreme care to avoid touching or even looking at a large jug full of water I'd brought in to wash the sleep out of my eyes.

I whispered to Devon, "I wonder where the bitter pill is in all this candy."[2]

"Only think, Grundle," he whispered back, sighing rapturously, "in a few days I'll be with Sabia!"

He hadn't heard a word I'd said! And I'll wager he hadn't heard Haplo either, for that matter. Which just goes to show you how love—at least among humans and elves—can addle the brain. Thank the One we dwarves are different! I love Hartmut down to the last strand of hair in his beard, but I'd be ashamed to let my feelings reduce my mental capacities to the consistency of gruel.

But, there, I shouldn't talk that way. Now that—

No, I'm getting ahead of myself.

"All right, but remember, no one ever gets something for nothing," I said, but I said it into my whiskers. I was afraid that if Alake heard me, she'd scratch my eyes out.

As it was, I think Haplo did hear me. He has sharp ears, that one. I was glad. Let him know that one of us isn't planning to swallow this without chewing on it first. He glanced at me and kind of half-smiled in that dark way of his that gives me the shivers.

When he finished eating, he said we were free to leave. We could take all the food and presents with us. At this, I saw even Alake was offended.

"No amount of gold or precious jewels can bring back the people those monsters murdered, or make up for what we have

---

[2] A reference to the elven practice of hiding bad-tasting medicine in sugared rose petals.

suffered," she said, casting a disdainful glance at the mounds of riches and wealth.

"I would sooner toss such blood money in the Goodsea, except it might poison the fish," Devon said angrily.

"Suit yourselves." Haplo shrugged again. "But you might need it, when you sail to your new homeland."

We looked at each other. We'd been so frightened and worried about the dragon-snakes, we'd completely forgotten about another danger that loomed over our people—the loss of the seasun.

"Will the dragon-snakes let us build more sun-chasers?" I asked dubiously.

"Better than that. They've offered to use their magic to fix the ones they destroyed. And they've given me information about this new homeland, important information."

We badgered him with questions, but Haplo refused to answer, saying that it would not be proper to tell us before discussing a matter of this importance with our parents. We were forced to admit he was right.

Alake looked at the gold, said it was a shame it should go to waste. Devon remarked that several bolts of the silken fabric were Sabia's favorite colors. I'd already pocketed some of the jewels (as I wrote earlier, we dwarves are a practical lot), but I gladly took a few more, just so the others wouldn't think I was being snooty.

We loaded ourselves, the presents, and the food on board the submersible. I checked the ship over thoroughly. Admittedly, the dragon-snakes were strong on magic, but I mistrusted that they knew anything about shipbuilding. However, the snakes appeared to have put it back together exactly the way it was before they broke it and I decided it was safe to sink in.

We each took up residence in our old rooms. Everything was as it had been when we left. I even found this—my journal, exactly where I left it. No water damage. Not a drop of ink smeared. Astounding! It made me kind of queasy. I wondered, more than once on that journey, if it had all really happened or if it had only been a strange and terrible dream.

The ship launched itself, under the same magical power as before, and we were headed back home.

I'm certain the journey took the same amount of time going as coming, but it seemed far longer to us. We laughed and talked excitedly about the first things we'd do when we reached our homelands and how we'd probably be considered heroes and what everyone would make of Haplo.

We spent a lot of time talking about Haplo. At least Alake and I did. She came into my cabin quite late the first night of our trip back home. It was that quiet period just before you go to bed when the aching for home comes over you so badly sometimes that it makes you think you'll die of it. I was feeling the same way myself, and I must admit that maybe a tear or two had trickled into my whiskers when I heard Alake's gentle tap on my door.

"It's me, Grundle. Can I talk to you? Or are you sleeping?"

"If I was, I'm not now," I told her grumpily, to hide the fact that I'd been crying. For all I knew, she'd dose me with herbs or something.

I opened the door. Alake came in and sat on the bed. I took one look at her—she was shy and proud and fluttery and happy—and I knew what this conversation was going to be about.

She sat on the bed, twisting the rings on her fingers. (I saw that she'd forgotten to take off her funeral jewelry. We dwarves aren't particularly superstitious, but if there was ever a bad omen, that was it. I meant to tell her, but just as I was about to say something she started to talk, and I never had the chance.)

"Grundle," she said, making up her mind to astonish me. "I'm in love."

I decided to amuse myself a little. It's fun to tease Alake, because she takes everything so seriously.

"I'm sure I wish you two all the best," I said slowly, stroking my whiskers, "but how do you think Sabia will take it?"

"Sabia?" Alake was startled. "Why, I suppose she'll be happy for me. Why shouldn't she?"

"She's unselfish. We all know that. And she loves you dearly, Alake, but she's pretty fond of Devon, too, and I don't think—"

"Devon!" Alake could barely speak for shock. "Do you . . . Did you think I meant I was in love with Devon?"

"Who else?" I asked as innocently as possible.

"Devon's very nice," Alake was going on, "and he's been very kind and helpful. And I will always think of him with the highest regard, but I could never fall in love with him. After all, he's little more than a boy."

A boy who's about one hundred Times older than you, I could have said, but I kept my mouth shut. Humans tend to be touchy about their age.

"No," Alake continued softly, her eyes glowing like candlelight at dusk, "I'm in love with a man. Grundle . . ." She gulped, swallowed, then said, in a rush, "It's Haplo!"

Of course, she expected me to fly backward around the room in shock and was considerably put out when I didn't.

"Humpf," was all I said.

"You're not surprised?"

"Surprised! Try painting 'I love you' in white paint across your forehead next time," I suggested.

"Oh, dear. Has it been that obvious? Do you . . . do you think *he* knows? It would be dreadful if he did."

Alake glanced at me sidelong, pretending to be afraid, but I could tell that deep down she was hoping I'd say, "Yes, of course, he knows."

Which I could have said truthfully, because the man would have to be blind, deaf, and dumb and a fool on top of it not to have known. I could have said this and it would have made Alake happy, but, of course, I didn't. It was all wrong and I knew it and I knew Alake would get hurt and the whole thing made me cross.

"He's old enough to be your father," I pointed out.

"He is not! And what if he is?" Alake argued, with the sort of logic one comes to expect from humans. "I've never met another man as noble and brave and strong and handsome. He stood there alone, Grundle. In front of those horrible creatures, naked, no weapons, not even his magic.

"You see, I know about the water and how it affects his magic, so don't say anything to me about that!" she added defiantly. "We humans can't do rune-magic ourselves, but our legends tell about people who could once, long ago. Haplo obviously wants to hide his power, and so I've said nothing.

"He was prepared to die for us, Grundle."

(No use my saying a word. She wouldn't have heard me.)

"How could I *not* love him? And then, to see those dreadful dragon-snakes bow down to him! He was magnificent! And now they're sending us home, giving us gifts, promising us a new homeland! And all because of Haplo."

"That may be," I said, feeling crosser than ever because I was forced to admit that what she said was true, "but what is he getting out of this? Have you asked yourself that? What does he mean, coming around asking me how many men my father has in his army and asking Devon if he thinks the elves would fight if they had to and whether or not they still remembered how to make magical weapons and wanting to know if your Coven could persuade the dolphins and whales to be on our side if it came to war?"

It occurs to me that I have forgotten to mention that Haplo had been asking those very questions of us that day.

"Grundle, you are mean-spirited and ungrateful!" Alake cried, and burst into tears.

I hadn't meant to make her cry. I felt about as low as a dragon-snake's belly. Going over to her, I patted her hand.

"I'm sorry," I said awkwardly.

"I asked him why he wanted to know such things," Alake continued, between sobs, "and he said that we should always be prepared for the worst and though this new homeland might look like a perfect place, it might be dangerous . . ." She stopped to wipe her nose.

I said I understood, which I did. What Haplo said made sense. What he said always made sense. And that made this nagging, rotten feeling of distrust and suspicion inside me all the harder to bear. I apologized again, and teased Alake until she cheered up and dried her eyes.

But dwarves are always truthful, and I couldn't help but tell her, "The only reason I said those things is that . . . well . . . it's just that . . . Haplo doesn't love you, Alake."

I cringed, waiting for another storm. To my surprise, however, Alake was quite calm. She even smiled, sadly, but it was a smile.

"Oh, I know that, Grundle. How could I expect him to love me? He must have thousands of women longing for him."

I thought I should encourage this line of thinking.

"Yes, and maybe he's got a wife somewhere—"

"He doesn't," Alake said quickly, too quickly. She looked down at her hands. "I asked him. He said he'd never found the right one, yet. I'd love to be the right one for him, Grundle. But I know I'm not worthy now. Perhaps someday I will be, if I keep trying."

She looked up at me, her eyes shining with her tears, and she was so lovely and seemed older and more mature than I'd ever known her and she glowed with a kind of inner light.

I said, then and there, that if love could do that for her then it must not be bad, no matter what happened. Besides, maybe when we reach home, Haplo will leave, go back to wherever it is he came from. After all, what could he possibly want with us? But I kept this thought to myself.

We hugged each other and had a good cry and I didn't say anything else awful about Haplo. Devon heard us and came in and Alake broke down and told him and he said he thought love was the most wonderful, beautiful thing in the whole world and we talked about Sabia and then they both made me confess that I wasn't a stranger to love myself and I broke down and told them about Hartmut and we all laughed and all cried and couldn't wait to get home.

Which made what happened when we got there all the more terrible.

I've been putting off writing this. I wasn't certain I could do it, for one thing. It makes me so terribly sad. But I've told everything and I can't very well go on with this story and leave out the most important part.

Being saved from the dragons and returning safely to our homelands would constitute a happy ending in most tavern tales I've heard. But the ending wasn't happy. And I have a feeling it isn't the end, yet, either.

The moment our submersible left the dragon-snakes' lair, we were besieged by—what else—a bunch of pesky dolphins. They wanted to know everything, all about what had happened, how we'd escaped. We'd barely told them before they swam off, eager to be the first to spread the news. There never was a more gossip-loving fish.

At least our parents would hear the good news and have time to recover from their initial shock at learning we were still alive and well. We started arguing among ourselves, trying to decide which of us got to go home first, but that was soon settled. The dolphins returned with a message saying that we were to meet our parents together on Elmas, the elven seamoon.

This suited us fine. To be honest, we were a bit nervous, now, as to our parents' reaction. We knew they'd be happy to have us back again, but after the kisses and tears we figured we could expect a severe scolding, if not worse. We had, after all, disobeyed their orders and run off without thinking of the suffering and misery we'd cause.

We even went so far as to mention this to Haplo, hinting that he would do us another great service if he would stay with us and smooth things over with our mothers and fathers.

He only grinned and said he'd protected us from the dragon-snakes, but when it came to parental wrath, we were on our own.

But we weren't thinking about stern lectures and punishment when the submersible landed and the hatch opened and we saw our parents standing there, waiting for us. My father took me in his arms and held me close and I saw, for the first time in my life, tears in his eyes. I would have listened to the sternest lecture, then and there, and loved every word.

We introduced them to Haplo. (The dolphins had, of course, already told our parents how he had saved us.) Our parents were grateful, but it was obvious that all of them were a little overawed by the man and his blue-marked skin and his air of quiet self-assurance. They managed to get out only a few, broken words of gratitude, which he accepted with a smile and a shrug, saying that we'd rescued him from the sea and that he'd been happy to return the favor. He said nothing more, and our parents were glad to turn back to us.

For a while, it was all embraces and words of affection. Devon's parents were there, waiting for their son. They were as glad to have him back as any of the other parents, but I saw, when I was in shape to see anything, that they still seemed sad, when they should have been overjoyed. The elven king was there, too, to welcome Devon, but Sabia wasn't.

Then I noticed, for the first time, that her father was dressed in white—the elven color of mourning. I saw all the elves around us—and there were many, waiting to welcome us—were clad in white, something that happened only when one of the royal family has died.

A chill constricted my heart. I looked at my father with what must have been a wild and terror-stricken expression, because he only shook his head and put his finger to my lips, to silence my questions.

Alake had been asking for Sabia. Her eyes met mine, and they were wide with fear. We both looked at Devon. Blind with joy, his vision clouded by rainbows, he hadn't seen a thing. He broke free of his parents' embrace (was it my imagination or were they trying to hold him back?) and went to the elven king.

"Where is Sabia, Sire?" Devon asked. "Is she mad at me for striking her? I'll make it up to her, I promise! Tell her to come out . . ."

The One lifted the clouds from his eyes. He saw the white clothing, saw the elven king's face scarred and ravaged by grief, saw the petals of white flowers that had been scattered over the Goodsea.

"Sabia!" Devon shouted, and he started to run toward the coral castle that stood shimmering behind us.

Eliason caught hold of him.

Devon struggled violently, then he collapsed in the man's arms. "No!" he cried, sobbing. "No! I never meant . . . I wanted to save her . . ."

"I know, my son, I know," Eliason said, stroking Devon's hair, soothing him as he might have soothed a child of his own. "It wasn't your fault. Your intentions were the best, the noblest. Sabia"—he could not speak her name without a catch in his throat, but he mastered himself—"Sabia is with the One. She is at peace. We must take comfort in that. And now, I think it is time for the families to be alone together."

Eliason took charge of Haplo with the gracious dignity and politeness that is characteristic of the elves, no matter what personal sorrows afflict them. Unhappy king. How he must have longed to be alone with his child!

Once we were inside, in a new part of the castle that had grown during our absence, my mother explained to me what had happened.

"The moment she woke up, Sabia knew what Devon had done. She knew he had sacrificed his own life for her and that his death would be a terrible one. From then on," my mother said, wiping her eyes on the hem of her sleeve, "the poor girl lost all interest in living. She refused to eat, refused to leave her bed. She drank water only when her father sat beside her and held the glass to her lips. She wouldn't talk to anyone, but lay for hours, staring out her window. When she slept at all, her sleep was broken by horrible dreams. They said her cries could be heard throughout the castle.

"And then one day, she seemed to be better. She got up out of bed, dressed herself in the dress she'd been wearing when you three were last together, and went about the castle singing. Her songs were sad and strange and no one liked to hear them, but they hoped this meant she was well again. Alas, it meant quite the opposite.

"That night, she asked her duenna to fetch her something to eat. The woman, thrilled that Sabia was hungry, hurried off, unsuspecting. When she returned, Sabia was gone. Frightened, the duenna woke the king. They searched."

My mother shook her head, unable to continue for her tears. Finally, she had recourse to the sleeve again, and went on.

"They found her body on the terrace where we met that day, the terrace where you overheard us talking. She'd thrown herself out a window. She was lying on almost the very same place where the elf messenger died."

I'm going to have to end this for now. I can't go on without crying.

The One guards your sleep now, Sabia. Your terrible dreams are at an end.

CHAPTER ♦ 18

SURUNAN

CHELESTRA

♦

THE LIBRARY OF THE SARTAN HAUNTED ALFRED, PURSUED HIM LIKE the specter in some old wives' tale. It reached out its cold hand to touch him and wake him in the night, crooking a beckoning finger, tried to draw him to his doom.

"Nonsense!" he would say to himself and, turning over, would attempt to banish the ghost by burying it in slumber.

This worked for the night, but the shade did not disappear with morning's light. Alfred sat at breakfast, pretending to eat, when in reality all he could think about was Ramu examining that one compartment. What was in it that was so closely guarded?

"Curiosity. Nothing more than curiosity." Alfred scolded himself. "Samah is right. I've lived around the mensch far too long. I'm like that girl in the ghost stories Bane's nurse used to tell him. 'You may go into any room in the castle except the locked room at the top of the stairs.' And is the fool girl satisfied with all the other one hundred and twenty-four rooms in the castle? No, she can't eat or sleep or have any peace at all until she's broken into the room at the top of the stairs.

"That's all I'm doing to myself. The room at the top of the stairs. I'll stay away from it. I won't think about it. I'll be satisfied with the other rooms, rooms that are filled with so much wealth. And I will be happy. I *will* be happy."

But he wasn't. He grew more unhappy with each day that passed.

He attempted to keep his restlessness hidden from his host and hostess and succeeded, or so Alfred fondly imagined. Samah watched him with the attentiveness of a Geg watching a leaky steam valve on the Kicksey-winsey, wondering when it's going to erupt. Intimidated by Samah's awe-inspiring and daunting presence, humbled by the fact that he knew he'd been in the wrong, Alfred was cringing and subdued in the Councillor's presence, barely able to lift his eyes to Samah's stern and implacable face.

When Samah was gone from home, however—and he was gone a great deal of the time on Council business—Alfred relaxed. Orla was generally on hand to keep him company, and the haunting spirit was not nearly as bothersome when he was with Orla as it was during the infrequent times when he was on his own. It never occurred to Alfred to wonder that he was rarely left alone anymore or to think it odd that Orla herself wasn't involved in Council business. He knew only that she was sweet to devote so much time to him—a thought that made him feel all the more wretched on the occasions when the ghost of the library reappeared.

Alfred and Orla were seated on her terrace, Orla busying herself by softly singing protective runes on the fabric of one of Samah's robes. Chanting the words, she traced the patterns with her deft fingers on the cloth, putting her love and concern for her husband into each sigil that sprang up at her command.

Alfred watched sadly. Never in his life had a woman sung the protective runes for him. One never would now. Or, at least, not the one he wanted. He was suddenly wildly and insanely jealous of Samah. Alfred didn't like the way the Councillor treated his wife—so cold and unresponsive. He knew Orla was hurt by it, he'd witnessed her silent suffering. No, Samah wasn't good enough for her.

And I am? he asked dolefully.

Orla glanced up at him, smiling, prepared to continue their conversation on the healthy state of her rosebushes.

Alfred, caught, was unable to hide the images of the ugly, tangled, thorny vines that were twisting around inside him— and it was painfully obvious he hadn't been meditating on the roses.

Orla's smile faded. Sighing, she laid aside her work.

"I wish you wouldn't do this to me . . . or to yourself."

"I'm sorry," said Alfred, looking and feeling wretched.

His hand went to pet the dog, who, seeing his friend's unhappiness, offered sympathy by laying its head on his knee.

"I must be an extraordinarily wicked person. I'm well aware that no Sartan should have such improper thoughts. As your husband says, I've been corrupted by being around mensch too long."

"Perhaps it wasn't the mensch," suggested Orla softly, with a glance at the dog.

"You mean Haplo." Alfred stroked back the dog's ears. "Actually Patryns are very loving, almost fiercely loving. Did you know that?"

His sad gaze was on the dog and he missed Orla's look of astonishment.

"They don't think of it as such. They call love by other names: loyalty, a protective instinct to ensure the survival of their race. But it is love, a dark sort of love, but love nevertheless, and even the worst of them feels it strongly. This Lord of the Nexus—a cruel, powerful, and ambitious man—risks his own life daily to go back into the Labyrinth to aid his suffering people."

Alfred, caught up in his emotion, forgot where he was. He stared into the dog's eyes. Liquid, brown, they drew him in, held him until nothing else seemed real to him.

"My own parents sacrificed their lives to save me, when the snogs were chasing us. They might have escaped, you see, but I was only a child and I couldn't keep up with them. And so they hid me and lured the snogs away from me. I saw my parents die. The snogs tortured them. And later, strangers took me in, raised me as their own."

The dog's eyes grew soft, sad. "And I have loved," Alfred heard himself saying. "She was a Runner, like myself, like my parents. She was beautiful, strong, and lean. The blue runes twined around her body that pulsed with youth and life beneath my fingers when I held her in my arms at night. We fought together, loved, laughed. Yes, there is sometimes laughter, even in the Labyrinth. Often it is bitter laughter, the jests dark and grim, but to lose laughter is to lose the will to live.

"She left me, eventually. A village of Squatters, who had

offered us shelter for the night, was attacked, and she wanted to help them. It was a stupid, foolish notion. The Squatters were outnumbered. We would have only died ourselves, most likely. I told her so. She knew I was right. But she was frustrated, angry. She'd come to love those people, you see. And she was afraid of her love, because it made her feel weak and powerless and hurting inside. She was afraid of her love for me. And so she left me. She was carrying my child. I know she was, though she refused to admit it. And I never saw her again. I don't even know if she is dead, or if my child lives—"

"Stop it!"

Orla's cry startled Alfred, shocked him out of his reverie. She had risen from her seat, was backing away, staring at him in horror.

"Don't do this to me anymore!" She was deathly pale, struggled for breath. "I can't bear it! I keep seeing those images of yours, the wretched child, watching his parents raped, murdered, their bodies torn apart. And he can't scream, he's so afraid. I see that woman you talk about. I feel her pain, her helplessness. I know the pain of bearing a child and I think of her alone, in that terrible place. She can't scream, either, afraid that her cries will bring death to her and her baby. I can't sleep nights for thinking of them, for knowing that we . . . I . . . I am responsible!"

Orla covered her face with her hands, to blot out any more images, and began to sob. Alfred was appalled at himself, uncertain how those images—that were really Haplo's memories—got into his head.

"Sit . . . Good dog," he said, shoving the animal's head (was it grinning at him?) off his knee.

Hurriedly, he approached Orla. He had some vague notion of offering her his handkerchief. But his arms appeared to have other ideas. He watched in amazement to see them steal around the woman's body, pull her close. She rested her head on his breast.

A tingling thrill shot through him. He held her, loved her with every fiber of his being. He stroked her shining hair with an awkward hand and, because he was Alfred, said something stupid.

"Orla, what knowledge is in the library of the Sartan that Samah doesn't want anyone to know about?"

She struck him, shoved him back so violently that he tripped over the dog and fell into the rosebushes. Her anger blazed in her eyes and burned in her cheeks—anger and . . . was it Alfred's imagination or did he see the same fear in her eyes that he'd seen in Samah's?

Without a word, Orla turned and left him, walking from her garden in hurt, offended dignity.

Alfred struggled to disentangle himself from the thorns that were pricking him painfully. The dog offered assistance. Alfred glared at it.

"It's all your fault!" he said crossly.

The animal cocked its head, looked innocent, denied the charge.

"It is, too. Putting such ideas into my head! Why don't you go off and find that blasted master of yours and leave me alone! I can get myself into quite enough trouble without your help."

Cocking its head in the other direction, the dog appeared to agree that this was true. It seemed to think the conversation had reached its logical conclusion, however, for it stretched luxuriously, bending forward over its forepaws, back over its hind end, and finally shook itself all over. Then, it trotted over to the garden gate, looked at Alfred expectantly.

Alfred felt himself go hot and cold, both at the same time— a most uncomfortable sensation.

"You're telling me that we're alone now, aren't you? No one's with us. No one's watching us."

The dog wagged its tail.

"We can . . ." Alfred swallowed. "We can go to the library."

The dog wagged its tail again, its expression long-suffering and patient. It obviously considered Alfred slow and thickheaded, but was magnanimously willing to overlook these minor faults.

"But I can't get inside. And if I could, I can't get back out. Samah would catch me . . ."

The dog was afflicted by a sudden itch. Plopping down, it scratched vigorously, fixed Alfred with a stern gaze that seemed to say, *Come, come. It's me, remember?*

"Oh, very well."

Alfred cast a furtive glance around the garden, half-expecting Samah to leap out of the rosebushes and lay violent hands upon his person. When no one came, Alfred began to sing and dance the runes.

He stood outside the library. The dog dashed up to the door, sniffed at it with interest. Alfred slowly followed, gazed at the door sadly. The warding runes had, as Samah had promised, been strengthened.

" 'Due to the current crisis situation and the fact that we cannot spare the staff needed to assist our patrons, the library is closed until further notice.' " Alfred read the sign aloud.

"It makes sense," he insisted. "Who's interested in doing any research anyway. They're spending all their time trying to rebuild and establish their city, trying to decide what to do about the Patryns, and wondering where the rest of our people are and how to get in touch with them. They have to deal with the necromancers on Abarrach and these dragon-snakes . . ."

The dog didn't agree.

"You're right," Alfred heard himself arguing, his own inner being as rebellious as his limbs and appendages. "If I had all those problems to solve, where would I turn? To the wisdom of our people. Wisdom recorded in there."

Well, the dog demanded, bored with sniffing at the door, *what are we waiting for?*

"I can't get inside," Alfred said, but the words came out a whisper—a halfhearted, faint, and ineffectual lie.

He knew how to get in without being detected. The idea had come to him, suddenly, last night.

He hadn't wanted it to come. And when it did, he'd told it in no uncertain terms to go away. But it wouldn't. His stubborn brain had gone right ahead making plans, examining the risks and deciding (with a cold-bloodedness that shocked Alfred) that the risks were minimal and worth running.

The idea had come to him because of that stupid story told by Bane's nurse. Alfred caught himself hoping irritably that she'd come to a bad end. She had no business telling such nightmare tales to a susceptible child. (Never mind the fact that Bane himself was a nightmare personified.)

Thinking about that tale, Alfred had found himself remembering Arianus and the time he'd lived at the court of King Stephen. One memory led to another memory, and that led to another, until his mind had carried him, without him being aware of where he was headed, to the time the thief broke into the treasure vault.

Money is water, on Arianus, where the life-sustaining liquid is in short supply and is, therefore, considerably valuable. The royal palace had stockpiles of the precious commodity, kept for use in times of emergency (such as when the elves succeeded in cutting off the water shipments). The vault where the barrels were stored was located in a building behind the palace walls, a building of thick walls and heavy bolted doors, a building guarded day and night.

Guarded—except on the roof.

Late one night, a thief, using a most ingenious system of ropes and pulleys, managed to make his way from a neighboring roof to the top of the water vault. He was drilling through the hargast-wood timbers when one gave way with a shattering crash, literally dropping the unlucky thief into the arms of the guards below.

How the thief had proposed to get away with enough water to make this dangerous feat worth his while was never learned. It was assumed he had accomplices, but, if so, they escaped and he never revealed them, not even under torture. He met his death alone, accomplishing nothing except to ensure that guards now patrolled the roof.

That and he'd provided Alfred with a plan for breaking and entering the library.

Of course, it was always possible that Samah had enveloped the entire building in a magical shell, but, knowing the Sartan as he did, Alfred considered it unlikely. They had considered runes politely advising people to keep out sufficient protection and they would have been, had not Alfred's wayward feet flung him inside. The Councillor had strengthened the magic, but the thought that anyone (much less Alfred) would have the temerity to deliberately enter a place he'd been commanded to avoid would be unthinkable.

It is unthinkable, Alfred thought miserably. I am corrupt. This is insanity!

"I . . . I must get away from here . . ." he said faintly, mopping his forehead with his lace cuff.

He was firm, resolved. He was going to leave. He didn't care what was in the library.

"If there is anything—which there probably isn't—then surely Samah has an excellent reason for not wanting stray scholars to poke at it—although what that reason could be is beyond me—not that it's any of my business."

This monologue continued for some time, during which Alfred made up his mind to leave and actually turned around and started down the path, only to find himself walking up it again almost immediately. He turned back, started home, found himself walking to the library.

The dog trotted after him, back and forth, until it grew tired, flopped down about halfway either direction, and watched Alfred's vacillation with considerable interest.

Finally, the Sartan made up his mind. "I'm not going inside," he said decisively, did a little dance, and began to sing the runes.

The sigla wove their magic around him, lifted him up into the air. The dog jumped excitedly to its feet, and began to bark loudly, much to Alfred's consternation. The library was located far from the center of the Sartan city, far from the homes of the inhabitants, but it seemed to the nervous Alfred that the animal's yelps must be audible in Arianus.

"Shush! Nice dog! No, don't bark. I—"

Attempting to hush the dog, Alfred forgot where he was going. Or at least that was the only explanation he could give for finding himself hovering over the roof of the library.

"Oh, dear," he said weakly, and dropped like a rock.

For long moments, he cowered on top of the roof, terrified that someone had heard the dog and that crowds of Sartan would be flocking around, wondering and accusing.

All was quiet. No one came.

The dog licked his hand and whined, urged him to once more take to the air, a feat the animal found highly entertaining.

Alfred, who had forgotten the dog's unique ability to show up where least expected, nearly crawled out of his skin at the unexpected slobber of a wet tongue.

Sitting back weakly against the parapet, he petted the animal with a shaking hand and looked around. He had been right. The only sigla visible were the perfectly ordinary runes of strength and support and protection from the elements that could be found on the roofs of any Sartan building. Yes, he'd been right, and he hated himself for being right.

The roof was constructed of massive beams of some tree Alfred didn't recognize, but they gave off a faint, woodsy, pleasing aroma. Probably a tree that the Sartan had brought with them from the ancient world, through Death's Gate.[1] These large beams were placed at intervals along the roof; smaller planks crisscrossed beneath, filling in the gaps. Intricate sigla, traced on the planks and the beams, would keep out rain and rodents and wind and sun, would keep out everything . . .

"Except me," Alfred said, gazing at the sigla unhappily.

He sat for long moments, unwilling to move, until the larcenous part of his nature reminded him that the Council meeting could not last much longer. Samah would return home and expect to find Alfred there, become suspicious if Alfred was not.

"Suspicious," said Alfred faintly. "When did one Sartan ever use that word about another? What is happening to us? And why?"

Slowly, he leaned over and began to draw a sigil on the wooden beam. His voice accompanied his work, his chant sad and heavy. The runes sank down through the wooden beams of a tree never known in this world, and they carried Alfred down into the library with them.

Orla paced about her house, restless, ill at ease. She wished Samah were at home, was perversely glad he wasn't. She knew she should go back out into the garden, should go back out to Alfred, apologize for behaving like such a fool, smooth the incident over. She should have never let it affect her like that, should have never let him affect her like that!

"Why did you come?" she demanded of his absent figure sadly. "All the turmoil and unhappiness was over. I could once more hope for peace. Why did you come? And when will you go?"

Orla took another turn about the room. Sartan dwellings are large and spacious. The rooms are made of cool, straight lines, bent, here and there, into perfect arches supported by upright

[1] Most likely cedar.

columns. The furniture is elegant and simple, providing only what is necessary for comfort, nothing for show or display. One could walk among the few furnishings with ease.

That is, a normal person could walk among them with ease, she amended, straightening a table that Alfred had knocked askew.

She put the table to rights, knowing Samah would be extremely irritated to find it out of its proper order. But her hand lingered on it; she smiled to herself, seeing, once again, Alfred blundering into it. The table stood next to a couch, was well out of the flow of traffic. Alfred had been far away from it, with no intention of being anywhere near it. Orla recalled watching in wonder those too-large feet of his veering off in the direction of the table, stumbling over each other in their haste to reach it and knock it over. And Alfred, watching in bemused bewilderment, like a nursemaid with a flock of unruly children. And he had looked at Orla in helpless, pleading apology.

I know I'm responsible, his eyes said, *but what can I do? My feet simply won't behave!*

Why did that wistful expression of his tug at her heart? Why did she long to hold those clumsy hands, long to try to ease the burden that rested on those stooped shoulders?

"I am another man's wife," she reminded herself. "Samah's wife."

They had loved each other, she supposed. She'd borne him children, they must have . . . once.

But she remembered the image Alfred had conjured for her, an image of two people loving each other fiercely, passionately, because this night was all they had, because all they had was each other. No, she realized sadly. She'd never truly loved.

She felt no pain inside her, no ache, nothing. Only spacious, large emptiness, defined by cool, straight lines, supported by upright columns. What furniture existed was neat, orderly, occasionally shifting position, but never actually rearranged. Until those too-large feet and those wistful, searching eyes and those clumsy hands blundered into her and threw everything into wild disarray.

"Samah would say that it is a mothering instinct, that since I am past my childbearing years, I have the need to mother something. Odd, but I can't remember mothering my own child.

I suppose I did. I suppose I must have. All I seem to remember is wandering about this empty house, dusting the furniture."

Her feelings for Alfred weren't motherly, however. Orla remembered his awkward hands, his timid caresses, and blushed hotly. No, not motherly at all.

"What is there about him?" she wondered aloud.

Certainly nothing visible on the surface: balding head, stooped shoulders, feet that seemed intent on carrying their owner to disaster, mild blue eyes, shabby mensch clothes that he refused to change. Orla thought of Samah: strong, self-possessed, powerful. Yet Samah had never made her feel compassion, never made her cry for someone else's sorrow, never made her love someone for the sake of loving.

"There is a power in Alfred," Orla told the straight and uncaring furniture. "A power that is all the more powerful because he is not aware of it. If you accused him of it, in fact"—she smiled fondly—"he would get that bewildered, astonished look on his face and stammer and stutter and . . . I'm falling in love with him. This is impossible. I'm falling in love with him."

And he's falling in love with you.

"No," she protested, but her protest was soft and her smile did not fade.

Sartan did not fall in love with other people's spouses. Sartan remained faithful to their marriage vows. This love was hopeless and could come only to grief. Orla knew this. She knew she would have to remove the smiles and tears from her being, straighten it up, return it to its straight lines and empty dustiness. But for a short time, for this one moment, she could recall the warmth of his hand gently stroking her skin, she could cry in his arms for another woman's baby, she could feel.

It occurred to her that she'd been away from him an interminable length of time.

"He'll think I'm angry at him," she realized, remorseful, remembering how she'd stalked off the terrace. "I must have hurt him. I'll go explain and . . . and then I'll tell him that he has to leave this house. It won't be wise for us to see each other anymore, except on Council business. I can manage that. Yes, I can definitely manage that."

But her heart was beating far too rapidly for comfort, and she was forced to repeat a calming mantra before she was relaxed enough to look firm and resolved. She smoothed her hair and wiped away any lingering traces of tears, tried a cool, calm smile on her face, studied herself anxiously in a mirror to see if the smile looked as strained and borrowed as it felt.

Then she had to pause to try to think how to bring the subject into conversation.

"Alfred, I know you love me . . ."

No, that sounded conceited.

"Alfred, I love you . . ."

No, that would certainly never do! After another moment's reflection, she decided that it would be best to be swift and merciless, like one of those horrid mensch surgeons, chopping off a diseased limb.

"Alfred, you and the dog must leave my house this night."

Yes, that would be best. Sighing, not holding out much hope that this would work, she returned to the terrace.

Alfred wasn't there.

"He's gone to the library."

Orla knew it as well as if she could look across the miles and peer through the walls and see him inside. He'd found a way to enter that wouldn't alert anyone to his presence. And she knew that he would find what he sought.

"He won't understand. He wasn't there. I must try to make him see *my* images!"

Orla whispered the runes, traced the magic with her hands, and departed on its wings.

The dog growled, warningly, and jumped to its feet. Alfred looked up from his reading. A figure clad in white was approaching, coming from the back of the library. He couldn't see who it was: Samah, Ramu? . . .

Alfred didn't particularly care. He wasn't nervous, wasn't assailed by guilt, wasn't afraid. He was appalled and shocked and sickened and he was, he was startled to discover, glad to be able to confront someone.

He rose to his feet, his body trembling, not with fear, but with his anger. The figure stepped into the light he had magically created to read by.

The two stared at each other. Quick indrawn breaths slipped

to sighs, eyes silently exchanged words of the heart that could
never be spoken.

"You know," said Orla.

"Yes," answered Alfred, lowering his gaze, flustered.

He'd been expecting Samah. He could be angry with Samah.
He felt a need to be angry, to release his anger that bubbled
inside him like Abarrach's hot lava sea. But how could he vent
his anger on her, when what he truly wanted to do was take
her in his arms? . . .

"I'm sorry," Orla said. "It makes things very difficult."

"Difficult!" Fury and indignation struck Alfred a blow that
left him reeling, addled his brain. "Difficult! That's all you can
say?" He gestured wildly to the scroll[2] lying open on the table
before him. "What you did . . . When you knew . . . This records everything, the arguments in the Council. The fact that
certain Sartan were beginning to believe in a higher power. How
could you . . . Lies, all lies! The horror, the destruction, the
deaths . . . Unnecessary! And you knew—"

"No, we didn't!" Orla cried.

She strode forward, came to stand before him, her hand on
the table, the scroll, that separated them. The dog sat back on
its haunches, looking at each with its intelligent eyes.

"We didn't know! Not for certain! And the Patryns were
growing in strength, in power. And against their might, what
did we have? Vague feelings, nothing that could ever be
defined."

"Vague feelings!" repeated Alfred. "Vague feelings! I've
known those feelings. They were . . . it was . . . the most wonderful experience! The Chamber of the Damned, they called it.
But I knew it as the Chamber of the Blessed. I understood the
reason for my being. I was given to know I could change things
for the better. I was told that if I had faith, all would be well. I
didn't want to leave that wonderful place—"

---

[2] Why, if Samah feared the scroll's discovery, didn't he burn it?

"I believe," writes Alfred, in an addendum to this section, "that Samah
had an innate regard for the truth. He tried to deny it, attempted to suppress it, but he could not bring himself to destroy it."

"But you did leave!" Orla reminded him. "You couldn't stay, could you? And what happened in Abarrach when you left?"

Alfred, troubled, drew back from her. He looked down at the scroll, though he wasn't seeing it; his hand toyed with its edges.

"You doubted," she told him. "You didn't believe what you'd seen. You questioned your own feelings. You came back to a world that was dark and frightening, and if you *had* caught a glimpse of a greater good, a power vaster and more wondrous than your own, then where was it? You even wondered if it was a trick. . . ."

Alfred saw Jonathon, the young nobleman he'd met on Abarrach, murdered, torn apart by the hands of a once-loving wife. Jonathon had believed, he'd had faith, and he'd died horribly because of it. Now, he was probably one of those tormented living dead, the lazar.

Alfred sat down heavily in the chair. The dog, grieving for the man's unhappiness, padded silently over and nuzzled him with its nose. Alfred rested his aching head in his arms.

Gentle, cool hands slid around his shoulders. Orla knelt beside him. "I know how you feel. I truly do. We all felt the same. Samah, the rest of the Council. It was as if . . . How did Samah put this? We were like humans drunk on strong wine. When they're intoxicated, everything looks wonderful to them and they can do anything, solve any problem. But, when the effects of the spirits wear off, they're left sick and hurting and feeling worse than they did before."

Alfred raised his head, looked at her bleakly. "What if the fault is ours? What if I had stayed on Abarrach? Did a miracle happen there? I'll never know. I left. I left because I was afraid."

"And we were afraid, too." Orla's fingers tightened over his arm in her earnestness. "The darkness of the Patryns was very real and this vague light that some of us had experienced was nothing but the tiny flicker of a candle flame, likely to be blown out with a breath. How can we put our faith in this? In something we don't understand?"

"What is faith?" Alfred asked gently, not talking to her but to himself. "Believing in something you do not understand. And how can we poor mortals understand that vast and terrible and wonderful mind?"

"I don't know," she whispered brokenly. "I don't know."

Alfred grasped her hand. "This was what you fought over. You and the other Council members! You and . . . and"—it was difficult for him to say the word—"your husband."

"Samah didn't believe in any of it. He said it was a trick, a trick of our enemy's."

Alfred heard Haplo speaking, the Patryn's words were almost an echo. *A trick, Sartan! You tricked me . . .*

". . . opposed the Sundering," Orla was continuing. "We wanted to wait before taking such drastic action. But Samah and the others were afraid—"

"And with good cause, so it appears," came a grim voice. "When I returned home and discovered you both gone, I had an idea where you might be found."

Alfred quailed at the sound, shivered. Orla, very pale, rose slowly to her feet. She remained standing near him, however, her hand resting on his shoulder in protective support. The dog, having been negligent in its duties, was apparently attempting to make up for it by barking at Samah with all its energy.

"Shut the beast up," said Samah, "or I will kill it."

"You can't kill it," Alfred replied, shaking his head. "No matter how hard you try, you can't kill this animal or what it represents."

But he rested his hand on the animal's head. The dog suffered itself to be gentled into silence.

"At least now we know who and what you are," stated the Councillor, eyeing Alfred grimly. "A Patryn spy, sent to learn our secrets." His gaze shifted to his wife. "And corrupt the trusting."

Resolutely, with dignity, Alfred rose to his feet. "You are wrong. I am a Sartan, to my sorrow. And as for learning secrets"—he gestured to the scroll—"it seems the secrets I have discovered were meant to be kept from our own people, not from the so-called enemy."

Samah was livid with rage, unable to speak.

"No," Orla whispered, looking earnestly at Alfred, her hand biting into his arm. "No, you're wrong. The time wasn't right—"

"Our reasons for doing what we did are not his concern, Wife!" Samah interrupted. He paused, waiting to speak until he had mastered his anger. "Alfred Montbank, you will remain a prisoner here until the Council meets and we decide what measures to take."

"A prisoner? Is that necessary?" Orla protested.

"I deem it so. I was coming to tell you the news we have just received from the dolphins. This man's Patryn ally has been discovered. He is here in Chelestra and, as we feared, he is in league with the dragon-snakes. He has met with them, he and representatives from the mensch royal families."

"Alfred," said Orla, "can this be true?"

"I don't know," Alfred replied wretchedly. "Haplo might do something like this, I'm afraid, but you must understand that he—"

"Listen to him, Wife. Even now, he seeks to defend this Patryn."

"How can you?" Orla demanded, drawing away from Alfred, regarding him with mingled sorrow, pain. "You would see your own people destroyed!"

"No, he would see his own people victorious," said Samah coldly. "You forget, my dear, he is more Patryn than Sartan."

Alfred made no reply, but stood clasping and unclasping his hands over the back of the chair.

"Why do you stand there and say nothing?" Orla cried. "Tell my husband he's wrong! Tell me *I'm* wrong!"

Alfred lifted mild blue eyes. "What can I say that you would believe?"

Orla stared at him, started to reply, then shook her head in frustration. Turning her back on him, she walked out of the room.

Samah regarded Alfred grimly.

"This time, I will post a guard. You will be called."

He stalked off, accompanied by the dog's defiant growl.

Ramu appeared in his father's place. Coming to the table, the son cast Alfred a baleful glance and laid firm hands upon the scroll. Deliberately and with great care, he rolled it up tightly, slid it into the scrollcase, and returned it to its proper place. He then took up a position at the back of the room, as far from Alfred as a Sartan could get and still keep an eye on him.

There was no need to guard him, however. Alfred would not have attempted to escape had the door been left standing wide open. He sat despondent, hunched in misery—a prisoner of his own people, the people he had hoped so long to find. He was in the wrong. He'd done a terrible thing and he couldn't, for the life of him, imagine what had prompted him to do it.

His actions had angered Samah. Worse, Alfred had hurt Orla. And all for what? To meddle in affairs that were not any of his business, affairs that were beyond his understanding.

"Samah is far wiser than I am," he said to himself. "He knows what is best. He is right. I am not Sartan. I am part Patryn, part mensch. Even"—he added, with a sad smile for the faithful animal, lying at his feet—"a little bit of dog. Most of all, though, I'm a fool. Samah wouldn't attempt to suppress such knowledge. As Orla said, he was waiting for a more appropriate time. That's all.

"I will apologize to the Council," he continued, sighing, "and I will gladly do whatever they ask of me. And then I will leave. I can't stay here any longer. Why is it?" He looked at his own hands, shook them in frustration. "Why do I break everything I touch? Why do I bring ruin on those I care about? I'll leave this world and never return. I'll go back to my crypt in Arianus and I'll sleep. Sleep a long, long time. Perhaps, if I'm lucky, I'll never wake up.

"And you," said Alfred, glaring bitterly at the dog. "You're on your own. Haplo didn't lose you, did he? He sent you away deliberately. He doesn't want you back! Well, good riddance, I say. I'll leave you here, too. Both of you!"

The animal cringed at his angry tone and baleful stare. Ears and tail drooping, the dog sank down at Alfred's feet and lay there, watching him with sad, sorrowful eyes.

CHAPTER ♦ 19

PHONDRA

CHELESTRA

♦

MUCH TO HAPLO'S AMAZEMENT, THE ROYAL FAMILIES, REUNITED with their children, decided to depart. Each family, it seemed, intended to return home, to rest and relax and, when they felt strong enough, discuss the idea of making the Sun Chase.

"What is this? Where are you going?" Haplo demanded of the dwarves, about to board their submersible. The humans were heading for theirs.

"We are going back to Phondra," said Dumaka.

"Phondra!" Haplo stared at him, openmouthed. Mensch! he thought in disgust. "Listen, I know you've had a shock and I'm sorry for your loss. I truly am." His glance went to Alake, sobbing in her mother's arms. "But you don't seem to understand that important things are happening, things that involve you and your people. You've got to take action now!

"For instance," he said, hoping to catch their attention, "did you know that the seamoon you're planning to inhabit is already inhabited?"

Dumaka and Delu frowned, grew attentive. The dwarves halted, turned around. Even Eliason lifted his head, a vague flicker of disquiet in the elf's sunken eyes.

"The dolphins said nothing of this," returned Dumaka sternly. "How do you know? Who told you?"

"The dragon-snakes. Look, I know you don't trust them. I don't blame you. But I have reason to believe that this time they're telling the truth."

"Who is living there? Those horrible creatures?" Yngvar guessed, scowling.

"No, not the dragon-snakes, if that's who you mean. They have their own seamoon. They don't need or want another. The people living on the moon in which you're interested are not dwarven, elven, or human. I don't think you've ever heard of them. They call themselves Sartan."

Haplo glanced around quickly, saw no signs of recognition, and breathed an inward sigh of relief. That made things easier. It might have been difficult, had these people any distant memories of the Sartan, to get them to move against those they must consider gods. He hurried on, while he had their attention.

"The dragon-snakes have promised to rebuild your ships, using their own magic. They're sorry for what they did. It was all a misunderstanding. I'll explain it to you when there's more time.

"For now, I'll tell you this much, so you can start making plans. The seamoon is everything the dolphins told you. Actually, it isn't really a seamoon. It's a permanent structure. And it's huge, big enough for all your people to live on together. And you'll be able to live in this realm for generations, without having to worry about building more sun-chasers."

Dumaka looked dubious. "You are certain you are discussing . . . what was the name?"

"Surunan," supplied his wife.

"Yes, Surunan."

"Yeah, that's the place," said Haplo, not wanting to have to speak the Sartan name. "It's the only place anywhere near the seasun. It's there . . . or nowhere for your people, I'm afraid."

"Yes," said Eliason softly, "we had ourselves come to that determination."

"Which brings us to our problem. What the dolphins didn't tell you was that . . . this place . . . is now the home of these Sartan. To give the dolphins credit, I don't think they knew. The Sartan haven't lived there very long."

Well, they had, but now wasn't the time to go into all that.

The mensch exchanged glances. They seemed dazed, unable to cope with this new situation.

"But who are these Sartan? You speak of them as if they were horrible creatures, who will turn us away," said Delu. "How do you know they won't be glad to have us live on their realm?"

"And how many of these Sartan are there?" asked her husband.

"There aren't many, a thousand or so. They inhabit one city in the realm. The rest of the land is going to waste."

Yngvar brightened. "Then what do we have to worry about? There's room for all."

"I agree with the dwarf. We will make Surunan productive and prosperous."

Haplo shook his head. "Logically, what you say makes sense. And the Sartan should be agreeable to you moving in, but I'm afraid they may not. I know something of these Sartan. According to the dragon-snakes, a long, long time ago, when the seasun was new, your ancestors used to live in this same realm with the Sartan. And then, one day, the Sartan told your ancestors to leave. They put your people in ships and sent them out into the Goodsea, not knowing, not caring, whether your people lived or died. It's not likely the Sartan will be happy to see you come back again."

"But, if that's the only place for us to go, how could they turn us away?" Eliason looked amazed.

"I'm not saying they will," Haplo said, shrugging. "I'm just saying they might. And you need to think about what you'll do if they refuse to let you. That's why you need to meet together, make plans, decisions."

He looked at the mensch expectantly.

They looked at each other.

"I will not go to war," said the elven king.

"Come now, man!" Yngvar snorted. "No one wants to fight, but if these Sartan prove unreasonable—"

"I will not go to war," Eliason repeated with maddening calm.

Yngvar began to argue. Dumaka attempted to reason.

"The sun will not leave us for many cycles," said Eliason brokenly. He waved his hand. "I cannot think of such things now—"

"Can't think about the welfare of your own people!"

Grundle, tearstreaks drying on her face, stalked across the pier and came to stand before the elven king, her head about level with his waist.

"Grundle, you should not speak so to your elders," repri-

manded her mother, but she didn't say it very loudly and her
daughter didn't hear her.

"Sabia was my friend. Every cycle that passes from now to
the end of my life, I'll think of her and miss her. But she was
willing to give her life to save her people. It would be a disgrace
to her memory if you, her father, couldn't do as much!"

Eliason stood staring at the dwarf as if he were in a dream
and she some strange apparition sprung out of nowhere.

Yngvar, the dwarf king, sighed and tugged at his beard. "My
daughter speaks true words, Eliason, even if she does hurl them
with all the grace and charm of an ax-thrower. We share your
grief, but we also share your responsibility. The lives of our
people come first. This man, who has saved our children, is
right. We must meet and plan what is to be done, and soon!"

"I agree with Yngvar," Dumaka spoke up. "Let us hold the
meeting on Phondra, fourteen cycles hence. Will that give you
time enough to conclude the mourning period?"

"Fourteen cycles!"

Haplo was about to protest. He caught the dwarf's keen-eyed
glance warning him to keep silent, and shut his mouth. Later,
he would discover that the elven mourning period—during
which no elf related to the deceased by either blood or marriage
may conduct any type of business—generally lasted for months,
sometimes longer.

"Very well," said Eliason with a deep sigh. "Fourteen cycles.
I will meet you on Phondra."

The Elmas departed. The Phondrans and Gargans returned
to their submersibles, prepared to go back to their respective sea-
spheres. Dumaka, prodded by Alake, came up to Haplo.

"You must forgive him, sir, forgive us all if we seem ungrateful to you for what you've done. The tears of great joy and
terrible grief have drowned all gratitude. You would do honor
to my lodge, if you would agree to be our guest."

"I am the one who would be honored to share your dwelling,
Chief," Haplo answered solemnly, feeling strangely as if he were
back in the Labyrinth, talking to the headman of one of the
Squatter tribes.

Dumaka said the appropriate words of pleasure and motioned toward his submersible.

"Will Eliason come, do you think?" Haplo asked as they boarded the vessel, the Patryn taking considerable care to avoid stepping in any water.

"Yes, he will come," Dumaka replied. "He's very reliable, for an elf."

"How long has it been since the elves went to war?"

"War?" Dumaka was amused, his teeth flashed white against his dusky skin. "The elves?" He shrugged. "Forever."

Haplo expected to spend his time on Phondra chafing with impatience, fuming at the forced inaction. He was surprised, after his first day or two, to discover that he was actually, grudgingly, enjoying himself.

Compared to the other worlds in which he'd traveled, Phondra most closely resembled his own. And while Haplo had never supposed he would be homesick for the Labyrinth, life with Dumaka's tribe brought back memories of some of the few pleasant and restful times in the Patryn's harsh life—those spent in the camps of the Squatters.[1]

Dumaka's tribe was the largest on Phondra and the strongest, one reason he was chieftain over the entire human population. It had taken numerous wars to settle the question, apparently, but now he was undisputed ruler and, in general, most of the other tribes approved his leadership.

Dumaka did not hold power alone, however. The Coven wielded a strong influence in the community, whose people revered magic and all those who could use it.

"In the old days," Alake explained, "the Coven and the chieftains were often at odds, each believing they had the best right to govern. My father's own father died that way, murdered by a warlock, who thought that he should be chief. The war that followed was bitter and bloody. Countless numbers perished. My father swore that if the One made him chief, he would bring

---

[1]The people of the Labyrinth can be divided generally into two groups: the Runners and the Squatters. The Runners are those who, like Haplo, seek to escape the Labyrinth. They travel alone; their lives are restless, short. The Squatters have banded together to form tribes for protection and to provide for the continuance of the race. They are nomadic, but do not move as fast or far as the Runners. Survival, not escape, is their primary goal.

about peace between the tribes and the Coven. The One granted him victory over his enemies and it was then that he married my mother, daughter of the Priestess of the Coven.

"My parents divided the power between them. My father rules on all disputes that occur over land or possessions; he gives laws and stands in judgment. My mother and the Coven deal with all things magical. Phondra has been at peace for years now."

Haplo looked around at the tribal village—the lodges made of poles and thatched grass; the women, babies on their hips, laughing and talking; the younger men, honing weapons, preparing to set off in pursuit of some wild beast. A group of men too old to go on the hunt sat in the warm, waning sunlight, reliving hunts of long ago. The air was soft to the touch, scented with smells of smoked meat, alive with the shrill cries of children having a play hunt of their own.

"It seems a pity it must all end," Alake said softly, her eyes glimmering.

Yes, it was a pity, Haplo caught himself thinking. He tried to shake off the thought, but he could not deny that in this place, with these people, he felt at peace and relaxed for the first time in a very long time.

It was merely a reaction to his fear, he decided. A reaction to the initial terror of the dragon-snakes, to the even greater terror of believing he'd lost his magic.

I must have been weaker than I knew. I'll use this time to regain my strength, for I'll soon need it. When I face the ancient enemy. When we go to war against the Sartan.

There's nothing I can do to hurry it, anyway, he told himself. It won't do to offend these mensch. I need them, need their numbers, if not necessarily their skill at arms.

He had been thinking a lot about the forthcoming battle. The elves would be worse than useless. He must find something for them to do, keep them out of the way. The humans were warriors, trained and skilled and easily roused to blood lust. The dwarves, from what he had gathered from talking to Grundle, were solid, tough. Slow to anger, but that wouldn't be a problem. Haplo thought it likely that the Sartan would inadvertently provide all the provocation he needed.

His only concern was that these Sartan might prove to be

like Alfred. Haplo considered the matter briefly, shook his head. No, from what he knew of Samah, from the records left in the Nexus, the Councillor was as different from Alfred as the light and lush world of air differed from the dark, smothering world of stone.

"I'm sorry, but I must leave you alone for a time . . ."

Alake was saying something to him, something about having to go to her mother. She was looking at him anxiously, fearful of offending him.

Haplo smiled at her. "I'll be fine on my own. And you don't have to worry about entertaining me, much as I enjoy your company. I'll just look around." He waved a hand. "Get to know your people."

"You like us, don't you?" asked Alake, returning his smile.

"Yes," said Haplo and only when the word was spoken did he realize he meant it. "Yes, I like your people, Alake. They remind me . . . of someplace I was, once."

He fell silent, abruptly, not particularly welcoming some of the memories, yet oddly grateful to greet them after a long absence.

"She must have been very beautiful," said Alake, somewhat downcast.

Haplo looked up at her swiftly. Women! Mensch, Patryn, all alike. What gave them that uncanny ability to crawl inside a man's skull, inside the dark places he thought hidden to all?

"She was," he said, and he hadn't meant to say that either. It was this place. Too much like home. "You'd better run along. Your mother will be wondering where you are."

"I'm sorry if I hurt you," she said softly. Reaching out her hand, she touched his, clasped his fingers.

Her skin was smooth and soft, her hand strong. His fingers tightened over hers, he drew her hand closer, not thinking what he was doing. Only knowing that she was beautiful and she warmed some cold part of him.

"A little pain is good for us," he said to her. "Reminds us we're alive."

She didn't understand, but she was reassured by his manner, and left him. Haplo's gaze followed her until the hungry, lonely ache inside him made him feel just a little bit too much alive for comfort.

Standing up, stretching in the warm sun, he went off to join the young warriors in the hunt.

The hunt was long, exciting, strenuous. Whatever beast it was—and Haplo never did catch the name—was cunning, vicious, and savage. The Patryn deliberately refused to use his magic. He found he enjoyed the hard, physical exertion, enjoyed pitting wits and muscle against an enemy.

The stalking and chasing lasted for hours, the kill itself, involving nets and spears, was tense and danger-edged. Several of the men were injured; one came close to being gored by the swordlike horn on top of the brutish head. Haplo flung himself on the young man, dragged him out of harm's way. The horn grazed the Patryn's skin but, protected as he was by the runes, did no true damage.

Haplo had never been in any danger, but the humans didn't know that and acclaimed him the hero of the day. At the end of the hunt, when the young men returned, singing, to the camp, he enjoyed their comradeship, the feeling that he was, once again, one with a community.

This feeling wouldn't last long. It never had in the Labyrinth. He was a Runner. He would grow restless and uneasy, chafe against walls only he could see. But for now, he permitted himself the pleasure.

"I'm building up their confidence in me, their trust." That was his excuse. Pleasantly weary, he walked back to his hut, planning to lie down and rest before tonight's feasting. "These men will follow me anywhere, now. Even to war against a far superior enemy."

He lay on his pallet, the warm ache of fatigue relaxing his muscles and his mind. A unwelcome thought occurred to him— his lord's instructions.

You are to be an observer. Take no action that might give yourself away as a Patryn. Do not alert the enemy to our presence.

But the Lord of the Nexus could not have foreseen that Haplo would run into Samah the Councillor. Samah, the Sartan who had imprisoned the Patryns in the Labyrinth. Samah, who had been responsible for the deaths, the sufferings, the torments endured by Haplo's people through countless generations.

"When I return, it will be with Samah, and my lord will once again trust me and think of me as his son . . . ."

♦

Haplo must have fallen asleep, for he jerked awake, alarmed, aware of someone inside his hut with him. He reacted swiftly, instinctively, and startled Alake, who took an involuntary step or two back away from him.

"I'm . . . sorry," muttered Haplo, seeing, by the lambent light of the campfires outside his hut, who it was. "I didn't mean to jump at you. You took me by surprise, that's all."

"Never disturb the sleeping tiger," said Alake. "So my father says. I called out and you answered, but you must have been dreaming. I'm sorry for waking you. I will leave . . ."

Yes, it had been a dream. Haplo was still trying to calm the rapid beating of his heart.

"No, don't go."

The dream lurked, on the fringes of his mind. He wasn't anxious to let it get at him again.

"That smells good," he said, sniffing at savory odors drifting on the soft night air.

"I brought you some food," Alake said, gesturing outdoors. The Phondrans never ate inside the lodge, but always out in the open—a sensible precaution, one that kept the dwellings clean and free of rodents. "You missed supper and I thought . . . that is, my mother thought . . . you might be hungry."

"I am. Tell your mother thank you very much for her thoughtfulness," said Haplo gravely.

Alake smiled, pleased to have pleased him. She was always doing something for him, bringing him food, small gifts, something she'd made herself. . . .

"You have upset your pallet. I will straighten it for you."

She took a step forward. Haplo was walking toward the lodge entrance. Somehow, the two managed to collide. Before Haplo knew what was happening, soft arms encircled him, soft lips sought his, warmth and fragrance surrounded him.

Haplo's body reacted before his brain could take control. He was half in the Labyrinth, still. The girl was more a part of his dream than reality. He kissed her hard, fiercely, his passion that of a man, forgetting he held a child. He pressed her close, started to draw her down on his pallet.

Alake gave a faint, scared gasp.

Haplo's brain took charge, jerked him to his senses.

"Get out!" he ordered, thrusting Alake roughly away from him.

She stood, shivering, in the doorway, staring at him. She'd been unprepared for the ardence of his passion, perhaps unprepared for her own body's response to what had before been maiden dreams and fantasies. She was frightened of him, frightened of herself. But she had come to know, suddenly, her own power.

"You love me!" she whispered.

"No, I don't," Haplo returned harshly.

"You kissed me . . ."

"Alake—" Haplo began, exasperated, then stopped.

He swallowed the cold, callous words he'd been ready to speak. It wouldn't do to hurt the girl, who would almost assuredly go weeping to her mother. He couldn't afford to offend the rulers of the Phondrans and, as much as it irritated him to admit it, he didn't want to hurt Alake. What had happened had been his own damn fault.

"Alake," he began again, lamely, "I'm too old. I'm not even your race . . ."

"Then what are you? You're not elven or dwarven . . ."

I belong to people beyond your comprehension, child. A race of demigods, who might stoop to take a mensch for a toy, but would never take one for a wife.

"I can't explain, Alake. But, you know I'm different. Look at me! Look at the color of my skin. My hair and eyes. And I'm a stranger. You know nothing about me."

"I know all I need to know," the girl said softly. "I know that you save my life . . ."

"You saved mine."

She drew nearer, her eyes warm and glowing. "You are brave, the bravest man I've ever known. And handsome. Yes, you are different, but that is what makes you special. And you may be old, but I am old, too, for my years. Boys my own age bore me."

She reached out for him. Haplo kept his hands at his sides.

"Alake," he said, able at last to think rationally, saying what he should have said in the first place, "your parents would never approve."

"They might," she faltered.

"No." Haplo shook his head. "They will repeat everything that I have said to you. They would be angry and they would have a right to be angry. You are a royal daughter. Your marriage is very important to your people. You have responsibilities. You must marry a chieftain or a chieftain's son. I'm nobody, Alake."

She drooped. Her head bowed, her shoulders shook. Tears glimmered on her lashes. "You kissed me," she murmured.

"Yes, I couldn't help myself. You are very beautiful, Alake."

She lifted her head, looked at him, her heart in her eyes. "There will be a way. You will see. The One will not keep two who love each other apart. No," she said, raising a hand, "you need have no fear. I understand, and I will not tell my father or my mother. I will say nothing of this to anyone. It will be our secret, until the One shows me how we may be together."

She gave him a soft, tremulous kiss on his cheek, then turned and fled from his lodge.

Haplo stared after her, frustrated, angry at her, at himself, at the absurd circumstances that had dumped him into this situation. Would she keep her word, say nothing to her parents? He considered going after her, but he had no idea what he'd say. How could he tell her that he hadn't been kissing her, that he'd been kissing a memory conjured by his surroundings, the hunt, the dream?

CHAPTER ♦ 20

PHONDRA

CHELESTRA

♦

Haplo was on his guard the next cycle, waiting for the look or sign indicating Dumaka had discovered his guest trifling with his daughter's affections.

But Alake was true to her word, proving stronger than Haplo had suspected. When she was in his company (a circumstance Haplo went out of his way to avoid, but sometimes couldn't help), Alake was demure, polite, proper. She no longer brought him little presents, no longer selected the choicest morsels from the cooking pot for his pleasure.

And then he had other problems to worry about.

The dwarven contingent arrived on the twelfth cycle. Yngvar brought a large group, consisting of the Elders and several military officers.

The dwarves were welcomed formally by Dumaka, his wife, members of the tribal council and the Coven. A nearby cave, whose cool chambers were used for storing fruits and vegetables and a rather remarkable wine made by the humans, was cleared out and turned over to the dwarves for the duration of their stay on Phondra. As Yngvar told Haplo, no dwarf could sleep soundly beneath a roof covered with grass. He wanted the feel of something substantial—like a mountain—over his head.

Haplo was glad to see the dwarves. Their arrival took unwanted attention away from him and it meant that the time for action was that much nearer. Haplo was ready for action now, the incident with Alake having effectively managed to dispel his lapse into idyllic euphoria.

He was eager for news, and the dwarves brought some.

"The dragon-snakes are rebuilding the sun-chasers," stated Yngvar. "As he said they would." The dwarf gave a nod toward Haplo.

The heads of the royal houses met privately together after dinner. Formal discussions, involving all members of the respective governments, would not take place until the elves arrived. Haplo had been invited, because he was a guest. He took care to keep out of the conversation, watched and listened quietly.

"These are good tidings," said Dumaka.

The dwarf twisted his beard, frowning.

"What is wrong, Yngvar? Is the work progressing too slowly? Is it slipshod? Ill done?"

"Oh, it's done well enough," the dwarven king grumbled. He shifted one leg out from beneath the other, trying, in vain, to make himself comfortable.[1] "It's *how* it's done that bothers me. Magic."

He grunted, rolled over on one rump, groaned, and began to rub his leg. "I mean no offense, ma'am," he added, nodding brusquely at Delu, who had bristled at his disparaging tone, black eyes flashing indignantly. "We've been through this before. You elves and humans know how we dwarves feel about magic. We know how you feel. We have come, thank the One, to both respect each other's thinking and not try to change it. And if I had thought that either of your magics or both would have salvaged the sun-chasers, I would have been the first to suggest using it."

The dwarf's eyes narrowed, he forgot his discomfort. "But those ships were broken into a thousand bits. A thousand, thousand bits, if you will. I could have sat on the largest piece of all that was left and it would have been no more to me than a splinter in my arse!"

---

[1]Humans, when in their own homeland of Phondra, have no use for furniture. They sit on the ground, sleep on the ground—a practice both elves and dwarves consider barbaric and another reason that meetings of the royal houses were generally held on Elmas.

"My dear," rebuked his wife, flushing. "You're not in the tavern."

"Yes, yes. We understand. Go on," persisted Dumaka impatiently. "What are you saying? The work is progressing or it isn't?"

Yngvar was not to be hurried, despite the fact that his toes had gone numb. He rose abruptly to his feet, marched over to what appeared to be a large ceremonial drum, and plopped himself down on it with a sigh of relief. Delu looked considerably shocked; her husband silenced her words of protest with a look.

"The work," said the dwarf slowly, glowering from beneath his bushy eyebrows, "is finished."

"What?" Dumaka exclaimed.

"The ships were built"—Yngvar snapped his fingers—"in less time than it took me to do that."

Haplo smiled, well pleased.

"That is not possible," argued Delu. "You must be mistaken. Our most powerful sorcerers—"

"—are as children compared to these dragon-snakes," stated Yngvar bluntly. "I am not mistaken. I have never seen such magic. The sun-chasers were so many splinters, floating on the water. The dragon-snakes came up to look at the ships, surrounded them. Their green eyes glowed red, brighter than the furnace in which we forge our axes. They spoke strange words. The sea boiled. The pieces of wood flew into the air and, as if one knew another, rushed together as a bride rushes to the arms of her groom. And there they stand—the sun-chasers. Exactly as we built them. Except that now"—the dwarf added, glowering—"none of my people will go near them. And that includes me."

Haplo's satisfaction turned instantly to gloom. Damn! Another problem! He should have foreseen the mensch reaction. As it was, even Delu looked troubled.

"This truly is a wondrous feat," she said in a low voice. "I would like to hear it described in more detail. Perhaps, if you could meet with the Coven tomorrow . . ."

Yngvar snorted. "If I never see another wizard, it will be too soon. No, I will not argue. I have said all I am going to say on the subject. The sun-chasers are there, floating in the harbor. The Coven is welcome to come look at the ships, sink them, dance in them, fly them, if you have a mind to. No dwarf will set so much as a hair of his beard on a single plank. This I swear!"

"Are the dwarves prepared to let themselves be turned into blocks of ice?" Dumaka asked, glowering.

"We have boats enough of our own—boats built with sweat, not magic—to take our people off our doomed seamoon."

"And what about us?" Dumaka shouted.

"Humans are not the concern of the dwarves!" Yngvar shouted back. "Use the cursed boats if you want."

"You know perfectly well we need a dwarven crew—"

"Superstitious fools!" Delu was saying.

Haplo got up, walked out. From the sounds of the argument raging behind him, no one was likely to notice his absence.

He stalked off toward his own lodge and nearly fell over Grundle and Alake, crouched in a grove of trees.

"What the— Oh, it's you," Haplo said irritably. "I thought you two'd had your fill of listening in on other people's conversations?"

They'd chosen a secluded spot, near the back end of the chieftain's lodge, shadowed from the bright light of the camp-fires that shone full on their faces when they stood up.

Alake looked ashamed. Grundle only grinned.

"I wasn't going to listen," Alake protested. "I came to see if my mother needed me to fetch more wine for our guests and I found Grundle hiding here. I told her it was wrong, that we shouldn't do this anymore, that the One had punished us—"

"The only reason you found me hiding here was that you came planning to hide here yourself!" Grundle retorted.

"I did not!" Alake whispered indignantly.

"You did so. What else were you doing traipsing around the back of the longhouse instead of the front?"

"Whatever I was doing is my business—"

"Both of you go on home," Haplo ordered. "It's not safe here. You're away from the firelight, too close to the jungle. Go on, now."

He waited until he saw them headed on their way, then started for his own lodge. Footsteps echoed his. He glanced around, saw Grundle tagging along behind.

"Well, what are you going to do about our parents?" she asked him, jerking a thumb in the direction of the longhouse.

Loud, angry voices could be heard, echoing through the night air. People passing by looked at each other worriedly.

"Shouldn't you be somewhere else?" Haplo said irritably. "Won't someone miss you?"

"I'm supposed to be in the cave asleep, but I stuffed a bag of potatoes in my blanket roll. Everyone'll think it's me. And I know the guard on duty. His name's Hartmut. He's in love with me," she said matter-of-factly. "He'll let me back in. Speaking of love, when's the wedding?"

"What wedding?" Haplo asked, his thoughts on how to solve the current problem.

"Yours and Alake's."

Haplo came to a stop, glared at the dwarf.

Grundle gazed back, smiling, innocent. Numerous tribe members were eyeing them curiously. Haplo caught hold of the dwarf's arm, hustled her into the privacy of his lodge.

"Uh-oh," she said, shrinking away from him in mock terror. "You're not going to try to seduce me, now, are you?"

"I didn't seduce anybody," Haplo said grimly. "And keep your voice down. How much do you know? What did Alake tell you?"

"Everything. Mind if I sit? Thanks." She plopped herself on the floor, began plucking leaves out of her side whiskers. "Whew! It was really hot, squatting in that bush. I could have told those dragon-snakes they were making a mistake, showing off their power like that. Not that they would have listened to me."

She shook her head, her expression suddenly grave, solemn. "Do you know, I think they did it on purpose. I think they knew magic like that would frighten my people. I think they meant to frighten them!"

"Don't be ridiculous. Why would they want to frighten you when they're trying to save you? And never mind that now anyway. What did Alake tell you? Whatever she said, I didn't try to take advantage of her."

"Oh, I know that." Grundle waved a deprecating hand. "I was just teasing. I have to admit . . ." she added grudgingly.

"You treated Alake better than I expected you to. I guess I misjudged you. I'm sorry."

"What did she tell you?" Haplo asked for the third time.

"That you two were going to be married. Not now. Alake's not a fool. She knows that this crisis is no time for her to bring up matrimony. But when the sun-chasers take us all to a new realm—if that ever happens, which now I'm beginning to doubt—then she figures you'll both be free to get married and start a new life together."

So, Haplo said to himself bitterly, here I've been thinking all along that she'd come to her senses. All she's been doing, apparently, is entrenching herself deeper in her fantasies.

"Do you love her?" Grundle askd.

Haplo turned, frowning, thinking the dwarf was teasing him again. He saw, instead, that she was very much in earnest.

"No, I don't."

"I didn't think so." Grundle gave a small sigh. "Why don't you just tell her?"

"I don't want to hurt her."

"Funny," said the dwarf, studying him shrewdly, "I'd have said you were the kind of man who didn't much care whether he hurt other people or not. What's your real reason?"

Haplo squatted down on his haunches, eyes level with the dwarf maid. "Let's say that it wouldn't be in anybody's best interests if I did anything to upset Alake. Would it?"

Grundle shook her head. "No, I guess you're right."

He breathed a sigh, stood up. "Listen, the shouting's stopped. I'd say the meeting's broken up."

Grundle clambered hastily to her feet. "That means I better get going. If I'm caught missing, Hartmut's the one who'll end up in trouble. I hope my parents settled everything with the humans. Deep down, you know, my father really respects Dumaka and Delu. It's just that the snakes frightened him so badly."

She started to dart out the door. Haplo caught hold of her, pulled her back.

Yngvar was stumping past, his face a sullen red in the firelight, arms swinging wildly as he muttered to himself. His wife tromped along at his side, her lips pressed together tightly, too angry to speak.

"I don't think they resolved anything," said Haplo.

Grundle shook her head. "Alake's right. The One sent you to us. I will ask the One to help you."

"The same One whose oath I swore?" asked Haplo.

"What else?" said Grundle, looking at him in astonishment. "The One who guides the waves, of course."

The dwarf dashed out the door, her short legs pumping as she ran off into the night. He watched the small figure bob among the campfires, saw that she would easily outdistance her parents. Yngvar's anger carried him along at a swift pace, but Haplo guessed the rotund king would soon get winded. Grundle would reach the cave in plenty of time to replace the sack of potatoes with her own stout body, save lover Hartmut from having his beard cut off or whatever form of punishment was measured out to guards derelict in their duties.

Haplo turned from the door, flung himself on his pallet, stared into the darkness. He thought about the dwarves and their reliance on this One, wondered if he could somehow use this to his advantage.

" 'The One who guides the waves'!" he repeated, amused.

He closed his eyes, relaxed. Sleep began to sever the ties that bound brain to body, snipping them one by one to let the mind drift free until dawn would catch it, drag it back. But before the last cord was cut, Haplo heard an echo of Grundle's words in his mind. But it wasn't the dwarf's voice that spoke them. The words seemed, in fact, to come to him out of a very bright white light, and they were slightly different.

The One who guides the Wave.

Haplo blinked, jerked to wakefulness. He sat up, stared into the darkness of his lodge.

"Alfred?" he demanded, then wondered irritably why he should have the feeling the Sartan was present.

He lay back down, shoved the dwarves, Alake, the Sartan, the One, the dragon-snakes, and whoever else was crowded into his lodge out into the night, and gave himself up to sleep.

CHAPTER ♦ 21

PHONDRA

CHELESTRA

♦

THE ELVES WERE TWO CYCLES LATE—TO THE SURPRISE OF NO ONE, except possibly Haplo.

Dumaka hadn't expected Eliason *that* soon, was astonished beyond measure when the dolphins brought word that the elves were sailing into Phondran waters. He sent everyone in the village into a mad scramble to open, clean out, and prepare the elven guesthouses.

These houses were special, having been built exclusively to house the elves, who—like the dwarves—demanded special arrangements. For example, no elf would consider sleeping on the ground. This was not a matter of comfort. Long ago, elven alchemists, perhaps in a vain attempt to try to harness the drifting seasun, had discovered the nature of the chemical reaction between seasun and seamoon that produced the breathable air surrounding the moons.

The chemical reaction, so the alchemists deduced, took place between the surface of the seamoon and the seasun. The next logical step was that a similar reaction would naturally take place between anything that rested on the surface for any length of time—this included elves or any other living creature.

Only inanimate objects were ever permitted to rest on the ground in the elven kingdom, and then the most valuable of these was moved periodically to prevent any unfortunate alteration.[1] Animals that slept on the ground were not encouraged in Elmas and had been gradually phased out, in favor of birds, monkeys, cats, all those who live in trees.

Elves will eat no food that has been grown on the ground or in it. They will not stand long in one place, nor stand long at all, if they can help it, but will sit down and pull their feet up into the chair.

One of the earliest and most devastating wars between the Phondrans and the Elmas was the War of the Bed. An elven prince had traveled to human lands to open negotiations to avert a war. All went well until the human chieftain led the elf to his quarters for the night. The elf took one look at the pallet spread on the bare ground, assumed the human was out to murder him,[2] and declared war on the spot.

Since then, humans and elves have come to respect, if not agree with, each other's beliefs. Elven guesthouses in Phondra are furnished with crude beds made of tree limbs lashed together with rope. And, in their own homelands, the elves have learned to avert their eyes when their human guests take the blankets from the bed and spread them out on the floor. (Eliason had even ceased the practice of attempting to shift his sleeping human guests into beds without their knowledge, ever since one fell out during the night and broke his arm.)

The guest quarters in the village were barely finished by the time the elven ship docked. Dumaka and Delu were on hand to greet their guests. Yngvar was there, as well, though the dwarven contingent and the humans kept well apart. Grundle and Alake were present, but separated, each standing with her own family.

---

[1] One reason the elves are extremely amenable to the constantly shifting nature of their coral dwellings. All furniture, clothing, bedding, and such-like would have to be moved anyway.

[2] It is a widely held belief among the Elmas that the short life span of humans is due entirely to their unfortunate habit of sleeping on the ground. Phondrans, on the other hand, view the tall elven beds with horror, are terrified that they will roll off in the night and kill themselves. The Gargan find the entire argument ridiculous. As long as there is solid stone above him, a dwarf could sleep standing on his head. Unfortunately, however, this is one reason many dwarves do not travel comfortably by ship.

The rift between the two races had deepened. Both sets of parents forbade their daughters to talk to one another. Haplo, seeing the two girls exchange secretive, flashing-eyed glances, guessed just how long that rule would be obeyed. He hoped grimly that they wouldn't get caught, precipitate another crisis. At least, the enforced separation had given Alake something else to think about besides the Patryn. He supposed he should be grateful.

The royal families greeted each other with every show of friendship—for the sake of their followers. Dumaka included Haplo as a highly honored guest and the Patryn was at least relieved to note that even the dwarf thawed out somewhat in Haplo's presence. But none of them could hide the fact that they were not meeting in peace as they would have normally. Handshakes were formal and stiff, voices were cold and carefully modulated. No one called anyone by his or her given name.

Haplo could have cheerfully drowned every one of them.

The dolphins had been the cause of this latest trouble. They had gleefully carried the news about the dwarves refusing to travel in the sun-chaser to the elves. Eliason was disposed to side with Dumaka, although, elflike, he had sent word that he would not be rushed into making a decision. This pleased neither. Consequently, Eliason had managed to anger both dwarves and humans before he even arrived.

All of which caused Haplo to literally gnash his teeth in frustration. He had one bit of consolation and it was negative—the dragon-snakes were nowhere to be seen. He was afraid the sight of the formidable creatures might harden the dwarves' determination against them.

A time for a meeting was set, later that evening, and then Yngvar and his contingent stomped off.

Eliason looked after the angry dwarf sadly, shook his head. "What is to be done?" he asked Dumaka.

"I have no idea," the human chieftain growled. "If you ask me, his beard's grown into his brain. He claims he and his people would rather freeze to death than set foot on the sun-chasers. They probably would, too. They're just stubborn enough."

Haplo, unobtrusive and silent, kept his distance, but lingered near, hoping to hear something that would help him figure out what to do.

Dumaka put a hand on Eliason's shoulder. "I am sorry, my friend, to add this trouble to the heavy burden of your sorrow. Although," he added, studying the elf intently, "you carry it better than I would have thought possible."

"I had to let the dead go," replied Eliason softly, "in order to look after the living."

The young elf, Devon, stood on the pier, staring out over the water. Alake was beside him, talking to him earnestly. Grundle, with a wistful glance at both of them, had been dragged off by her parents.

But it was obvious that Alake's words were falling on deaf ears. Devon paid no attention to her, didn't respond in any way.

Dumaka's grim expression softened. "So young, to be dealt such a heavy blow."

"Three nights running," said Eliason, in low tones, "we discovered him in that room where my daughter . . . where she . . ." He swallowed, turned exceedingly pale.

Dumaka squeezed his arm in silent sympathy, to indicate he understood.

Eliason drew a deep breath. "Thank you, my friend. We found him . . . there, staring out the window at the stones below. You can imagine what terrible deed we feared he contemplated. I brought him with me, hoping that the company of his friends would draw him out of the shadows that surround him. And it was for his sake I left earlier than I had intended."

"Thank you, Devon," Haplo muttered.

Alake, after a helpless glance at her father, finally suggested that Devon might want to see his quarters, and offered to show him the way. He responded like one of the automatons the Gegs used on Arianus, trailing after Alake with listless step and bowed head. He didn't know where he was, obviously cared less.

Haplo remained hanging about Eliason and Dumaka, but it was soon apparent that the two rulers were going to talk of Devon and his sorrows and nothing of major importance.

Just as well, Haplo decided, leaving them. They're not likely to get into a fight over that subject. And I have at least two out of five mensch speaking to each other.

He couldn't help but think back to his time spent on Arianus, time spent trying to spread discord between elves and humans and dwarves. Now he was working twice as hard to bring the three mensch races together.

"I might almost believe in this One," he said to himself. "Somebody must be getting a big laugh out of all this."

The ceremonial drum was beating, calling the royal families to conference. Everyone in the village turned out to watch the various parties wend their way to the longhouse. At any other time, such a meeting would have been cause for jubilation; the Phondrans would have been chattering among themselves, pointing out to their children such curiosities as the remarkable length of dwarven beards, the sunlight blondness of elven hair.

But this day, the Phondrans stood in silence, quieting irritably the children's high-pitched questions. Rumor had blown through Phondra like the embers of a campfire, stirred by a high wind. Wherever it fell, small blazes started up, spread rapidly through the tribes of the realm. Other humans from other tribes had traveled here in their long narrow boats, to witness the meeting.

Many of these were witches and warlocks, belonging to the Coven, and were welcomed by Delu, made guests of her own lodgehouse. Others were chieftains, owing their loyalty to Dumaka, and were welcomed by him. Still others were nobody in particular, just curious. These invariably had some guestfriend or relative among the tribe. Nearly every lodge had at least one extra blanket spread on its floor.

All gathered to watch the procession, consisting of the three royal families, representatives of other Phondran tribes, the Phondran Coven, the Elmas Guildsmen, the Gargan Elders—all of the latter acting as witnesses for their people. The humans were silent, faces strained and tense, worried and anxious. Everyone knew that no matter what was decided in the meeting, their fate—for good or ill—depended on the outcome.

Haplo had started for the lodge early, intending to slip inside before any of the dignitaries arrived. But, glancing out to sea, he was disconcerted and none too pleased to see the long sinuous necks and green-red slit eyes of the dragon-snakes.

He couldn't help feeling a qualm, an uncomfortable tight-ening of stomach muscles, a chill in his bowels. The sigla on his skin began to glow a faint blue.

Haplo wished irritably the snakes hadn't come, hoped none of the others saw them. He'd have to remember to try to keep everyone from the water's edge.

The drum beat loudly, then stopped. The members of the three families met outside the lodgehouse, were making a show of friendship—grudging on the part of the dwarves, stiff and constrained on the part of everyone else.

Haplo was wondering how he could manage to evade getting caught up in the formalities, when two figures, one tall and one short, loomed in his path. Hands grabbed his arms. Alake and Grundle dragged him into the jungle shadows.

"I don't have time for games—" he began impatiently, then took a good look at their faces. "What's happened?"

"You've got to help us!" Alake gasped. "We don't know what to do! I think we should tell my father—"

"That's the last thing we want to do!" Grundle snapped. "The meeting's just getting started. If we break it up now, who knows when they'll ever get back together?"

"But—"

"What's happened?" Haplo demanded.

"Devon!" Alake's eyes were wide and frightened. "He's . . . disappeared."

"Damn!" Haplo swore beneath his breath.

"He's gone for a walk. That's all," Grundle said, but the dwarf's nut-brown complexion was pale, her side whiskers trembled.

"I'm going to tell my father, he'll call out the trackers." Alake started to run away.

Haplo caught hold of her, hauled her back.

"We can't afford to interrupt the meeting. I'm a fair tracker myself. We'll find him, bring him back quietly, without fuss. Grundle's right. He's probably just gone off for a walk, to be by himself. Now, where and when did you last see him?"

Alake had been the last to see him.

"I took him to the elven guesthouse. I stayed with him, tried to talk to him. Then Eliason and the other elves returned to prepare for the meeting and I had to leave. But I waited around, hoping to get a chance to talk to him when Eliason and the rest left. I went back to the guesthouse. He was there, alone."

"I told him that Grundle and I had found a place in back of the longhouse where we could . . . well, that is . . ."

"Listen in?" Haplo suggested.

"We have a right," Grundle stated. "This all happened because of us. We should be there."

"I agree," said Haplo quietly, to calm the irate dwarf. "I'll see what I can do. Now, finish telling me about Devon."

"At first, he seemed almost angry to see me. He said he didn't want to listen to anything our parents said. He didn't care. Then, suddenly, he cheered up. He was almost too cheerful, somehow. It was . . . kind of awful." She shuddered.

"He told me he was hungry. He knew dinner would be a long time coming, what with the meeting and all, and he asked me if I could find him something to eat. I told him I could and tried to persuade him to come with me. He didn't want to leave the guesthouse, he said. The people staring at him made him nervous.

"I thought it would be good if he ate something; I don't think he's eaten in days. And so I left to fetch food. There were other elves with him. On the way, I ran into Grundle, looking for me. I brought her along, thinking she might be able to cheer up Devon. When we got back to the lodge"—Alake spread her hands—"he was gone."

Haplo didn't like the sounds of any of this. He'd known people in the Labyrinth who suddenly couldn't take it anymore, couldn't stand the pain, the horror, the loss of a friend, a mate. He'd seen the ghastly cheerfulness that often came after a severe despondency.

Alake saw the grim expression on his face. She moaned, covered her mouth with her hand. Grundle tugged at her side whiskers in black gloom.

"He's probably just taking a walk," Haplo repeated. "Did you look for him in the village? Maybe he went after Eliason?"

"He didn't," said Alake softly. "When we got back to the guesthouse, I searched around back. I found . . . tracks. His tracks, I'm certain. They lead right into the jungle."

That clinches it, thought Haplo. Aloud, he added, "Keep

quiet. Try to act as if nothing's the matter, and take me there, quickly."

The three hurried back to the elven guesthouse. They took a circuitous route, kept to the fringes of the crowds, avoided the assembly gathered around the longhouse.

Haplo could see Dumaka, greeting the dwarven dignitaries. He was glancing about, perhaps in search of the Patryn. At that moment, Eliason stepped forward, prepared to present his party. Haplo was thankful to note that there were numerous elves present; he hoped they all had long names.

Alake led him to the back of the guesthouse, pointed to the moist ground. The tracks were footprints—too long and narrow for dwarves—and undoubtedly made by booted feet. Phondrans, without exception, all went barefoot.

Haplo swore silently beneath his breath.

"Have the other elves in the guesthouse missed him yet?"

"I don't think so," Alake replied. "They're all outside, watching the ceremony."

"I'll go look for him. You two stay here, in case he comes back."

"We're going with you," said Grundle.

"Yes. He's our friend." Alake joined her.

Haplo glared at them, but the dwarf's jaw was set firm, her small arms crossed defiantly over her chest. Alake regarded him calmly, steadfastly. There would be an argument, and he didn't have time.

"Come on, then."

The two girls started down the path, stopped when they realized Haplo wasn't following.

"What is it? What are you doing?" Alake asked. "Shouldn't we hurry?"

Haplo had squatted down, was quickly tracing sigla in the mud over the elf's footprints. He breathed soft words; the sigla flashed green, and suddenly began to grow and sprout. Plants and weeds sprang up, covering the path, obliterating any sign of the elf's footprints.

"This is no time," snapped Grundle, "to start a garden."

"They'll be looking for him soon." Rising to his feet, Haplo watched the plants completely overrun the path. "I'm making

certain no one comes after us. We'll do what needs to be done,
tell whatever story we need to tell. Agreed?"

"Oh!" murmured Alake, biting her lip.

"Agreed?" Haplo stared at the two grimly.

"Agreed," Grundle said, subdued.

"Agreed," Alake repeated unhappily.

They left the campsite behind, followed the elf's footprints
into the jungle.

At first, Haplo thought that perhaps Grundle might have inadvertently guessed the truth. It appeared that the despondent
young elf *was* simply intent on trying to walk off his misery.
The tracks kept to the open path. Devon hadn't bothered to
conceal his whereabouts, he wasn't attempting to hide from
anyone, and he must have known that Alake, at least, would
come after him.

And then, abruptly, the tracks ended.

The path continued on, smooth, unmarked. The plant life on
each side was dense, too dense to penetrate without leaving
some sort of trace, and not a leaf was disturbed, not a flower
crushed, a stalk bent.

"What'd he do? Grow wings?" the dwarf grumbled, peering
into the shadows.

"So to speak," said Haplo, looking up into the trailing vines.

The elf must have taken to the trees. A swift glance farther
into the jungle's dark shadows showed him something else.

His first thought was, Damn! Another elven mourning
period!

"You girls go back now," he said firmly, but suddenly Alake
gave a shriek, and before he could stop her, she had plunged
into the undergrowth.

Haplo jumped after her, dragged her back, shoved her hard
into Grundle. The two fell over each other. Haplo ran on, glancing back over his shoulder to make certain he'd delayed the two
from following.

The dwarf, in her thick boots, had become entangled in the
vines. Alake seemed prepared to leave her friend to fend for
herself, started after Haplo. Grundle set up a howl of rage that
could be heard for miles.

"Shut her up!" Haplo ordered, crashing through the thick
jungle foliage.

Alake, anguish twisting her face, turned back to help Grundle.

Haplo reached Devon.

The elf had formed a noose out of vines, wrapped it around his neck, and jumped from a tree limb to what he had hoped would be his death.

Looking at the limp body, swinging grotesquely in a spiral on its vine, Haplo thought at first the young man had succeeded. Then he saw two of the elf's fingers twitch. It might be a death spasm, it might not.

Haplo shouted the runes. Blue and red sigla flashed through the air, burst on the vine, severed it. The body plunged down into the undergrowth.

Reaching the young man, Haplo grabbed hold of the vine around the neck, wrenched it loose. Devon wasn't breathing. He was unconscious, his face discolored, lips blue. The vine had cut into the flesh of his slender neck, left it bruised and bleeding. But, Haplo saw after a swift, cursory examination, the elf's neck wasn't broken, the windpipe wasn't crushed. The vine had slipped, apparently, sliding up the neck instead of snapping it, as Devon had undoubtedly intended. He was still alive.

But he wouldn't be alive long. Haplo felt for a pulse, life fluttered faintly beneath his fingers. The Patryn sat back on his heels, considering. He had no idea if what he intended would work or not. As far as he knew, it had never been tried on a mensch. But he seemed to remember Alfred saying something about using his magic to heal the child, Bane.

If Sartan magic worked on a mensch, Patryn magic should work as well . . . or better.

Haplo took hold of the elf's flaccid hands, Devon's left hand in Haplo's right, the Patryn's left hand holding the elf's right hand fast. The circle was joined.

Haplo shut his eyes, concentrated. He was dimly aware, behind him, of Alake and Grundle. He heard them come to a halt, heard Alake whimper, Grundle's breath whistle through her teeth. Haplo paid no attention to them.

He was giving his own life strength to Devon. Runes on his arms glowed blue. The magic flowed from him to the elf, carried Haplo's life with it, carried Devon's pain and suffering back to Haplo.

The Patryn experienced, vicariously, the terrible grief, the burning guilt, the bitter, gnawing regret that had tormented Devon, sleeping and waking, and had finally driven him to seek solace in oblivion. Haplo felt the shriveling fear right before the jump—the brain's instinct for self-preservation making a last desperate attempt to fight back.

Then the decision. Pain, the horrible feeling of suffocation, the knowledge, peaceful and serene, that death was near and the torment would soon all be over . . .

Haplo heard a groan, heard the rustle of the plants. He gasped for breath, opened his eyes.

Devon stared up at him, face anguished, twisted, bitter. "You had no right," he whispered hoarsely, his throat sore and bruised from the vine's grip. "I want to die! Let me die, damn you! Let me die!"

Alake cried out. "No, Devon! You don't know what you're saying!"

"He knows," said Haplo grimly. He sat back on his heels, wiped his hand across his sweaty forehead. "You and Grundle go on back to the path. Let me talk to him."

"But—"

"Go!" Haplo yelled angrily.

Grundle tugged on Alake's hand. The two made their way back slowly through the trampled leaves and slashed plants to the path beyond.

"You want to die," Haplo said to the elf, who averted his head, shut his eyes. "Go ahead, then. Hang yourself. I can't stop you. But I'd appreciate it if you'd wait until after we get all this business about the sun-chasers settled, because I assume there'll be another long period of grieving over you, and the delay could endanger your people."

The elf refused to look at him. "They'll be all right. They have something to live for. I don't." His words were a hoarse croak. He grimaced at the pain.

"Yeah? Well, what do you think your parents will have to live for after they cut your body down from that tree limb? You have any idea what their last memory of you will be? Your face bloated, skin discolored, black as rotting fungus; your eyes bugged out of your head, your tongue sticking out of your mouth?"

Devon blanched, cast Haplo a hate-filled glance, and turned his head again. "Go away," he muttered.

"You know"—Haplo continued as if he hadn't heard—"if your body hangs there long enough, the carrion birds'll come. The first thing they go for is the eyes. Your parents may not even recognize their son—or what's left of him, when the birds are finished, not to mention the ants and the flies—"

"Stop!" Devon tried to shout, but it came out a sob.

"And there's Alake and Grundle. They lost one friend, now they'll lose another. You didn't give them a thought, either, I suppose? No, just yourself. 'The pain, I can't bear the pain,' " Haplo mimicked the elf's light, piping voice.

"What do you know about it?" Devon cried.

"What do I know about it . . . about pain," Haplo repeated softly. "Let me tell you a story, then I'll leave you to kill yourself, if that's what you want. I knew a man, once, in the Laby— a place I lived. He was in a fight, a terrible fight, for his life. In that place, you have to fight to stay alive, you don't fight to die. Anyway, this man was hurt horribly. Wounds . . . all over his body. His suffering was beyond belief, beyond endurance.

"The man defeated his enemies. The chaodyn lay dead around him. But he couldn't go on. He hurt too much. He could have tried to heal himself with his magic, but it didn't seem to him to be worth the effort. He lay on the ground, letting the life seep out of him. Then something happened to change his mind. There was a dog . . .

"The dog." Haplo paused, a strange, lonely ache constricting his heart. All this time, how could he have forgotten the dog?

"What happened?" Devon whispered, blue eyes intent upon the man. "What happened . . . with the dog?"

Haplo frowned, rubbed his chin; sorry, in a way, he'd brought it up, glad, in a way, to remember.

"The dog. The animal had fought the chaodyn and it had been hurt, too. It was dying, in such pain that it couldn't walk. Yet, when the dog saw the man's suffering, it tried to help him. The dog didn't give up. It started to crawl, on its belly, to get help. Its courage made the man feel ashamed.

"A dumb brute, with nothing to live for—no hopes or dreams or ambitions—and it fought to go on living. And I had everything. I was young, strong; I'd won a great victory. And I was about to throw it all away . . . because of the pain."

"Did the dog die?" Devon asked softly. Weak as a sick child, like a child, he wanted to hear the end of the story.

The Patryn wrenched himself back from his memories.

"No, the man healed the dog, healed himself." He hadn't noticed his lapse, hadn't noticed that he and "the man" had gotten rather mixed. "He rose to a position of power among his people. He changed the course of people's lives . . ."

"Saved people from dragon-snakes? Or maybe themselves?" Devon asked, with a twisted, rueful smile.

Haplo stared at him, then grunted. "Yeah, maybe. Something like that. Well, what's it going to be? Shall I leave you here to try again?"

Devon glanced up at the cut vine, dangling over his head. "No. No, I'll come . . . with you." He tried to sit up, and fainted.

Haplo reached out his hand, felt for the pulse. It was stronger, steadier. He brushed aside a lock of flaxen hair caught in the dried blood on the neck.

"It will get better," he told the unconscious young man. "You won't forget her, but the remembering won't hurt as much."

CHAPTER ♦ 22

PHONDRA

CHELESTRA

♦

THE MEETING OF THE ROYAL FAMILIES OPENED WITH STIFF FORMALI-
ties, cold glances, unspoken resentment. From there, it moved
to open hostility, hot words, and bitter recriminations.

Eliason's position against war had not altered with the passage of time.

"I am quite willing to set sail in the sun-chasers and find this
new realm," he stated. "And I will undertake to negotiate with
these . . . er . . . Sartan, since all know that elves are skilled in
such diplomatic endeavors. I cannot see how these Sartan could
refuse such a reasonable request, particularly when we explain
how we will bring them much-needed goods and services. My
advisers, having given the matter considerable study, have determined that this Sartan race must be relatively new to this realm
themselves. We think it likely they'll actually be quite glad to
see us."

Eliason's face darkened. "But if not, if the Sartan refuse, well,
after all, it *is* their realm. We will simply look elsewhere."

"Fine," said Dumaka sourly. "And while you are looking,
what will you eat? Where will you find the food to feed your
people? Will you grow corn in the cracks in the deck? Or has
elven magic come up with a way to pull bread out of air? We
have calculated that we can carry barely enough supplies for the
journey as it is, considering all the mouths we'll have to feed.
There will be room for no more."

"The supply of fish is plentiful," said Eliason mildly.

"Of course," Dumaka retorted, "but not even an elf could live exclusively on a diet of fish! Without fruits and vegetables, the mouth-sickness[1] will come upon our people."

Yngvar looked horrified at the mere thought of being forced to live on fish.[2] The dwarf planted his feet firmly on the ground, glared round at the assembly. "You argue over who stole the pie when the pie hasn't even been cooked yet! The sun-chasers are cursed; the dwarves will have nothing to do with them. And, after consultation with the Elders, we have determined that we will allow no one to have anything to do with them, lest the curse will come back on us. It is our intention to scuttle the things, send them to the bottom of the Goodsea. We will build more ourselves, without the help of snakes."

"Yes, that's a good idea," said Eliason. "There will be time—"

"There will *not* be time!" Dumaka fumed. "You elves were the ones who figured up how many cycles we had—"

"You dwarves are worse than superstitious children!" Delu was arguing loudly. "The ships are no more cursed than I am!"

"And who's certain about you, Witch?" Hilda flashed back, side whiskers bristling.

At that moment, one of the doorkeepers, attempting to give the impression he was deaf and blind to the turmoil around him, crept into the longhouse and whispered something to Dumaka. The chieftain nodded, gave an order. Everyone else had ceased talking, wondering what this interruption portended. No one ever disturbed a royal meeting unless it was a matter of life and death. The doorkeeper departed swiftly on his errand. Dumaka turned to Eliason.

"Your guards have discovered the young man, Devon, to be missing. They've searched the camp, but no trace of him can be found. I've called out the trackers. Don't worry, my friend," the chief said, his anger forgotten at the sight of the elf's anxiety. "We'll find him."

---

[1]A reference to what the dwarves know as scurvy.

[2]Dwarves have a low regard for fish and eat it only when no other, more substantial, food is available. A slang word among dwarves for fish is *elmas-fleish*, or "elf-meat."

"A young fool's gone for a walk!" Yngvar snapped irritably. "Why all the fuss?"

"Devon has been very unhappy of late," said Eliason in a low voice. "Very unhappy. We fear . . ." His voice failed. He shook his head.

"Ach!" said Yngvar gravely, in sudden understanding. "That's the way of it, is it?"

"Grundle!" Hilda called out sharply, loudly. "Grundle! Come in here, this instant!"

"What are you doing, Wife? Our daughter's in the cave—"

"Take the sack off your head,"[3] Hilda retorted. "Our daughter's no more in that cave than I am." She stood up, raised her voice threateningly. "Grundle, I know you're out there, spying! Alake, this is serious. I won't tolerate any more nonsense from you girls!"

But there was no answer. Yngvar looked solemn, tugged at his beard. Stepping outside, he motioned to one of his attendants, a young dwarf named Hartmut, and sent him off toward the cave.

Yngvar returned to the longhouse, where Eliason was also on his feet. "I should go help search—"

"And do what? End up losing yourself in the jungle? Our people will find him. All will be well, my friend—we pray to the One."

"We pray to the One," Eliason repeated, and sat back down, his head in his hands.

Then Yngvar spoke, "Aye, but where's that Haplo got to? Has anybody seen *him*? Wasn't he supposed to be here? This meeting was his idea in the first place."

"You dwarves are suspicious of everything!" Dumaka shouted. "First, the dragon-snakes' magic. Now Haplo! And after he saved our children—"

"He saved our children, but what do we truly know of him, Husband?" Delu asked. "Perhaps he brought them back, only to carry them off again!"

---

[3]Reference to a popular dwarven drinking game, the rules of which are far too complex to describe and probably wouldn't be believed anyway.

"She's right!" Hilda came to stand by the human woman's side. "I say your trackers start looking for this Haplo!"

"Fine!" said Dumaka, exasperated. "I'll send the trackers out looking for everyone—"

"Chief!" The doorkeeper shouted, "They've found them! All of them!"

Elves, humans, and dwarves rushed out of the longhouse. By this time, everyone in camp knew either what had occurred or what was rumored to have occurred. The royal families joined a throng heading toward the elven guesthouse.

Human trackers escorted Haplo, Grundle, and Alake from the jungle. Haplo carried Devon in his arms. The elf had regained consciousness, smiled weakly, shamefaced at the attention.

"Devon! Are you hurt? What happened?" Eliason shouldered his way through the crowd.

"I'm . . . fine," Devon managed, his voice coming out a croak.

"He'll be all right," Haplo said. "He had a nasty fall, got hung up in a vine. Let him rest. Where shall I put him?"

"This way." Eliason led the Patryn to the elven guesthouse.

"We can explain everything," Grundle announced.

"I've no doubt of that," her father muttered, eyeing his daughter grimly.

Haplo carried Devon into the guesthouse, deposited the young man on his bed.

"Thank you," said Devon softly.

Haplo grunted. "Get some sleep."

Devon, taking the hint, closed his eyes.

"He needs rest," said Haplo, coming to stand between Eliason and the young elf. "I think we should let him alone."

"But I want my physician to see to him—" Eliason began anxiously.

"That won't be necessary. He's going to be all right. But now he needs rest," Haplo repeated.

Eliason looked past Haplo at the young elf lying exhausted, disheveled, on the bed. The girls had cleaned him up, washed the blood away, but the burns and marks left by the vine were plainly visible on his neck. The elven king looked back at Haplo.

"He fell," the Patryn repeated coolly. "Got tangled in a vine."

"Will it happen again, do you think?" Eliason asked quietly.

"No." Haplo shook his head. "I don't think so. We had a talk . . . about the dangers of climbing trees in the jungle."

"Thank the One," Eliason murmured.

Devon had fallen asleep. Haplo led the elven king back outside the guesthouse.

"Alake and I took Devon for a walk," Grundle was explaining to an attentive crowd. "I know I disobeyed you, Father"—the dwarf gave Yngvar a sidelong glance—"but Devon looked so unhappy and we thought this might cheer him—"

"Humpf!" Yngvar snorted. "Very well, Daughter. We will discuss your punishment later. For now, go on with your story."

"Grundle and I wanted to speak to Devon alone," Alake said. "There were too many people in the village, too much going on, and so we suggested a walk in the jungle. We talked and talked and it was hot and we were thirsty and then I noticed that one of the sugarjuice trees had fruit on it. I guess what happened was my fault, because I suggested that Devon climb up—"

"And he was nearly at the top," inserted Grundle, gesturing dramatically, "when he slipped and down he went, headfirst into a tangle of chokevines."

"They wrapped around his neck! He was caught. I . . . we didn't know what to do!" Alake's eyes were wide. "I couldn't get him down. He was too far off the ground. Grundle and I ran back to the village to get help. The first person we found was Haplo. He came with us and cut Devon down from the vines."

Alake looked at Haplo, standing on the edge of the crowd. Her eyes shone.

"He saved Devon's life," she said softly. "He used his magic and healed him! I saw it. Devon wasn't breathing. The vines had wrapped around his neck. Haplo put his hands on him and his skin glowed blue and suddenly Devon opened his eyes and . . . he was alive."

"Is this true?" Dumaka asked Haplo.

"She's exaggerating, she was upset." The Patryn shrugged. "The boy wasn't dead. He was out cold. He would have come around. . . ."

"I was upset," Alake said, smiling, "but I wasn't exaggerating."

Everyone began to talk at once: Yngvar halfheartedly scolded his daughter for running away. Delu stated that it was foolish to attempt to climb a sugarjuice tree by oneself and that Alake should have known better than to allow it. Eliason said he thought the girls showed good sense in running for help and that they should thank the One Haplo had been there to avert another tragedy.

"The One!" said Grundle, pouncing on the startled elven king. "Yes, you thank the One, who sent us this man"—she pointed her short, stubby finger at Haplo—"and then you turn around and toss the rest of the gifts the One provides into the Goodsea!"

Everyone in camp fell silent, stared at the dwarf maid.

"Daughter," Yngvar began sternly.

"Hush!" Hilda counseled, treading on his foot. "The child makes sense."

"And why will you throw these blessings away?" Grundle glared round at all of them. "Because you don't understand them and so you're afraid of them." A scathing glance at the dwarves. "Or because you might have to fight to obtain them." The elves came in for their share of her ire.

"Well, we decided—Alake, Devon, and I. We're taking the sun-chaser with Haplo. We're sailing to Surunan. We'll go alone, if we have to—"

"No, you won't, Grundle," Hartmut said stoutly, coming to stand beside her. "I'll go with you."

"We'll go!" cried several young humans and "We'll come, too!" shouted numerous young elves.

The cry was taken up by almost all the young people around. Grundle exchanged glances with Alake. The dwarf-maid turned to her parents.

"Well, what have you started now, Daughter?" her father asked dourly. "Open rebellion against your own father?"

"I'm sorry, Father," Grundle answered, flushing. "But I truly believe it's for the best. You wouldn't let our people freeze . . . or the humans . . ."

"Of course, he wouldn't," said Hilda. "Admit it, Yngvar. Your feet grew too big for your head. You were looking for a way to back down. Our daughter's given you one. Will you take it?"

Yngvar rumpled his beard. "I don't see that I have much choice," he said, trying hard to frown and not quite succeeding. "The lass will be leading my own army against me, if I'm not careful."

He grunted and stomped off. Grundle looked after him anxiously.

"Relax, dear," said Hilda, smiling. "He's really quite proud of you."

And, indeed, Yngvar was stopping on his way to tell everyone, *"That's* my daughter!"

"And my people will go." Eliason bent down and kissed the dwarf soundly. "Thank you, Daughter, for showing us our folly. May the One bless and guide you always." His eyes filled with tears. "And now, I must return to Devon."

Eliason left hurriedly.

Grundle was tasting power, obviously found it sweeter than sugarjuice, more intoxicating than dwarven ale. She glanced around, elated, for Haplo, saw him standing in the shadows, watching quietly.

"I did it!" she cried, running over to him. "I did it! I said what you told me! They're going! All of them!"

Haplo kept silent, his face was dark, expression impenetrable.

"It was what you wanted, wasn't it?" Grundle demanded, irritated. "Wasn't it?"

"Yeah, sure. It was what I wanted," Haplo answered.

"It's wonderful!" Alake came over to him, her smile dazzling. "All of us, sailing to new lives!"

Two muscular humans ran over, lifted the dwarf-maid to their shoulders, and bore her off in triumph. Alake began to dance. A procession started, the humans chanting, elves singing, dwarven deep bass rivaling the booming of the drum.

Sailing to new lives.

Sailing to death.

Haplo turned on his heel, walked into the darkness, leaving the bright firelight and revelry behind.

CHAPTER ♦ 23

SURUNAN

CHELESTRA

♦

ALFRED HAD NOT BEEN FORCED TO SPEND ALL THIS TIME A PRISONER in the library. The Sartan Council met not once but on numerous occasions; the members were apparently having difficulty arriving at a decision concerning Alfred's transgression. Alfred was permitted to leave the library, return to the house. He would be confined to his room until the Council had reached a decision concerning him.

The Council members were forbidden to discuss the proceedings, but Alfred was certain that Orla was the one coming to his defense. The thought warmed him, until he noticed that the wall between husband and wife had grown even higher, thicker. Orla was grave and reserved. Her husband cold with anger. They rarely spoke to each other. Alfred's resolve to leave strengthened. He wanted only to make his apologies to the Council, then he would be gone.

"There is no need to lock me inside my room," Alfred told Ramu, who served as his guard. "I give you my word as a Sartan that I will not attempt to escape. I ask only one favor of you. Could you see to it that the dog is allowed fresh air and exercise?"

"I suppose we must comply," Samah said ungraciously to his son, when Alfred's request was reported.

"Why not dispose of the animal?" Ramu asked indifferently.

"Because I have plans for it," Samah replied. "I believe I will ask your mother to perform the task of walking the creature." He and his son exchanged significant glances.

Orla refused her husband's request. "Ramu can walk the animal. I want nothing to do with it."

"Ramu has his own life now," her husband reminded her sternly. "He has his family, his own responsibilities. This Alfred and his dog are our responsibility. One for which you have only yourself to thank."

Orla heard the rebuke in his voice, was conscious of her guilt for having failed in that responsibility once already. And she had failed her husband again, tying up the Council with strings of arguments.

"Very well, Samah," she agreed coldly.

She went early to Alfred's room the next morning, prepared to undertake the onerous task. She was cool, aloof, reminded herself that no matter what she had said in his defense to the Council, she was angry with this man, disappointed in him. Orla rapped sharply on his door.

"Come in," was the meek reply.

Alfred didn't ask who it was, didn't suppose, perhaps, he had the right to know.

Orla entered the room.

Alfred, standing by the window, flushed crimson when he saw her. He took a tentative step toward her. Orla raised a warding hand.

"I've come for the dog. I suppose the animal will accompany me?" she said, regarding it dubiously.

"I . . . I think so," said Alfred. "G-good dog. Go with Orla." He waved his hand and, much to his astonishment, the animal went. "I want to thank—"

Orla turned and walked out of the room, careful to shut the door behind her.

She led the dog to the garden. Sitting down on a bench, she looked expectantly at the animal. "Well, play," she said irritably, "or whatever it is you do."

The dog made a desultory turn or two about the garden, then returned and, laying its head on Orla's knee, gave a sigh and fixed its liquid eyes on her face.

Orla was rather nonplussed at this liberty, and was uncomfortable with the dog so near. She wanted very much to be rid of it and barely resisted an impulse to leap to her feet and run off. But she wasn't certain how the dog might react, seemed to vaguely recall, from what little she knew about the animals, that sudden movement might startle them into vicious behavior.

Gingerly, reaching down her hand, she patted its nose.

"There . . ." she said, as she might have spoken to an annoying child, "go away. There's a good dog."

Orla had intended to ease the dog's head off her lap, but the sensation of running her hand over the fur was pleasant. She felt the animal's life-force warm beneath her fingers, a sharp contrast to the cold marble bench on which she rested. And when she stroked its head, the dog wagged its tail, the soft brown eyes seemed to brighten.

Orla felt sorry for it, suddenly.

"You're lonely," she said, bringing both hands to smooth the silky ears. "You miss your Patryn master, I suppose. Even though you have Alfred, he's not really yours, is he? No," Orla added with a sigh, "he's not really yours.

"He's not mine, either. So why am I worried about him? He's nothing to me, *can* be nothing to me." Orla sat quietly, stroking the dog—a patient, silent, and attentive listener, one who drew from her more than she'd intended to reveal.

"I'm afraid for him," she whispered, and her hand on the dog's head trembled. "Why, why did he have to be so foolish? Why couldn't he have left well enough alone? Why did he have to be like the others? No," she pleaded softly, "*not* like the others. Let him not be like the others!"

Taking the dog's head in her hand, cupping it beneath the chin, she looked into the intelligent eyes that seemed to understand. "You must warn him. Tell him to forget what he read, tell him it wasn't worth it—"

"I believe you are actually growing to like that animal," Samah said accusingly.

Orla jumped, hurriedly withdrew her hand. The dog growled. Rising with dignity, she shoved the animal aside, tried to wipe its drool from her dress.

"I feel sorry for it," she said.

"You feel sorry for its master," said Samah.

"Yes, I do," Orla replied, resenting his tone. "Is that wrong, Samah?"

The Councillor regarded his wife grimly, then suddenly relaxed. Wearily, he shook his head. "No, Wife. It is commendable. I am the one who is the wrong. I've . . . overreacted."

Orla was still inclined to be offended, held herself aloof. Her husband bowed coldly to her, turned to leave. Orla saw the lines of tiredness on his face, saw his shoulders slump with fatigue. Guilt assailed her. Alfred had been in the wrong, there was no excusing him. Samah had countless problems on his mind, burdens to bear. Their people were in danger, very real danger, from the dragon-snakes, and now this . . .

"Husband," she said remorsefully, "I am sorry. Forgive me for adding to your burdens, instead of helping to lift and carry them."

She glided forward, reached out, laid her hands on his shoulders, caressing, feeling his life-force warm beneath her fingers, as she'd felt the dog's. And she yearned for him to turn to her, to take her in his arms, to hold her fast. She wanted him to grant her some of his strength, draw some of his strength from her.

"Husband!" she whispered, and her grasp tightened.

Samah stepped away from her. He took hold of her hands in his, folded them one on top of the other, and lightly, dryly, kissed the tips of her fingers.

"There is nothing to forgive, Wife. You were right to speak in this man's defense. The strain is telling on both of us."

He released her hands.

Orla held them out to him a moment longer, but Samah pretended not to see.

Slowly, she lowered her hands to her sides. Finding the dog there, pressing against her knee, she absently scratched it behind its ear.

"The strain. Yes, I suppose it is." She drew a deep breath, to hide a sigh. "You left home early this morning. Has there been more news of the mensch?"

"Yes." Samah glanced about the garden, not looking at his wife. "The dolphins report that the dragon-snakes have repaired the mensch ships. The mensch themselves held a joint meeting and have decided to set sail for this realm. They are obviously planning on war."

"Oh, surely not," Orla began.

"Of course they mean to attack us," Samah interrupted impatiently. "They are mensch, aren't they? When, in their entire bloody history, did they ever solve a problem except by the sword?"

"Perhaps they've changed . . ."

"The Patryn leads them. The dragon-snakes are with them. Tell me, Wife, what do *you* think they intend?"

She chose to ignore his sarcasm. "You have a plan, Husband?"

"Yes, I have a plan. One I will discuss with the Council," he added, with an emphasis that was perhaps unconscious, perhaps deliberate.

Orla flushed, faintly, and did not reply. There had been a time when he would have discussed this plan with her first. But not now, not since before the Sundering.

What happened between us? She tried to remember. What did I say? What did I do? And how, she wondered bleakly, am I managing to do it all over again?

"At this Council meeting, I will call for a vote to make our final decision concerning the fate of your 'friend,' " Samah added.

Again the sarcasm. Orla felt chilled, kept her hand on the dog to urge it to stay near her.

"What will happen to him, do you think?" she asked, affecting nonchalance.

"That is up to the Council. I will make my recommendation." He started to turn away.

Orla stepped forward, touched him on the arm. She felt him flinch, draw back from her. But, when he faced her, his expression was pleasant, patient. Perhaps she had just imagined the flinch.

"Yes, Wife?"

"He won't be . . . like the others?" she faltered.

Samah's eyes narrowed. "That is for the Council to decide."

"It wasn't right, Husband, what we did long ago," Orla said determinedly. "It wasn't right."

"Are you suggesting that you would defy me? Defy the decision of the Council? Or, perhaps, you already have?"

"What do you mean?" Orla asked, staring at him blankly.

"Not all who were sent arrived at their destination. The only way they could have escaped their fate was to have foreknowledge of it. And the only people who had that knowledge were the members of the Council . . ."

Orla stiffened. "How dare you suggest—"

Samah cut her short. "I have no time for this now. The Council will convene in one hour. I suggest you return that beast to its keeper and tell Alfred to prepare his defense. He will, of course, be given a chance to speak."

The Councillor walked out of the garden, heading for the Council building. Orla, perplexed, troubled, watched him, saw Ramu join him, saw them put their heads together in serious and earnest conversation.

"Come," she said, sighing, and led the dog back to Alfred.

Orla entered the Council chamber strong with resolve, her attitude defiant. She was prepared to fight now as she should have fought once before. She had nothing to lose. Samah had practically accused her of complicity.

What stopped me then? she asked herself. But she knew the answer, though it was one she was ashamed to admit.

Samah's love. A last, desperate attempt to hold onto something I never truly had. I betrayed my trust, betrayed my people, to try to cling with both hands to a love I only truly held with the tips of my fingers.

Now I will fight. Now I will defy him.

She was fairly certain she could persuade the others to defy Samah, as well. She had the impression several of them were feeling not quite right about what they'd done in the past. If only she could overcome their fear of the future . . .

The Council members took their places at the long marble table. When all were present, Samah entered, sat in his chair at the center.

Prepared for a stern and judgmental Councillor, Orla was astonished and surprised to see Samah relaxed, cheerful, pleasant. He gave her what might be taken for an apologetic smile, shrugged his shoulders.

Leaning over to her, he whispered, "I'm sorry for what I said, Wife. I'm not myself. I spoke hastily. Bear with me."

He seemed to wait with some anxiety for her reply.

She smiled at him tentatively. "I accept your apology, Husband."

His smile broadened. He patted her hand, as if to say, *Don't worry, my dear. Your little friend will be all right.*

Astonished, puzzled, Orla could only sit back in her chair and wonder.

Alfred entered, the dog trotting along faithfully at his heels. The Sartan took his place—again—before the Council. Orla could not help thinking how shabby Alfred looked—gaunt, stooped-shouldered, poorly made. She regretted she hadn't spent more time with him before the meeting, hadn't urged him to change out of the mensch clothes that were obviously having an irritating effect on the other Council members.

She'd left him hurriedly after returning the dog, though he'd tried to detain her. Being with him made her uncomfortable. His eyes, clear and penetrating, had a way of breaking down her guard and sneaking inside her in search of the truth, much as he'd sneaked inside the library. And she wasn't ready for him to see the truth inside her. She wasn't prepared to see it herself.

"Alfred Montbank"—Samah grimaced over the mensch name, but he had apparently given up his attempts to urge Alfred to reveal his Sartan name—"you are brought before this Council to answer two serious charges.

"The first: You willfully and knowingly entered the library, despite the fact that runes of prohibition had been placed on the door. This offense you committed two times. On the first occasion," Samah continued, though it seemed Alfred wanted to speak, "you claimed you entered by accident. You stated that you were curious about the building and, on approaching the door, you . . . um . . . slipped and fell through it. Once inside, the door shut and you couldn't get out, and you entered the library proper searching for the exit. Is this testimony that I've repeated subtantially true?"

"Substantially," Alfred answered.

His hands were clasped before him. He did not look directly at the Council, but darted swift glances at them from beneath lowered eyes. He was, Orla thought unhappily, the very picture of guilt.

"And on this occasion, we accepted this explanation. We explained to you why it was that the library was prohibited to our people, and then we left, trusting that we would have no need to say anything further on the subject.

"Yet, in less than a week, you were again discovered in the library. Which brings us to the second, and more serious, charge facing you: This time, you are accused of entering the library deliberately and in a manner which indicates you feared apprehension. Is this true?"

"Yes," said Alfred sadly, "I'm afraid it is. And I'm sorry. Truly very sorry to have caused all this trouble, when you have other, greater worries."

Samah leaned back in his chair, sighed, and then rubbed his eyes with his hand. Orla sat regarding him in silent astonishment. He was not the stern, awful judge. He was the weary father, forced to administer punishment to a well-loved, albeit irresponsible, child.

"Will you tell the Council, Brother, why you defied our prohibition?"

"Would you mind if I told you something about myself?" Alfred asked. "It would help you understand . . ."

"No, please, Brother, go ahead. It is your right to say whatever you like before the Council."

"Thank you." Alfred smiled, faintly. "I was born on Arianus, one of the last Sartan children born on Arianus. That was many hundred years after the Sundering, after you went to your Sleep. Things weren't going well for us on Arianus. Our population was decreasing. Children weren't being born, adults were dying untimely, for no apparent reason. We didn't know why then, though, perhaps," he said softly, almost to himself, "I do now.[1] That, however, is not why we're here.

"Life for the Sartan on Arianus was extremely difficult. There was so much needed to be done, but not enough people to do it. The mensch populations were increasing rapidly. They had

---

[1] Reference to the startling and horrifying discovery that the dead were being brought to life in Abarrach, recounted in *Fire Sea*, vol. 3, *The Death Gate Cycle*. It is theorized that for one person to be brought to life untimely, another will die untimely.

gained in magical talent and in mechanical skills. There were far too many of them for us to control. And that, I think, was our mistake. We weren't content to advise or counsel, offer our wisdom. We wanted to control. And since we couldn't, we left them, retreated below ground. We were afraid.

"Our Council decided that since there were so few of us remaining, we should place some of our young people in stasis, to be brought back to life some time in the future when, hopefully, the situation had improved. We were confident, you see, that by then we would establish contact with the other three worlds.

"There were many of us who volunteered to enter the crystal chambers. I was one of them. It was a world," Alfred said quietly, "I was glad to leave.

"Unfortunately, I was the only one to come back."

Samah, who had seemed to be only half-listening, a patient, indulgent expression on his face, sat up straight at this and frowned. The other members of the Council murmured among themselves. Orla saw the anguish, the bitter loneliness of that time, reflected on Alfred's face, felt her heart wrung with compassion, pity.

"When I woke, I discovered that all the others, all my brothers and sisters, were dead. I was alone in a world of mensch. I was afraid, terribly afraid. I feared the mensch might find out who and what I was, discover my talent for magic, try to make me use that talent to aid them in their ambitions.

"At first, I hid from them. I lived . . . I don't know how many years of my life in the underground world to which the Sartan had retreated long ago. But, during those rare times I visited the mensch in the worlds above, I couldn't help but see what dreadful things were happening. I found myself wanting to help them. I knew I *could* help them, and it occurred to me that helping them was what we Sartan were supposed to be doing. I began to think that it was selfish of me to hide myself away, when I might, in some small way, try to make things right. But, instead, as usual, I only seemed to have made things all wrong."[2]

---

[2] A reference to Alfred's adventures with the child Bane, the assassin Hugh the Hand, and his first meeting with Haplo, recounted in *Dragon Wing*, vol. 1 of *The Death Gate Cycle*.

Samah stirred, somewhat restlessly. "Truly your story is tragic, Brother, and we are grieved to have lost so many of our people on Arianus, but much of this we knew already and I fail to see—"

"Please, bear with me, Samah," Alfred said, with a quiet dignity that was, Orla thought, most becoming to him. "All that time I spent with the mensch, I thought of my people, missed them. And I knew, to my regret, that I'd taken them for granted. I had paid some attention to their stories of the past, but not enough. I had never asked questions, I wasn't interested. I knew, I realized, very little about being a Sartan, very little about the Sundering. I grew hungry for that knowledge. I'm still hungry for it."

Alfred gazed at the members in wistful pleading. "Can't you understand? I want to know who I am. Why I'm here. What I'm expected to do."

"These are mensch questions," said Samah, rebuking. "Not worthy of a Sartan. A Sartan knows why he is here. He knows his purpose and he acts upon his knowledge."

"Undoubtedly, if I had not been so much on my own, I would have never been forced to ask such questions," Alfred answered. "But I didn't have anyone to turn to." He stood tall, no longer crushed with awe, no longer meek, apologetic. He was strong with the rightness of his cause. "And it seems, from what I read in the library, that others asked the same questions before me. And that they found answers."

Several Council members glanced uneasily at each other, then all eyes turned to Samah.

He looked grave and sad, not angry. "I understand you better now, Brother. I wish you had trusted us enough to tell us this before."

Alfred flushed, but did not lower his gaze to his shoes, as he was wont. He regarded Samah steadily, intently, with that clear-eyed gaze that had often disturbed Orla.

"Let me describe our world to you, Brother," said the Councillor, leaning forward, fingertips together on the top of the table. "Earth, it was called. Once, many thousands of years ago, it was ruled exclusively by humans. Consistent with their warring, destructive nature, they unleashed a dreadful war upon themselves. The war did not destroy the world, as so many had feared and predicted. But it changed the world irretrievably. New races, they say, were born out of the cataclysmic smoke and flame. I doubt the truth of that. I believe these races were always present, but had remained hidden in the shadows, until the light of a new day should dawn.

"Magic came into the world then, supposedly, though all know that this ancient force has been in existence since the beginning of time. It, too, was waiting for the dawn.

"There had been many religions in the world over the centuries; the mensch being glad to toss all their problems and frustrations into the lap of some nebulous Supreme Being. Such Beings were numerous and varied. They were never seen, capricious, demanded to be taken on faith and faith alone. No wonder, when we Sartan came to power, the mensch were thankful to switch their allegiance to us, to flesh and blood beings, who laid down strict laws that were fair and just.

"All would have been well, had it not been that our opposite number, the Patryns, rose to power at the same time.[3] The mensch were confused, many began to follow the Patryns, who rewarded their slaves with power and wealth seized at the expense of others.

"We fought our enemy, but battle proved difficult. The Patryns are subtle, tricky. A Patryn would never be crowned king of a realm, for example. They left that to the mensch. But you would be sure to find one of their number acting in the role of 'adviser' or 'councillor.' "

"And yet," Alfred inserted mildly, "from what I have read, the Sartan were often to be found in such roles themselves."

Samah frowned at the implication. "We were *true* advisers; we offered counsel and wisdom and guidance. We did *not* use the role to usurp thrones, to reduce the mensch to little more than puppets. We sought to teach, to elevate, to correct."

"And if the mensch didn't follow your advice," Alfred asked in a low voice, clear eyes unwavering, "you punished them, didn't you?"

"It is the responsibility of the parent to chastise the child who

---

[3]A more complete history of the Patryns can be found in *Fire Sea*, vol. 3 of *The Death Gate Cycle*.

has behaved heedlessly, foolishly. Certainly we made the mensch see the error of their ways. How would they learn otherwise?"

"But what about freedom of will?" Alfred took several steps toward Samah, passion carrying him forward. "Freedom to learn on their own? To make their own choices? Who gave us the right to determine the fate of others?"

He was earnest, articulate, confident. He moved with grace, with ease. Orla thrilled to hear him. He was speaking aloud the questions she had asked often in her own heart.

The Councillor sat silent during the onslaught, cold, unassailable. He let Alfred's words hang in the quiet, tense atmosphere for a moment, then caught and returned them with studied calm.

"Can a child raise itself, Brother? No, it cannot. It needs parents to feed it, teach it, guide it."

"The mensch are not our children," Alfred returned angrily. "We did not create them! We did not bring them into this world. We have no right to try to rule their lives!"

"We did not try to rule them!" Samah rose to his feet. His hand flattened on the table, as if he might have struck it, but he controlled himself. "We permitted them to act. Often, we watched their actions with deep sadness and regret. It was the Patryns who sought to rule the mensch. And they would have succeeded, but for us!

"At the time of the Sundering, the power of our enemy was growing exceedingly strong. More and more governments had fallen under their sway. The world was embroiled in wars, race against race, nation against nation, those who had nothing slitting the throats of those who had everything. No darker time had ever been and it seemed worse must come.

"And then it was that the Patryns managed to discover our weakness. Through vile trickery and magic, they convinced some of our people that this nebulous Supreme Being, whom even the mensch had now ceased to worship, actually did exist!"

Alfred started to speak.

Samah raised his hand. "Please, let me continue." He paused a moment, put his fingers to his forehead, as if it ached. His face was drawn, fatigued. With a sigh, he resumed his seat, looked back at Alfred. "I do not fault those who fell victim to this subterfuge, Brother. All of us, at one time or another, long to rest our head upon the breast of One stronger, wiser than ourselves; to surrender all responsibility to an All-Knowing, All-Powerful Being. Such dreams are pleasant, but then we must wake to reality."

"And this was your reality. Tell me if I'm wrong." Alfred regarded them with pity, his voice soft with sorrow. "The Patryns were growing stronger. The Sartan were splintering into factions. Some of them began denying their godhood. They were prepared to follow this new vision. And they threatened to take the mensch with them. You were on the verge of losing everything."

"You are not wrong," Orla murmured.

Samah cast her an angry glance that she felt but did not see. She was looking at Alfred.

"I make allowances for you, Brother," the Councillor said. "You were not there. You cannot possibly understand."

"I understand," said Alfred clearly, firmly. He stood straight and tall. He was, Orla thought, almost handsome. "At last, after all these years, I finally understand. Who did you truly fear?"

His gaze swept over the Council. "Was it the Patryns? Or did you fear the truth: the knowledge that you *aren't* the moving force in the universe, that you are, in fact, no better than the mensch you've always despised? Isn't *that* what you truly feared? Isn't that why you destroyed the world, hoping to destroy truth as well?"

Alfred's words echoed throughout the silent hall.

Orla caught her breath. Ramu, face dark with suppressed fury, cast a questioning glance at his father, as if seeking permission to do or say something. The dog, who had flopped down at the Sartan's feet to doze through the boring parts, sat up suddenly and glared around, feeling threatened.

Samah made a slight, negating gesture with his hand, and his son reluctantly settled back in his chair. The other Council members looked from Samah to Alfred and back to their Councillor again, more than a few shaking their heads.

Samah stared at Alfred, said nothing.

The tension in the room grew.

Alfred blinked, seemed suddenly to realize what he'd been saying. He began to droop, his newfound strength seeping from him.

"I'm sorry, Samah. I never meant—" Alfred shrank backward, stumbled over the dog.

The Councillor rose abruptly to his feet, left his chair, walked around the table and came to stand beside Alfred. The dog growled, ears flattened, teeth barred, tail swishing slowly side to side.

"Shush!" said Alfred unhappily.

The Councillor reached out his hand. Alfred cringed, expecting a blow. Samah put his arm around Alfred's shoulders.

"There, Brother," he said kindly, "don't you feel better now? Finally, you have opened up to us. Finally, you trust us. Think how much better it would have been for you if you had come to me or to Ramu or Orla or any of the Council members with these doubts and problems! Now, at last, we can help you."

"You can?" Alfred stared at him.

"Yes, Brother. You are, after all, Sartan. You are one of us."

"I'm s-sorry I broke into the library," Alfred stammered. "That was wrong. I know. I came here to apologize. I don't . . . don't know what got into me to say all those other things—"

"The poison has been festering inside you long. Now it is purged, your wound will heal."

"I hope so," Alfred said, though he seemed dubious. "I hope so." He sighed, looked down at his shoes. "What will you do to me?"

"Do to you?" Samah appeared puzzled. "Ah, you mean punish you? My dear Alfred, you have punished youself far more than such an infraction of the rules warrants. The Council accepts your apology. And any time you would like to use the library, you have only to ask either myself or Ramu for the key. I think you would find it extremely beneficial to study the history of our people."

Alfred gaped at the man, all power of speech lost in unparalleled astonishment.

"The Council has some additional, minor business," Samah said briskly, removing his hand from Alfred's shoulders. "If you will seat yourself, we will attend to our work swiftly and then we can depart."

At a gesture from his father, Ramu silently brought Alfred a chair. He collapsed into it, sat huddled, drained, dazed.

Samah returned to his place, began to discuss some trivial matter that could well have waited. The other Council members, obviously uncomfortable and eager to leave, weren't listening.

Samah continued to talk, patiently, quietly. Orla watched her husband, watched his deft, facile handling of the Council, watched the play of intelligence on his strong, handsome face. He had successfully won over poor Alfred. Now, slowly, surely, he was winning back the loyalty and confidence of his followers. The Council members began to relax under the influence of their leader's soothing voice; they could even laugh at a small joke.

They will leave, Orla thought, and the voice they hear will be Samah's. They will have forgotten Alfred's. Odd, I never noticed before how Samah manipulates us.

Except now it is them, not us. Not me. Not anymore.

Not anymore.

The meeting came to an end at last.

Alfred didn't listen, he was lost in troubled reveries, was roused only when people began to move.

Samah stood up. The other Council members were at ease, feeling better. They bowed to him, to each other (not to Alfred, they ignored Alfred), and took their leave.

Alfred wavered unsteadily to his feet.

"I thought I had the answer," he said to himself. "Where did it go? How could I lose it so suddenly? Perhaps I was wrong. Perhaps the vision was, as Samah said, a trick of Haplo's."

"I have noticed that our guest seems extremely fatigued," Samah was saying. "Why don't you, Wife, take Alfred back to our house and see to it that he relaxes and eats something."

The Council members had all filed out by now. Only Ramu lingered behind.

Orla took Alfred's arm. "Are you all right?"

He still felt dazed, his body shook, feet stumbled over themselves. "Yes, yes," he answered vaguely. "I think I would like to rest, however. If I could just go back to my room and . . . lie down."

"Certainly," said Orla, concerned. She glanced around. "Are you coming with us, Husband?"

"No, not just yet, my dear. I need to arrange with Ramu to

attend to that small matter on which the Council just voted. You go ahead. I will be home in time for dinner."

Alfred let Orla guide him toward the door. He was almost out of the Council Chamber when it occurred to him that the dog wasn't following. He glanced around for the animal, could not, at first, find it. Then he saw the tip of a tail, sticking out from under the Council table.

An unwelcome thought came to him. Haplo had trained the dog to act as a spy. He often ordered it to tag along with unsuspecting people, whose words were then carried through the dog's ears to the Patryn's. Alfred knew, in that moment, that the dog was offering this very same service to him. It would stay with Ramu and Samah, listen in on what they said.

"Alfred?" said Orla.

The Sartan jumped, guilt assailing him. He whirled around, didn't watch where he was going, and smashed nose first into the doorframe.

"Alfred . . . Oh, dear! What have you done? Your nose is bleeding!"

"I seem to have run into the door . . ."

"Tilt your head back. I'll sing you a rune of healing."

I should call the dog! Alfred trembled. I should never permit this. I am worse than Haplo. He spied on strangers. I'm spying on my own kind. I have only to say the word, call it, and the dog will come to me.

Alfred looked back. "Dog—" he began.

Samah was watching him with disdainful amusement, Ramu with disgust. But both were watching him.

"What were you saying about the dog?" Orla asked, looking anxious.

Alfred sighed, closed his eyes. "Only that I . . . I sent it home."

"Where you should be right now," Orla told him.

"Yes," said Alfred. "I'm ready to leave."

He had reached the outer door of the Council hall, when he heard, through the dog's ears, father and son start to talk.

"That man is dangerous." Ramu's voice.

"Yes, my son. You are right. Very dangerous. Therefore we must never relax our vigilance over him again."

"You think that? Then why did you let him go? We should do to him what we did to the others."

"We cannot now. The other Council members, especially your mother, would never agree. This is all part of his clever plan, of course. Let him think he has fooled us. Let him relax, think himself unwatched, unsuspected."

"A trap?"

"Yes," Samah answered complacently, "a trap to catch him in the act of betraying us to his Patryn friend. Then we will have enough evidence to convince even your mother that this Sartan with the mensch name means to encompass our downfall."

Alfred sank onto a bench, just outside the Hall of the Council of Sartan.

"You look terrible," said Orla. "I think your nose must be broken. Are you faint? If you don't feel able to walk, I can—"

"Orla." Alfred looked up at her. "I know this is going to sound ungrateful, but could you please leave me?"

"No, I couldn't possibly—"

"Please. I need to be alone," he said gently.

Orla studied him. Turning, she looked back toward the hall, stared into the shadowy interior intently, as if she could see within. Perhaps she could. Perhaps, though her ears did not hear the voices inside the hall, her heart did. Her face grew grave and sad.

"I'm sorry," she said, and left him.

Alfred groaned and rested his head in his shaking hands.

CHAPTER ♦ 24

PHONDRA

CHELESTRA

♦

EVENTS HAVE HURTLED DOWN ON US LIKE BOULDERS FROM THE mountaintop. Some seemed likely to flatten us, but we managed to duck and so survived.[1]

We spent several more days on Phondra, for we had a great deal of planning to do, as you may well imagine. Many factors had to be determined: how many people were to be in each sunchaser, what we could and could not take with us, how much food and water would be necessary for the duration of the journey, and a lot of other details that I won't bother to put down. It was bad enough having to listen and worry about them all.

Alake and I have finally been allowed to sit in on the royal meetings. It was an extremely proud moment for us.

During the first meeting, Alake and I concentrated on being serious, solemn, and earnest. We paid strict attention to every word and we were ready with our opinions, despite the fact that no one ever asked us for them.

But by the next afternoon, when my father and Dumaka were

---

[1]The next several pages of Grundle's journal chronicle events previously related. Since—with one exception—they correspond with Haplo's account, these passage will be deleted. The exception is Devon's attempted suicide, which Grundle describes as an "accident while picking sugarfruit." It is interesting to note that even in her own private writings, she loyally perpetuates the deception.

busy drawing—for the sixth time—a diagram of one of the sun-chasers in the dirt to determine how many water barrels could be safely stowed in the hold, Alake and I began to discover that being a ruler was, as she put it, a royal pain.

Here we were, stuck inside the longhouse, which was hot and stuffy, forced to listen to Eliason drone on about the merits of fish oil and why casks of it were considered an absolute necessity by the elves. Outdoors (we could see plainly through the slats in the log walls) the most interesting things were going on.

Alake's quick eye caught sight of Haplo, pacing restlessly about the camp. Devon walked with him. Our elf friend had almost completely recovered from his accident. The scars on his neck were healing. Other than an extremely raspy voice, he was back to being his old self. (Well, almost. I guess he will never be the merry, carefree Devon we once knew, but then I suppose none of us will ever be the same again.)

Devon spent most of his time with Haplo. They never seemed to say much to each other, but each seemed glad of the other's company. At least, I assume Haplo liked having the elf around. It's hard to tell what Haplo's thinking. For example, he's been in an extremely dark humor these past few days, which is odd, considering everything worked out the way he wanted. But then, I got the distinct feeling he was impatient, in a hurry to be gone, and was fed up with the delay.

I was watching the two of them walk past, thinking regretfully that if Alake and I had been spying, as usual, we would have left long before this (or fallen asleep!), when I saw Haplo suddenly stop in midstride, look in our direction. His face was grim. Turning, nearly bowling over the startled elf, he headed for the longhouse.

I perked up, having the feeling something was about to happen. Alake had seen him coming, too, and was smoothing her hair and adjusting her ear-jangles. She sat up straight and pretended to look deeply interested in the subject of fish oil, when only a moment before she'd been rolling her eyes and trying not to yawn. It was enough to make a cat laugh. As it was, I snorted and caught a stern, reproving look from my mother.

The doorkeeper entered, apologized for interrupting, and announced that Haplo had something to say. Of course, he was graciously received. (He'd been invited to attend these meetings, but he had better sense.)

He began by saying he hoped we were making progress, reminding us again that we didn't have much time. I thought his look, as he said this, was dark.

"What are you discussing?" he asked, his gaze going to the diagram on the floor.

None of the others seemed inclined to answer, so I told him. "Fish oil."

"Fish oil," Haplo repeated. "Every day, the Sartan grow stronger, your sun drifts farther, and you sit here yammering about fish oil."

Our parents looked ashamed. My father ducked his head, chewed on his beard. My mother sighed loudly. Eliason, his pale skin flushed, started to say something, floundered, and fell silent.

"It is hard to leave our homelands," said Dumaka finally, staring down at the diagram of the boat.

At first, I couldn't figure out what that had to do with fish oil, but then it occurred to me that all of the arguing and discussion over petty details were just our parents' way of stalling, of refusing to face the inevitable. They knew they had to leave, but they didn't want to. I felt suddenly like bursting into tears.

"I think we were hoping for a miracle," said Delu.

"The only miracle you're going to get is the one you make yourselves," Haplo answered irritably. "Now, look, here is what you take and how you take it."

He told them. Squatting down on the floor near the diagram, he explained everything. He told us what to take, how to pack it, what each man, woman, and child could carry, how much room to allot, what we'd need when we reached Surunan, what we could leave behind because we could make it when we got there. He told what we'd need in case of war.

We listened, dazed. Our parents presented feeble arguments.

"But what about—"

"Not necessary."

"But we should take—"

"No, you should not."

In less than an hour, everything was settled.

"Be ready to sail for your homes tomorrow. Once there, send out the word for your people to start gathering at the appointed locations." Haplo stood up, brushed the dirt off his hands. "The dwarves will sail the sun-chasers to Phondra and Elmas. Allow a full cycle at each city or village for loading everyone on board.

"The fleet will reassemble at Gargan in"—Haplo made a swift calculation in his head—"fourteen cycles' time. We should travel together; there's safety in numbers. Any who lag behind"—a stern glance at the elves—"will be left behind. Understood."

"Understood," said Eliason, with a faint smile.

"Good. I'll leave you all to work out the final details. Which reminds me, I'm in need of a translator. I want to ask the dolphins some questions concerning Surunan. I was wondering if I could borrow Grundle?"

"Take her," my father said, with what sounded suspiciously like relief.

I was on my feet, glad to escape, and heading for the door when I heard a smothered sound, caught sight of Alake's pleading eyes. She'd give every ear-jangle she owned and probably her ears along with them to go with Haplo.

I tugged at the sleeve of his shirt. "Alake speaks dolphin a lot better than I do. In fact, I don't speak it at all. I think she should come with us."

He gave me an exasperated look, but I ignored him. After all, Alake and I were friends. He couldn't go on avoiding her forever.

"Besides," I said, out of the corner of my mouth, "she'll only follow us." Which was true enough and got me off the hook.

So he said, not very graciously, that he'd be pleased if Alake would come, too.

"And Devon?" I asked, seeing the elf hanging about, lost and forlorn.

"Why not?" I thought I heard him mutter. "Invite the whole damn village. Have a parade."

I waved to Devon, whose face brightened. He joined us eagerly. "Where are we going?"

"Haplo wants to talk to the dolphins. We're going along to translate. By the way," I added, something just occurring to me, "the dolphins speak our languages, you know. And so do you. Why don't you talk to them yourself?"

"I tried. They won't talk to me."

"Really?" Devon stared at him, amazed. "I never heard of such a thing."

I had to admit I was pretty surprised, myself. Those gossipy fish will talk to anyone. Usually you can't get them to shut up.

"I'll speak with them," offered Alake. "Perhaps it's just because they've never seen anyone quite like you."

Haplo grunted, said nothing more. He was, as I have stated, in a dark and morose mood. Alake looked at me, worried, raised her eyebrows. I shrugged my shoulders, glanced at Devon, who shook his head. None of us had a clue what was bothering the man.

We reached the seashore. The dolphins were hanging about, as usual, hoping for someone to come along and toss them a juicy tidbit of news or cod or listen to whatever it was they had to say. But, when they saw Haplo coming, they all flipped their tails, turned, and swam out to sea.

"Wait!" Alake cried, standing on the shore and stomping her foot. "Come back here."

"There, you see." Haplo waved his hand impatiently.

"What do you expect? They're only fish," I said.

He stood glaring at them in frustration and at us in resentment. It occurred to me that he didn't really want us there, probably didn't want us to hear whatever it was he thought he might hear, but he didn't have much choice.

I went down to the water's edge, where Alake was talking with one of the dolphins who had slowly and reluctantly swum back. Haplo stayed behind, keeping well away from the water.

"What's the problem?" I asked.

Alake squeaked and whistled. I wondered if she knew how truly ridiculous she sounded. You'd never catch me lowering myself to fish-talk. She turned around.

"Haplo's right. They're refusing to talk to him. They say he's in league with the dragon-snakes, and they hate and fear the dragon-snakes."

"Listen, fish," I said to the dolphin, "we're not crazy about the dragon-snakes ourselves, but Haplo has some sort of hold on them. He got them to let us go and made them repair the sun-chasers."

The dolphin shook its head violently, splattering water all over both of us. It began to squeak shrilly, alarmingly, flapping its flippers in the water.

"What's the matter with it?" Devon came over to join us.

"That's nonsense!" Alake cried angrily. "I don't believe you. I won't stay here and listen to such talk." She turned her back on the frantic dolphin and walked up the beach to where Haplo was standing.

"It's useless," she said. "They're behaving like spoiled children. Let's go."

"I need to talk to them," Haplo said.

"What did the thing say to her?" I asked Devon softly.

He glanced over at the two of them, motioned me closer.

"It said that the dragon-snakes are evil, more evil than we can imagine. And that Haplo's just as evil as they are. He has a private hatred for these Sartan. Once, long ago, his people fought the Sartan and lost. Now, he wants revenge. He's using us to get it. When we've destroyed the Sartan for him, he'll turn us over to the dragon-snakes."

I stared at him. I couldn't believe it, and yet, in a way, I could. I felt sick inside and afraid. Judging by his looks, Devon wasn't faring much better. Dolphins often exaggerate the truth, or sometimes come up with only part of the truth, but it is, generally, the truth. I've never known one to lie. We both eyed Haplo, who was trying to persuade Alake to return and talk to the dolphins again.

"What do you think?" I asked Devon.

The elf took his time answering. "I think the dolphins are wrong. I trust him. He saved my life, Grundle. Saved my life by giving me some of his own."

"Huh?"

That made no sense at all. I was about to say as much to Devon, when he shushed me. Alake was returning to the water's edge, followed by Haplo. Seeing him this near the sea, in danger of being splashed, I concluded the matter must be serious.

Alake summoned the dolphin before her with her best imperious air, bracelets clashing, arm stabbing downward. Her eyes flashed, her voice was stern. Even I was impressed. The dolphin swam to her meekly.

"Listen to me," Alake said, "you will answer the questions this man puts to you to the best of your ability or from this moment on, you dolphins will be shunned by every human, elf, and dwarf."

"Exceeding our authority a bit, aren't we?" I poked her in the ribs.

"Shut up." Alake pinched me. "And agree to go along."

We did. Both Devon and I stoutly insisted that no elf or dwarf would ever talk to a dolphin again. At this dire threat, the dolphins gasped and floundered and flopped around in the water, sounding agonized and swearing that they were only interested in our welfare. (Overdoing it, if you ask me.) Finally—after pathetic bleatings, which we ignored—one of the fish agreed to talk to Haplo.

And then, after all this, what do you suppose was Haplo's question? Did he ask about Sartan defenses? About how many men manned the battlements? About how good they were at ax-heaving? No.

Alake, having cowed the dolphins, looked at him expectantly. Haplo spoke the fish's language fluently.

"What he's saying?" I asked Devon.

Devon looked dazed. "He's asking them how the Sartan are dressed!"

Well, of course, Haplo could have asked nothing that would have caught the dolphins' fancy more (which, it occurs to me, may have been the reason he asked it). Dolphins have never understood our strange propensity for draping the body in cloth, just as they've never understood our other odd habits, such as living on dry land and expending all that energy walking when we might be swimming.

But, for some reason, they find the wearing of clothing particularly hilarious and, as such, are continually fascinated by it. Let an elf matron attend a ball in a puffed-sleeve gown when long tight sleeves are in fashion and every dolphin in the Goodsea will have heard about it by morning.

As it was, we were treated to a graphic account (Alake translating, for my benefit) of what the Sartan were wearing, which—all in all—I thought sounded pretty boring.

"The dolphins say that the Sartan all dress alike. The males wear robes that fall in long, loose folds from the shoulders and the females wear a similar design, except that theirs are cinched around the waist. The robes are plain-colored, either white or gray. Most have simple designs along the bottom, and some are trimmed in gold. The dolphins suspect that the gold denotes some type of official ranking. They don't know what."

Devon and I sat down in the sand, both of us glum and uncommunicative. I wondered if he was thinking about what I was thinking about. I had my answer when I saw him frown and heard him repeat, "He saved my life."

"The dolphins don't think much of the Sartan," Alake was saying to me, in low tones. "Apparently, the Sartan ask the dolphins continually for information, but when the dolphins ask the Sartan questions, the Sartan refuse to answer."

Haplo nodded; this information obviously didn't surprise him much. In fact, I could see he wasn't surprised by anything he heard, as if he knew it all beforehand. I wondered why he asked, why he bothered. He had joined us, sitting in the sand, his arms propped up on his bent knees, hands clasped. He looked relaxed, prepared to sit here for several signe.

"Is there . . . anything else you want to know?" Alake glanced at him then over at us to see if we knew what was going on.

We weren't any help. Devon was busy digging holes in the sand, watching them fill with water and tiny sea creatures. I felt angry and unhappy and began tossing rocks at the dolphin, just to see how close I could come to hitting it.

The stupid fish, tickled by the dress question, I suppose, swam out of my range, started to giggle and cavort.

"What's so funny?" Haplo asked. He seemed relaxed, but from where I was seated, I could see a glint in his eye, a bright flash like sun off hard, cold steel.

Of course, the dolphin was eager to tell.

"What?" I asked.

Alake shrugged. "Only that there is one Sartan who dresses much differently from the others. He looks different from the others."

"Different? How?"

Casual conversation, except I saw that Haplo's hands had tightened.

The dolphins were eager to describe it. Several more swam up at this point, all talking at once. Haplo listened intently. It took Alake some moments to sort out who was squeaking what.

"The man wears a coat and knee breeches, like a dwarf, only he's not a dwarf. He's much taller. He has no hair on the top of his head. His clothes are shabby and worn out, and the dolphins say he seems as worn out as his clothes."

I watched Haplo out of the corner of my eye; a shiver crept over me. His expression had changed. He was smiling, but his smile was unpleasant, made me want to look away. The fingers of his hands were clasped so tightly together that the knuckles, beneath their blue marks, had all turned white. This was what he'd wanted to hear. But, why? Who was this man?

"The dolphins don't think that this man is a Sartan."

Alake continued talking in some perplexity, expecting every moment for Haplo to end what seemed a boring conversation. He listened with quiet interest, however, saying nothing, encouraging the dolphins silently to continue.

"He doesn't go around with the Sartan. The dolphins see him walking on the pier alone a lot. They say he looks much nicer than the Sartan, whose faces seem to have stayed frozen when the rest of them thawed out. The dolphins would like to talk to him, but he has a dog with him that barks at them when they come too close—"

"Dog!"

Haplo's whole body flinched, as if someone'd hit him. And I'll never forget, if I live to be four hundred, the tone of his voice. It made my hair stand on end. Alake was staring at him in astonishment. The dolphins, sensing a choice morsel of gossip, swam as close as they possibly could without actually beaching themselves.

"Dog . . ." Devon's head jerked up. I don't think he'd been paying much attention, up to this point. "What about a dog?" he whispered to me.

I shook my side whiskers at him, to keep him quiet. I didn't want to miss whatever Haplo was going to do or say next. He didn't say or do anything, however. Just sat there.

For some reason, I recalled a recent evening spent at our local tavern, enjoying the usual brawl. One of my uncles was hit over the head with a chair. He sat on the floor for quite a while, and the expression on his face was identical to the expression on Haplo's.

First my uncle looked dazed, stunned. Pain brought him to his senses; his face kind of twisted, and he moaned a little. But by then, too, he realized what had happened to him, and he was so angry he forgot that he hurt. Haplo didn't moan. He didn't make any sound that I heard. But I saw his face twist, then darken in anger. He jumped to his feet and, without a word, stalked off back toward camp.

Alake cried out, and would have run after him, if I hadn't been holding onto the hem of her dress. As I told you, the Phondrans don't believe in buttons or anything of that type. They wrap the cloth around themselves. While ordinarily the folds are quite secure, one good tug in a strategic location can pretty well undo the whole business.

Alake gasped, grappled with folds of falling fabric, and by the time she was properly redraped, Haplo was out of sight.

"Grundle!" She pounced on me. "What did you do that for?"

"I saw his face," I answered. "Obviously, you didn't. Believe me, he wanted to be alone."

I thought she was going to fly off after him and I was on my feet, prepared to stop her, when she sighed, suddenly, and shook her head.

"I saw his face, too," was all she said.

The dolphins were squeaking in excitement, begging to know the gory details.

"Go on! Get out of here!" I said, and began chucking rocks in earnest.

They swam off, with hurt and offended squeaks. But I noticed that they only swam out of range of my throwing arm and that they kept their heads out of the water, mouths open, beady little eyes watching eagerly.

"Stupid fish!" snapped Alake, tossing her head, making her ear-jangles clash like bells. "Vicious gossips. I don't believe anything they say."

She kept glancing at us uneasily, wondering if we'd overheard what the dolphins said about Haplo and the dragonsnakes. I tried to look innocent, but I must not have succeeded.

"Oh, Grundle! Surely you don't think for a moment what they said was true! That Haplo's using us! Devon"—Alake turned to the elf for support—"tell Grundle that she's wrong. Haplo wouldn't do . . . what they said. He just wouldn't! He saved your life, Devon."

But Devon wasn't listening. "Dog," he repeated thoughtfully. "He said something to me about a dog. I wish I . . . I just can't remember . . ."

"You have to admit, Alake," I said reluctantly, "that we don't know anything about him. Where he comes from, even what he is. Now this man with no hair on his head and the shabby clothes. Haplo obviously knew the man was with the Sartan; he wasn't the least surprised to hear about him. He *was* surprised about the dog, though, and from the look of him, the surprise wasn't pleasant. Who is this strange man? What does he have to do with Haplo? And what's the big deal about a dog?"

I looked hard at Devon as I spoke.

The elf was no help. He only shrugged. "I'm sorry, Grundle. I wasn't feeling very good at the time . . ."

"I know all about Haplo I need to know," said Alake angrily, twitching the folds of her dress back into place. "He saved our lives, saved you twice, Devon!"

"Yes," said Devon, not looking at Alake, "and how nicely it all worked out for him."

"It did, didn't it?" I said, thinking back. "He was the hero, the savior. No one's ever questioned a thing he says. I think we should tell our parents—"

Alake stomped her foot. Bracelets and ear-jangles rang wildly. I'd never seen her so angry. "You do, Grundle Heavybeard, and I'll never speak to you again! I swear it by the One!"

"There's a way we can find out for certain," Devon said soothingly, to calm her down. He stood up, brushed the sand off his hands.

"What's that?" Alake demanded, sullen, suspicious.

"Spy—"

"No! I forbid it! I won't have you spying on him—"

"Not on him," said Devon. "On the dragon-snakes."

Now I felt as if *I'd* been hit over the head with a chair. The very idea took my breath away.

"I agree with you, Alake," Devon argued persuasively, "I want to believe in Haplo. But we can't get around the fact that dolphins generally know what's going on—"

" 'Generally'!" Alake repeated bitterly.

"Yes, that's what I mean. What if they've got part of it wrong and part of it right? What if, for example, the dragon-snakes are using Haplo? What if he's in just as much danger as we are? I think, before we tell our parents or anybody, we should find out the truth."

"The elf's got a point," I admitted. "At least for now, the dragon-snakes seem to be on our side. And snakes or no snakes, we can't stay on the seamoons. We've got to reach Surunan. And if we bring this up . . ."

I didn't need to finish my sentence. We could picture, all too well, how this information would start the squabbling and the distrust and the suspicion all over again.

"Very well," said Alake.

The thought of Haplo being in danger had won her over, of course. I regarded Devon with newfound admiration. Eliason had been right. Elves did make good diplomats.

"We'll do it," Alake said. "But when? And how?"

Trust a human. Always had to have a plan.

"We'll have to wait and watch for a time," Devon said. "There's bound to be opportunity on the trip."

A sudden, horrible thought struck me. "What if the dolphins tell our parents what they told us?"

"We'll have to watch them, see that they don't talk to our parents or anyone else for that matter," said Alake, after a moment's pondering, during which none of us came up with anything more helpful. "With any luck, our people will be too busy to take time out to gossip."

A forlorn hope. I didn't mention that it was not only probable but logical that our parents would ask the dolphins for information before we set out on the journey. I was surprised they hadn't thought to do it yet, but I guess they had more important things on their minds—like fish oil.

We all agreed to keep close watch, be ready with arguments in case we failed. Alake was to warn Haplo, discreetly, without giving anything away, that it might be best if no one spoke to dolphins for a while.

After that, we parted, to make preparations for the great journey and to begin keeping an eye on our parents.

It's a good thing they have us around. I've got to go. More later.[2]

---

[2]This is, however, the last entry in Grundle's journal.

CHAPTER ♦ 25

PHONDRA

CHELESTRA

♦

His DOG WAS WITH ALFRED.

There was no doubt in Haplo's mind that the dog the dolphins mentioned was *his* dog and it was with Alfred. The thought irritated Haplo, bothered him more than he cared to admit, rankled like a poisoned barb in his flesh. He found himself thinking about the dog when he should have been concentrating on more important matters—such as the journey ahead, the war against the Sartan.

"It's only a damn dog," he told himself.

Elves and dwarves were boarding their submersibles, preparing to travel back to their homelands and ready their people for the great Sun Chase. Haplo stayed with them until the last possible moment, reassuring the dwarves, prodding the elves to action, solving problems both real and imaginary. They hadn't all agreed to go to war, not yet. But he was leading them toward it, gently, without their being aware of his intent. And Haplo had little doubt that the Sartan would finish whatever it was he started.

The humans, with typical human impetuosity, wanted to sail the submersibles to Surunan directly, land their people on the shore, and then open up negotiations.

"We will be arguing from a position of strength," stated Dumaka. "The Sartan will see our numbers, see that we have already established a foothold. They will see, too, that we arrive in peace with peaceful intent. They will look out over the walls of their city and see women and children . . ."

"They'll look out over their walls and see an army," Yngvar growled. "They'll grab their axes first and think about talking later."

"I agree with Yngvar," said Eliason. "We don't want to intimidate these Sartan. I suggest that we halt the fleet near Surunan, close enough for the Sartan to see our ships and be impressed by our numbers, but far enough away that they do not feel threatened. . . ."

"And what's wrong with a little threatening?" Dumaka argued. "I suppose you elves plan to go groveling and crawling in on your bellies, prepared to wash their feet."

"Certainly not. We elves know how to behave politely, present our proposals in a civilized manner without loss of dignity."

"Now you're saying we humans are not civilized!" Dumaka flared.

"If the boot fits . . ." Yngvar began, at which point Haplo intervened.

"I think it would be best to go with Eliason's plan. What if, as Yngvar suggests, the Sartan decided to attack? You'd have your families strung out on the beaches, defenseless. Far better to keep on board the ships. There's a place to moor the submersibles not far from Draknor, where the dragon-snakes live.

"Don't worry," Haplo added hastily, noting the scowls that met this proposal, "you won't be that close to the snakes. You can take advantage of their air bubble to bring your ships to the surface. And by the time you reach this point, you'll be glad to breathe fresh air again. Once you're here, you ask the Sartan for a meeting, and then open negotiations."

His plan was accepted. Haplo smiled quietly. He could almost certainly count on the mensch to talk themselves into trouble.

Which brought him to his next topic of conversation: weapons. In particular, magical elven weapons.

No weapon made by mensch, magic or otherwise, could stand up against the power of the Sartan rune-magic. But Haplo had devised a plan that would make everyone equal, a plan that would, in fact, give the mensch the edge. He hadn't told anyone about his plan yet, not the mensch, not even his allies, the dragon-snakes. Too much was at stake: victory over the ancient enemy, Samah helpless and at the Patryn's mercy. Haplo would tell everyone when they needed to know and not a moment before.

Although no elf living could remember a time of warfare, the magical weapons they'd once developed were celebrated in story and legend. Eliason knew all about them, described them all to Haplo. The two of them endeavored to determine which weapons the elves could manufacture swiftly, which weapons they could learn to use effectively—or at least learn how to inflict more damage on an enemy than on themselves.

After some discussion, Haplo and Eliason settled on the bow and arrow. The elven king was quite enamored of archery—a sport still used by some elves as a form of entertainment at parties. The magical arrows hit whatever target they were ordered to hit after being fired and therefore aim wasn't all that critical.

The humans were already skilled in the use of bow and arrow, plus numerous other weapons. And although their weapons weren't magically enhanced (nor would the humans use elven weapons, considering them suitable only for weaklings), the Coven had the power to summon the elements to assist in the battle.

This point settled, the Gargans, Phondrans, and Elmas took friendly leave of each other. Dwarves and elves sailed off to their homelands, and Haplo breathed a sigh of relief.

Walking back to his lodge, he was thinking to himself that, at last, everything seemed to be working out.

"Haplo," said Alake. "May I speak with you? It's about the dolphins."

He glanced at her impatiently, irritated at the interruption. "Yes? What about them?"

Alake bit her lip, looked abashed. "It's urgent," she said softly, in apology. "Otherwise I wouldn't bother you. I know what important matters you have on your mind . . ."

It occurred to Haplo that the dolphins might have told the girl things she hadn't told him. He had no way of knowing, he'd been involved in meetings since then.

He forced himself to pause, to smile at the girl, seem glad to see her. "I'm going back to my lodge. Will you walk with me?"

Alake returned his smile—how easy it was to please her—

and fell into step beside him, moving gracefully to the pleasing silvery sounds of the bells and beads she wore.

"Now," he said, "tell me about the dolphins."

"They don't mean any harm, but they do like to stir up excitement and, of course, it's difficult for them to understand how important it is for us to find a new seamoon. The dolphins can't figure out why we want to live on land. They think we should live in the water, as they do. And then they're really frightened of the dragon-snakes . . ."

Alake wasn't looking at him while she talked. Her eyes were averted; her hands, he noted, were nervously twisting the rings on her fingers.

She knows something, Haplo concluded grimly. Something she isn't telling.

"Sorry, Alake," he said, still smiling at her, "but I'm afraid I don't find fish much of a threat."

"But I thought . . . that is, we thought . . . Grundle and Devon agree . . . that if the dolphins talked to our people, they might say things. The dolphins, I mean. Things that would upset our parents and maybe cause more delays."

"What things, Alake?" Haplo came to a halt. They were near his lodge, no one else was around. "What did the dolphins say?"

The girl opened her eyes wide. "Nothing!" she began, faltered, hung her head. "Please don't make me tell you."

It was well she couldn't see the expression on Haplo's face. He drew a deep breath, controlled the impulse to seize the girl and shake the information out of her. He did take hold of her, but his touch was gentle, caressing.

"Tell me, Alake. The lives of your people could be at stake."

"It doesn't have anything to do with my people—"

"Alake." Haplo's grip on her tightened.

"They said terrible things about . . . about you!"

"What things?"

"That the dragon-snakes were evil, that you were evil. That you're only using us." Alake raised her head, her eyes flashed. "I don't believe it! I don't believe a word. Neither do Grundle and Devon. But if the dolphins were to tell my parents . . ."

Yes, Haplo thought, that would finish it. Of all the damn, fool, stupid things to happen! His grand design, about to be wrecked by a bunch of fish!

"Don't worry," she said quickly, seeing the dark expression on his face. "I have an idea."

"What is it?" Haplo was only half-listening, trying to figure out how to solve this latest crisis.

"I thought," Alake suggested shyly, "that I might tell the dolphins to go on ahead of us . . . act as scouts. They'd like that. They love to feel important. I could say it was my father's suggestion. . . ."

Haplo considered. It would keep the fish from causing trouble. By the time the mensch reached Surunan, it would be too late for them to back out, no matter what the dolphins told them.

"That's a good idea, Alake."

Her face was radiant. It took so little effort to make her happy, would take so little. A voice, which sounded very much like the voice of his lord, spoke in Haplo's ear.

You could get this girl to do anything you want. Be nice to her. Give her a few trinkets, whisper sweet things to her in the night, promise her marriage. She would become your slave, do anything for you, even die for you. And, when you're finished, you can always cast her aside. After all, she is only a mensch.

The two were still standing outside his lodge. Haplo had his hands on the girl's arms. Alake moved closer, pressing her body nearer. He had only to draw her inside his hut and she would be his. She'd been startled the first time, taken by surprise. But now she'd had time to dream about lying in his arms. Her fear had been subdued by desire.

And in addition to the pleasure she would give him, she would be useful, too. A spy on her parents, on the dwarves and the elves. She would report back to him every word, every thought. And he would ensure that what she knew, she'd keep to herself. Not that she was likely to betray him, but this would make it certain. . . .

He fully intended to go through with her seduction, was surprised to watch himself pat her on the arms, as if she were an obedient child.

"A good idea," he repeated. "We don't have a moment to lose. Why don't you go take care of the dolphins right now?" He took a step backward, away from her.

"Is that what you want?" she asked him, her voice low and breathless.

"You said yourself how important this was, Alake. Who knows but that, even now, your father isn't on his way to talk to the dolphins."

"He isn't," she said, drooping. "He's in the lodge, talking with Mother."

"Then now's a perfect time."

"Yes," she said, but she lingered a moment longer, perhaps hoping he'd change his mind.

She was young, lovely.

Haplo turned from her and entered his hut, flung himself on his pallet as if exhausted. He waited, unmoving, in the cool darkness until he heard her soft footfalls passing through the dust. She was hurt, but not nearly as hurt as she would have been.

"After all, since when do I need a mensch to help me? I work alone. And damn Alfred, anyway," he added incongruously. "This time, I'll finish him."

The sun-chasers arrived on schedule. Two stayed to take aboard Dumaka's tribe. Others traveled around the shores of the seamoon, gathering up the remainder of the human population of Phondra.

Haplo was pleasantly surprised at the dispatch and efficiency of the humans, who managed to collect everyone on board the submersibles with a minimum of fuss and confusion. Looking around the deserted camp, he was reminded of how easily the Squatters had been able to pack up their belongings and move on.

"Our people used to be nomads," Dumaka explained. "We traveled to different parts of Phondra, following the game, gathering fruits and vegetables. Such a life caused wars, however. Men always imagine that the antelope are fatter in another man's portion of the jungle.

"Peace has come to us slowly, we have worked long and hard for it. I am saddened to think we may be forced to go back to war."

Delu came to him, put her arm around him. The two of them looked wistfully around their now-empty, all-but-deserted village.

"All will be well, Husband. We are together. Our people are

together. The One who guides the waves is with us. We'll carry peace in our hearts and offer it to these Sartan as our greatest gift."

Hopefully, they'll spit in your face, Haplo thought. His one worry was Alfred. Alfred would not only take these mensch into his home, he'd give them the shabby velvet coat off his back. But Haplo was coming to think Alfred wasn't a typical Sartan. The Patryn expected better things of Samah.

Once the humans were taken on board the submersibles, they shed only a few tears at leaving their homeland. Those tears soon dried in the excitement of the trip, the anticipation of a new and purportedly rich world.

There was no sign of the dragon-snakes.

Haplo sailed on the largest of the submersibles with the chief and his family, friends, and members of the Coven. The sun-chaser was similar to the much smaller submersible he'd sailed in before, except that it boasted several levels.

They reached Gargan, found the dwarves packed and ready to go, but did not find the elves, to no one's surprise. Even Haplo had made allowances for them to be late; his dire threat of leaving them behind had only been intended to prod them on.

"It'll be chaos," Yngvar predicted dourly. "But I've sent my best men to captain the vessel and thrown in the army to boot. We'll have them here *in* time, if not *on* time."

The elven contingent arrived only four cycles late; the submersibles moving slowly, rolling in the sea like overfed whales.

"What's the meaning of this?" Yngvar demanded.

"We're overloaded, that's what, Vater!" the dwarven captain raved, on the verge of tearing out his beard. "It would have been easier to drag the seamoon behind us. We might as well. The blasted elves brought along everything else! See for yourself!"

The dwarves had taken care to build bunks for the elves, but the Elmas took one look at them and refused to sleep in anything so crude. They had then attempted to bring their own heavy, ornately carved wooden bed frames aboard, at which the dwarven captain told them there was either room for the beds or for the elves, take their pick.

"I was hoping for the beds," said the dwarf dourly to Yngvar. "At least they don't make any noise."

The elves eventually agreed to sleep in the bunks, then proceeded to drag aboard goose-feather mattresses, lace-edged sheets, silk blankets, and down pillows. And this was only the beginning. Every elven family had valuable heirlooms that simply could not be left behind—everything from fanciful magical clocks to harps that played themselves. One elf arrived with a full-grown tree in a pot; another with twenty-seven songbirds in twenty-seven silver cages.

Finally, everyone and everything was stowed aboard. The elves were, for the most part, satisfied, though it was impossible to move through the sun-chaser without tripping over something or someone.

Then began the truly difficult part—leaving their homeland. The humans, accustomed to constant moving about, had been matter-of-fact. The dwarves, though giving up their beloved caves was a wrench, took the departure with stoic calm. The elves were shattered. One dwarf captain reported that with all the tears shed in his ship, he had more water on the inside than the out.

At last, however, the huge fleet of sun-chasers was assembled and ready to sail to their new homeland. The heads of the royal households gathered on the deck of the flagship to lead the people in prayer, asking the One to grant them a safe journey and a peaceful landing.

Their prayers concluded, the dwarven sea captains began exchanging a flurry of signals and the submersibles sank beneath the waves.

They had only traveled a short distance when a first officer, face white and panicked, approached Yngvar, knuckled his forehead to the dwarven king, and said something to him in low tones.

Yngvar frowned, glanced at the others. "Dragon-snakes," he reported.

Haplo had been aware of the snakes' presence a long time: the sigla on his skin itched and burned. He rubbed at it irritably; the runes on his hands glowed a faint blue.

"Let me talk to them," he said.

"How can any of us 'talk' to them?" Yngvar demanded gruffly. "We're underwater!"

"There are ways," said Haplo and headed off for the bridge,

accompanied—whether he wanted them or not—by the mensch royalty.

The warning blue glow of the runes shone through his shirt, reflected in the wide eyes of the mensch, who'd heard this phenomenon described by their children, but who'd never witnessed it.

It was useless for Haplo to try to tell himself that the dragon-snakes did not present a threat. His body was reacting to them as centuries of instinct had trained it to react. The only thing he could do was ignore the warning and hope that over time, his body would come to understand.

He entered the steerage, found the dwarven crew huddled together, muttering among themselves. The captain pointed out to sea.

The dragon-snakes hung in the water, huge bodies undulating with sinuous grace, eyes red slits in the green water.

"They're blocking our way, Vater. I say we turn back."

"And go where?" Haplo asked. "Back to your homeland and sit waiting for the ice to come? I'll talk to them."

"How?" Yngvar asked again, but the word came out a gargle.

A shimmering, ghostly image of a dragon-snake appeared on the bridge. Fear flowed from it like chill water. Those members of the dwarven crew who could still move did so, fleeing the bridge with loud cries. Those who were frozen in terror stood staring, shivering. The captain held his ground, though his beard quivered and he was forced to keep his hand on the wheel to steady himself.

The royal families remained, too, for which courage Haplo gave them grudging credit. His own instinct was to run, swim, tear the wooden planks apart with his bare hands in order to escape. He fought against his fear, and managed to subdue it, though he had to work to find saliva enough in his mouth to speak.

"The sun-chaser fleet is assembled, Royal One. We are sailing for Surunan as we planned. Why do you stand in our path?"

Slit eyes—merely a reflection of the real eyes—glowed red, gazed steadfastly at Haplo.

"The distance is far, the way is long. We have come to guide you, Master."

"A trick!" breathed Yngvar, teeth clicking together.

"We can find our own way," added Dumaka.

Delu raised her voice suddenly in a chant, held up some kind of rock she wore on a chain around her neck, probably some crude mensch form of protective magic.

The red eyes of the dragon-snake narrowed to slits.

"Shut up, all of you!" Haplo snarled. He kept his own gaze fixed on the dragon-snake. "We thank you for your offer, Royal One. And we will follow. Captain, keep your vessel in the dragon's wake, order all the other sun-chasers to do likewise."

The dwarf looked to his king for confirmation. Yngvar's face was dark with anger and terror; he started to shake his head.

"Don't be a fool," Haplo warned him in a quiet undertone. "If they wanted to kill you, they would have done so long before now. Accept their offer. It's no trick. I guarantee it . . . with my life," he added, seeing the dwarf king still hesitate.

"We have no choice, Yngvar," said Eliason.

"And you, Dumaka?" the dwarf demanded, breathing heavily. "What do you say?"

Husband and wife exchanged glances. Delu shrugged in bitter acquiescence. "We have our people to consider."

"Go ahead, then." Dumaka agreed, frowning.

"Very well," stated Yngvar. "Do as he says."

"Yes, Vater," the captain answered, but he cast Haplo a sullen glance. "Tell the creature it must take itself off my bridge. I can't run my ship without a crew."

The dragon-snake was already starting to disappear, fading from view slowly, leaving behind the vague uneasiness and half-remembered fears that assail a sleeper waking suddenly from a bad dream.

The mensch breathed deep sighs of relief, though their dark looks did not brighten. The submersible's crew and officers returned, shamefaced, avoiding their captain's irate glare.

Haplo turned and left. On his way out, he nearly ran down Grundle, Alake, and Devon, emerging rather hastily from the shadows of a nearby doorway.

"You're wrong!" Alake was saying to Devon.

"For your sake, I hope I—"

"Shush!" Grundle caught sight of Haplo.

The three fell silent. He had obviously interrupted an important conversation, and he had the feeling it was about him. The other two had heard the dolphins, too, apparently. Devon looked ashamed, kept his gaze averted. Grundle, however, stared at Haplo defiantly.

"Spying again?" he said. "I thought you'd learned your lesson."

"Guess not," muttered Grundle, as he passed.

The remainder of the voyage was peaceful. They didn't see the dragon-snakes, their dread influence could no longer be felt. The submersible sailed along in the wake left by the huge bodies, swimming far ahead.

Life aboard ship was boring, claustrophobic, uneventful.

Haplo was certain that the three mensch were up to something. But, after a few days of keeping a close eye on them, he concluded he must be mistaken.

Alake avoided him, devoted herself to her mother and her studies of magic, in which she had developed a renewed interest. Devon and a host of younger elves spent their time practicing shooting arrows at a target they had set up. Grundle was the only one who gave Haplo cause for concern, and then only as a minor annoyance, like a gnat.

More than once, he caught her trailing after him, staring at him, her expression grave and thoughtful, as if she was having difficulty making up her mind about him. And when she discovered him looking at her, she'd give him an abrupt nod or shake her side whiskers at him, turn around, and stump off. Alake had said Grundle didn't believe the dolphins. Apparently, Alake'd been wrong.

Haplo didn't waste time trying to argue with the dwarf. After all, what the dolphins had told the young people was true. He *was* using the mensch.

He spent most of his waking hours with them, molding them, shaping them, leading them to do what he wanted. His task wasn't easy. The mensch, terrified of their dragon-snake allies, might come to greatly admire the would-be enemy.

This was Haplo's one fear, the one toss of the rune-bone that would end his game. If the Sartan welcomed the mensch with open arms, clasped them to their bosoms, so to speak, Haplo was finished. He'd escape, of course. The dragon-snakes would see to that. But he'd have to go back to the Nexus empty-handed, make a humiliating report to his lord.

Faced with that choice, Haplo wasn't certain he would go back at all. Better to die . . .

Time passed quickly, even for the Patryn, impatient to at last meet his greatest foe. He was lying in his bed when he heard a grinding sound, felt a jolt pass through the ship. Voices cried out in alarm, only to be reassured the next moment by their king.

The submersibles floated upward, broke through the water. Open air and sunshine—bright sunshine—surrounded them.

The sun-chasers had caught the sun.

CHAPTER 26

SURUNAN

CHELESTRA

♦

Aᴌғʀᴇᴅ sᴘᴇɴᴛ ᴍosᴛ oғ ʜɪs ᴅᴀʏ ᴀɴᴅ ᴀ ɢʀᴇᴀᴛᴇʀ ᴘoʀᴛɪoɴ oғ ʜɪs night listening to the echo of the conversation he'd overheard between Samah and his son. He heard it all, over and over again in his mind, but one portion kept returning to him, louder and more persistent than the rest.

We should do to him what we did to the others.

What others?

Those who had discovered that they were not gods, that they were (or should be) worshipers? Those who had found out that the Sartan were not the sun, but just another planet? What had happened to them? Where were they?

He glanced around, almost as if he expected to find them sitting in Orla's garden. The heretics weren't in Chelestra. They weren't on the Council. Despite the fact that there was some division, the Council members, with the exception of Orla, appeared to be solidly behind Samah.

Perhaps all Ramu meant was that the heretics had been counseled, finally converted back to proper Sartan ways of thinking. This was a comforting thought, and Alfred wanted very much to believe it. He spent almost an entire hour convincing himself it must be true. That nagging unfortunate part of him that seemed to be always going off on its own (and taking his feet with it) argued that he was, as usual, refusing to face reality.

The internal argument was wearing, left him worn out and unhappy. He was tired of it, tired of being by himself, forced to argue with himself. He was immeasurably cheered at the sight of Orla entering the garden in search of him.

It had seemed to Alfred as if she had been avoiding him.

"Ah, here you are." Orla spoke briskly, impersonally. She might have been talking to the dog, snoozing at Alfred's feet. The animal opened an eye to see who was here, yawned, rolled over, and went back to sleep.

Startled by Orla's detached tone, Alfred sighed. She obviously loathed him now. He supposed he couldn't really blame her.

"Yes, I'm here," he replied. "Where did you think I would be—the library?"

Orla flushed in anger, then paled. She bit her lip. "I'm sorry," she said, after a moment. "I suppose I deserved that."

"No, I'm the one who is sorry," Alfred said, appalled at himself. "I don't know what's come over me. Won't you please sit down?"

"No, thank you," Orla said, her flush deepening. "I can't stay. I came to tell you that we've received a message from the mensch. They have arrived on Draknor." Her voice hardened. "They want to arrange a meeting."

"What is Draknor? One of the durnai?"

"Yes, poor creature. The durnai were meant to hibernate until the seasun drifted away, then we would wake them and they would follow it. Most durnai, after we left, never woke up. I doubt if even the mensch, who have lived on the durnai all this time, are aware that they have been living on a living being.

"Unfortunately, the dragon-snakes realized at once that the durnai were alive. They attacked one, woke it, and have tormented the durnai ever since. According to the dolphins, the dragon-snakes have devoured it slowly, gnawed at it bit by bit. It lives in perpetual agony and fear.

"Yes," Orla added, seeing Alfred grow pale with horror. "It is these creatures who have allied themselves with your Patryn friend. And with the mensch."

Alfred was sickened. He glanced down at the dog, slumbering peacefully. "I can't believe it. Not even of Haplo. He is a Patryn—ambitious, hard, cold. But he's not a coward. He's not cruel. He takes no delight in tormenting the helpless, he does not enjoy inflicting pain."

"Yet he is there, in Draknor, and the mensch are with him. But they won't be content to stay there. They want to move here, to this realm." Orla looked around her garden, lush and beautiful in night's soft darkness. "That is what this meeting is about."

"Well, of course, they can't stay on Draknor. It must be dreadful. There is plenty of room for them here," said Alfred, feeling more cheerful than he had in days.

He was actually looking forward to being in company with the mensch again. They might be quarrelsome, disruptive, but they were interesting.

Then he saw the expression on Orla's face.

"You do plan to let them move onto Surunan, don't you?" he asked.

He saw the answer in her eyes, and stared at her, appalled. "I can't believe it! You'd turn them away?"

"It isn't the mensch, Alfred," Orla said. "It's those who are with them. The Patryn. He's asked to come to the meeting."

"Haplo?" Alfred repeated in astonishment.

At the sound of the name, the dog sprang to its feet, ears pricked, eyes searching.

"There, there," said Alfred, petting the animal, calming its excitement. "There, there. He's not here now. Not yet."

The dog gave a little whimper, and settled back down, nose on paws.

"Haplo, coming to a meeting of the Sartan," Alfred mused, disquieted by the news. "He must be very confident, to reveal himself to you. Of course, you already know he's on Chelestra, and he's probably aware that you know. Still, this isn't like him."

"Confident!" Orla snapped. "Of course he's confident! He's got the dragon-snakes, not to mention several thousand mensch warriors—"

"But perhaps the mensch only want to live in peace," Alfred suggested.

"Do you honestly believe that?" Orla looked at him in wonder. "Can you be that naive?"

"I admit I'm not as wise or as intelligent as the rest of you," Alfred stated humbly. "But shouldn't you at least listen to what they have to say?"

"Of course the Council will listen to them. That's why Samah has agreed to the meeting. And he wants you to be present. He sent me to tell you."

"Then you didn't come to me on your own," Alfred said softly, staring down at his shoes. "I was right. You have been avoiding me. No, don't worry about it. I understand. I've made things difficult enough for you. It's just that I missed talking to you, I missed hearing your voice. I missed"—he lifted his eyes— "looking at you."

"Alfred, please, don't. I've said this to you before—"

"I know. I'm sorry. I think it would be a good idea if I left this house, perhaps even left Chelestra."

"Oh, Alfred, no! Don't be ridiculous. You belong here, with us, with your people—"

"Do I?" Alfred asked her seriously, so seriously he stopped the words on her lips. "Orla, what happened to the others?"

"Others? What others?" she asked, perplexed.

"The others, the heretics. Before the Sundering. What happened to them?"

"I . . . I don't know what you mean," she said.

But Alfred saw that she did. She had gone extremely pale; her eyes were wide and frightened. Her lips parted, as if she would say something more, but no sound came from them. Turning hurriedly, she almost ran from the garden.

Alfred sat down unhappily on the bench.

He was beginning to be extremely frightened . . . of his own people.

The meeting between the Sartan and the mensch was arranged by the dolphins, who, as Alake had said, loved to feel important. What with swimming back and forth from one group to another, suggesting times, changing times, confirming times, discussing where and how and with whom, the dolphins were quite busy and did not think to mention their suspicions concerning Haplo and the dragon-snakes.

Or perhaps, in the excitement of the occasion, the dolphins simply forgot all about the Patryn. As Grundle said, what do you expect from the mind of a fish?

Haplo was on guard, always present when the dolphins were around, careful to request that the dolphins speak one of the mensch languages so that he knew what was being said.

It was a needless precaution.

The royal heads of household had far more urgent worries, didn't have time to listen to idle gossip. The mensch were currently arguing over where to hold the meeting with the Sartan: on Sartan ground, as the Sartan wanted, or to insist that the Sartan sail out and meet the representatives of the three races midway.

Dumaka, who had already decided he didn't like these Sartan, was in favor of forcing them to come to him.

Eliason said it would be more polite for them to go to the Sartan. "We're the ones coming as beggars."

Yngvar grumbled that he didn't care where the meeting was held as long as it was on dry land. He was sick and tired of living in a damn boat.

Haplo sat quietly nearby, watching, listening, saying nothing. He would let them argue, get it out of their systems, and then he would step in and tell them what to do.

As it turned out, the Sartan insisted that the meeting be held on Surunan or there would be no meeting.

Haplo smiled quietly. Out in a ship, in the magic-nullifying waters of the Goodsea, the Sartan would be completely at the mercy of the mensch . . . or anyone the mensch happened to have with them.

But it was early days for thinking of that. The mensch were in no mood to fight. Not yet.

"Meet the Sartan on Surunan," Haplo advised. "They want to try to impress you with their strength. It won't hurt if you allow them to think they've succeeded."

"Impress *us!*" Delu repeated in disdain.

The dolphins sped back with the mensch agreement, returned to say that the Sartan had invited the royal representatives to come early the next morning. They were to appear before the Sartan Council, present their requests in person to that august body.

The royal representatives agreed.

Haplo returned to his berth. He had never, in his life, experienced such excitement. He needed quiet, solitude, to calm his racing heart, burning blood.

If all his plans worked out, and he could see—at this point— no reason why they shouldn't, he would return to the Nexus in triumph, with the great Samah as prisoner. This victory would vindicate him, pay for his mistakes. Once again, he would be held in high esteem by his lord, the man he loved and revered above all others.

And, while he was at it, Haplo intended to get his dog back, too.

CHAPTER ◆ 27

SURUNAN

CHELESTRA

◆

Alfred knew quite well why he'd been invited to attend the meeting between the mensch and the Sartan Council members, a meeting to which, under normal circumstances, he would have never been asked. Samah knew that Haplo would be accompanying the mensch. The Councillor would be watching Alfred carefully, closely, in an attempt to catch some sort of communication between them.

Had Alfred and Haplo met under normal circumstances, Alfred would have had no cause to worry. Haplo would have disdained to acknowledge Alfred's presence at all, much less speak to him. But now Alfred had the dog. How he had managed to end up with the dog, how Haplo had managed to lose the dog, were questions beyond the Sartan's ability to answer.

Alfred had the feeling that once Haplo saw the dog, he would demand the dog back. Samah would most likely get what he wanted tonight—evidence that Alfred was in collusion with a Patryn. And there wasn't anything Alfred could do to stop it.

He considered not attending the meeting, considered hiding himself somewhere in the city. He considered, wildly, fleeing back through Death's Gate. He was forced to reject all these ideas for a variety of reasons—the main one being that Ramu attached himself to Alfred, stayed with him everywhere he went.

Ramu marched Alfred and the dog to the Council hall, led them both into the Council chambers. The other Council members were present, already seated. They glanced at Alfred, looked severe, and averted their gazes. Ramu indicated a chair, requested that Alfred be seated, then stood directly behind him. The dog curled up at the Sartan's feet.

Alfred attempted to catch Orla's eye, but failed. She was quiet, composed, as cold as the marble table on which she rested her hands. She, like the others, refused to look at him directly. Samah, however, more than made up for his colleagues.

Alfred glanced in the Councillor's direction and was disconcerted to find Samah's stern eyes glaring straight at him. Alfred tried not looking at the Councillor, but that was worse, for he could feel the eyes, if he could not see them, and their hard, suspicious glare made him shrivel up inside.

Absorbed in his own vague terrors, yet having no idea what he feared, Alfred wasn't aware of the mensch's arrival until he heard those Council members around him start to mutter and whisper.

The mensch walked into the Council Chamber. Heads held high, they walked proudly, tried not to look awed and daunted at the marvelous sights they'd seen on their way.

The Council members weren't paying all that muttering attention to the mensch, however. Their eyes were fixed on one figure, on the blue-tattooed skin of the Patryn, who entered last and who kept back behind the mensch, retreating to a shadowy corner of the large room.

Haplo knew they were watching him. He smiled quietly, folded his arms across his chest, leaned back comfortably against the wall. His eyes flicked over the Council members, rested briefly on Samah, then their gaze came to rest on one person.

Blood rushed to Alfred's face. He could feel the heat, hear it beating in his ears, wondered miserably that it wasn't gushing out his nose.

Haplo's smile tightened. He glanced from Alfred to the dog slumbering quietly beneath the table, unaware that it's master had entered. The Patryn's eyes came back to Alfred.

Not yet, Haplo said to him silently. *I won't do anything yet. But just wait.*

Alfred groaned inwardly, his arms and legs curled up like those of a dead spider. Now everyone in the room was staring at him: Samah. Orla. Ramu. All the other Council members. He saw scorn, contempt, in every gaze except Orla's. But in hers, he saw pity. If Death's Gate had been anywhere nearby, he would have hurled himself into it without a second thought.

He paid no attention to the proceedings. He had the vague impression that the mensch said some polite words, introduced themselves. Samah rose to his feet, was responding, introduced the Council members (not using their true Sartan names, but giving the mensch equivalent).

"If you do not mind," Samah added, "I will speak the human language. I find it the language best suited to conduct such business as this. I will, of course, provide translations for the elves and dwarves—"

"There is no need for that," said the elf king, speaking flawless human. "We all understand each other's languages."

"Indeed?" Samah murmured, lifting an eyebrow.

By this time, Alfred had calmed himself enough to study the mensch, listen to what they were saying. He liked what he saw and heard. The two dwarves—husband and wife—had the fierce pride and dignity of the best of their race. The humans—again husband and wife—had the quick movements and quicker tongues of their people, but these were tempered by intelligence and common sense. The elf was alone and looked pale and sorrowful—recently bereaved, Alfred guessed, noting the man's white clothing. The elven king had the wisdom of his years, and he had, in addition, the wisdom his people had accumulated over the years—a wisdom Alfred had not seen in many of the elves of other worlds.

And the three disparate races were unified! This was not a hastily arranged alliance, made for the sake of the moment, but a unity that had obviously lasted a long, long time. One that had been carefully nurtured until it had taken root and was now strong and unbending. Alfred was very favorably impressed, and he could only suppose that Samah and the rest of the Sartan must be impressed as well.

The Council members, who had risen to be introduced, returned to their chairs.

"Please, be seated," Samah said to the mensch, with a gracious wave of his hand.

The mensch glanced around. There were no chairs.

"Is this some type of joke?" Dumaka demanded, scowling. "Or are we to sit on the cold stone floor?"

"What do you— Ah, an oversight. I apologize," Samah said, apparently just now realizing his mistake.

The Councillor sang several runes. Chairs made of solid gold sprang into existence, one directly behind each mensch. The dwarf, feeling something suddenly touching his backside, jumped in alarm. Turning, seeing the chair where no chair had been before, he sucked in a deep breath, let it out in a curse.

The humans were momentarily stunned. The elf alone remained calm, unperturbed. Coolly, Eliason took a seat in the chair. Folding his hands in his lap, he drew his legs off the floor, as was the elven custom.

Delu sat down with graceful dignity, yanked her glowering husband down into his chair. Dumaka's fist was clenched, the veins stood out sharply beneath his glistening skin.

Yngvar gave the chair a dark glance, the Sartan an even darker one.

"I will stand," said the dwarf.

"As you please." Samah was about to continue speaking, when the elf interrupted.

"What about a chair for Haplo? Our friend?"

Eliason made a graceful gesture, nodded at the Patryn, who was still standing.

"You refer to this man as 'friend,' do you?" Samah asked, a dangerous edge to his voice.

The mensch heard the danger, failed to understand.

"Yes, certainly, he is our friend," Delu replied. "That is," she amended, with a warm glance at Haplo, "we would be honored if he considered himself as such."

" 'Savior' is what my people call him," said Eliason quietly.

Samah's eyes narrowed. He leaned forward slightly, hands folded on the table before him. "What do you know about this man? Nothing, I'll wager. Do you know, for instance, that he and his people have long been our most bitter enemies?"

"We were all once bitter enemies," said Yngvar. "Dwarves, humans, elves. We made peace. Perhaps you should do the same."

"We could help negotiate, if you like," Eliason offered, obviously in earnest.

The unexpected response took Samah by surprise, left him momentarily at a loss for words. Alfred fought a sudden wild impulse to applaud. Haplo, standing in the corner, smiled quietly.

Samah recovered himself. "Thank you for the offer, but the differences that divide his people and ourselves are beyond your comprehension. Heed my warning. This man is a danger to you. He and his people want only one thing and that is complete rule over you and your world. He will stop at nothing to attain his goal: tricks, deceits, treachery, lies. He will appear to be your friend but, in the end, he will prove to be your deadliest enemy."

Dumaka bounded to his feet in anger. Eliason forestalled him, the elf's smooth words soothing the human's anger like oil over rough seas.

"This man, at the risk of his own life, saved the lives of our children. He negotiated a peaceful settlement between our people and the dragon-snakes. He was in large part responsible for bringing us here safely to a realm where we hope we can establish our homes. Are these the acts of an enemy?"

"These are the tricks of an enemy," Samah replied coldly. "However, I will not argue with you. I see he has completely deluded you."

It seemed the mensch would have spoken. The Councillor raised his hand imperiously for silence, continued on.

"You have come requesting that we share our realm with you. We grant your request. Your people will be allowed to move onto those portions of Surunan designated for your habitation. We will establish a government for you, provide laws for you to follow. We will work with you to help improve your economic situation. We will educate you and your children. All this and more we will do for you, provided that you do something for us in return."

Samah glanced pointedly at Haplo. "You will rid yourselves of this man. Order him to leave. If he is your 'friend,' as you claim, he will understand that we have only your best interests at heart and he will be happy to comply."

The mensch stared at the Councillor, so shocked that for long moments they could not speak.

"Best interests!" Dumaka managed at last to find words for his astonishment. "What do you mean—best interests?"

"Government over us? Laws for us?" Yngvar thumped himself on the chest. "Dwarves govern dwarves, no one else makes decisions for us—not humans, not elves, not you!"

"No matter how many golden chairs you can pull out of the air!" Hilda sniffed.

"We humans choose our own friends. And we choose our enemies!" Delu cried passionately.

"Peace, friends," said Eliason mildly. "Peace. We agreed I was to speak?"

"Go ahead, then," Dumaka growled, resuming his seat.

The elven king rose to his feet, took a step forward, made a graceful bow.

"We seem to be laboring under a misunderstanding. We came to ask you and your people if you would be kind enough to share your realm with our peoples. Surunan is certainly large enough for all. Looking around, as we sailed in, we could see that much of this precious land is now going to waste.

"We will develop the land, make Surunan prosperous. We will provide you with many goods and services you undoubtedly now lack. We will, of course, be more than pleased to include your people in our alliance. You will have an equal vote—"

"Equal!" Samah's astonishment was boundless. "We are not your equals! In intelligence, magical power, wisdom, we are far superior. I make allowances," he said, pausing to regain his composure, "because you do not know us as yet—"

"We know enough." Dumaka was again on his feet, Delu standing at his side. "We came in peace, offering to share this realm with you in peace, in equal partnership. Do you accept our offer or not?"

"Partnership! With mensch!" Samah's hand struck the marble table. "There will be no equal partnership. Take yourselves back to your boats and find another realm where you can all be 'equal.' "

"You know very well that there is no other realm," said Eliason gravely. "Our request is reasonable. There is no reason why you should not grant it. We do not seek to take over your land, only use that portion of it that you are not using."

"We consider such demands unreasonable. We are not just 'using' this world. We created it! Your ancestors worshiped us as gods!"

The mensch stared at Samah, incredulous.

"If you will excuse us, we will take our leave," said Delu, with dignity.

"We worship one god," Yngvar stated. "The One who created this world. The One who guides the waves."

The One who guides the waves. Alfred, who had been hunched miserably in his chair, angry, frustrated, longing to intervene but fearing only to make matters worse, sat suddenly bolt upright. A jolt surged through his body. *The One who guides the waves.* Where had he heard that before? What other voice had spoken it?

Or something like it. For that wasn't quite right.

The One who guides the waves.

I am in a room, seated at a table, surrounded by my brothers and sisters. White light shines down upon us, peace and serenity envelop me. I have the answer! I have found it, after all these years of fruitless searching. I know it now, and so do all the others. Haplo and I . . .

Alfred's gaze went irresistibly to Haplo. Had he heard? Did he remember?

Yes! Alfred saw it in Haplo's face—in the eyes, dark and suspicious, returning Alfred's stare, in the grimly tightened lips. He saw it in the tattooed arms folded across the chest, barring entry. But Alfred knew the truth. He remembered the Chamber of the Blessed on Abarrach, he remembered the shining light, the table. He remembered the voice, the One . . .

The One who guides the Wave!

"That's it!" Alfred cried, leaping out of his chair. "The One who guides the Wave! Haplo, don't you remember? On Abarrach? In the chamber? The light! The voice that spoke. It was in my heart, but I heard it clearly and so did you. You must remember! You were sitting beside . . ."

Alfred's voice faded. Haplo was gazing at him with bitter hatred and enmity. *Yes, I remember,* he said silently. *I can't forget, no matter how much I want to. I had everything figured out. I knew what I wanted, how to get it. You destroyed all that. You made me doubt my lord. You made me doubt myself. I'll never forgive you.*

At the sound of the beloved name, the dog had wakened. Its tail wagged violently, it stood up on trembling legs, stared at its master.

Haplo whistled, slapped his thigh. "Here, boy," he called.

The dog began to whine. It crept out from beneath the table, started forward, then looked back at Alfred. The dog stopped. Whimpering, it looked back at Haplo. Then it made a complete circle, returned to where it had started, at the feet of the Sartan.

Alfred reached down his hand. "Go on," he urged. "Go to him."

The dog whined again, started for Haplo again, made another circle, came back.

"Dog!" Haplo commanded sharply, angrily.

Alfred was concentrating his attention on the Patryn and the dog, but he was also uncomfortably aware of Samah, who was watching the entire incident. Alfred recalled the words he'd just said to Haplo, realized how they must sound to the Councillor, foresaw more questions, more interrogation, and he sighed heavily.

For the moment, however, none of that was important. What was important was the dog . . . and Haplo.

"Go with him," Alfred pleaded, gave the dog a gentle push on its hind end.

The animal refused to budge.

Haplo cast Alfred a look that would have been a blow, had he been close enough. Turning on his heel, the Patryn stalked out the door.

"Wait, Haplo!" Alfred cried. "You can't leave him! And you. You can't let him go," he said to the dog.

But the animal wouldn't move and Haplo didn't stop walking.

"They must be brought back together!" Alfred said to himself, fondling the grieving animal. "And it must be soon. He remembers the dog now and he wants it back—a good sign. If Haplo should ever completely forget . . ."

Alfred sighed, shook his head gloomily.

The humans started to walk out after Haplo.

Samah glared at the mensch. "If you leave now, if you follow after your 'friend,' you will never be allowed back."

Eliason said something to the others, speaking in low tones. Dumaka shouted "No!" angrily, but his wife rested a restraining hand on his arm. "I don't like it," Yngvar was heard to mutter. "We have no choice," his wife replied. Eliason cast them all one last, questioning glance. Dumaka turned away. Delu nodded mutely.

Eliason turned back to the Sartan. "We accept your offer. We accept all your terms, with one exception. We will not ask this man, our friend, to leave us."

Samah raised an eyebrow. "Then in that case, we are at an impasse. For we will not allow you to set foot upon this land so long as you harbor a Patryn among you."

"You can't mean that!" cried Alfred, shocked into speaking. "They've agreed to the rest of your demands—"

Samah glanced at him coldly. "You are not part of the Council, Brother. I thank you not to interfere with Council business."

Alfred went pale, gnawed his lower lip, but kept silent.

"And where would you have our people go?" Dumaka demanded.

"Ask your friends," Samah answered. "The Patryn and the dragon-snakes."

"You sentence us to death," Eliason said quietly. "And perhaps you sentence yourselves. We came to you in peace and in friendship. We made what we considered a reasonable request. In turn, we have been humiliated, patronized, treated like children. Our people are peaceful. I did not believe, before this, that I would ever advocate the use of force. But now—"

"Ah, at last the truth is told." Samah was cool, haughty. "Come, come. This is what you intended all along, wasn't it? You and the Patryn have this all planned—war. You want to destroy us. Very well. Go to war against us. If you are fortunate, you *might* live to regret it."

The Councillor spoke the runes. Sigla, blazing red and yellow, sizzled in the air, burst above the startled mensch with the ferocity of a thunderclap. Heat burned their skin, dazzling light blinded them, shock waves knocked them to the floor.

The magical spell ended abruptly. Silence fell over the Council Chamber. Dazed and shaken by this exhibition of magical power—a power beyond their comprehension—the mensch looked around for the Councillor.

Samah had disappeared.

Frightened and angry, the mensch picked themselves up and stalked out.

"He doesn't mean it, does he?" Alfred turned to Orla. "He can't possibly be serious—going to war against those weaker than ourselves, those we were meant to protect? Never has such a vile thing happened. Never in our history. He can't mean it!"

Orla refused to meet his eyes, acted as if she hadn't heard him. She gave the departing mensch a fleeting glance, then left the Council Chamber without answering Alfred.

He didn't need an answer. He knew it already. He'd seen the expression on Samah's face, when the Councillor worked his terrifying magic.

Alfred recognized that expression. He'd felt it on his own face countless times, had seen it reflected in the mirror of his own soul.

Fear.

CHAPTER ♦ 28

NEAR DRAKNOR

CHELESTRA

♦

"OUR PARENTS ARE BACK." GRUNDLE[1] CREPT AS SILENTLY AS A dwarf possibly could into the small cabin Alake shared with her parents. "And they don't look happy."

Alake sighed.

"We have to find out how the meeting went," said Devon. "Will they come here, do you think?"

"No, they're in Eliason's cabin, right next door. Listen." Grundle cocked her head. "You can hear them."

The three leaned near the wall. Muffled voices could be heard, but they were low and their words indistinguishable.

Grundle pointed to a small knothole.

Alake understood her meaning, placed her hand on the knothole, and began to run her fingers round and round the edge, whispering. The hole gradually, imperceptibly, grew larger. Alake peered through it, turned to her companions, motioned them near.

"We're in luck. One of Mother's feathered staves is standing right in front of it."

The three gathered close, ears to the wall.

---

[1]As stated previously, Grundle leaves us no record of later events. We must refer, therefore, to this account, which is taken from Haplo's *Chelestra: World of Water*, volume four, *Death Gate Journals*.

"I have never seen magic like that." Delu's voice was heavy with defeat. "How can we fight against such awesome power?"

"We won't know until we try," stated her husband. "And I am for trying. I would not speak to a dog the way they spoke to us."

"Ours is a terrible choice," said Eliason. "The land is theirs, by right. It is the right of these Sartan to refuse us permission to move into their realm. But, by so doing, they doom our people to death! And it does not seem to me that they should have the right to do that. I do not want to fight them, neither can I watch my people die."

"You, Yngvar," Haplo said. "What do you think?"

The dwarf was silent a long time. Grundle, standing on tiptoe, put her eye to the knothole. Her father's craggy face was stern. He shook his head.

"My people are brave. We would fight any human or elf or whatever these call themselves"—he waved a disparaging hand in the general direction of the Sartan—"if they fought fairly, using ax and sword and bow. My people are not cowards."

Yngvar glowered around, daring someone to accuse him of such a thing. Then he sighed. "But against magic such as we saw today? . . . I don't know. I don't know."

"You don't have to fight their magic," said Haplo.

They stared at him.

"I have a plan. There's a way. I wouldn't have brought you here otherwise."

"You . . . knew about this?" Dumaka asked, frowning with suspicion. "How?"

"I told you. My people and theirs are . . . similar." He pointed to the sigla, tattooed on his skin. "This is my magic. If it gets wet with seawater, my magic fails. I'm helpless. More helpless than any of you. Ask your daughter, Yngvar. She saw me. She knows. And the same thing happens to the Sartan."

"What are we supposed to do?" Grundle whispered gruffly. "Invade the city with a bucket brigade?"

Devon pinched her. "Shush!"

But their elders looked almost as perplexed.

"It's simple. We flood the city with seawater," Haplo explained.

All stared at him, silently digesting this strange notion. It sounded far too easy. There must be something wrong. Each mulled it over in his or her mind. Then, slowly, hope began to kindle fire in eyes that had been dark with gloom.

"The water doesn't hurt them?" Eliason asked anxiously.

"No more than it hurts me," said Haplo. "The water makes us all equal. And no blood is shed."

"It does seem that this is the answer," said Delu hesitantly.

"But all the Sartan have to do is keep from getting wet," Hilda inserted. "Beings as powerful as these can surely manage that."

"The Sartan may avoid the rising water for a time. They could all fly to the rooftops, roost like chickens. But they can't stay up there forever. The water will rise higher and higher. Sooner or later, it must engulf them. And when it does, they will be helpless. You can sail your submersibles into Surunan, take over, never swing an ax, never shoot an arrow."

"But we can't live in a world full of water," Yngvar protested. "When it drains off, the Sartan's magic will come back, won't it?"

"Yes, but by that time, there will be a change of leadership among the Sartan. He doesn't know it yet, but the Councillor you met today is going to be taking a trip." Haplo smiled quietly. "I think you'll find it far easier to negotiate when he's gone. Especially if all you have to do is remind the Sartan that you have the power to bring the seawater back anytime you choose."

"And will we?" Delu was dazed. "Will we have the power?"

"Of course. You simply ask the dragon-snakes. No, no, wait! Hear me out. The dragon-snakes bore holes into the rock foundation. Water flows in, rises, 'dampens' the spirits of the Sartan, and, when they surrender, the dragon-snakes cause the water to recede. The dragon-snakes can use their magic to erect gates at the bore holes, to keep the water out. Any time you ask them, the dragon-snakes can reopen the gates, do it all over again, if necessary. As I said, I don't think it will be."

Grundle pondered, examined the idea from all angles, as she knew her father and mother were doing, searching for a flaw. She could find none and, apparently, neither could those listening to Haplo in more conventional fashion.

"I'll talk to the dragon-snakes, explain the plan to them," Haplo was offering. "I'll go to Draknor, if I can use one of your boats. I won't bring the serpents on board your ship again," he added hastily, seeing faces pale at the thought.

Alake was radiant.

"It's a splendid plan! No one will get hurt. And you thought he was in league with the dragon-snakes." She glared at Grundle.

"Shhh," said the dwarf maid irritably, and pinched Alake.

Humans, elves, dwarves, looked relieved, spoke hopefully.

"We will make it up to the Sartan," Eliason said. "They don't know us yet, that's the problem. When they see that all we want is to live peaceful, productive lives and not bother them in the least, they will be happy to let us stay."

"*Without* their laws and *without* their godhood," Dumaka stated grimly.

The others agreed. The talk reverted to plans of moving onto Surunan, of who would live where and how. Grundle had heard all this before; the rulers had discussed little else during the entire voyage.

"Shut that thing," she said. "I've got a plan of my own."

Alake shut the knothole. She and Devon looked at the dwarf expectantly.

"This is our chance," said Grundle.

"Chance for what?" Devon asked.

"Chance to find out what's really going on," the dwarf said in a low voice, with a meaningful glance at her companions.

"You mean . . ." Alake couldn't finish.

"We follow Haplo," said Grundle. "We'll find out the truth about him. He might be in danger," she added hastily, seeing Alake's dark eyes glitter in anger. "Remember?"

"That's the only reason I'll condone this," Alake said in lofty tones. "The only reason I'll go."

"Speaking of danger," Devon said somberly. "What *about* the dragon-snakes? We couldn't even get close to the bridge the time the dragon-snake came on board. When Haplo first confronted them. Remember?"

"You're right," Grundle admitted, subdued. "We were all of us scared silly. I couldn't move. I thought you were going to faint."

"And *that* dragon-snake wasn't even real," Alake pointed out. "Just a . . . a reflection or some such thing."

"If we do get close, our teeth will be chattering so loudly we won't be able to hear what they're saying."

"At least we'll be able to defend ourselves," Devon said. "I'm a fair shot with my bow—"

Grundle snorted. "Arrows, even magic ones, won't have any effect on those monsters. Right, Alake?"

"What? I'm sorry, I was thinking. You mentioned magic. I've been working on my spells. I've learned three new defensive ones. I can't tell you about them, because they're secret, but they worked beautifully against my teacher."

"Yeah, I saw him. Has his hair grown back yet?"

"How dare you spy on me, you little beast!"

"I wasn't. As if I cared! I happened to be passing by, when I heard a sound and smelled smoke. I thought the ship was on fire and so I looked through a keyhole—"

"There! You've admitted it—"

"The dragon-snakes," inserted Devon with elven diplomacy. "And Haplo. They're what's important. Remember?"

"I remember! And a fat lot of good magic arrows or magic fire or magic anything's going to do us if we can't get close to the blasted creatures anyway."

"She's got a point, I'm afraid." Devon sighed.

"And Alake's got an idea," said Grundle, eyeing her friend closely. "Haven't you?"

"Maybe. It's something we shouldn't do. We could get into real trouble."

"Yes, so?" Grundle and Devon brushed aside such mundane considerations.

Alake glanced around, although there was no one in the small cabin except themselves. Motioning her friends near, she leaned in toward them.

"I've heard my father tell that in the old days, when one tribe fought another, some of the warriors chewed an herb that took away fear. My father never used it. He said that fear was a warrior's best weapon in a fight, it sharpens his instincts—"

"Pah! If your insides feel like they're going to be your outsides any minute, it doesn't matter how sharp your instincts are—"

"Hush, Grundle!" Devon squeezed the dwarf's hand. "Let Alake finish."

"I was about to say, before I was interrupted"—Alake glanced sternly at Grundle—"that in this case we really don't need to have particularly sharp instincts because we don't intend to fight anything. We just want to sneak up on the dragon-snakes, listen to what they talk about, and then sneak away. This herb would help take away our fear of them."

"Is it magic?" Grundle asked suspiciously.

"No. Just a plant. Like lettuce. Its properties are inherent. All you have to do is chew it."

The three looked at each other.

"What do you think?"

"Sounds good to me."

"Alake, can you get hold of it?"

"Yes, the herbalist brought some along with her. She thought some of the warriors might want it if we went to war."

"All right, then. Alake gets the herb for us. What's it called?"

"No-fear weed."

"Weed?" Grundle frowned. "I don't think—"

Voices out in the passageway interrupted them. The meeting was breaking up.

"When will you leave, Haplo?" Dumaka's deep tones carried clearly through the closed door.

"Tonight."

The three companions exchanged glances.

"Can you get the weed by then?" Devon whispered.

Alake nodded.

"Good, then. It's all settled. We go." Grundle held out her hand.

Devon placed his hand over the dwarf's. Alake grasped both.

"We go," each said firmly.

Haplo spent the remainder of the day ostensibly learning how to operate one of the small, two-person submersibles, used by humans and elves for fishing. He studied the operation of the dwarven boat carefully, asked questions—far more than would have been needed simply to sail the vessel the short distance to Draknor. He went over every inch of the craft, rousing the suspicions of dwarves by his intense interest.

But the Patryn was profuse in his praise of dwarven carpentry and navigation skills, and, eventually, the captain and crew were looking for things to impress him.

"This will serve my purpose well," said Haplo, glancing around the submersible in satisfaction.

"Of course," growled the dwarf. "Yer only taking her far as Draknor. You ain't plannin' to circumnavigate the bleedin' world."

Haplo smiled quietly. "You're right, friend. I'm not planning to circumnavigate the world."

He was planning to leave it. Just as soon as the dragon-snakes flooded Surunan, which he hoped would be tomorrow. He'd capture Samah. This ship would carry him—and his prisoner—through Death's Gate.

"I'll put the runes of protection on the inside of the vessel, instead of the outside," he said to himself, once he was alone, back in his cabin. "That should solve the problem of the seawater.

"And that reminds me. I'll need to take back a sample of the water to my lord, have it analyzed, determine if there isn't some way to nullify its debilitating effects against us. And perhaps he can discover how this strange water came into existence. I doubt if the Sartan created it. . . ."

Haplo heard a thump in the corridor outside his cabin.

"Grundle," he guessed, shaking his head.

He'd spotted the mensch trailing behind him all day. Her heavy tread, heavier boots, and her huffing and snorting would have alerted a blind and deaf man to her presence. The Patryn wondered vaguely what mischief she was up to now, but gave the matter little thought. One nagging concern continued to prey on his mind, drove all else out.

The dog. Once *his* dog. Now, apparently, Alfred's.

Haplo took from his belt two daggers, given to him by Dumaka, and laid them on the bed, examined them carefully. Good weapons, well-made. He called on his magic. The sigla on his skin glowed blue, flared red. Haplo spoke the runes, placed his finger on the flat of the knife's blade. The steel hissed and bubbled, smoke drifted upward in a thin line. Runes of death began to form on the blade, beneath Haplo's tracing finger.

"Let the damn dog do what it wants." Haplo took extreme

care drawing the runes on which his life might depend, yet he'd done this so many times he could allow his mind to turn to other matters. "I lived for a long time without the animal and I can do it again. The dog came in handy, admittedly, but I don't need it. I don't want it back. Not now. Not after it's been living with a Sartan."

Haplo completed his work on one side of the dagger. He sat back, studied it carefully, searching for the tiniest flaw, the smallest break in the intricate pattern. There wouldn't be any, of course. He was good at what he did.

Good at killing, cheating, lying. He was even good at lying to himself. Or at least he'd been good once. He used to actually believe his own lies. Why couldn't he believe them anymore?

"Because you're weak." He sneered at himself. "That's what my lord would say. And he'd be right. Caring about a dog. Caring about mensch. Caring about a woman who left me long ago. Caring about a child of mine who might be stranded back there in the Labyrinth. A child alone. And I don't have the courage to go back and search for it . . . for her!"

A mistake. A broken, incomplete sigil. None of the rest would work now. Haplo swore savagely, bitterly, swept the daggers off the bed.

The brave Patryn, risking his life to enter Death's Gate, risking his life to explore new, uncharted worlds.

Because I'm afraid to go back to one world I do know. That's the real reason I was ready to give up and die that long time ago in the Labyrinth.[2] I couldn't take the loneliness. I couldn't take the fear.

And then, he'd found the dog.

And now, the dog was gone.

Alfred. It was all Alfred's doing. Damn him to hell and back again.

A loud drumming, which sounded suspiciously like the heels of heavy boots beating against a wooden deck, came from outside Haplo's cabin. Grundle must be getting bored.

---

[2]Reference to Haplo's fight with the chaodyn, *Dragon Wing*, vol. 1 of *The Death Gate Cycle*.

The Patryn stared grimly at the daggers lying on the deck. Work botched. He was losing control.

Let Alfred have the damn dog. He was welcome to it.

Haplo picked up the daggers, carefully began his work over again, this time giving it his full and undivided attention. At last, he etched the final sigil onto the dagger's blade. Sitting back, he studied the dagger. This time, all was correct. He started to work on the next.

Task complete, he wrapped the two rune-enhanced daggers safely and securely in what the dwarves called oilcloth. The cloth was completely waterproof; Haplo knew, he'd tested it. The oilcloth would protect the daggers, keep them from losing *their* magic, just in case something happened and he lost his.

Not that he was expecting trouble, but it never hurt to be prepared. To be honest—and he supposed bitterly that this must be his day for honesty—he didn't trust the dragon-snakes, though logic told him he had no reason not to. Perhaps his instincts knew something his brain didn't. He'd learned, in the Labyrinth, to trust his instincts.

Haplo walked to the door, flung it open.

Grundle tumbled inside, falling flat on her face. Nonplussed, she picked herself up, dusted herself off, then glared at Haplo.

"Shouldn't you be going?" she demanded.

"Just now," he said, with his quiet smile.

He thrust the oilskin pouch into the belt around his waist, hiding it beneath the folds of his shirt.

"About time," Grundle snorted, and stomped off.

That afternoon, Alake went to the herbalist, complaining of a sore throat and cough. While the herbalist was preparing an infusion of chamomile and peppermint and droning on about how terrible it was that most young people didn't seem to have any respect these days for the old ways and how nice it was that Alake was different, Alake managed to pluck several leaves of the no-fear weed the herbalist had growing in a small tub.

Clutching the leaves in one hand, keeping that hand hidden behind her back, Alake accepted the tea, listened carefully to instructions that the brew was to be drunk without delay, the dose repeated again before bedtime.

She promised she would, as well as she could speak considering her bad cough. On leaving, she added the no-fear weed leaves to the tea mixture, returned hastily to her room.

That night, Devon and Grundle met in Alake's quarters.

"He's gone," Grundle reported. "I watched him board the submersible. He's a strange one. I heard him inside his cabin, talking to himself. I couldn't understand much, but he sounded upset. You know, I don't think he's coming back."

Alake scoffed. "Don't be silly. Of course he's coming back. Where else would he go?"

"Maybe back to wherever he lives."

"That's nonsense. He promised to help our people. He wouldn't leave us now."

"What makes you think so, Grundle?" Devon asked.

"I don't know," the dwarf replied, unusually solemn and thoughtful. "Something about the way he looked . . ." She sighed gloomily.

"We'll find out, soon enough," Devon predicted. "Did you get the herbs?"

Alake nodded, handed each a leaf of the no-fear weed. Grundle stared at the gray-green leaf in disgust,[3] sniffed at it, sneezed. Holding her nose, she popped it into her mouth, chewed it rapidly, and gulped it down.

Devon licked the leaf delicately with the tip of his tongue and nibbled at it.

"You look like a rabbit!" Grundle laughed nervously.

Alake, solemn and serious, placed her leaf in her mouth with a reverent air. Closing her eyes, she said a silent prayer before she chewed and swallowed it.

Then all three sat and stared at each other, waiting for their fear to go away.

---

[3]Dwarves do not like green vegetables; the potato, the carrot, and the onion are the only vegetables in the dwarven diet, and even these they will not eat raw.

CHAPTER ♦ 29

DRAKNOR

CHELESTRA

♦

"WHERE DO YOU THINK YER TAKING THAT THERE BOAT?"

The dwarven deckhand had popped up out of nowhere seemingly, was glowering at the three young people.

"You are speaking to a royal chieftain's daughter, sir," said Alake, drawing herself up imperiously. "And to the daughter of your king."

"That's right," said Grundle, marching forward.

The deckhand, abashed, snatched the shapeless hat off his head and bobbed from the waist. "Pardon, missy. But my orders are to watch over these here boats. No one takes one without the Vater's permission."

"I know that," Grundle snapped. "And we've got my father's permission. Show him, Alake."

"What?" Alake jumped, stared at her.

"Show him the permission letter from my father." Grundle winked, glanced significantly at the pouch that hung from a braided belt encircling the human's waist.

The top edges of several small, tightly rolled parchments were barely visible, peeping out over the edge.

Alake flushed, her eyes narrowed. "These are my spells!" she mouthed angrily. "I'm not showing them to anyone."

"Women," said Devon hurriedly, taking hold of the deckhand's arm and drawing him away. "They never know what they have in their pouches."

"It's all right," Grundle shot back. "You can show him. He can't read!"

Alake glared at her.

"Come on! We don't have much time! Haplo's probably left by now."

Alake sighed. Reaching into her pouch, she drew forth one of the parchments.

"Will this do?" she asked, unrolling it, thrusting it beneath the deckhand's nose, snapping it back up again before he could do more than blink.

"I . . . I guess so." The dwarf ruminated. "Just to be on the safe side, I think I'll go ask the Vater himself. You don't mind waiting, do you?"

"No, go ahead. Take your time." Grundle was gracious.

The deckhand departed. The moment his back was turned, the three climbed through a hatch in the hull and from there into the small submersible, which hung onto the side of the mothership rather like a young dolphin clinging to its parent. Grundle shut both hatches—the one on the hull and the one in the submersible, and detached the vessel from the sun-chaser.

"Are you sure you know how to operate this thing?" Alake had as much use for mechanical devices as Grundle had for magic.

"Sure," Grundle said promptly. "I've been practicing. I thought, if we ever got a chance to spy on the dragon-snakes, we'd need a boat to do it."

"Very clever," Alake conceded magnanimously.

The water around Draknor, unlike the rest of the Goodsea, was dark and murky.

"Like swimming through blood," Devon remarked, peering out the porthole in search of Haplo's small vessel.

The two girls agreed complacently. The no-fear weed had lived up to its reputation.

"What's he doing?" Alake wondered uneasily. "He's been inside his ship the longest time."

"I told you," Grundle said. "He's not coming back. He's probably fixing it up to live in for a while—"

"There he is," Devon cried, pointing.

Haplo's submersible was easily recognized: it belonged to Yngvar and was therefore marked with the royal crest.

Assuming that Haplo knew where he was going, which they did not (none of them having been taught the mysteries of navigating the Goodsea[1]), the mensch tagged along behind.

"Maybe he'll see us. Grundle, keep back," Alake said worriedly.

"Pooh. In this muck, he can't see us. Not even if we were on his—"

"—tail," said Devon hurriedly.

Grundle was steering. Alake and Devon stood behind her, peering eagerly over her shoulder. The no-fear weed was working quite effectively. They were agreeably tense and excited but not afraid. Suddenly, however, Grundle turned around to her friends with a stricken look.

"I just thought of something!"

"Watch where you're going!"

"Do you remember the last time we saw the dragon-snake? It talked with Haplo. Remember?"

Both nodded.

"And it spoke *his* language. We couldn't understand a word! How can we find out what they're saying when we don't know what they're saying?"

"Oh, dear," said Alake, looking downcast. "I hadn't thought of that."

"So what do we do?" Grundle asked, deflated, her excitement for the adventure gone. "Go back to the sun-chaser?"

"No," said Devon decisively. "Even if we can't understand what they're saying, we can use our eyes and maybe we'll learn something that way. Besides, Haplo might be in danger. He might need our help."

---

[1] Sound is the most reliable form of communication in the sea. Ship captains know and utilize the various distinct sounds that the seamoons—the durnai—make as they drift through the water. These sounds are detected by "elf ears," magical devices made by elven wizards that pick up the sounds and transmit them through a hollow tube to the ship's captain. By noting the various locations of these sounds and their distances, the position of the ship can be determined.

Unfortunately, however, the captains would be familiar only with their own local waters. Out of those waters, they must now rely on the dragon-snakes for guidance.

"And my side whiskers might grow until they touch my feet!" Grundle retorted.

"Well, what do you want to do?" Devon asked.

Grundle looked at her friend. "Alake?"

"I agree with Devon. I say we go on."

"I guess we go on," said Grundle, shrugging. Then she cheered up. "Who knows? We might find some more of those jewels."

Haplo sailed the submersible slowly toward Draknor, taking his time, trying to avoid running aground again. The water was dark and foul-looking. He could barely see through it, had no idea where he was or which direction he was headed. He was letting the dragon-snakes guide him, letting them draw him toward them.

The sigla on his skin glowed bright blue. It took enormous force of will for him to steer the ship closer to Draknor's shore, when every instinct screamed for him to turn around and sail away.

The submersible surfaced, bobbed up out of the water, with a suddenness that startled him. A large stretch of beach was visible, white sand glowing in the darkness with an eerie, ghostly light that emanated from some unknown source, perhaps the crushed and crumbled rock itself.

No welcoming fire burned this time. Either he was unexpected, which Haplo couldn't believe, or he was unwelcome. He adjusted the oilskin pouch, felt it press heavy and reassuring against his skin.

Beaching the vessel, Haplo jumped from the deck to the shore, being careful to avoid getting his feet wet. He landed safely on the white sand, took a moment to get his bearings.

The beach extended several leagues before him. Tall rock formations, their jagged peaks black against the Goodsea, rose up out of the sand.

Odd mountains, Haplo thought, eyeing them with disgust. They reminded him of gnawed and broken bones. He glanced around, wondering where the dragon-snakes were. His gaze glanced across a dark opening in the side of one of the mountains. A cave.

Haplo began to walk across the deserted, barren beach. The sigla on his skin burned like fire.

The three mensch sailed into the cove so close behind Haplo they were practically nose to rudder. Once there, however, they kept their distance.

Peering with difficulty through the dark water, they saw the Patryn beach his ship, watched him jump out, then stop and look around, as if wondering which way to go.

Apparently, he made a decision. He started walking purposefully along the shoreline.

When he was out of earshot, the three guided their small submersible into shore, tied it to a formation of coral that thrust up out of the water like "a finger, warning us away," Grundle said.

The three laughed.

They waded through the shallow water, forced to hurry to keep Haplo in sight.

Tailing him was easy. The Patryn's skin gave off a radiant blue glow.

They crept after him silently.

Or rather, Devon crept after Haplo silently. The elf glided over the sand with graceful ease, treading so lightly his feet never seemed to touch the ground.

Grundle fondly imagined she was emulating Devon, and she did manage to move quietly—for a dwarf. Her thick boots clumped, her breath came in wheezing huffs, and she only spoke when she should have kept quiet half-a-dozen times.

Alake could move nearly as softly as the elf, but she had forgotten, in the excitement of the moment, to take off her ear-jangles and her beads. One of her magic spells required a small silver bell, wrapped in a pouch. Alake slipped once, the bell gave out a small, muffled ring.

The three froze, holding their breaths, certain Haplo must have heard them. The only fear that the no-fear weed had not been able to dispel was the fear that the Patryn would catch them and send them home.

Haplo kept walking. He obviously hadn't heard. The three breathed a sigh of relief and continued on.

That the dragon-snakes might have heard them was a thought that never crossed their minds.

Haplo came to a dead standstill outside the cavern. He'd only experienced terror like this once before, standing with his lord outside the Gate of the Labyrinth. His lord had been able to enter.

Haplo had not.

"Enter, Patryn," hissed a voice from the darkness. "Have no fear. We bow before you."

Sigla flared red and blue on Haplo's skin, its light illuminating the darkness beyond. Comforted more by the sight of the power of his magic than by the serpent's assurance, Haplo walked to the cavern's opening.

Looking in, he saw them.

The light of his runes reflected off the dragon-snakes' shining scales. Their bodies were draped over each other in a hideous, tangled coil, making it impossible to tell where one left off and the other began.

It seemed that most were asleep, for their eyes were closed. Haplo moved silently as a Patryn learns to move in the Labyrinth, but he had barely set foot in the cavern when two of the slit red eyes opened, fixed their red-green gaze upon him.

"Patryn," the king snake said. "Master. You honor us with your presence. Please, come closer."

Haplo did as the serpent requested, the sigla on his skin itching and burning, nearly driving him wild. He scratched the back of his hand. The reptile's giant head loomed over him; its body remained resting comfortably on the back of one of its neighbors.

"How did the meeting go between the mensch and the Sartan?" the dragon-snake asked, blinking its eyes lazily.

"As well as you might expect," Haplo said shortly. He intended to explain his plan, give the snakes their orders, then depart. He loathed these creatures. "The Sartan—"

"Pardon me," the serpent interrupted, "but could we speak human? We find that conversing in your language wearies us. Admittedly the human language is crude and awkward, but it does have its moments. If you don't mind. . . ."

Haplo did mind. He didn't like it, wondered what was behind this sudden change. They'd spoken his language well enough the first time they'd met, spoken it at length. He considered refusing, just to assert his own authority, decided that was pointless. What did it matter what language they talked? He didn't want to draw this out any longer than necessary.

"Very well," he said, and continued to explain his plans, speaking the human tongue.

The three mensch watched Haplo enter the cave. His skin was a bright, flaring blue.

"That must be where the snakes live," exclaimed Grundle.

"Hush!" Devon clapped his hand over her mouth.

"We can't go in after him," Alake whispered, worried.

"Maybe there's a back entrance."

The three circled around the side of the mountain. They poked and prodded among huge, fallen boulders. Walking was treacherous. The ground was wet and slick with a dark liquid that oozed out of the rocks. They stumbled and fell, Grundle cursed beneath her breath.

The mountainside was covered with huge gouges. "As if something had taken large bites out of it," Alake said. But none of these gouges led them inside the cavern.

Growing discouraged, they were about to give up when, suddenly, they found exactly what they'd hoped to find.

A small tunnel opened directly into the side of the mountain. The three crept in, examined it. The cave was dry, the way smooth and easy to travel.

"I hear voices!" Grundle said excitedly. "It's Haplo!"

She listened closely, her eyes grew wide. "And I can understand what he's saying. I've learned to speak his language!"

"That's because he's speaking human," said Alake.

Devon hid his smile. "At least now we'll know what they're saying. I wonder if we can get any closer."

"Let's follow this," said Grundle, pointing. "It seems to be heading the right way."

The three entered the tunnel which, by the most remarkable chance, appeared to lead them exactly the direction they wanted to go. They hurried along it eagerly. Haplo's voice became louder and clearer to them each moment, as did the voices of the dragon-snakes. The sides of the tunnel gave off a lovely, phosphorescent glow, lighting their way.

"You know," said Alake, pleased, "it's almost as if this had been constructed exactly for us."

"So this means war," the dragon-snake said.

"Did you have any doubts, Royal One?" Haplo gave a brief laugh.

"Some, I must admit. The Sartan are unpredictable. There *are* those of their race who are truly selfless, who would welcome the mensch with arms outstretched, would take them into their own dwellings, even though it meant they went without a roof above their heads."

"Samah isn't one of those," said Haplo.

"No, we never supposed he was."

The dragon-snake seemed to smile, though how it was possible for the reptilian face to alter expression was beyond Haplo.

"And when will the mensch attack?" the dragon-snake pursued.

"That's what I came to talk to you about, Royal One. I want to make a suggestion. I know this doesn't go along with the plan we originally discussed, but I think this will work out better. All we have to do—to defeat the Sartan—is flood their city with seawater."

Haplo explained, in much the same terms as he had explained it to the mensch. "The seawater will nullify their magic, leave them easy prey for the mensch. . . ."

"Who can then go in and slaughter them indiscriminately. We approve." The dragon-snake nodded its head lazily.

Several of its neighbors opened their eyes, blinked in sleepy agreement.

"The mensch won't slaughter anyone. I was thinking more in terms of surrender—total and unconditional. And I don't want the Sartan to die. I intend to take Samah and maybe a few more back to my lord for questioning. It would be helpful if they were alive enough to answer," the Patryn concluded wryly.

The slit eyes narrowed dangerously. Haplo tensed, wary.

The serpent sounded almost jocular, however. "And what would the mensch do with the sodden Sartan?"

"By the time the water drains away and the Sartan have dried out, the mensch will have moved onto Surunan. The Sartan will have a tough time evicting several thousand or so humans, elves, and dwarves who have already set up housekeeping. And then, of course, the mensch, with your assistance, Royal One, could always threaten to open the seagates and flood the city again."

"We would be curious to know why you formulated such a plan, in opposition to our own. What did you find wrong with forcing the mensch into open warfare?"

The hissing voice was cold, its tone lethal. Haplo couldn't understand. What was wrong?

"These mensch can't fight," he explained. "They haven't fought a war in who knows how long? Oh, the humans skirmish among themselves, but hardly anyone gets hurt. The Sartan, even without their magic, could inflict serious casualties. I think my way is better, easier. That's all."

The dragon-snake lifted its head slightly, slid its body down off its reptile pillow, and slithered across the cavern floor toward Haplo. He stood his ground, kept his gaze fixed firmly on the slit red eyes. Instinct told him that to give in to his fear, to turn and run, would mean his death. His only chance was to face this out, try to discover whatever it was the serpents were truly after.

The flat, toothless head halted an arm's length from him.

"Since when," asked the dragon-snake, "does a Patryn care how mensch live . . . or how they die?"

A shudder went through Haplo, starting at the core of his being, twisting his insides. He opened his mouth, was about to make some reply.

"Wait!" the dragon-snake hissed. "What have we here?"

A form began to coalesce out of the dank cavern air. It shimmered and shifted, faded in, faded out again, wavering either in its magic or in its decision or perhaps some of both.

The dragon-snake watched with interest, though Haplo noted it slid back, moved nearer the knot of its fellows.

The Patryn saw enough of the wavering figure to know who it was—the one person he didn't need. What the devil was he doing here? Perhaps it's a trick. Perhaps Samah sent him.

Alfred stepped out of thin air. He glanced around vaguely, eyes blinking in the darkness, and immediately spotted Haplo.

"I'm so glad I found you!" Alfred sighed in relief. "You can't imagine how difficult that spell is—"

"What do you want?" Haplo demanded, tense, on edge.

"I'm returning your dog," said Alfred cheerfully, with a wave of his hand at the animal materializing in the air behind him.

"If I'd wanted the beast, which I don't, I would have come for it myself—"

The dog, being somewhat quicker on the uptake than Alfred, caught sight of the dragon-snakes. It began to bark in wild, frantic alarm.

Alfred realized, apparently for the first time, where his magic had taken him. The dragon-snakes were now all wide awake. Bodies writhing, they loosed themselves from their tangled knot with slippery speed.

"Oh . . . m-m-my gracious," stammered Alfred, and dropped to the ground in a dead faint.

The king dragon-snake's head darted toward the dog.

Haplo leapt over the comatose body of the Sartan, caught hold of the animal by the scruff of its neck.

"Dog, quiet!" he commanded.

The dog whined, looked at Haplo plaintively, as if uncertain of its welcome. The dragon-snake pulled back.

The Patryn jerked a thumb in Alfred's direction. "Go to him. Keep an eye on your friend."

The dog obeyed, first casting a threatening glance at the dragon-snakes, warning them to keep their distance. Padding over to Alfred, the animal began to lick the Sartan's face.

"Does that annoying creature belong to you?" asked the dragon-snake.

"It used to, Royal One," Haplo stated. "But now it's his."

"Indeed." The serpent's slit eyes flared, quickly cooled. "It still seems attached to you."

"Forget the damn dog!" Haplo snarled, patience wearing thin, rubbed by his fear. "We were discussing my plan. Will you—"

"We discuss nothing in the presence of the Sartan," interrupted the dragon-snake.

"You mean Alfred? But he's out cold!"

"He is very dangerous," hissed the dragon-snake.

"Yeah," said Haplo, looking at the Sartan, lying in a crumpled heap on the ground.

The dog was licking Alfred's bald head.

"And he seems to know you quite well."

Haplo's skin prickled with danger. Damn and blast that fool Sartan anyway! I should have killed him when I had the chance. I will kill him, my very next opportunity . . .

"Kill him now," said the dragon-snake.

Haplo tensed, stared grimly at the creatures. "No."

"Why not?"

"Because he may have been sent to spy on me. And if he was, I want to know why, who sent him, what he planned to do. You should want to know, too, since you think he's so dangerous."

"It matters little to us. And he *is* dangerous, but we can take care of ourselves. He is a danger to you, Patryn. He is the Serpent Mage. Do not let him live! Kill him . . . now."

"You call me 'master,' " said Haplo coolly. "And yet you're giving me orders. Only one man, my lord, has such power over me. Someday perhaps, I will kill the Sartan, but that day will come in my own time, at my own choosing."

The red-green flame in the serpent's eyes was almost blinding. Haplo's own eyes burned and stung. He fought the impulse to blink. If once he looked away, he had the feeling he would see nothing but his own death.

Then suddenly it was dark. The dragon-snake's eyelids closed over the flame.

"We are concerned solely for your own well-being, Master. Of course, you know best. Perhaps, as you suggest, it would be wise to question him. You may do so now."

"He won't talk if you're around. In fact, he won't regain consciousness if you're around," Haplo added. "If you don't mind, Royal One, I'll just take him out. . . ."

Moving slowly, purposefully, keeping an eye on the dragon-snake, Haplo took hold of Alfred's flaccid arms and hefted the man, who was no lightweight. Haplo positioned the Sartan's limp body on his shoulder.

"I'll carry him to my boat. If I find out anything from him, I'll let you know."

The dragon-snake's head weaved back and forth slowly, sinuously.

Debating whether or not to let me go, Haplo thought. He

wondered what he'd do if the snake refused, ordered him to stay. He supposed he could throw Alfred to them. . . .

The snake's eyes closed, flared open. "Very well. In the meantime, we will confer on your plan."

"Take all the time you need," Haplo grunted. He had no intention of coming back. He started out the cave.

"Pardon me, Patryn," said the dragon-snake, "but you seem to have forgotten your dog."

Haplo hadn't forgotten. That had been his plan. Leave the animal behind, let it act as his ears for him. He glanced back at the dragon-snakes.

They knew.

"Dog, come here."

Haplo clasped his arm around Alfred's legs. The Sartan dangled down the Patryn's back, arms flopping like some ungainly, grotesque doll. The dog trotted along after them, now and then giving the Sartan's hand a comforting lick.

Once outside the cave, Haplo sighed deeply, wiped his forehead with his hand. He was unnerved to find himself shaking.

Devon, Alake, and Grundle arrived at the tunnel's outlet in time to see Alfred stumble out of the air. Crouching prudently in the shadows, concealed behind several large boulders, the three watched and listened.

"The dog!" breathed Devon.

Alake clasped his hand, counseled silence. She shivered, and looked uneasy when the dragon-snakes ordered Haplo to kill Alfred, but her face cleared when the Patryn told him he would do so in his own time.

"A trick," she whispered to the other two. "It's a trick to rescue the man. I'm sure Haplo doesn't mean to really kill him."

Grundle looked as if she'd like to argue, but Devon took hold of *her* hand and squeezed it warningly. The dwarf subsided into a muttering silence. Haplo left, taking Alfred with him. The dragon-snakes began talking.

"You saw the dog," said their king, continuing to speak human, even among themselves.

The three young people, accustomed to hearing the human

language by now, never gave this odd occurrence a second
thought.

"You know what the dog means," the dragon-snake continued ominously.

"I don't!" whispered Grundle loudly.

Devon squeezed her hand again. The dragon-snakes nodded
their understanding.

"This will not do," their king said. "This does not suit. We
have been lax, the terror has subsided. We trusted that we had
found the perfect tool in this Patryn. He has proven weak,
flawed. And now we find him in company with a Sartan of
immense power. A Serpent Mage, one whose life the Patryn
held in his hands and yet did not take!"

Hisses of anger breathed through the darkness. The three
young people exchanged puzzled glances. Each was beginning
to notice a faint flutter in the stomach, a chill creeping over the
body—the no-fear weed was wearing off, and they had not
thought to bring more with them. They huddled near each other
for comfort.

The king dragon-snake raised its head, twisted round to take
in everyone in the cave. Everyone.

"And this war he proposes. Bloodless! Painless! He talks of
'surrender'!" The serpent hissed the words in derision. "Chaos
is our life's blood. Death our meat and drink. No. Surrender is
not what we had in mind. The Sartan grow more frightened
every day. They now believe that they are alone in this vast
universe they created. Their numbers are few, their enemies
many and powerful.

"The Patryn did have one good suggestion, and I am in-
debted to him for it—flood their city with seawater. What subtle
genius. The Sartan will watch the water rise. Their fear will
change to panic. Their only hope—escape. They will be forced
to do what they were strong enough to resist doing ages before.
Samah will open Death's Gate!"

"And what of the mensch?"

"We will trick them, turn friends into enemies. They'll
slaughter each other. We will feed off their pain and terror
and grow strong. We will need our strength, to enter Death's
Gate."

Alake was shivering. Devon put his arm around her, comfortingly. Grundle was crying, but she did so silently, her lips clamped tight. She wiped away a tear with a grimy, trembling hand.

"And the Patryn?" asked one. "Does he also die?"

"No, the Patryn will live. Remember: chaos is our goal. Once we pass through Death's Gate, I will visit this self-styled Lord of the Nexus. I will endear myself to him by bringing him a present—this Haplo, a traitor to his own kind. A Patryn who befriends a Sartan."

Fear grew on the three young people, invaded their bodies, an insidious disease. They burned and chilled, limbs shook, stomachs clenched with sickness. Alake tried to speak. Her facial muscles were stiff with fright, her lips quivered.

"We must . . . warn Haplo," she managed to gasp.

The others nodded in agreement, neither being able to respond aloud. But they were too terrified to move, afraid the slightest sound would bring the dragon-snakes down upon them.

"I must go to Haplo," Alake said faintly. She reached out her hands, grasped the cavern wall, and dragged herself to her feet. Her breath came in short, sharp pants. She started to try to leave.

But whatever light had shone them their way here was gone. A terrible smell, of living flesh rotting away, nearly made her gag. She seemed to hear, far away, a dismal wail, as of some huge creature, crying in agony.

Alake walked ahead into the noisome shadows.

Devon started to follow, discovered he couldn't free his hand from Grundle's panicked, deathlike grip.

"Don't!" she pleaded. "Don't leave me." The elf's face was chalk white, his eyes glittered with unshed tears. "Our people, Grundle," he whispered, swallowing. "Our people."

The dwarf gulped, bit her lip. She let go—reluctantly—of his hand.

Devon fled. Clambering to her feet, Grundle stumbled after.

"Are the mensch children leaving?" asked the king dragon-snake.

"Yes, Royal One," answered one of his minions. "What is your command?"

"Kill them slowly, one at a time. Allow the last survivor to remain alive long enough to tell Haplo what they overheard."

"Yes, Royal One." The dragon-snake's tongue flickered with pleasure.

"Oh," added the king dragon-snake offhandedly, "make it appear as if it was the Sartan who murdered them. Then return the bodies to their parents. That should end all thought of a 'bloodless war.' "

CHAPTER ♦ 30

DRAKNOR

CHELESTRA

♦

THE SUBMERSIBLE LOOKED STRANGELY PATHETIC AND HELPLESS, beached on the shoreline, like a dying whale. Haplo dumped the unconscious Alfred none too gently on the ground. The Sartan flopped and groaned. Haplo stood over him grimly. The dog kept some distance from both, watched each anxiously, uncertainly.

Alfred's eyes flickered open. For a dazed moment, he obviously had no idea where he was or what had happened. Then memory returned, and so did his fear.

"Are . . . are they gone?" he asked in a quavering voice, propping himself up on bony elbows and staring around in a panic.

"What the hell were you trying to do?" Haplo demanded.

Seeing no dragon-snakes, Alfred relaxed, looked rather shamefaced. "Return your dog," he said meekly.

Haplo shook his head. "You honestly expect me to believe that. Who sent you? Samah?"

"No one sent me." Alfred gathered the various parts of his gangling body together and, putting them into some semblance of order, managed to stand up. "I left of my own accord, to return the dog. And to . . . to talk with the mensch." He faltered some, on this last statement.

"The mensch?"

"Yes, well, that was my intent." Alfred flushed in embarrassment. "I commanded the magic to take me to you, assuming that you would be on board the sun-chasers with the mensch."

"I'm not," said Haplo.

Alfred ducked his head, glanced around nervously. "No, I can see that. Shouldn't . . . shouldn't we be leaving?"

"*I'll* be leaving soon enough. First you're going to tell me why you followed me. When I leave, I don't want to walk into some Sartan trap."

"I told you," Alfred protested. "I wanted to return your dog. It's been very unhappy. I thought you would be with the mensch. It never occurred to me that you might be somewhere else. I was in a hurry. I didn't think—"

"I can believe that!" Haplo said impatiently, cutting off the excuses. He eyed Alfred intently. "But that's about all I believe. Oh, you're not lying, Sartan, but, as usual, you're not telling the truth, either. You came to return my dog. Fine. And what else?"

Alfred's flush deepened, flooding his neck and the top of his balding head.

"I thought I would find you with the mensch. And I would be able to talk to them, urge them to be patient. This war will be a terrible thing, Haplo. A terrible thing! I must stop it! I need time, that's all. The involvement of those . . . those hideous creatures . . ."

Alfred looked again toward the cave, shuddered, glanced back at Haplo, at the sigla on his skin that glowed a vibrant blue. "You don't trust them, either, do you?"

Once again, the Sartan was in Haplo's mind, sharing his thoughts. The Patryn was damn sick and tired of it. He'd said the wrong thing in that cavern. *These mensch can't fight. . . . The Sartan could . . . inflict serious casualties.*

And he heard again the hissing response. *Since when does a Patryn care how mensch live . . . or how they die?*

Since when?

I can't even blame that on Alfred. It all happened before he bumbled in. It was my doing. My undoing, Haplo thought bitterly. The danger was present from the beginning. But I wouldn't admit it. My own hatred blinded me. Just as the serpents knew it would.

He eyed Alfred, who, sensing some sort of inner battle within Haplo, kept quiet, waited anxiously for the outcome.

Haplo felt the dog's cold nose press against his hand. He glanced down. The animal looked up, wagged its tail gently. Haplo stroked its head, the dog crowded near him.

"The war with the mensch is the least of your problems, Sartan," Haplo said finally.

He gazed back at the cave, which could be clearly seen, despite the darkness, a hole of black torn out of the side of the mountain. "I've been near evil before. In the Labyrinth. . . . But never anything like that." He shook his head, turned back to Alfred. "Warn your people. As I'm going to warn mine. These dragons don't want to conquer the four worlds. They want to destroy them."

Alfred blanched. "Yes . . . Yes. I sensed that. I'll talk to Samah, to the Council. I'll try to make them understand—"

"As if we would talk with a traitor!"

Runes flared, sparkling in the night like a cascade of stars. Samah stepped from the midst of the magic.

"Why am I not surprised." Haplo smiled grimly, glanced at Alfred. "I almost trusted you, Sartan."

"I swear, Haplo!" Alfred cried. "I didn't know— I didn't mean—"

"There is no need to continue to try to deceive us, Patryn," said Samah. "Every move this 'Alfred'—your compatriot— makes has been watched. It must have been quite easy for you to seduce him, to draw him into your evil designs. But surely, considering his ineptness, by now you must be regretting your decision to make use of such a clumsy, bumbling oaf."

"As if I'd sink so low as to make use of any of your weak and sniveling race," Haplo scoffed. Silently, he was saying, If I could capture Samah, I could leave this place now! Leave the dragon-snakes and the mensch, leave Alfred *and* the damn dog. The submersible's ready, the runes will take us safely back through Death's Gate. . . .

Haplo cast a sidelong glance at the cavern. The dragon-snakes were nowhere to be seen, although they must have known of the presence of the Sartan Councillor on their isle. But Haplo knew they were watching, knew it as surely as if he could see the green-red eyes glowing in the darkness. And he felt them urging him on, felt them eager for the battle.

Eager for fear, chaos. Eager for death.

"Our common enemy's in there. Go back to your people, Councillor," Haplo said. "Go back and warn them. As I intend to go back and warn mine."

He turned, started walking toward his ship.

"Halt, Patryn!"

Glowing red sigla exploded, a wall of flame blocked Haplo's escape. The heat was intense, scorched his flesh, seared his lungs.

"I'm going back and you're coming back with me, as my prisoner," Samah informed him.

Haplo turned to face him, smiled. "You know I won't. Not without a fight. And that's just what *they* want." He pointed toward the cave.

Alfred extended trembling, pleading hands. "Councillor, listen to him! Haplo's right—"

"Silence, traitor! Don't you think I understand why you side with this Patryn? His confessions will seal your guilt. I am taking you with me to Surunan, Patryn. I prefer that we go peacefully, but, if you choose to fight . . ." Samah shrugged. "So be it."

"I'm warning you, Councillor," Haplo said quietly. "If you don't let me go, the three of us will be lucky to escape with our lives." But as he talked, he was already beginning to construct his magic.

Anciently, open warfare between Patryn and Sartan had been rare. The Sartan—maintaining as they did to the mensch that warfare was wrong—had their image to consider and would generally refuse to be drawn into a fight. They found subtler means to defeat their enemy. But occasionally battle could not be avoided and a contest would be waged. Such battles were always spectacular, generally deadly. They were held secretly, in private. It would never do for the mensch to see one of their demigods die.

Battle between two such opponents is long and tiring, both

mentally and physically.[1] Some warriors were known to collapse
from sheer exhaustion alone. Each opponent must not only prepare his own offense, drawing his magic from the countless possibilities that are present at that particular moment, but he must
also prepare a defense against whatever magical attack his opponent might be launching.

Defense is mainly guesswork, although each side claimed to
have developed ways to fathom the mental state of an opponent
and therefore be able to anticipate his next move.[2]

Such was the battle both were proposing to wage. Haplo had
been dreaming of it, yearning for it, all his life. It was every
Patryn's dearest wish, for though much had been lost to them
through the eons, they had held fast to one thing: hatred. But
now that the moment he'd lived for was finally here, Haplo
could not savor it. He tasted nothing but ashes in his mouth.
He was conscious of the audience, of the slit red eyes, watching
every move.

Haplo forced the thought of the dragon from his mind, forced
himself to concentrate. Haplo called upon the magic, felt it answer. Elation surged through him, submerged all fear, all
thoughts of the dragons. He was young and strong, at the height
of his power. He was confident of victory.

The Sartan had one advantage that the Patryn didn't anticipate. Samah must have fought in such magical battles before.
Haplo had not.

The two faced each other.

"Go on, boy," Haplo said quietly, giving the dog a shove.
"Go back to Alfred."

The animal whimpered, didn't want to leave.

"Go!" Haplo glared at it.

The dog, ears drooping, obeyed.

"Stop it! Stop this madness!" Alfred cried.

He dashed forward with some wild intent of hurling himself
bodily between the combatants. Unfortunately, Alfred wasn't

---

[1]For further information on these magical battles, see Appendix I.

[2]Extremely unlikely, considering the wide degree of difference in the magical constructs of each race. Most battles were won through sheer luck,
though you would never find the victor who would admit it.

watching where he was going and fell, headlong, over the dog. The two went down in a confused and yelping tangle in the sand.

Haplo cast his spell.

The sigla on the Patryn's skin flared blue and red, twisted suddenly into the air, wound together to form a chain of steel that glimmered red in the firelight. The chain streaked out with the speed of lightning to bind Samah in its strong coils, Patryn rune-magic would render him helpless.

Or that was how it was supposed to work.

Samah had apparently anticipated the possibility that Haplo would try to take him prisoner. The Councillor invoked the possibility that when the Patryn's attack was launched against him, he wouldn't be there to receive it. And he wasn't.

The steel chain wrapped around air. Samah stood some distance away, regarding Haplo with disdain, as he might have regarded a child throwing stones at him. The Councillor began to sing and dance.

Haplo recognized an attack. He was faced with an agonizing decision, and one that had to be made in a heartbeat. He could either defend against an attack—and to do so would require that he instantly sort through myriad possibilities open to his enemy—or he could launch another attack himself, hoping to catch Samah defenseless, in midspell. Unfortunately, such a maneuver would leave Haplo defenseless, as well.

Frustrated and angry over being thwarted by an enemy he'd considered a pushover, Haplo was anxious to end the battle swiftly. His steel chain still hung in the air. Haplo instantly rearranged the magic, altered the sigla's form into that of a spear, and hurled it straight at Samah's breast.

A shield appeared in Samah's left hand. The spear struck the shield; the chain of Haplo's magic began to fall apart.

In the same instant, a gust of wind sprang up off the waters. Taking the shape and form of a huge fist, the wind smote Haplo, buffeted him, sent him reeling.

The Patryn landed heavily on the sandy beach.

Groggy and dazed from the blow, Haplo swiftly regained his feet, his body reacting with the instincts learned in the Labyrinth, where to give in to even a moment's weakness meant death.

Haplo spoke the runes. The sigla on his body flared. He opened his mouth to give the command that would end this bitter contest. His command changed to a startled curse.

Something wrapped itself tightly around his ankle. It began tugging at him, trying to yank him off his feet.

Haplo was forced to abandon his spell. He looked to see what had hold of him.

A long tentacle of some magical sea creature had reached out of the water. Preoccupied with his own spell-casting, Haplo had not noticed it sliding across the beach toward him. Now it had him; its coils, shining with Sartan runes, wound around and around Haplo's ankle, his calf, his leg.

The creature's strength was incredible. Haplo fought to free himself, but the more he struggled, the tighter the tentacle grasped. It jerked him off his feet, flung him to the sand. Haplo kicked at it, tried to wriggle free. Again, he was faced with a terrible decision. He could expend his magic to free himself, or he could use his magic to attack.

Haplo twisted to get a look at his enemy. Samah watched complacently, a smile of triumph on his lips.

How the hell can he think he's won? Haplo wondered angrily. This stupid monster isn't deadly. It's not poisoning me, crushing the life out of me.

It's a trick. A trick to gain time. Samah figures I'll expend my energy trying to free myself instead of attacking. Surprise, Samah!

Haplo's full mental powers concentrated on re-forming the spell he had been about to cast. The sigla flared in the air, were coming together, humming with power, when the Patryn felt water wash over the toe of his boot.

Water . . .

Suddenly Haplo saw Samah's ploy. This was how the Sartan would defeat him: simple, yet effective.

Dunk him in seawater.

The Patryn cursed, but refused to give way to panic. He commanded the rune structure to shift their target, altered them to a flight of flaming arrows, sent them darting into the creature that had hold of him.

The creature's tentacle was wet with seawater. The magical arrows struck it, sizzled, and went out.

Water lapped over Haplo's foot, up his leg. Frantic now, he dug his hands into the sand, tried to hold on, to stop himself from being pulled into the sea. His fingers left long tracks behind them. The creature was too strong and Haplo's magic was weakening, the complex rune-structures starting to break apart, unravel.

The daggers! Flipping over onto his back, squirming in the grasp of the ever-tightening coils, Haplo ripped open his shirt, grabbed the oilskin, and feverishly began to unwrap the weapons.

Cold logic stopped him, the logic of the Labyrinth, the logic that had led more than once to his survival. The water was up to his thighs. These daggers were his only means of defense and he had been about to get them wet. Not only that, but he would reveal their existence to his enemy . . . enemies. He couldn't forget their audience, who must be disappointed to see the end of the show.

Better to accept defeat—bitter though it was—and retain the hope of fighting back, then risk all in a desperate strike that would get him nowhere.

Clasping the oilskin pouch tightly to his breast, Haplo closed his eyes. The water surged up over his waist, his breast, his head, engulfed him.

Samah spoke a word. The tentacle released its hold, disappeared.

Haplo lay in the water. He had no need to look at his skin to know what he would see: bare flesh, a sickly white in color.

He lay so long and so still, the waves gently lapping over his body, that Alfred must have become alarmed.

"Haplo!" he called, and the Patryn heard clumsy, shuffling footsteps heading his direction, heading inanely into the seawater.

Haplo raised up. "Dog, stop him!" he shouted.

The dog dashed after Alfred, caught hold of his coattails, dragged him backward.

Alfred fell. Legs spraddled, arms akimbo, he sat down heavily in the sand. The dog stood next to him, looking pleased with itself, though it occasionally glanced Haplo's way with an anxious air.

Samah gave Alfred a look of contempt and disgust.

"The animal has more brains than you do, seemingly."

"But . . . Haplo's hurt! He might be drowning!" Alfred cried.

"He's no more hurt than I am," Samah replied coldly. "He's shamming, most likely plotting some evil, even now. Whatever it is, he must do it without his magic."

The Councillor walked to the shore, maintaining a safe distance from the waterline. "Stand up, Patryn. You and your cohort will accompany me back to Surunan, where the Council will decide what to do with you."

Haplo ignored him. The water had destroyed his magic, but it had also calmed him, calmed his fever, his rage. He could think clearly, begin to try to sort out his options. One question came insistently to mind: Where were the dragon-snakes?

Listening . . . Watching . . . Savoring the fear, the hatred. Hoping for a deadly conclusion. They wouldn't intervene, not as long as the battle raged. But the battle had ended. And Haplo had lost his magic.

"Very well," said Samah. "I will take you with me as you are."

Haplo sat up in the water. "Try it."

Samah began to sing the runes, but his voice cracked. He choked, coughed, tried again. Alfred stared at the Councillor in astonishment. Haplo watched, smiled grimly.

"How—" Samah rounded on the Patryn furiously. "You have no magic!"

"Not me," said Haplo calmly. "Them." He pointed a wet finger at the cave.

"Bah! Another trick!" Samah again attempted to cast his spell.

Haplo stood up, splashed through the water, back toward the shore. He was being watched. They were all being watched.

He groaned in pain, glared at Samah. "I think you've broken one of my ribs."

His hand pressed against his side, pressed against the hidden daggers. His skin would have to be dry, in order to use the weapons. But that shouldn't be too difficult to manage.

He groaned again, stumbled, and fell; dug his hands deep into the warm, dry sand. The dog watched him, whined and whimpered in sympathy.

Alfred, his forehead wrinkled in concern, was heading in Haplo's direction, his own hands outstretched.

"Don't touch me!" Haplo snarled. "I'm wet!" he added, hoping the fool would take the hint.

Alfred, looking hurt, backed away.

"You!" Samah accused. "You are the one blocking my magic!"

"Me?" Alfred gaped, gabbled incoherently. "I . . . I . . . Me? No, I couldn't possibly—"

Haplo had one thought: to return to the Nexus, to carry the warning. He lay on the warm sand, hunched over, groaned as if in acute agony. His hand, dry from the sand, slid inside his shirt, inside the oilcloth.

If Samah tries to stop me, he'll die. Lunge, stab for the heart. The dagger's runes will unravel any protective magic he's cast around himself.

Then the real fight begins.

The dragons. They had no intention of letting any of them escape.

If I can make it to the submersible, its magic should be powerful enough to keep them at bay. Long enough for me to make it back safely to Death's Gate.

Haplo's hand closed over the dagger's hilt.

A terror-filled scream pierced the air. "Haplo, help us! Help!"

"That sounds like a human's voice!" Alfred cried in astonishment, peering through the darkness. "What are mensch doing here?"

Haplo paused, dagger in his hand. He had recognized the voice: Alake's.

"Haplo!" she cried again, desperate, frantic.

"I see them!" Alfred pointed.

Three mensch, running for their lives. The dragon-snakes slithered behind, driving their victims like sheep to the slaughter, teasing them, feeding off their panic.

Alfred ran to Haplo, extended his hand to help him up. "Quickly! They don't stand a chance!"

An odd sensation stole over Haplo. He'd done this, or something like this, before. . . .

. . . The woman gave Haplo her hand, helped him to stand. He didn't thank her for saving his life. She didn't expect it.

Today, maybe the next, he'd return the favor. It was that way in the Labyrinth.

"Two of them," he said, looking down at the corpses.

The woman yanked out her spear, inspected it to make certain it was still in good condition. The other had died from the electricity she'd had time to generate with the runes. Its body still smoldered.

"Scouts," she said. "A hunting party." She shook her chestnut hair out of her face. "They'll be going for the Squatters."

"Yeah." Haplo glanced back the way they'd come.

Wolfen hunted in packs of thirty, forty creatures. There were fifteen Squatters, five of them children.

"They don't stand a chance." It was an offhand remark, accompanied by a shrug. Haplo wiped the blood and gore from his dagger.

"We could go back, help fight them," the woman said.

"Two of us wouldn't do that much good. We'd die with them. You know that."

In the distance, they could hear hoarse shouts—the Squatters calling each other to the defense. Above that, the higher-pitched voices of the women, singing the runes. And above that, higher still, the scream of a child.

The woman's face darkened, she glanced that direction, irresolute.

"C'mon," urged Haplo, sheathing his dagger. "There may be more of them around here."

"No. They're all in on the kill."

The child's scream rose to a shrill shriek of terror.

"It's the Sartan," said Haplo, his voice harsh. "They put us in this hell. They're the ones responsible for this evil."

The woman looked at him, her brown eyes flecked with gold. "I wonder. Maybe it's the evil inside us."

A terror-filled scream, the cry of a child. A hand stretched out to him. A hand not taken. Emptiness, a sadness for something irretrievably lost.

The evil inside us.

Where did you come from? . . . Who created you? Haplo recalled his words to the dragon-snakes.

You did, Patryn.

The dog barked sharp warning. It ran up to him, eager, anxious, begging to be ordered to attack.

Haplo scrambled to his feet. "Don't touch me," he told Alfred harshly. "Keep away from me. Don't get any water on you! It'll disrupt your magic," he explained impatiently, seeing Alfred's confusion. "For whatever that's worth."

"Oh, yes!" Alfred murmured, and backed up hastily.

Haplo drew his dagger, drew both daggers.

Instantly, Samah spoke a word. This time, his magic worked. Glowing sigla surrounded the Patryn, closed like manacles over his hands and bound his feet. The dog jumped back with a startled yelp, fled to Alfred.

Haplo could hear almost hear the dragon's gloating laughter. "Let me go, you fool! I might be able to save them."

"I will not fall for your trickery, Patryn." Samah began to sing the runes. "You don't expect me to believe you care about these mensch!"

No, Haplo didn't expect Samah to believe it, because Haplo didn't believe it himself. It was instinct, the need to protect the helpless, the weak. The look on his mother's face as she shoved her child into the bushes and turned to fight her enemy.

"Haplo, help us!"

Alake's screams rang in his ears. Haplo fought to escape his bonds, but the magic was too strong. He was being carried off. The sand, the water, the mountains began to fade from his sight. The cries of the mensch grew faint and far away.

And then, suddenly, the spell ended. Haplo found himself back standing on the beach. He felt dazed, as though he'd been dropped from a great height.

"Go on, Haplo," said Alfred, standing beside him, stooped body upright, thin shoulders squared. "Go to the children. Save them, if you can."

A hand closed over his. Haplo looked down at his wrists. The manacles were gone. He was free.

Samah was cold with rage, his face contorted in fury. "Never in all the history of our people has a Sartan helped a Patryn. This dooms you, Alfred Montbank! Your fate is sealed!"

"Go on, Haplo." Alfred ignored the Councillor's ravings. "I'll see to it that he doesn't interfere."

The dog was racing in circles around Haplo, barking warnings, darting a few steps toward the dragon-snakes, dashing back to urge his master on.

His master, once again.

"I owe you one, Alfred," said Haplo. "Though I doubt if I'll live to repay it."

He drew the daggers, their runes flared red and blue. The dog sped off, heading straight for the dragon-snakes.

Haplo followed.

CHAPTER ♦ 31

DRAKNOR

CHELESTRA

♦

THE DRAGON-SNAKES HAD ALLOWED THE MENSCH TO LEAVE THE
cave safely, kept them in sight the entire time. The three reached
the shoreline. They could see Haplo and his ship. Fear was dis-
pelled. Hope returned. The three began to run toward him.

The dragon-snakes poured out of the cave, a hundred sinuous bodies surged over the ground in a writhing, slime-covered
mass.

The three mensch heard their hissing, turned around in
terror.

The serpents' red-green gaze caught the three, held them,
fascinated. Tongues flicked out, tasting the air, smelling, savoring fear. The dragon-snakes closed in on their prey. But it
was not their intent to kill swiftly.

Fear made them strong, terror gave them power. They were
always disappointed to see a victim die.

The snakes lowered their flame-eyed gazes, slowed their advance to a lazy crawl.

The mensch, freed of the paralyzing fascination, screamed
and began running across the beach.

The dragon-snakes hissed in pleasure and slid rapidly
behind.

They kept close to the young people, close enough to let
them smell the dank, putrid odor of the death they brought,
close enough to let them hear the sounds that would be the last
sounds they heard—except their own, dying screams. The giant

bodies, sliding over the sand, ground it beneath them. Flat heads, looming over the mensch, cast horrid, swaying shadows before them.

And the dragon-snakes watched, in glee, the battle between Patryn and Sartan, thrived on the hatred, and grew stronger still.

The mensch were weakening and, as their bodies weakened, so did their sheer terror. The dragon-snakes needed to prod their prey a bit, stir them back to action.

"Take one," commanded the king dragon-snake, from his place at the head of the advance. "The human. Kill her."

Day was dawning. Night was fading, the darkness lifting, as much as it could lift from this place of darkness. The sun's light glimmered over the murky water. Haplo cast a shadow as he ran.

"We must help him!" Alfred urged Samah. "You can help him, Councillor. Use your magic. Between us, maybe we can defeat the dragons . . ."

"And while I fight dragons, your Patryn friend escapes. Is that your plan?"

"Escape?" Alfred blinked watery blue eyes. "How can you say that? Look! Look at him! He's risking his life—"

"Bah! He's in no danger! The foul creatures are his to command! His people created them."

"That's not what Orla told me," Alfred retorted angrily. "That's not what the dragon-snakes said to you on the beach, is it, Councillor? 'Who created you?' you asked them. 'You did, Sartan.' That was their answer, wasn't it?"

Samah's face was livid. He raised his right hand, started to trace a sigil in the air.

Alfred raised his left, traced the same sigil, only in reverse, nullified the magic.

Samah moved sideways in a sliding dance step, murmuring words beneath his breath.

Alfred slid gracefully the opposite direction, repeated the same words, backward.

Again, Samah's magic was nullified.

But, behind him, Alfred could hear a furious hissing, the thrashing of reptile bodies, Haplo's hoarse voice shouting instructions to the dog. Alfred longed to look to see what was happening, but he did not dare move his complete attention from Samah.

The Councillor, drawing upon all his power, began to weave another spell. The magic rumbled in the distance, runes crackled. The tremendous, confusing storm of possibilities was coming down, full force, upon Alfred.

He began to feel faint.

Haplo's only goal was to rescue the mensch. Once he had them, however, he had no idea what to do, no plan of attack. Why bother? he demanded of himself bitterly. The battle was hopeless from the start. It was taking all his concentration to rid himself of the fear that threatened to lay hold of him, wring him inside out, drop him, retching up his guts, in the sand.

The dog had outdistanced him, reached the mensch already. The three were nearly finished, exhaustion and terror had drained them of their strength. Ignoring the serpents, the dog dashed around the mensch, herded them together, urged them on when it seemed they might lag.

One of the snakes came too close. The dog dashed toward it, growling a warning.

The dragon-snake slid back.

Devon collapsed onto the ground. Grundle grasped him by the shoulder, shook him.

"Get up, Devon!" she pleaded. "Get up!"

Alake, with a courage born of despair, stood over her fallen friend and turned to face the dragon-snakes. She raised a hand that trembled, but did not loose its firm grip on the object it held—a wooden stick. She presented it boldly, and began to cast her spell, taking time to speak the words clearly and distinctly, as her mother had taught her.

The stick burst into magical flame. Alake waved the firebrand in the eyes of the dragon-snakes, as she would have waved it in the eyes of some predator cat, stalking her chickens.

The dragon-snakes hesitated, drew back. Haplo saw their game, forgot his fear in his rage. Devon, with Grundle's assistance, was regaining his feet. The dog barked and jumped, trying to draw the serpent's attention to itself, away from the mensch.

Alake, proud, beautiful, exultant, thrust the firebrand at the snakes. "Leave this place! Leave us!" she cried.

"Alake, get down!" Haplo shouted.

The snake struck with incredible swiftness, head darting forward faster than the eye could follow, the brain could comprehend. It was a blur, nothing more. A blur that darted out and darted back.

Alake screamed, fell, writhing in pain, to the ground.

Grundle and Devon knelt down beside her. Haplo almost stumbled over them. He grasped the dwarf by the shoulder, jerked her to her feet.

"Run ahead!" he shouted. "Get help!"

Help. What help? Alfred? What am I thinking? Haplo asked himself angrily. It had been a reflexive response. But, at least, it would get the dwarf out of the way.

Grundle blinked, understood, and, after a wild, despairing look at Alake, the dwarf turned and took off for the water's edge.

The dragon-snake's head hovered in the air, loomed over its victim, over Haplo. Its eyes were on the Patryn, on the blue-flaring, rune-lit daggers in his hands. The snake was confident, but wary. It had little respect for the Patryn, but was smart enough not to underestimate its enemy.

"Devon," said Haplo, keeping his voice deliberately calm, "how's Alake?"

The elf's choked sob answered him. He could hear the girl's screams. She wasn't dead, more was the pity. Poisoned, he guessed, her flesh torn by the dragon's bone-hard mouth.

He risked a quick glance back. Devon gathered Alake in his arms, and held her close, soothing her. The dog was by his side, growling menacingly at any snakes that looked their direction.

Haplo placed his body between the serpent and the mensch. "Dog, stay with them."

He faced the dragon-snake, daggers raised.

"Take him," ordered the king.

The dragon-snake's head dove down. Jaws gaped wide, venom dripped. Haplo dodged it, as best he could, but several drops fell on him, burned through the wet shirt and into the skin.

He was aware of searing pain, but it wasn't important now. He kept his gaze and his attention fixed on his target.

The serpent lunged for him.

Haplo leapt backward, brought both hands together, drove both daggers into the dragon's skull, between the slit red eyes.

The rune-enhanced blades bit deep. Blood spurted. The dragon-snake roared in pain, reared its head up and back, carrying Haplo, trying to hang onto the daggers, with it.

His arms were nearly ripped from their sockets. He was forced to let go and dropped to the ground. Crouching low, he waited.

The wounded dragon-snake flailed and thrashed about blindly in its death throes. At last, with a shudder, it lay still. The slit-eyes were open, but the fire was gone. The tongue lolled from the toothless mouth. The daggers remained firmly entrenched in the bloody head.

"Go for your weapons, Patryn," said the king dragon-snake, red-green eyes gleaming with pleasure. "Seize them! Fight on! You've killed one of us. Don't give up now!"

It was his only chance. Haplo lunged, hand outstretched, made a desperate grab.

A snake's head swooped down. Pain exploded in his arm. Bone shattered, blood burned with the poison. His right hand fell useless. Haplo kept going, made another try with his left.

The serpent started for him again. A hissed command from its king halted it.

"No, no! Don't end it yet! The Patryn is strong. Who knows? He might be able to reach his ship."

If I *could* make it to my ship . . .

Haplo laughed at the thought. "That's what you want, isn't it? You want to see me turn and run. And you'll let me get— how far? Within arm's reach? Maybe even set my foot on it. And then what? Snatch me away. Take me into that cave?"

"Your terror will feed us a long, long time, Patryn," whispered the dragon-snake.

"I'm not going to play. You'll have to find your fun somewhere else."

Deliberately, Haplo turned his back on the snakes, crouched down beside the two young people. The dog posted guard behind its master, growling at any serpent that came too close.

Alake was quiet now, she no longer moaned. Her eyes were closed, her breathing ragged and shallow.

"I . . . I think she's better," said Devon, swallowing hard.

"Yes," Haplo said quietly. "She's going to be well soon." He heard, behind him, the huge bodies slide close. The dog's growl intensified.

Alake opened her eyes, smiled up at him.

"I am better," she breathed. "It . . . doesn't hurt anymore."

"Haplo!" Devon said warningly.

Haplo glanced behind him. The snakes had begun to circle around, some moving to the left, others moving to the right. Their bodies slid over the ground, curving, coiling, flat heads always facing his direction. Slowly, inexorably, they were surrounding him. The dragon-snakes began to hiss—soft, sibilant whispers of death. The dog ceased to growl, crept back to be near its master.

"What's the matter?" Alake whispered. "You killed the dragon-snake. I saw you. They're gone now, aren't they?"

"Yes," said Haplo, taking her hands in his. "They're gone. The danger's over. Rest easy, now."

"I will rest easy. You will watch over me? . . ."

"I will watch over you."

She smiled, closed her eyes. Her body shuddered, then lay still.

Samah spoke the first rune, started to speak the second. The magic was gathering around him in a light-spangled cloud.

A small person, howling at the top of her lungs, sprang on him, clutched at him, her momentum nearly carrying them both over.

His spell disrupted, Samah stared down at a young female dwarf. Her grimy hands tugged at his robes, practically dragged them off him.

"Rescue . . . Alake fell . . . Haplo alone . . . dragons . . . he needs . . . help!" The dwarf panted, pulled on Samah's robes. "You . . . come!"

Saman thrust the mensch aside. "Another trick."

"Come! Please!" the dwarf begged, and burst into tears.

"I will help," said Alfred.

The dwarf gulped, looked at him dubiously. Alfred turned to face Samah.

The Councillor was speaking the runes again, but this time

Alfred did not stop him. Samah's body shimmered, started to fade.

"Go to the aid of your Patryn friend!" he called. "See what thanks you get!"

The Councillor disappeared.

The dwarf maid was too upset and frightened to be startled. She clasped Alfred's wrinkled hand. She had, more or less, regained her breath.

"You must help! The dragon-snakes are killing him!"

Alfred started forward, intent on doing what he could, although what that would be, he wasn't certain. But he had forgotten, in his preoccupation with Samah, the horror of the creatures. Now, he stared at them, aghast: long reptile bodies whipping and lashing in the sand, eyes red as flame, green as the ugly sea, toothless jaws slavering, tongues dripping venom.

The weakness swept again over Alfred. He recognized it, fought against it, but not very hard. Swaying, he let go, let it take him away from the fear . . .

Small fists pummeled him.

Alfred, dazed, opened his eyes. He was lying in the sand.

A dwarf stood over him, beating him on the breast with her fists, shouting at him. "You can do magic! I saw you! You brought him his dog! Help him, damn you! Help Alake and Devon! Damn you! Damn you!"

The dwarf collapsed, buried her face in her hands.

"There . . . don't cry," said Alfred, reaching out timidly, awkwardly to pat the small, heaving shoulder. He looked back at the dragon-snakes and his heart nearly failed him. "I want to help," he said pathetically, "but I don't know how."

"Pray to the One," the dwarf said fiercely, raising her head. "The One will give you strength."

"Perhaps you're right," said Alfred.

"Alake!" Devon cried, shaking the lifeless body. "Alake!"

"Don't wish her back," Haplo said. "Her pain is over."

Devon raised a stricken face. "Do you mean she's . . . But you can save her! Bring her to life! Do it, Haplo! Like you did for me!"

"I don't have my magic!" Haplo shouted harshly. "I can't save her. I can't save you. I can't even save myself!"

Devon laid Alake's body gently on the ground. "I was afraid to live. Now I'm afraid to die. No, I don't mean that. It's not the dying. That's easy." He reached out, took hold of Alake's chill hand. "It's the pain, the fear . . ."

Haplo said nothing. There was nothing to say, no comforting words to offer. Their end was going to be a horrible one. He knew it, so did Devon, so did Grundle.

Grundle? Where was she?

Haplo remembered. He'd sent her back for help. For Alfred. The Sartan was hopelessly inept, but Haplo had to admit he'd seen Alfred do some fairly remarkable things . . . if he hadn't passed out first.

Haplo jumped to his feet. His sudden movement startled the dog, startled the dragon-snakes. One of them lashed out from behind him, its forked tongue flicked across his back like a whip of flame, seared the flesh from his bones. The pain was intense, paralyzing; every nerve in his body sizzled with the agony. He slumped to his knees, defeated.

Grundle stood on the shoreline, alone—a small, pathetic figure. No sign of Alfred.

Haplo pitched down flat on the sand. He was vaguely aware of Devon crouching over him, of the dog making a heroic, if futile, dash at the snake who had attacked him. Nothing was real now except the pain. It burned in his vision, filled his mind with fire.

The serpent must have struck him again, because suddenly the pain intensified. And then the dog was licking his face, nuzzling his neck, yelping and whining eagerly. It no longer sounded frightened.

"Haplo!" Devon shouted. "Haplo, don't go! Come back! Look and see!"

Haplo opened his eyes. The black mists that had been closing over him receded. He looked around, saw the pallid face of the elf, turned skyward.

A shadow passed across Haplo, a shadow that cooled the flames of the snake's venom. Blinking, trying to clear his vision, Haplo gazed upward.

A dragon flew above them, a dragon such as Haplo had never seen in all his life. Its beauty made the soul shrink in awe. Green polished scales flashed like emeralds. Its wings were golden leather, its mane of gold shone and glistened brighter than Chelestra's water-bound sun. The body was enormous, its wingspan seemed, to Haplo's dazed mind, to extend from horizon to horizon.

The dragon flew low, screamed in warning, dove down on the snakes. Devon ducked, involuntarily raised an arm over his head. Haplo didn't move. He lay still, watching. The dog barked and yelped like a thing possessed. Leaping in the air, it snapped playfully at the beast as it thundered overhead.

The rushing beat of dragon's wings stirred up clouds of sand. Haplo coughed, sat up to try to see.

The dragon-snakes fell back. Bodies flattening, they slid away, reluctantly, from their victims. Slit-eyes aimed malevolently at this new threat.

The dragon soared far above the serpents, wheeled, and dove again, taloned claws extended.

The king snake reared its head to meet the challenge. It spewed venom, attempted to hit the dragon's eyes.

The dragon struck, pinioned the snake's body. Claws sank deep into the scaled flesh.

The serpent writhed and twisted in fury. Its head coiled around, it snapped at the dragon, but the dragon was careful to keep just out of reach of the venomous jaws. Other snakes were rushing to their leader's aid. The dragon, great wings straining, lifted the king snake from the ground, soared into the air. The serpent dangled from its claws.

The king snake fought, lashing with its tail, striking out again and again with its head.

The dragon flew higher, until it was almost lost to Haplo's sight. Far up over the craggy mountains of Draknor, the dragon loosed its hold on the snake, let it fall.

The dragon-snake plummeted, twisting and shrieking, down onto the mountain, onto the sharp bones of the tormented creature it had used for its lair. The seamoon shook with the force of the snake's fall. Rocks cracked and splintered, the mountain caved in on top of the snake's carcass.

The dragon came back, circled overhead, glittering eyes seeking another kill.

The serpents coiled in defensive posture, the red-green eyes darted uneasy glances at each other.

"If we can catch the dragon on the ground, attack it in a body, we can defeat it!" hissed one.

"Yes," said another. "A good idea. You challenge it, lure it down from the sky! Then I'll attack it."

"Why me? You challenge it!"

They argued among themselves, none of them daring to commence the fight that would lure the dragon down from its safe haven in the air. None was willing to risk its own slimy skin to save its fellows, and they had no king, now, to command them. Leaderless, faced with a powerful enemy, the like of which they had never encountered, they deemed it best to make a strategic retreat. The dragon-snakes slid rapidly across the sand, heading for the dark safety of what was left of their shattered mountain.

The dragon pursued them, harassing them, harrying them, until it had driven every one of them into the cave. Then it wheeled, flew back, hovered over Haplo. He tried to look directly at it, but the shining light of its being made his eyes water.

You are wounded. Yet you must find the strength to return to your ship. The dragon-snakes are disorganized for the moment, but they will soon regroup and I do not have the power to fight them all.

The dragon didn't speak aloud. Haplo heard the voice in his mind. It sounded familiar, but he couldn't place it.

He forced his pain-racked body to stand. Yellow flares burst in his eyes; he staggered, would have lost his balance.

Devon was there beside him, the elf holding him, propping him up. The dog pattered around him, anxious and wanting to help. Haplo remained standing quietly, until the weakness passed, then he nodded, unable to speak, and took a feeble step. Suddenly, he stopped.

"Alake," he said, and looked down at the body. His gaze shifted grimly to the cave where he could see the slits of red eyes, watching.

The dragon understood him. *I will care for her. Have no fear. They will not disturb her rest.*

Haplo nodded again, wearily, and shifted his gaze to his goal, his submersible. And there was Grundle, standing in the sand, apparently rooted to the spot.

They lurched across the beach. The slender elf, finding reserves of strength he never knew he had, guided the injured

Patryn's faltering steps, held him up when he would have fallen. Haplo lost sight of the dragon, forgot about it, forgot the snakes, concentrated on fighting the pain, fighting to remain conscious.

They came level with Grundle, who still had not moved. She was staring at them with wide eyes. She made no sound, only a garbled rattle.

"I can walk . . . from here!" Haplo gasped.

He staggered forward, caught himself on the submersible's wood prow. Propping himself up, he pointed back at the stammering dwarf. "Go . . . get her."

"What's the matter with her, do you think?" Devon asked, worried. "I've never seen her like that."

"Scared silly, maybe." Haplo groaned. He had to climb on board, quick. "Just grab her . . . bring her along."

Hand over hand, he pulled himself along the rail of the ship's upper deck, heading for the hatch.

"What about *him*?" He heard Grundle cry shrilly.

Haplo glanced back, saw a huddled figure lying in the sand. Alfred.

"It figures," Haplo muttered bitterly.

He was about to say, "Leave him," but, of course, the dog had raced over to sniff at, paw over, and lick the unconscious Sartan. Well, after all, Haplo remembered grudgingly, I do owe him.

"Bring him along, if you must."

"He turned into the dragon," Grundle said, voice quivering in awe.

Haplo laughed, shook his head.

"He did!" the dwarf averred solemnly. "I saw him. He . . . turned himself into a dragon!"

The Patryn looked from the dwarf to Alfred, who had regained his senses—what senses were his to regain.

He was making feeble, flapping motions with his hands, trying to temper the dog's wet, enthusiastic welcome.

Haplo turned away, too weak to care or argue.

Finally persuading the dog to let him alone, Alfred reassembled himself and tottered to his feet. He stared blankly around at everything and everyone. His gaze wandered to the cave, and he remembered. He cringed.

"Are they gone?"

"You should know!" Grundle yelled. "You chased them away!"

Alfred smiled wanly, deprecatingly. He shook his head, glanced down at the impression his body had left in the sand.

"I'm afraid you're mistaken, child. I wasn't much help to anyone, not even myself."

"But I saw you!" the dwarf continued stubbornly.

"Hurry up, Sartan, if you're coming," Haplo called out. Only a few more steps . . .

"He's coming, Patryn. We will see to that. You will have company in your prison."

Haplo stopped, leaned against the rail. He had barely strength enough to lift his head.

Samah stood before him.

CHAPTER ♦ 32

SURUNAN

CHELESTRA

♦

Haplo came back to consciousness slowly, reluctantly, knowing he must wake to pain within and without, knowing he must wake to the knowledge that his carefully ordered life had been consumed in flames, scattered like ashes on the seawater.

He lay for long moments without opening his eyes, not from wariness or caution, as he might have done under similar circumstances, but from sheer weariness. Living, from now on, was going to be a constant struggle for him. When he'd started this journey, long ago, on Arianus, he'd had all the answers. Now, at the finish, he was left with nothing but questions. He was no longer confident, no longer sure. He doubted. And the doubt frightened him.

He heard a whine; a shaggy tail brushed against the floor. A wet tongue licked his hand. Haplo, eyes still closed, rubbed the dog's head, ruffled the ears. His lord would not be pleased to see the animal return. But then, there was a lot his lord wasn't going to be pleased to see.

Haplo sighed and, when it became apparent he couldn't go back to sleep, groaned and opened his eyes. And, of course, the first face he would see on awakening belonged to Alfred.

The Sartan hovered over him, peered down at him anxiously. "Are you in pain? Where does it hurt?"

Haplo was strongly tempted to shut his eyes again. Instead, he sat up, looked around. He was in a room in what must be a private house, a Sartan house—he knew it by instinct. But now it was no longer a house, it was a Sartan prison. The windows sparkled with warding runes. Powerful sigla, burning with a vivid red light, enhanced the closed and barred door. Haplo glanced down ruefully at his arms and body. His clothes were wet, his skin bare.

"They've been bathing you in seawater—Samah's orders," said Alfred. "I'm sorry."

"What are you apologizing for?" Haplo grunted, glowering at the Sartan in irritation. "It's not your fault. Why do you insist on apologizing for things that aren't your fault?"

Alfred flushed. "I don't know. I guess I've always felt that they *were* my fault, in a way. Because of who and what I am."

"Well, it isn't, so quit sniveling about it," Haplo snapped. He had to lash out at something and Alfred was the closest thing available. "*You* didn't send my people to the Labyrinth. *You* didn't cause the Sundering."

"No," said Alfred sadly, "but I didn't do much to set right what I found wrong. I always . . . fainted."

"Always?" Haplo glanced at the Sartan sharply, reminded suddenly of Grundle's wild tale. "How about back there on Draknor. Did you faint then?"

"I'm afraid so," said Alfred, hanging his head in mortification. "I'm not sure, of course. I don't seem to be able to remember much of anything that went on. Oh, by the way." He cast Haplo an uneasy, sidelong glance. "I'm afraid I . . . er . . . did what I could for your injuries. I hope you won't be too angry, but you were in terrible pain—"

Haplo looked down again at his bare skin. No, he wouldn't have been able to heal himself. He tried to be angry, it would have felt good to be angry, but he couldn't muster the energy to feel much of anything now.

"You're apologizing again," he said, and lay back down.

"I know. I'm sorry," said Alfred.

Haplo glared at him.

Alfred turned around and headed back across the small room to another bed.

"Thank you," Haplo said quietly.

Alfred, astonished, looked to see if he'd heard correctly. "Did you say something?"

Haplo damn well wasn't going to repeat himself. "Where are we?" he asked, though he already knew. "What happened after we left Draknor? How long have I been out?"

"A day and night and half another day. You were badly hurt. I tried to convince Samah to allow your magic to return, to let you use it to heal yourself, but he refused. He's frightened. Very frightened. I know how he feels. I understand such fear."

Alfred fell silent, stared long at nothing. Haplo shifted restlessly. "I asked you—"

The Sartan blinked and came out of his reverie.

"I'm sorry. Oh! There I go, apologizing again. No, no. I won't do it anymore. I promise. Where was I? The seawater. They have been bathing you in it twice a day." Alfred glanced at the dog and smiled. "Your friend there put up quite a fight whenever anyone came near you. He nearly bit Samah. The dog will listen to me now. I think the animal's beginning to trust me."

Haplo snorted, didn't see the need to pursue that subject further. "What about the mensch? They get home safely?"

"As a matter of fact, no. That is, they're safe enough," Alfred amended hastily, seeing Haplo frown, "but they didn't go home. Samah offered to take them. He's been quite good to them, in fact, in his own way. It's just that he doesn't understand them. But the mensch—the dwarf maid and the elven lad—refused to leave you. The dwarf was extremely stubborn about it. She gave Samah a piece of her mind."

Haplo could picture Grundle, chin outthrust, shaking her side wiskers at the Sartan Councillor. The Patryn smiled. He wished he could have seen it.

"The mensch are here, staying in this house. They've been to see you as often as the Sartan would allow. In fact, I'm surprised they haven't come to visit before now. But, then, of course, this is the morning of the—"

Alfred stopped in some confusion.

"The what?" Haplo demanded, suddenly suspicious.

"I really hadn't intended to mention it. I didn't want to worry you."

"*Worry* me?" Haplo gazed at the Sartan in amazement, then burst out laughing. He laughed until he felt tears burn in his eyes, drew in a deep, shuddering breath. "I'm in a Sartan prison, stripped of my magic, taken captive by the most powerful Sartan wizard who ever lived, and you don't want to worry me."

"I'm sor—" Alfred caught Haplo's baleful gaze, gulped, and kept quiet.

"Let me guess," said Haplo grimly. "Today is the day the Council meets to decide what to do with us. That's it, isn't it?"

Alfred nodded. Returning to his bed, he sat down, long, ungainly arms dangling dejectedly between his legs.

"Well, what can they do to you? Slap you on the wrist? Make you promise to be a good boy and stay away from the nasty Patryn?"

It was supposed to have been a joke. Alfred didn't laugh.

"I don't know," he said in low, fearful tones. "You see, I overheard Samah talking once and he said—"

"Hush!" Haplo warned, sat up.

A voice, a female voice, had begun to chant outside the door. The glowing runes of warding faded, began to disappear.

"Ah," said Alfred, brightening, "that's Orla!"

The Sartan was transformed. Stooped shoulders straightened, he stood up tall, looked almost dignified. The door opened and a woman, ushering two mensch before her, stepped inside.

"Haplo!" Grundle cried, and, before the Patryn knew what was happening, she dashed forward and flung herself into his arms.

"Alake's dead!" she wailed. "I didn't mean for her to die. It's all my fault!"

"There now," he said, patting her awkwardly on the broad, solid back. She clung to him, blubbering.

Haplo gave her a little shake. "Listen to me, Grundle."

The dwarf gulped, sniffed, gradually quieted.

"What you three did was dangerous, foolhardy," Haplo said sternly. "You were wrong. You shouldn't have gone there by yourselves. But you did, and nothing can change that. Alake was a princess. Her life was dedicated to her people. She died for her people, Grundle. For her people"—the Patryn looked at Sartan—"and maybe for a lot of other people, as well."

The Sartan woman who had come in with them put her hand to her eyes and turned her face away. Alfred, going to her, hung about her timidly, his arm starting of its accord to steal around the woman's shoulders, to offer her comfort. The arm hesitated, drew back.

Blast the man! thought Haplo. He can't even make love to a woman properly.

Grundle snuffled a little, hiccuped.

"Hey, come on, now," Haplo told her gruffly. "Cut it out. Look, you're upsetting my dog."

The dog, who appeared to have taken this personally, had been adding his howls to hers. Grundle wiped away her tears, and managed a wan smile.

"How are you, sir?" Devon asked, sitting on the end of the bed.

"I've been better," Haplo said. "But so have you, I'll wager."

"Yes, sir," Devon answered.

He was pale and unhappy. His terrible ordeal had left its mark on him. But he seemed more assured, more confident. He had come to know himself.

He wasn't the only one.

"We have to talk to you!" Grundle said, pulling on Haplo's wet sleeve.

"Yes, it's very important," Devon added.

The two exchanged glances, looked over at the Sartan: Alfred and the woman he called Orla.

"You want to be alone. That's all right. We'll leave." Alfred started to shuffle off.

The woman, smiling, laid her hand on his arm. "I don't think that would be possible." She cast a significant glance at the door. The warding runes were not alight, but footsteps could be heard pacing outside—a guard.

Alfred seemed to shrivel up. "You're right," he said in a low voice. "I wasn't thinking. We'll sit here and we won't listen. We promise."

He sat down on the bed, patted a place beside him. "Please, sit down."

The woman looked at the bed, then at Alfred. She flushed deeply. Haplo thought back to Alake, looking the same, reacting the same.

Alfred turned a truly remarkable shade of red, jumped to his feet.

"I never meant— Of course, I wouldn't— What must you think? No chairs. I only intended—"

"Yes, thank you," said Orla faintly, and sat down at the end of the bed.

Alfred resumed his seat at the opposite end of the bed, gaze fixed on his shoes.

Grundle, who had been watching with considerable impatience, took hold of Haplo's hand, dragged him off into a corner, as far from the Sartan as possible. Devon followed. The two, serious and solemn, began to tell their tale in loud whispers.

It might have seemed impossible, being in the same room with three people having an intense discussion and not listening, but the two Sartan managed it admirably. Neither of them heard a word spoken, both being far too intent on voices within to pay much attention to those without.

Orla sighed. Her hands twisted together nervously and she glanced at Alfred every few seconds, as if trying to make up her mind whether or not to speak.

Alfred, sensing her tension, wondered at the cause. A thought occurred to him.

"The Council. It's meeting now, isn't it?"

"Yes," Orla answered, but without a voice.

"You're . . . you're not there?"

She started to reply, but ended up only shaking her head. "No," she said, after a moment's pause. Lifting her chin, she spoke more firmly. "No, I'm not there. I quit the Council."

Alfred gaped. To his knowledge, no Sartan had ever done such a thing. None had ever even contemplated it, so far as he knew.

"Because . . . of me?" Alfred asked timidly.

"Yes. Because of you. Because of him." She looked at the Patryn. "Because of them." Her gaze went to the mensch.

"What did— How did Samah—?"

"He was furious. In fact," Orla added complacently, with a smile, "I'm on trial myself now, along with you and the Patryn."

"No!" Alfred was appalled. "He can't! I won't allow you to—"

"Hush!" Orla rested her hand on his lips. "It's all right." She took hold of Alfred's hand, the hand that was clumsy, rawboned, too large. "You've taught me so much. I'm not afraid anymore. Whatever they do to us, I'm not afraid."

"What *will* Samah do?" Alfred's fingers closed over hers. "What happened to others, my dear? What happened to those of our people, who, long ago, discovered the truth?"

Orla turned to face him. Her eyes met his steadily, her voice was calm.

"Samah cast them into the Labyrinth."

CHAPTER 33

SURUNAN

CHELESTRA

♦

"WE HEARD THE DRAGON-SNAKES SAY THAT, HAPLO," GRUNDLE asserted, looking frightened at the memory. "They said it was all a trick and they were going to make our people slaughter each other and they were going to take you prisoner—"

"To your lord," Devon struck in. "The dragon-snakes plan to take you back to your lord and denounce you as a traitor. They said all that. We heard them."

"You have to believe us!" Grundle insisted.

The Patryn had listened closely, frowned at what he heard, but he hadn't spoken.

"You do believe us, don't you?" Devon asked.

"I believe you."

Hearing conviction in his voice, the two relaxed, looked reassured. Haplo heard the echo of the snake's words. *Chaos is our life's blood. Death our meat and drink.*

On Abarrach, he'd found evidence that there might be a power for a greater good. If that was true, then he thought it quite likely that here, on Chelestra, he had discovered its opposite.

He wondered if Alfred had heard, and glanced across the room. Obviously not. The Sartan looked as white if he'd just taken a spear through the heart.

"Sartan!" Haplo said sharply. "You need to hear this. Tell

them what you told me," he urged Grundle, "about the dragon-snakes and Death's Gate."

Alfred turned his head toward the dwarf. Shaken, he was obviously only half-listening. Orla, more composed, gave Grundle serious attention.

Abashed at this audience, Grundle began her story somewhat flustered, grew more confident as she went along.

"I didn't understand hardly any of it. I did, at the beginning, all about how they planned to flood your city with seawater and that would ruin your magic and you'd have to escape. But then they began to talk about something called 'Death's Gate'?"

She looked to Devon for verification. The elf nodded.

"Yes, that was it. 'Death's Gate.' "

Alfred was suddenly attentive. "Death's Gate? What about Death's Gate?"

"You tell them," Grundle urged the elf. "You know the exact words they used. I never can remember."

Devon hesitated, to make certain he had it right. "They said: 'They will be forced to do what they were strong enough to resist doing ages before. Samah will open Death's Gate!' And then they said something after that about entering Death's Gate . . ."

Orla gasped, rose to her feet, her hand pressed to her breast. "That's what Samah means to do! He talks of opening Death's Gate if the mensch attack us!"

"And that will unleash this terrible evil on the other worlds," Haplo said. "The dragon-snakes will grow in numbers and in power. And who will be left to fight them?"

"Samah must be stopped," said Orla. She turned to the dwarf and the elf. "Your people must be stopped."

"We don't want war," Devon returned gravely. "But we must have a place to live. You leave us little choice."

"We can work it out. We'll bring everybody together, negotiate—"

"It is late for that, 'Wife.' " Samah appeared, standing in the doorway. "War has begun. Hordes of mensch are sailing for our city. They are being led by the dragon-snakes."

"But . . . that's not possible!" Grundle cried. "My people are afraid of the dragon-snakes."

"The elves would not follow the dragon-snakes without good

reason," stated Devon, eyeing Samah narrowly. "Something must have happened to force them to make such a drastic decision."

"Something *did* happen, as you well know. You and the Patryn."

"Us!" Grundle exclaimed. "How could we do anything! We've been here with you! Though we'd *like* to do something," she added, but it was a mutter, into her whiskers.

Devon poked her in the back, and she subsided.

"I think you should explain yourself, Samah," Orla intervened, "before you accuse children of starting a war."

"Very well, 'Wife.' I will explain."

Samah used the word as a whip, but Orla did not flinch beneath it. She stood calmly beside Alfred.

"The dragon-snakes went to the mensch and told them that *we* Sartan were responsible for the unfortunate death of the young human female. The dragons claimed that we took the other two children captive, that we are holding them hostage."

His cold gaze turned to Devon and Grundle. "All very well planned—the way you two persuaded us to take you along. The Patryn's idea, of course."

"Yeah, sure," muttered Haplo tiredly. "I though it up right before I passed out."

"We didn't plan anything like that!" Grundle protested, her lower lip quivering. "We told you the truth! I think you're a wicked man!"

"Hush, Grundle." Devon put his arms around her. "What are you going to do to us?"

"We do not make war against children," said Samah. "You will be returned safely to your families. And you will carry with you this message for your people: Attack us at your own peril. We know all about your plan to flood our city with seawater. You think that this will weaken us, but your 'friends' the Patryn and his evil minions, have willfully misled you. You will not find a city of a few helpless Sartan. You will find a city of thousands of Sartan, armed with the power of centuries, armored by the might of other worlds—"

"You're going to open Death's Gate," said Haplo.

Samah did not deign to respond. "Repeat my words to your

people. I want it to be remembered that we gave them fair warning."

"You can't be serious!" Alfred extended pleading hands. "You don't know what you're saying! Opening Death's Gate would mean . . . disaster. The dragon-snakes would be able to enter other worlds. The dreadful lazar on Abarrach are waiting for just such a chance to enter this one!"

"So is my lord," Haplo said, shrugging. "You'd be doing him a favor."

"This is what the dragons want you to do, Samah," Orla cried. "These children know. They overheard the dragons' plotting."

"As if I'd believe them . . . or any of you." Samah glanced around at them all in disdain. "At the first breach in the walls, I will open Death's Gate. I will summon our brethren from the other worlds. And there *are* Sartan on other worlds. You cannot fool me with your lies.

"As for your lord"—Samah turned to Haplo—"he will be cast back into the Labyrinth along with the rest of your evil race. And this time, there will be no escape!"

"Councillor, don't do this." Alfred's voice was calm, sad. "The true evil isn't out there. The true evil is here." He placed his hand on his heart. "It is fear. I know it well. I've given way to its power most of my life.

"Once, long ago, Death's Gate was meant to stand open, to lead us from death into a new and better existence. But the time for that is past. Too much has changed. If you open Death's Gate now, you will discover, to your bitter sorrow and regret, that you have uncovered a darker and more sinister aspect to the name Death's Gate—a name that was once meant to stand for hope."

Samah listened in silence, with exemplary patience.

"Are you finished?" he asked.

"I am," replied Alfred humbly.

"Very well. It is time these mensch were returned to their families." Samah gestured. "Come, children. Stand together. Don't be afraid of the magic. It will not harm you. You will seem to sleep, and when you wake up, you will be safely with your people."

"I'm not afraid of you." Grundle sniffed. "I've seen better magic than you could ever hope to make."

Glancing conspiratorially at Alfred, she winked.

Alfred looked extremely confused.

"You remember what is it you have to say to your people?" Samah asked.

"We remember," said Devon, "and so will our people. We'll remember your words as long as we live. Farewell, Haplo." The elf turned to him. "Thank you not only for my life, but for teaching me to live it."

"Good-bye, Haplo," said Grundle. She went over to him, hugged him around his knees.

"No more eavesdropping," he said severely.

Grundle heaved a sigh. "I know. I promise."

She stood a moment, fumbling at something she had tucked inside a pocket of her dress. The object was large, too large for the pocket, and now it was stuck fast. Grundle tugged, the pocket tore. Wrenching the object loose, she held it out to Haplo. It was a book, its leather-bound cover worn and stained with what might have been tears.

"I want you to have this. It's a journal I kept when we left to go to the dragon-snakes. I asked the lady"—Grundle nodded at Orla—"to fetch it for me. She did. *She's* nice. I was going to write some more in it, I was going to write the end, but . . . I couldn't. It's too sad.

"Anyway," she continued, wiping away a stray tear, "just ignore all the bad things I say about you at the beginning. I didn't know you then. I mean . . . You'll understand? . . ."

"Yes," said Haplo, accepting the gift. "I'll understand."

Devon took Grundle's hand, the two stood together before Samah. The Councillor sang the runes. Fiery trails of sigla formed in the air, encircled the dwarf and the elf. Their eyes closed, heads drooped, they leaned against each other. The runes flared, and the two were gone.

The dog gave a dismal howl. Haplo rested his hand on the animal's head, counseling silence.

"That's accomplished," said Samah briskly. "Now, we have a most unpleasant task. The sooner we get it done, the better.

"You, who call yourself Alfred Montbank. Your case has been brought before the Council. After careful deliberation, we have found you guilty of consorting with the enemy, of plotting against your own people, of attempting to deceive us with lies, of speaking heresy. We have passed sentence upon you. Do you, Alfred Montbank, concede that the Council has the right and the wisdom to pass such sentence upon you that will enable you to learn from your mistakes and make reparation for them?"

The speech was a mere formality, always asked of each person who came before the Council. But Alfred listened to it intently, appeared to be considering each word carefully.

" 'Learn from my mistakes and make reparation for them,' " he repeated to himself. He looked up at Samah and when he answered, his voice was firm and steadfast. "Yes, Councillor, I do."

"Alfred , you can't!" Orla flung herself upon her husband. "Don't go through with this, Samah! I beg you! Why won't you listen?"

"Be silent, Wife!" Samah thrust her back, away from him. "Your sentence, too, has been passed. You have a choice. You can go with him or remain among us. But either way, you will be stripped of your powers of magic."

Orla stared at him, her face livid. Slowly, she shook her head. "You're insane, Samah. Your fear has driven you mad."

Coming to stand beside Alfred, she took hold of his arm. "I choose to go with him."

"No, Orla," Alfred told her, "I can't allow it. You don't know what you're saying."

"Yes, I do. You forget," she reminded him, smiling at him tremulously, "I've shared your visions." She looked over at the Patryn. "I know what we face and I'm not afraid."

Haplo wasn't paying attention. The Patryn had been studying the Sartan who stood guard at the door, calculating the odds on jumping the man and making good his escape. The chances were slim, almost hopeless, but it beat hanging around here, waiting for Samah to give him another bath.

He tensed, prepared to attack. Samah turned suddenly, spoke to the guard. Haplo forced himself to relax, tried to look nonchalant.

"Ramu. Take these two to the Council Chamber and make them ready for the sending. We must cast this spell immediately, before the mensch attack. Gather together all the members of the Council. They will all be needed to perform magic of this magnitude."

"What spell of sending?" Haplo was instantly on his guard, thinking it had something to do with him. "What's going on?"

Ramu entered, stood beside the door.

Alfred walked forward, Orla at his side. The two moved calmly, with dignity. And for once, Haplo noted in wonder, Alfred didn't fall over anything.

Haplo moved to block Alfred's path. "Where are they sending you?"

"To the Labyrinth," Alfred answered.

"What?"

Haplo laughed, thinking this was some bizarre plot to trap him, though for what purpose he couldn't imagine. "I don't believe it!"

"Others were sent before us, Haplo. We are not the first. Long ago, during the Sundering, the Sartan who discovered and embraced the truth were cast into prison along with your people."

Haplo stared, dazed. It didn't make sense. It wasn't possible. And yet he knew Alfred was telling the truth. The Sartan couldn't lie.

"You can't do this!" Haplo protested to Samah. "You're sentencing them to death!"

"Drop the concerned act, Patryn. It will gain you nothing. You will be joining your 'friend' soon enough, after we have questioned you fully concerning this so-called Lord of the Nexus and his plans."

Haplo ignored the man, turned to Alfred. "You're going to let him send you to the Labyrinth? Just like that? You've been there! In my mind! You know what it's like. You won't last two minutes. You or her! Fight, damn it! For once in your life, stand up and fight!"

Alfred paled, looked troubled. "No, I couldn't . . ."

"Yes, you can! Grundle was right. *You* were the dragon, weren't you? You saved our lives on Draknor. You're powerful, more powerful than Samah, more powerful than any Sartan who has ever lived. The dragon-snakes know it. Serpent Mage, they call you. *He* knows it. That's why he's getting rid of you."

"Thank you, Haplo," Alfred said gently, "but even if what

you say is true, and I did turn myself into a dragon, I can't remember how I did it. No, it's all right. Please, understand."

He reached out, rested a hand on the Patryn's muscle-clenched arm. "All my life I've been running away from what I am. Either that, or fainting. Or apologizing." He was calm, almost serene. "I'm not running anymore."

"Yeah," said Haplo harshly. "Well, you better not faint either. Not in the Labyrinth." He jerked his arm away from the Sartan's touch.

"I'll try to remember." Alfred smiled.

The dog whimpered, crowded close, rubbing its muzzle against Alfred's leg. He patted it gingerly. "Take care of him, boy. Don't lose him again."

Ramu stepped between them, began to chant the runes.

Sigla flashed, blinding Haplo. The heat drove him back. When he could see again, the red runes of warding burned before the door, blocked the windows.

The Sartan were gone.

CHAPTER ♦ 34

SURUNAN

CHELESTRA

♦

Haplo lay back down on the bed. Nothing he could do except wait. His skin was starting to dry. The sigla on his body were visible once again, faintly. It would take a long time for his magic to return fully, time he guessed he didn't have. The Sartan would be back soon, douse him with water, then try to force him to talk.

That should prove entertaining.

In the meantime, he supposed, he should try to get what rest he could. The loss of his magic made him feel tired, weak. He wondered if this was a real, physical reaction or only in his mind. He wondered about other things, lying on his back, attempting to comfort the grieving dog.

Sartan men and women in the Labyrinth. Sent there with their enemies. What had happened to them? Presumably, of course, the Patryns, in their fury, would have turned on them, killed them.

But what if they didn't? Haplo mused. What if those longtime enemies were forced to put aside their hatred and their anger and work together in order to survive? And what if, during the long, dark nights, they lay down together; sought comfort in each other's arms, a respite from their terror? Could it be that, long ago, Patryn and Sartan blood had mingled?

The thought staggered Haplo. It was too overwhelming to comprehend. The possibilities it presented were too confusing.

His hand stroked the dog's head, which rested on his chest. The animal's eyes closed, it sighed and nestled near him, on the bed. Haplo was almost asleep himself when the world rippled.

His eyes flared open. He tensed, alarmed, panicked by the terrifying sensation, yet unable to move a muscle to combat it. The ripple effect began at his feet, spread upward, carried sickness and dizziness with it. He could only watch, feel it, helpless to act.

Once before, he'd experienced this. Once before, the world around him had rippled. Once before, he had seen himself, without shape or dimension, pasted flat against his surroundings that were themselves as thin and brittle as a dead leaf.

The waves spread above him, bending the room, bending the walls, the ceiling. The red warding runes that barred the doors and windows winked out, but Haplo could not take advantage of their absence. He couldn't move.

Last time, the dog had vanished, too. He grabbed hold of it. This time, it remained, dozing quietly, sleeping through everything.

The ripple effect passed as swiftly as it had come. The red warding runes flared again. The dog snored.

Drawing a deep breath, letting it out, Haplo stared up at nothing.

The last time the world had rippled, Alfred had been the cause. Alfred had entered Death's Gate.

The Patryn woke suddenly, body tingling with alarm. It was night, the room was dark or would have been, but for the glowing runes. He sat up, trying to remember, isolate the sound that had brought him wide awake from a deep sleep. He was so intent on listening that he didn't notice, at first, the sigla on his skin gleaming a bright blue.

"I must have slept a long time," he said to the dog, who had itself been roused from slumber. "I wonder why they didn't come for me? What do you suppose is going on, boy?"

The dog seemed to think it had some idea, for it jumped off the bed and padded over to the window. Haplo, having the same idea, followed. He drew as close to the runes as he could, ignoring the magical heat that burned his skin, his own magic unable to protect long against it. Shielding his eyes with his hand, he squinted against the sigla's flaring brilliance, tried to look outside.

He couldn't see much in the night; shadows running through the shadows, darker shapes of darkness. But he could hear their shouts; it was the shouting that had wakened him.

"The wall is breached! The water is flooding our city!"

Haplo thought he heard footsteps at the door. He tensed, turned, prepared to fight. It was foolish of them to have allowed him to regain his magic. He'd teach them how foolish.

The footsteps hesitated a moment, then began to retreat. Haplo walked to the door, listened until the sound faded away. If there had been a Sartan guard, he wasn't there now.

The runes of warding were still strong, however, still powerful. Haplo was forced to draw back from the door; fighting the heat was draining his strength.

Besides, no need to waste his energy.

"Might as well relax, boy," he advised the dog. "We'll be out of here, soon enough."

And then where would he go? What would he do?

Back to the Labyrinth. To look for Alfred. To look for others . . .

Smiling quietly, Haplo returned to his bed, stretched out comfortably, and waited for the seawater to rise.

APPENDIX ♦ I

MAGICAL BATTLE

BETWEEN PATRYN AND SARTAN:

A FURTHER EXPLANATION

♦

BOTH SARTAN AND PATRYN MAGIC IS BASED ON THE THEORY OF POSsibilities.[1] A contest between the two can best be described as a lethal version of a children's game known as Knife, Paper, Stone.[2] In this game, each child provides himself with three objects: a small knife, a piece of paper, and a rock. These objects are hidden behind the back. Opponents face each other and, at a given signal, both grab an object and bring it forth in mock battle. The goal is to try to guess which weapon out of three possible weapons the opponent will use this round and be prepared to counter his attack.

The various outcomes are determined thus:

Knife cuts paper. (Whoever produces the knife wins this round.)

Stone crushes knife.

Paper covers stone.

---

[1] See "Magic in the Sundered Realms, Excerpts from a Sartan's Musing," in *Dragon Wing,* vol. 1 of *The Death Gate Cycle.*

[2] One theory holds that this game was played by mensch children desirous of emulating Sartan (or Patryn) heroes.

♦

Knife, Paper, Stone is, of course, an extremely simplified version of a magical battle between Patryn and Sartan, each of whom would have at his or her disposal innumerable possibilities for attack and defense.

Ancient duels between the two were rarely fought "in hot blood" as was the fight between Samah and Haplo. Both races had their images to consider and a battle would take place only after a challenge had been issued and accepted. A Patryn was always ready to fight in public view. A Sartan might agree, but only if he or she felt that such a public display of prowess and courage would prove instructive to the mensch.

Public duels were held in arenas and provided absolutely marvelous shows, although the presence of a crowd rather hampered some of the more spectacular magical effects. It would never do, for example, to call down a lightning bolt on one's enemy and mistakenly electrocute half the audience. Thus these public battles rarely ended in death, but were similar to a chess tournament where one opponent attempts to place the other in checkmate.

Private contests were much more serious, fought on a more lethal scale, and almost always ended in death for either one or both opponents. They were held in secret places, known only to the two races, where destructive forces could be unleashed without endangering innocent bystanders. Sometimes the two fought alone, but more often family members and members of the Council attended to serve as witnesses. They were never permitted to intervene.

It should be noted here that the Sartan Council was always publicly opposed to these duels and would endeavor, until the last moment, to stop the fight.

Despite the limitless number of possibilities available, most wizards generally followed a set pattern, based on the dictates of logic. The first spells to be cast were usually either defensive or distractive in nature. They were easy, requiring little effort on the part of the spellcaster, and enabled him to study and feel out his opponent. Thus, a Sartan wizard might attempt to distract his enemy by sending a million snakes into combat; the Patryn might counter by surrounding himself with a wall of fire.

Such distractions and defenses would give way to powerful offensive spells and equally powerful defenses. Opponents were required to see an attack coming and react to it within seconds, all the while guarding against attacks (such as lightning bolts) against which one could not defend oneself. The slightest miscalculation, the blinking of an eye, a momentary weakening, almost always proved fatal.[3]

[3]Excerpt from a treatise, untitled, discovered in the library of the Sartan on Chelestra.

APPENDIX ♦ II

STATUS AND PROMISE

OF THE DURNAI

♦

(From a report given by Ramu, son of Samah, to the Sartan Council of Seven. This report was submitted sometime early during the session in which Alfred first reported to the council. The text, as well as other artifacts, was later found in Alfred's possession. How he came by them remains a mystery. The footnotes appear to be Alfred's and are consistently expressed in the tongue of the mensch—an interesting fact in itself.)

Brother Sartan of the Council:

I beg to put before you, my brothers and sisters, a report on the state of our realm as it pertains to the seamoons it contains, known to us as the durnai. I humbly submit this report and beg your understanding should it fall short of your needs and expectations. May the runes grant us insight and wisdom in our governance of creation.[1]

I beg to set before you a summary of this realm's structure. I shall then endeavor with my limited and inadequate ability to compare its expected state with that currently found.[2]

---

[1] A Sartan cliché enshrining their magic as the ultimate source of power in all creation.

[2] Such self-denigrating and "bumble" language is expected in all reports to the Council. Ramu certainly harbored no such actual questions regarding his own abilities. Indeed, I doubt that Ramu ever believed he could fail at anything.

ORIGINAL GEOGRAPHY AND GEOLOGY
PLAN OF OUR REALM

Our Realm of Water consists of a great sea surrounded by ice. In the midst of this sea moves the seasun, a great glowing sphere of phosphorescent light that illuminates and warms the waters about it. Its motion melts the ice around it and leaves the sea to freeze again behind it. Many creatures inhabit this sea—greatest among them being the durnai, upon which the mensch live.

The Seasun

The seasun is powered primarily by energy coming through a rift[3] from the Realm of Fire. Until the Death Gates open at Jran-kri,[4] this rift provides only sufficient energy to keep this realm alive. Only by achieving Jran-kri will the durnai be awakened and the ice melted permanently.

The seasun moves in a predestined cycle through the water. This cycle is nearly one thousand years long, thus accounting for the long sleep[5] of our people and our recent revival. Originally this motion was intended to act to circulate the waters of

---

[3]Samah explained that the Sundered Realms are connected not only by the Death Gates but by many additional conduits known as rifts. Rifts are special passage dimensions used for the conveyance of matter/energy from one realm to the next. Generally, they move things in only one direction and are impossible for use of transport by living beings. The rifts were originally intended to tie all the Sundered Realms together into a unified and interdependent system. These rifts were the key of transporting wastes, resources, and products between the realms after the Death Gates were opened. They are only partially functional now.

[4]A Sartan phrase meaning "third part" or "phase 3," which has come to specifically mean the third phase of the Sundering. There were to be three such phases in all. Jran-ai (phase 1) refers to the actual Sundering magic whereby all creation was divided into its elements and the realms were created. The durnai were apparently created in the magic at that time. Jran-dus (phase 2) involved the occupation and organization of the realms under the guidance of the Sartan. Jran-kri (phase 3) was to herald the opening of the Death Gates and the final phase of universal cooperation. Jran-kri was never initiated.

[5]i.e., hibernation.

the great sea following Jran-kri. The durnai would circle the sea-sun, and the seasun would move about the water in a circular countermotion. The intention was to keep the waters circulating and to aid in the recycling of materials from other realms.

The Goodsea

Though it is thought of as a sea, it is actually not composed of water. The Goodsea is made up of a clear oxygenated emulsion liquid. Mammals may breathe it directly without drowning.

The Goodsea is filled with a variety of small prokaryotes, eukaryotes, plankton, and similar species designed specifically to react chemically with waste products that were to have been rift-dumped into this location after the Jran-kri. Forms of kelp were also grown in vast fields, creating free-floating forests. All of these produce useful byproducts naturally which are then absorbed as fuel energy by the durnai.

The effect of these small creatures is to perform the first stage in a refining process of waste materials. The byproducts of these sea creatures, being of lighter density than the sea, tend to float toward the nongravity[6] of the durnai. These byproducts are then absorbed as durnai food—the final process before exporting refined materials through another rift in the center of each durnai to the great refining mechanisms in the Realm of Sky.[7]

There are other creatures of the water as well. The dolphins, intelligent and rather overcommunicative, never have to surface for air as in our previous world,[8] as they breathe the emulsion directly. Other water mammals such as whales, serpents, mermen, seals, sea lions, and manatees abound. Normal sea creatures such as fish, kraken, hippocampus (water steeds), sea horses, rays, and other common marine creatures have been

---

[6]Ramu is mistaken in calling the repulsion effect of the durnai "nongravity." It might be more appropriately called reverse gravity.

[7]He is certainly referring to the Kicksey-winsey of Arianus. The Realm of Water—it appears—was to act as a distilling and recycling location for the waste of other worlds. It's hard to imagine such a beautiful place as a garbage dump.

[8]Refers to Earth before the Sundering.

adapted to this environment as well. Plankton in the emulsion absorb the carbon dioxide from the various creatures' exhalations and reprocesses it back to oxygen.

Biospheres (The Durnai)

In the Sundering, we created the durnai—biosphere creatures of titanic size—which were to float randomly in their hibernation sleep. These durnai are living beings, created by the Sartan at Jran-ai to be an integral part of their overall plan. During Jran-ai, the durnai would remain in hibernation, awaiting the increased luminance of the seasun to be brought about at Jran-kri.[9] Until Jran-kri, the durnai were to remain in this state of deep sleep, occasionally drifting back to be frozen in the ice, only to be thawed again eons later—still hibernating—as the seasun would complete its circuit through the ice.

The original plan was to have the mensch act as caretaker parasites working in a symbiotic arrangement inside the durnai. The mensch would cultivate the interior surfaces of the biospheres, which, in turn, would keep it healthy for its chemosynthesis.

Once awakened, the biospheres would interact with the emulsion sea to recycle biological and chemical waste products from the other worlds back into useful biosynthetics, gases, and chemicals. Drawing their energy from the phosphorescent sun in the realm, the durnai "mountain roots" would channel the chemicals from the sea to the underearth. These roots appeared to the inhabitants as craggy mountains thrusting up from the sea and into the cavern ceiling above. In fact, these "mountains" are more analogous to bones with marrow structures thrust into the sea. The roots would then pull the chemicals and waste products up into the durnai—not unlike the roots of a tree—and convert these into useful chemicals for their own life sustenance and, as a byproduct, chemicals and other substances that would be disposed of through the natural rift in the core of the biosphere. This rift, connected through netherspace to the Realm of Air, would then supply needed source materials to the great machine there.[10]

[9]See note 4 above.

[10]Again, the Kicksey-winsey.

The Shores / Outer Durnai Layer

Resembling craggy rock mountain walls thrusting down from the valley roof, the shores are analogous to bone structures pushing down from the biosphere's center. The shores both form pockets of atmosphere and penetrate the sea along great mountainous ranges.

These mountains curve down from the nongravity to form shores where the sea surges along in undulating waves. Here the transfer action presses the chemicals and other gathered materials into the bone channels, where it is conducted into the foundations of the durnai.

Most importantly, the crystalline formations at the base of the mountains act as gatherers of light energy from the phosphorescent sun in the realm, thus supplying the needed photosynthetic energy for the process of life in the durnai.

The Valleys (Warrens) / Outer Durnai Layer

Above the sea surface—meaning away from the water and toward the center of the durnai—and between the towering mountain walls curving away from the shores lay the valleys, or warrens. These warrens were intended as the primary habitat for most of the mensch in this realm. Here, atmospheric and ecological balances are maintained partially by the plants that live here and partially by the biosphere itself. The warrens act as a dynamic biological shock absorber that allows the biosphere to correct for minor changes in the sea surrounding it.

Atmosphere and temperature are partially maintained by the biosphere itself. The sphere naturally generates internal heat, which partially offsets the cool of the water outside. The biosphere also helps maintain the atmosphere. Both of these effects, however, rapidly decrease as the sphere drifts back into the ice.

The mountains to each side rise to a roof so far distant as to allow natural weather to occur. This is generated partially by the drifting rotation of the sphere through the water and its action against different currents in the sea that surrounds it. Rain is the most normal result, although snow is a common problem as a biosphere nears the ice.

The atmospheric pressure keeps the bottomless sea at bay. Many warrens are connected by fjords of towering mountains plunging into the eternal sea.

All warrens are lit by light coming up from the sea or by light produced by the mensch themselves.

Underneath / Inner Durnai Layer

Chemicals and other substances which are carried into the creature from the bone-mountains enter the core of the sphere to be processed by the various organs there. These processes utilize the photosynthetic processes along with chemosynthesis to produce its own life-giving energy. As byproducts, natural gas, nitrogen, carbon compounds, and certain biological organisms are produced. These useful byproducts are then moved by the biosphere to the rift at the sphere's center for expulsion.

The Rift

At the center of the creature is the rift, where all byproduct materials are sent. This rift is a netherspace conduit that takes these materials to Arianus for use by the great machine in manufacturing materials and devices for the use of all realms. This one-way conduit normally would transmit vast quantities of raw gases and chemicals to the machine.

The rift generates a nongravity field, pushing all mass objects away from the center of the durnai. (See diagram on page x.)

CURRENT ABERRANT STATUS OF THE REALM

Having now awakened, we Sartan confront many issues. The chief among these issues remains the questions of why the Jran-kri was never reached. Second is a question that remained unanswered in our own time before the sleep: What of the dragons?

JRAN-KRI NOT ESTABLISHED AS PLANNED

With the failure of the plan to attain Jran-kri, the durnai have remained in a dormant or hibernation state as they were when they were created. They perform their functions autonomically but do little more. They do not move of their own volition, as was originally planned, nor do they synthesize abundant gaseous and solid materials for the machine in the Realm of Air as they were designed to do. Without increased output from the seasun, the durnai will remain dormant, occasionally falling into the ice (deep hibernation) and being thawed out in the cycle of the seasun. In the current hibernation state, the amount of chemicals being produced and transmitted is negligible.

DRAGONS AND THE MAGIC-SUPPRESSION OF THE SEA

The origin of the dragons remains as much a mystery to us as do their purposes. For now, it is only certain that they are our most powerful enemy—and that they have somehow changed the Goodsea.

Due to some interference of the dragons, the emulsion of the Goodsea now acts as a damper on probability. It localizes reality as part of its own process of regeneration and, thus, prevents any magic—which requires alternate probabilities—from working. Runes of the Sartan fade and seem to disappear under the effects of the sea. This is because the runes themselves extend into the realms of probability. When the probabilities are localized by the sea into a single reality, then the runes cannot exist and they fade away, losing both presence and power.

Within our walls we are safe. Beyond we are helpless. I move that the Council consider these findings at once.

Most humbly and gratefully submitted.
Ramu

APPENDIX ◆ III

CHELESTRA

SUBMERSIBLES

◆

(From a recovered sales parchment found on Gargon with footnotes by Alfred the Sartan)

You don't want grace and elegance. Stop looking at your shoes![1] What you really want is dependable, profitable and, most importantly, SAFE transportation through the seas of Chelestra. Come to us an we'll provide!

Dwarven submersibles are transportation and cargo carriers built by the solid dwarven craftsmen utilizing a few key elven technomagic principles and technologies.[2] These submersibles are most often used in trade between the various worlds. Some humans and elves have ordered travel ships built and not a few military ships built as well. This craft—a light, swift cargo/transport—is a fine example of dwarven submersibles.

All submersibles currently utilize the gravity of the worlds[3] for

---

[1] A dwarven phrase meaning to be truthful rather than self-deluding.

[2] In point of fact, dwarves depend totally on elven technomagics to make their submersibles function.

[3] The mensch of Chelestra are unaware that they are living inside larger living organisms (called durnai by the Sartan) and thus refer to their habitats as "worlds." Gravity, to the mensch in Chelestra, is a force that pushes away from the center of their worlds—opposite of the attractive force known in all other worlds.

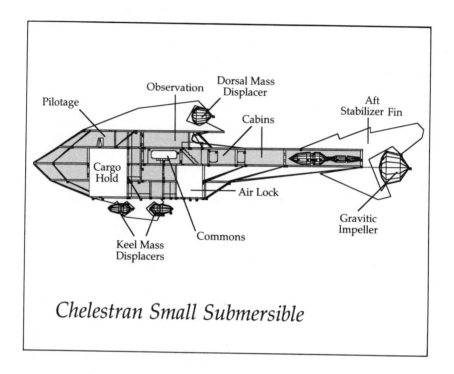

Chelestran Small Submersible

navigation, propulsion, and buoyancy control. As you know, the density of an object relative to the density of the water around it determines a ship's ability to float. Density is the weight of an object divided by its volume. Simply put, if the density of the ship is less than the density of the water it replaces, then the ship will float toward a world. If the density of the ship is more than the water it replaces, it sinks away from the world. More accurately, if the density of a ship is less than the density of the water it displaces, the ship will rise in the water through the surface until the amount of water displaced is equal to the density of the ship.

Submersibles control their buoyancy—and hence, their depth in the water—by changing their density. Elven magic provides the Gargon Submersibles with the combined means of altering their density at will as well as providing motive power for the ship through the Goodsea.

Crystals mounted in the keel of the ship generate various degrees of mass as directed from the bridge of the ship. Under normal, unpowered circumstances, the submersible is designed to float. In Gargon navigation terms, this means that a ship without the benefit of its keel mass-displacers would rise toward the nearest world. This is a natural safety feature much appreciated by all dwarves who know that even elven devices break down from time to time.[4]

When activated, the keel mass-displacers increase the density of the ship and, thus, cause it to sink into the sea—away from the world. Naturally, the farther from the biosphere one travels, the less the influence of the gravity those spheres produce. Occupants of the submersibles would become weightless—however, a side benefit of the increased mass from the displacers is the generation of a natural gravity field through the ship. Thus, those traveling aboard are not subject to the weightless condition at all—unless there is a problem with the keel displacers.

Similar crystals operating on the same principles are employed in the propulsion of the craft and its directional control. A system of these crystals is used as a gravitic impeller, which provides the motive force for the ship. Other mass-displacers, located as design requires, are placed for directional control. On this ship, the navigation displacer is easily noticeable since it is mounted on the dorsal fin of the ship. The keel displacers are used for navigation on the surface.

Although the Goodsea is breathable, it is not advisable to be outside the ship while under way, as the force of the liquid rushing past the ship could easily sweep you away from your craft. For this reason, submersibles are normally enclosed, although most do have decks for observation while the ship is at a stop and during surface operations. A large open area can be seen on this ship aft on deck 4 for this purpose.

Cargo for the ship is loaded through sealed hatches opening through the hull just around and below the pilot's compartment on deck 4. These hatches open directly into the hold extending down through decks 3, 2 and 1.

Additional access to the interior of the ship is through the large airlock located at the aft end and through decks 1 and 2.

---

[4]The reliability of the elven "technomagical devices" is statistically extremely high by all accounts I have studied. The dwarven author of this description is showing the cultural dwarf bias against all technology.

Large doors and a repeating set of navigation controls on deck 1 allow the operator to actually capture items from the sea without ever leaving the ship. The operator can utilize the keel mass-displacers to attract the object to the keel of the ship and then use their navigation controls to move the ship and airlock over the object. While requiring some practice, this technique is occasionally used to rescue dwarves who may have fallen into the sea.

A functional galley/commons area (deck 3), cabins (also deck 3) and an observation room (deck 4 aft of the pilot's compartment) completes the perfect craft for your transport and crew needs.

DECK 1

This is the lowest level of the ship. Its primary features are the airlock controls, atmosphere holding tanks, and cargo hold.

(1A)

The main cargo hold narrows with the bow plates of the ship to this bottom location. Overhead, the hold extends through two more decks to the twin sealed cargo hatches above. Pressure doors exit this location port and starboard to area 1B, and an access ladder is mounted to the aft bulkhead of this compartment extending up through the rest of the hold overhead.

(1B)

Storage lockers are located here for tools and other gear.

(1C)

The main access corridor of this deck. Forward can be seen the base of the main access shaft, which runs through all decks of the ship. At this shaft between each deck is a watertight hatch, which can close to seal off each deck in an emergency.

Aft of this corridor is a large observation window that looks into the airlock (1D) beyond. Here, too, are the controls that can navigate the ship, control the keel displacers, shift atmosphere and water in the airlock and open the doors to the airlock chamber.

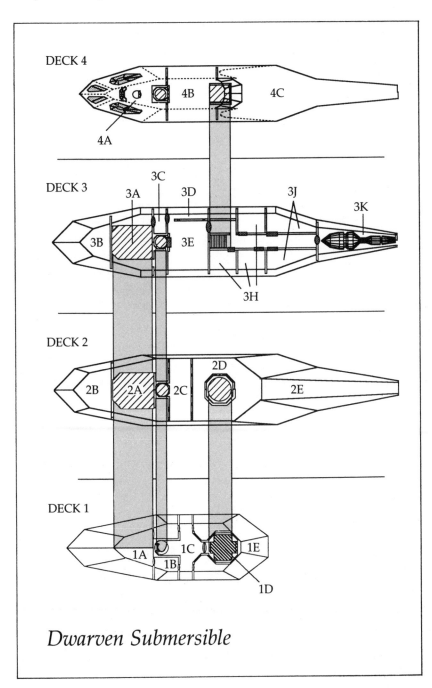

DECK 4

4A 4B 4C

DECK 3

3A 3C 3D 3J 3K

3B 3E 3H

DECK 2

2A 2B 2C 2D 2E

DECK 1

1A 1B 1C 1D 1E

Dwarven Submersible

(1D)

The airlock is the easiest means of entering and exiting the ship while submerged. Rolltop doors set into the keel open the two-deck-tall airlock to the sea. Special rods of elven design displace the atmosphere in the chamber to holding tanks located aft door storage (1E). Access to this chamber from the interior of the ship is from deck 2 (2D).

(1E)

Occasionally, atmosphere leaks from the ship. Atmosphere in the ship is as important as its mass-displacers, for if the ship interior is flooded, it loses it natural buoyancy safeguard.

This compartment holds additional atmosphere in compressed tanks. Air vacated from the airlock is magically transferred into these tanks as well. Whenever an area of the ship needs to be reclaimed from the invading sea, these tanks can be used to blow them clear of water.

DECK 2

This is a level of the ship comprised mostly of equipment. Here are found the compartments that support the work done on the other levels of the ship.

(2A)

The upper level of the cargo hold. Additional pressure doors lead aft to corridor 2C. Additional hatches lead forward to compartment 2B.

(2B)

The freshwater compartment. The seawater does not quench thirst, of course, so people aboard need a freshwater store. This also ballasts out the fuel compartment in the rear of the ship (2E).

(2C)

Access corridor. A large pressure door leads aft to the airlock room (2D). Forward is the main access shaft and ladder leading to all other decks.

(2D)

Airlock room. Often used as additional hold storage space, this room surrounds the top of the airlock from deck 1. A large pressure door on the starboard side allows access to the airlock interior from the ship.

(2E)

Fuel storage. This fuel room holds the lead shavings and graphite that operate the gravitic converts and, thence, all the machinery on the ship.

DECK 3 / MAIN DECK

The primary living quarters of the ship. The crew cabins (3H), commons room (3D) and galley (3E) are all located here. The impeller room (3K) is also located on this deck with its associated repair and tool rooms (3J) as well as the top of the cargo hold (3A and B).

(3A)

Overhead on the port and starboard sides are located a pair of large watertight hatches. These hatches can, when surfaced, open to allow access to the three-deck-tall cargo hold below. The hatches open outward and away from the ship for safety (impossible to open while submerged) and convenience (the hatches can easily be supervised from the pilot's compartment on deck 4 which they flank).

(3B)

Forward pantry. Here additional water stores and food are kept.

(3C)

Aft pantry. Items for immediate use are stored here, convenient to the galley compartment.

(3D)

The commons room. Comfortable and well appointed. Crew can relax and eat in this room amidships. Its location is not an accident—if the ship should encounter heavy undersea storms, this room is located nearest to the center of the ship's motion.[5]

(3E)

Galley. Long and cramped, it is designed for the preparation of food.

(3F)

Additional storage lockers.

(3G)

Main corridor. A large ladder leads up to the viewing/observation room on deck 4. The doors to the cabins are located here as well as an access hatch to the engine compartment (3K).

(3H)

Crew cabins. The beds are mounted on dual axial swivels so as to roll with the motion of the ship.

(3J)

Tool rooms. These hold various magical devices for repairing the gravitics should they break down.[6]

(3K)

Impeller room. A large turned crystal is mounted in this room with a variety of conduits extending from it. Its color is that of black

---

[5]An important factor of dwarven design—dwarves generally get violently motion sick in conveyances.

[6]Such "repairs" mostly constitute wholesale replacement of large magical components on dwarf ships. Dwarves do not perform the magic of the elves.

light—thus making it difficult to look at and impossible to focus on its surface. Some dwarves have gone mad attempting to do so.[7]

DECK 4 / PILOT DECK
This deck has only two functions: piloting the ship and observing the ocean world around it.

(4A)

Pilot's compartment. A free-standing pedestal stands near the center of the compartment. Above it is a large magical display in three dimensions showing navigational data. The navigation device can be told in advance where to go. In these circumstances, the ship is capable of navigating itself.

Also located in this room is a ladder up to the top of the ship. A small, personal airlock is located here.

(4b)

Observation room. The large ladder enters aft of the compartment from deck 3 below. Around it can be seen an observation window that looks out over the afterdeck and to the sea beyond. Watertight doors on either side of the descending ladder allow access to the afterdeck when the ship is surfaced.

(4C)

Afterdeck. Used when the ship is surfaced. A carved railing surrounds this deck back as far as the aft impeller fin.

CONCLUSIONS
You must agree[8] that the dwarven submersible is the safest means of travel between the worlds. Every crafthall and guild of dwarven workers put their sweat and brains into the dwarven submersible. You'll pay less elsewhere for a ship but you'll be sorry later.

---

[7] An old wives' tale or seafaring legend of the dwarves. It has no basis in fact.

[8] Dwarves prefer to be direct over condescending.

Lady Dark

Poetry by Kevin T. Stein

Music by Janet Pack

sha - dows' craft and 'flect my will,

stage! The sha dows'

X

To dance and laugh, to

craft and 'flect my will, To

X

own   fond ——   cage, ———————   The   Bard's   La - dy

own   fond   cage, ———————   The   Bard's—   La - dy ——

X   X

Dark,   and   the   flame ———   she   hones.

Dark, ——   and   the   flame   she ——   hones.

X X   X   X   X

A Muse is she to whom my heart is

A Muse is she, to whom my heart is

X   X

found,   Touch ____ her   flesh   would

found,   Touch ____ her   flesh ____ would

X X   X

I   sub - lime,   She   that steals my

I   sub - lime,   She   steals my

X   X

soul,   by mine own— hand   ground,   To

soul,   by mine own— hand   ground,   To

X   X   XX

life   she   doth   give _____ wings   and __

rhyme.   She   bids,   my   ears   but

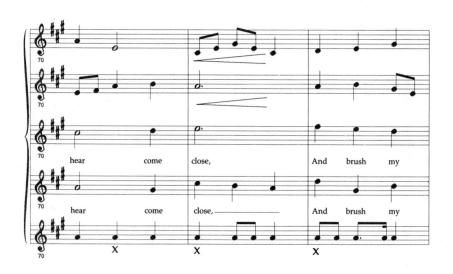

hear   come   close,   And   brush   my

hear   come   close, _____   And   brush   my

lips   like____   pet _____   al'd   rose.

lips____   like   pet _____   al'd   rose.

For Bonnie Ruth Anderson, with love.

10:96

DUE DATE			